PENGUIN POETS IN TRANSLATION
GENERAL EDITOR: CHRISTOPHER RICKS

# VIRGIL IN ENGLISH

PUBLIUS VERGILIUS MARO was born in 70 BC near Mantua in Cisalpine Gaul, the north of Italy, where his parents owned a farm. He was educated at Cremona, Milan and Rome. When the Civil War broke out in 49 BC he retired to Naples for most of his life. His father's estate was confiscated as part of the redistribution of land to returning veterans, but restored to him through influential friends. These included Maecenas, Augustus' chief minister, and the emperor himself. Virgil completed the *Eclogues* in 37 BC, the year in which he accompanied Horace to Brindisi. He finished the *Georgics* in 30 BC, and spent the rest of his life on the *Aeneid*. In his last year he set out for Greece, but fell ill at Megara and had to return to Italy. He died at Brindisi in 19 BC. He was buried near Naples and a tomb purporting to be his is still shown.

K. W. GRANSDEN is Reader Emeritus in English and Comparative Literature at the University of Warwick. He was educated at Jesus College, Cambridge, where he took a double First in Classics. His publications on Virgil include editions of *Aeneid* VIII and XI and a study of the *Aeneid* in the series 'Landmarks of World Literature', all published by Cambridge University Press. He has also published books on E. M. Forster, John Donne and Tennyson.

# VIRGIL IN ENGLISH

*Edited by* K. W. GRANSDEN

PENGUIN BOOKS

PENGUIN BOOKS

Published by the Penguin Group
Penguin Books Ltd, 27 Wrights Lane, London w8 5tz, England
Penguin Books USA Inc., 375 Hudson Street, New York, New York 10014, USA
Penguin Books Australia Ltd, Ringwood, Victoria, Australia
Penguin Books Canada Ltd, 10 Alcorn Avenue, Toronto, Ontario, Canada m4v 3b2
Penguin Books (NZ) Ltd, 182–190 Wairau Road, Auckland 10, New Zealand

Penguin Books Ltd, Registered Offices: Harmondsworth, Middlesex, England

First published 1996
10 9 8 7 6 5 4 3 2

Set in 10/12.5 pt Monotype Bembo
Typeset by Datix International Limited, Bungay, Suffolk
Printed in England by Clays Ltd, St Ives plc

# CONTENTS

# INTRODUCTION

## I THE POET

### Virgil's Achievement and Reputation

Virgil's poetry, especially the *Aeneid*, has generated a longer and
larger tradition of commentary than any other poetry in the entire
European canon. Commentary includes translation and imitation –
the means by which texts produced at a particular period of history
are continually renewed in subsequent ages. Translation is a major
form of revaluation: Virgil's poetry, like most Latin poetry, avow-
edly imitated Greek models, so that we may see Virgil himself as a
kind of translator, re-creating – in what for him was the vernacular –
stories, themes, characters and images from Greek literature. For
Virgil, as for all Roman writers, the Greeks were 'the classics': for
us, Virgil has himself become a classic, perhaps, as T. S. Eliot said,
'our classic, the classic of all Europe'.

   Virgil's unique place in the European tradition is partly owing to
historical circumstances. He was born near Mantua in 70 BC and
died at Brindisi in 19 BC. He lived through the period of civil war
which tore the Roman republic apart after the assassination of Julius
Caesar, and which was ended by the decisive victory of Octavian
over Antony and Cleopatra at the battle of Actium in 31 BC, events
familiar to us from Shakespeare's Roman plays. In 27 BC Octavian
took the title of Augustus Caesar, established peace (the 'Pax
Augusta') and laid the foundations of the Roman empire. He died
in AD 14, outliving his poets – Horace by more than twenty years,
Virgil by more than thirty. During his reign an event occurred of
which little official note was taken at the time; but in the long

perspective of history the Incarnation was to give new meaning to the words of Caesar in Shakespeare's *Antony and Cleopatra*: 'the time of universal peace is near'.

Virgil celebrated the Pax Augusta in several passages of his poetry. The panegyrics on Augustus in *Aeneid* I, VI and VIII may seem to us extravagant, but they reflect his contemporaries', and his own, heartfelt longing for peace, and gratitude to the one man who had proved able to secure it. In one early poem, the Fourth Eclogue, written in 40 BC, Virgil tells of the imminent birth of a boy child of divine origin, who is destined to rule over a world to which the peace and justice of the Golden Age (traditionally located in a lost order of time past) will return. Some of the imagery of this remarkable poem is traditional, and occurs in other prophetic texts, including the book of Isaiah, which Virgil is highly unlikely to have known, and the so-called Sibylline prophecies, written in Greek hexameters, which he would have known. Some of these, though of a later date than Virgil's time, are still extant. The Child has never been certainly identified: Virgil may have intended his poem primarily as a metaphor for the hoped-for coming of a new order. It was Constantine who first proposed that the Child was an intuition of Christ, but few have accepted this. There is a famous passage in *Aeneid* VI which also refers in 'Messianic' tones to the coming of a promised saviour, Augustus:

> hic vir, hic est, tibi quem promitti saepius audis,
> Augustus Caesar, divi genus, aurea condet
> saecula qui rursus Latio regnata per arva
> Saturno quondam, super et Garamantas et Indos
> proferet imperium; iacet extra sidera tellus,
> extra anni solisque vias . . .                    (Aeneid VI, 791–6)

> But next behold the Youth of Form Divine,
> Caesar himself, exalted in his Line:
> Augustus, promis'd oft and long foretold,
> Born to restore a better Age of Gold.
> Affrick and India shall his Pow'r obey,
> He shall extend his propagated sway
> Beyond the Solar Year, without the starry way.

(Dryden's version: its only fault is to translate '*divi genus*', 'child of a god', into the imprecise 'exalted in his Line'.)

There were a number of 'saviour-cults' in the first century BC, of which only Christianity was destined to survive. Hercules, to whom Augustus is compared a few lines later in that passage, and Aeneas himself, the hero of Virgil's epic, were saviour figures, labouring on behalf of civilization against barbarism, ridding the world of evil, bringing salvation to the afflicted, as Hercules did when he rescued the early settlers on the Palatine from the monster Cacus (see *Aeneid* VIII, where his exploits and his cult are described). All these saviour figures were of divine origin, and were deified after their death, as was Augustus.

In the Middle Ages, largely on the strength of the Fourth Eclogue, Virgil was revered as a 'magus' and his poetry consulted at random for advice and comfort (the *sortes Virgilianae*). In the early years of its existence, his poetry was the Bible of the pagan opposition to Christianity, and his immense fame during his lifetime and in the years following his death must be chiefly ascribed to Roman national pride in having at last produced, in the *Aeneid*, a heroic poem worthy to stand beside the epics of Homer. Comparison between the two poets became a commonplace of the Renaissance schools: Homer was held to excel in *ingenium* ('nature' or 'genius'), Virgil in *ars* ('art'): but modern criticism has long since discarded such frigid simplifications.

## The Eclogues and Georgics

The authentic canon of Virgil's works (some miscellaneous pieces attributed to him in antiquity are not now thought to be his) consists of the *Eclogues*, the *Georgics* and the *Aeneid*. The *Eclogues* or 'bucolics', a collection of ten short pastoral poems completed by 37 BC, have had an influence out of all proportion to their modest length. Beneath a surface of beguiling charm and elusive limpidity, they are highly sophisticated pieces, the product of an urban culture with nostalgic hankerings after lost innocence and rural simplicity. Apart from the unique Fourth Eclogue, discussed above, they are mainly dialogues between poets masquerading as shepherds, pasturing metaphorical sheep or goats, capping each other's songs and discussing art, love (often unrequited) and the delights of leisure (*otium*). Virgil's chief model for the *Eclogues* was the *Idylls* of the Greek pastoral poet Theocritus, but Virgil created his own landscape, a synthesis of the conventional pastoral myth of Arcadia and of the north Italian countryside remembered from his boyhood. This landscape is more than a backdrop: it reflects the emotions of its inhabitants. In Eclogue II the distraught Corydon leaves the cosy streams and woods and climbs into wild and uninhabited country in order to lament his lost love.

The poems have an intriguing autobiographical element. In Eclogues I and IX, the poet articulates the sadness of landholders whose farms were taken from them and given to veterans returning from the civil wars. Virgil himself experienced this but was reinstated by Augustus. In Eclogue I Virgil empathizes with the figure of Meliboeus, who must go into exile, more profoundly than he does with Tityrus, who (like the author) has been saved from eviction by Augustus. The theme of exile returns in the last and most pessimistic of the eclogues, in which the poet Gallus laments his lost love and rejects the consolations of Arcadia.

The *Georgics*, which followed the *Eclogues*, was completed about 30 BC. This poem too is about the countryside, but no longer the stylized Arcadia of the *Eclogues*: '*otium*' has been replaced by '*labor improbus*' ('damned hard work'). The poem, in four books, deals with various branches of agriculture. The underlying theme is man's life after the Fall. For just as in the myth of Eden man had to earn his bread by the sweat of his brow, so in Virgil's poem Jupiter ended the Golden Age (when nature produced all things spontaneously, for instance honey on tap) and obliged mankind to work the land to prevent it from reverting to wilderness. A famous passage in *Georgics* I describes the 'Jovian Fall' and its consequences.

But the poem is valued now not primarily for its practical advice on agriculture (though not all of this is out of date) but for its moral and philosophical excursions, praising the Italian countryside and the self-sufficient life of the farmer, and satirizing the luxury and corruption of metropolitan Rome: a contrast much exploited in the Renaissance, in the court–country antithesis familiar in works such as *As You Like It*, and also in the 'retirement' poetry of the eighteenth century. In these passages, too, Virgil introduces himself into his text, asking the Muses' aid in expounding the mysteries of the natural world and expressing a longing to live a secluded life without fame: '*inglorius*', his own word for himself, finds an echo in Gray's 'mute inglorious Milton'. In another famous passage, the poet reminisces about an old gardener he once knew, who exemplified the virtues of frugality and hard work. Those same virtues, transposed into the heroic world, permeate the *Aeneid*.

The poem ends with a long descriptive digression, telling the story of Orpheus and Eurydice, linked to the main theme of Book IV (beekeeping) through another myth, that of Aristaeus, who according to Virgil lost his swarm and learnt that this was a punishment for having tried to violate Eurydice. In running away from him, she was bitten by a snake and died. After suitable propitiation, a new swarm is spontaneously generated from the rotting carcasses of cattle ('out of the strong came forth sweetness'). By his discovery of this process, called *bugonia*, Aristaeus became one of the mythical benefactors of mankind: his practical contribution to apiculture is contrasted with the pathos of Orpheus' fruitless quest for Eurydice in the underworld. All Virgil's empathy is with the doomed poet, and in the haunting beauty of the underworld passage he transcends the mode of didactic epic, introduces human voices 'wild with pain' into his poem for the first time, and prepares for the underworld scenes of *Aeneid* VI, in which a number of verses from the Orpheus episode are used again.

The *Georgics* is modelled partly on the *Works and Days* of the Greek didactic poet Hesiod and partly on various prose works about agriculture, but Virgil has transformed his models into something unique in ancient literature. The poem displays a perfection of style not previously seen in Latin poetry, yet in the *Aeneid* he went far beyond this and, in the words of the Victorian scholar F.W.H. Myers, suggested 'possibilities in the Latin tongue which no successor has been able to realize'.

## The Aeneid

When Virgil died in 19 BC the *Aeneid* was finished but unrevised. He had intended to spend a further three years on it before devoting the rest of his life to philosophy. We know this from the fourth-century *Life* of the poet by Aelius Donatus (itself based on a lost biography by Suetonius). Further evidence for the poem's unrevised state is to be found in certain inconsistencies between episodes, and also in the. fifty-odd incomplete lines ('hemistichs') which occur throughout the text. These half-lines are generally ignored by translators, especially the coupleteers. Virgil appointed the poet Varius to be his literary executor, instructing him to destroy the manuscript in the event of his death. But Augustus set the poet's wishes aside, and the work was published posthumously, as it stood, to immediate critical acclaim. Its fame even predated its appearance: the poet Propertius wrote in 26 BC that 'something greater than the *Iliad*' was in preparation. It quickly became (and has remained) a school text, and also a handbook of poetic decorum: the Renaissance philosopher Peter Ramus drew many of his examples of tropes and figures from the *Aeneid*. Some early criticisms were levelled against both its content (plagiarism of Homer) and its style (an affected fondness for 'ordinary' words thought by some to be unsuitable to heroic verse). It has had other critics too, notably Shelley (who placed Lucretius above Virgil as a creator), Pound and Robert Graves. But its central place in European letters has never been seriously or for long impugned. The plagiarism of Homer might now be called 'creative imitation': in any case Homer was not widely read in the Middle Ages or even in the Renaissance, when the *Aeneid* became the heroic poem *par excellence*, the model and inspiration of the vernacular epics of Tasso, Ariosto, Spenser and Milton. As for the charge of affecting ordinary words, Virgil was ahead of his time: what some saw as a blemish now appears much more effective than the unvaryingly inflated diction of later Latin epic.

The *Aeneid* is modelled on Homer's two epics, the *Iliad* and the *Odyssey*. In neither of these poems is that crucial event of antiquity, the fall of Troy, described. The *Iliad* ends before the city's capture, with the death of Hector, while in the *Odyssey* the war is over and Odysseus is on his way home. In the *Aeneid* the fall of Troy is vividly recalled as a narrative in the first person by the defeated Trojan prince Aeneas, who fled from the burning ruins of the city to seek a new homeland in Italy as ordained by the gods. Throughout the first half of the poem Aeneas is a homeless wanderer and exile: Virgil returns to the theme of dispossession, first considered in the *Eclogues*, but now on a cosmic not a local scale. Aeneas lands safely in Italy, but is forced against his will to fight a war with some of the indigenous tribes, led by Turnus, prince of Ardea. The poem ends when Aeneas reluctantly kills Turnus and makes peace with the local king, Latinus: but the real ending lies beyond the poem, in various 'prophetic' passages which bring a legend of the Bronze Age right up to the coming of Augustus. Aeneas will marry Latinus' daughter Lavinia: their descendants, in whom is mixed the blood of Troy and Italy, will rule in Latium through the centuries which separate the fall of Troy (traditionally 1184 BC) from the founding of Rome by Romulus (traditionally 753 or 751 BC). Aeneas is the son of Venus, Romulus the son of Mars, and this conjunction of opposites (love and war) represents the dual ancestry of the Roman nation.

Aeneas' victory in Italy wiped out the defeat at Troy. Rome was destined to arise as a new and greater Troy, from the ashes of the old city. Troy represents the past ('*fuit Ilium*'), Rome the future, its founding an example of good coming out of evil, an event of universal significance preordained by the gods. Aeneas becomes a new kind of hero, not just a warrior and killer like Achilles (though he is a great warrior) but a founder of civilization, a creator not a destroyer, a man whose most famous virtue is *pietas*.

In Homer, the fall of Troy, though fated and inevitable, is not what Zeus wanted. He preferred the Trojans. But it was his wife Hera (the Roman Juno) whose implacable hatred of the Trojans forced his acquiescence in the city's fall. The cause of her hatred was the notorious judgement in which Paris awarded the prize in a divine beauty contest to Aphrodite (the Roman Venus), who had bribed him with the promise of Helen, wife of Menelaus, king of Sparta. Virgil refers to this story at the beginning of the *Aeneid*. Paris later eloped with Helen, which led to the Trojan war. That war reverberates throughout Greek tragedy, from the *Agamemnon* of Aeschylus to the *Trojan Women* of Euripides. Juno's hatred of the Trojans pursues Aeneas to the very end of Virgil's poem, when she finally accepts the inevitable and is reconciled by Jupiter to the destiny of Rome and to her future role as one of the great deities of the Roman pantheon.

The first half of the *Aeneid* contains the poem's three most popular and influential books: II (the fall of Troy), IV (the tragedy of Dido) and VI (the descent into the underworld). When the poem opens, Aeneas is shipwrecked off the north African coast at Carthage (the modern Tunis, as Gonzalo reminds us in *The Tempest*, a play with several Virgilian echoes). Here he is received by the queen ('the widow Dido'), to whom he tells the tale of his ordeal at Troy and his subsequent voyaging. Dido falls in love with Aeneas as Desdemona does with Othello:

> She loved me for the dangers I had passed,
> And I loved her that she did pity them.

Juno seeks to delay Aeneas' mission to reach Italy by engineering a marriage between the two lovers, but their dalliance is interrupted by divine messages and by the ghost of Aeneas' father Anchises reminding him of his duty (cf. *Hamlet*: 'this visitation/Is but to whet thy almost blunted purpose'). Aeneas sails; Dido kills herself. This story has always been the most frequently translated part of the *Aeneid*, and has inspired many romances about women deserted by their faithless lovers. But Virgil, while empathizing deeply with the tragic despair of Dido, justifies Aeneas' departure in terms of his divinely ordained mission and the enmity in historical times between Rome and Carthage. Books II and IV were chosen for translation by the Earl of Surrey: they represent the first versions of any part of the poem ever made in England. They also form the basis of Berlioz' opera *Les Troyens*.

The sixth book of the *Aeneid* has a special significance, because of Dante's 'reawakening' of Virgil from Limbo to be his guide through Hell and Purgatory in the *Divine Comedy*. For Dante, Virgil represented the furthest limits human insight could reach without the supervention of divine grace: hence Virgil's disappearance at the end of the *Purgatorio*, for he cannot enter the Christian heaven. But two thirds of Dante's poem is permeated with his love and reverence for Virgil, not only as 'l'altissimo poeta', but as the man who, in *Aeneid* VI, provided the first systematic guidance into the mysteries of the soul's progress after death, the judgement, the cycle of purification, the separation of the righteous in the Elysian Fields from the damned in Tartarus: all of these, based by Virgil on the teachings of Pythagoras and Plato, on the Orphic mystery cult and on Stoic philosophy, foreshadow the more elaborate structure of Christian eschatology.

In Virgil's poem Aeneas descends into the underworld to meet the shade of his father in the Elysian Fields. Virgil's poetic art is here at its most exalted, his spiritual insights at their most awe-inspiring: here we see into the mind of the poet himself as he reveals, through the personae first of the Sibyl, who guides Aeneas through the world of the dead, and then of Anchises, the mysteries of the hereafter. Anchises also shows his son a pageant of Rome's future heroes, culminating in Augustus. (A malevolent and distorted version of this pageant is the vision of Scotland's future kings shown to Macbeth by the witches.)

The second half of the *Aeneid* is described by Virgil as his 'greater work' (*maius opus*). 'My subject is war, and the pity of war. The poetry is in the pity.' Here are to be found some of the poem's finest passages: the funeral of Pallas, the story of Nisus and Euryalus, and the splendid description of Aeneas' shield, made for him by Vulcan at the instigation of Venus, and ornamented with scenes from the future history of Rome, culminating in the battle of Actium and the death of Cleopatra.

The structure of the *Aeneid* is complex. Legend coexists with events which occurred in the author's lifetime. The treatment is synchronic, not diachronic. Events far ahead of Aeneas' time are brought into the text through passages of prophecy, a technique which became a feature of later epics. A notable instance is Michael's prophecy to Adam in *Paradise Lost* XII, in which he foretells the course of human history after the Fall and up to the birth of Christ:

> . . . he shall ascend
> The Throne hereditary, and bound his Reign
> With earth's wide bounds, his Glory with the Heav'ns.  (XII, 369–71)

Milton here echoes words used by Jupiter in his prophecy to Venus of the coming of Augustus:

> imperium Oceano, famam qui terminet astris                    (I, 287)

> Whose Empire Ocean, and whose Fame the Skies
> Alone shall bound . . .                                        (Dryden)

Milton's Adam is to Christ as Virgil's Aeneas is to Augustus.

Virgil's vision of Rome's destiny, formulated by Anchises in his speech to his son in *Aeneid* VI, is

> To pacify, to impose the rule of law,
> To spare the conquered and war down the proud.

These words emphasize the virtue of magnanimity in victory for which, along with courage in adversity, Aeneas is conspicuous, and for which he became in the Renaissance the archetype of the good prince. But such sentiments, however admirable, do not in themselves account for the poem's enduring value. Sainte-Beuve wrote that Virgil 'gave a new form to tastes, passions and sensibilities . . . and at a decisive moment of world history foresaw what would appeal to the future'. Where Homer had celebrated the regularity and harmony of experience, Virgil explores its dislocations, dissonances and ambivalences. He is the poet of the unrealized, the word

not spoken, the thing not enacted. Behind the triumphalism of the
Augustan passages lie the doubts, despair and sadness of Aeneas, the
loneliest man in literature: he loses his home, his wife, his mistress
and most of his comrades, and never sees the future for which he
strives. Behind and beneath his story we hear, time and again, the
voice of the poet himself, a voice sometimes direct, sometimes
implied. When Jupiter says that the war stirred up by Juno between
the Trojans and the Latins is in defiance of his own will, we see
Virgil wrestling with the eternal question of how we explain the
existence of evil in a universe ruled by '*mens*' (rationality). In the
outcome of that conflict, and in the Pax Augusta, we have a happy
ending. But it is only 'for the time being'. It is lines like '*sunt
lacrimae rerum, et mentem mortalia tangunt*' – 'here are tears for things,
and mortality touches the heart' – which remain in the reader's
mind. Imperial Rome has followed Troy into the past, but the
sadness of human mortality is permanent.


## II THE TRANSLATORS

### The Early Translators

> And for ther is so great diversite
> In English and in writing of our tonge,
> So prey I God that non myswrite thee,
> Ne thee mismetre for defaute of tonge.
> And red wherso thou be, or elles songe,
> That thou be understonde, God I beseche!

> (Chaucer, *Troilus and Criseyde*, V, 1793–8)

We may begin this survey of Virgil's English translators with a
quotation from Chaucer, for two reasons. First, because he was the
earliest poet to attempt to versify Virgil, although he epitomized
rather than translated Aeneas' arrival in Carthage and his meeting
with Dido – first, in *The House of Fame*, and later in *The Legend of
Good Women*. For the latter he used for the first time the rhymed

decasyllabic couplet (the so-called 'heroic' couplet), a metre which went out of fashion in the early Renaissance, to return at the end of the sixteenth century as the dominant metre for English non-dramatic verse for the next two centuries.

But the lines from *Troilus and Criseyde* have a further importance. They remind us that English poets in the Middle Ages and the early Renaissance regarded their native tongue as a metrically unstable and linguistically inadequate instrument. Dryden in his prose writings refers frequently to the poverty and inferiority of English in comparison with Latin, and tells us that he often tested the accuracy of his own English by translating it into Latin, 'thereby trying what sense the words will bear in a more stable language' (*Epistle Dedicatory to 'Troilus and Cressida'*, 1679).

The challenge of rendering into English Virgil's unsurpassed mastery of Latin verse at the golden zenith of its maturity was bravely undertaken by men only too well aware that they had to make do with a language lexically, orthographically and metrically in a state of becoming rather than being.

The history of Virgil translations in these islands properly begins north of the border, with Gavin Douglas, whose pioneering version of the complete 'XIII bukes of Eneidos' into Scottish verse, using the medieval metre known as rhyme royal, was made around 1513 and first printed in 1553. He included the 'thirteenth book', an addition to Virgil's text giving the poem a 'romance' ending, written in pastiche Virgilian Latin by the humanist Maffio Veggio in the fifteenth century. (The Latin text of this continued to be printed in some editions of Virgil until the eighteenth century.)

Douglas is one of the great pioneers of translation. He inaugurated the Renaissance tradition of seeing the *Aeneid* primarily as a political poem. Sir Thomas Elyot in his *Boke Named the Governour* (1531), Sir Philip Sidney in his *Apology for Poetry* (1595) and Dryden in the dedicatory preface to his *Aeneis* (1697), all saw the poem as a political document in which Aeneas is portrayed as the ideal prince, excelling in arms but also the embodiment of justice, wisdom and magnanimity. Dryden went further and identified Aeneas with the Emperor Augustus, the '*buono Augusto*' of Dante's Virgil.

Douglas's version is a masterpiece of Renaissance humanism, imbued with the freshness of the courtly world. In reading it today, we can get behind the neoclassical Virgil of Dryden into a more imaginative world in some respects closer to that of Virgil himself. C. S. Lewis gives a good example: Virgil's '*rosea cervice refulsit*' is rendered by Douglas 'her nek shane like unto the rois in May', and by Dryden 'she turned and made appear her neck refulgent'. 'But', says Lewis, '"*refulsit*" *cannot possibly have had to a Roman ear the* "classical" *quality which* "refulgent" *has for the English. And* "*rosea*" *has completely disappeared . . . and with it half the sensuous vitality of the image.*' Another example, given by D. F. C. Coldwell, is Douglas's delightful rendering of '*laetitia exsultans*': 'hoppit up for ioy, he was so glad'. Dryden's 'exulting in his force' again falls back on translating a Latin word by using its English derivative. But 'exulting' has quite lost the original Latin sense of '*exsultans*', 'leap up' or 'dance', while '*laetitia*' (happiness, joy) is omitted altogether.

About forty years later Henry Howard, Earl of Surrey, translated *Aeneid* II and IV, the fall of Troy and the story of Dido. He made extensive use of Douglas, whose text, though unpublished in his lifetime, circulated in manuscript. Surrey too was a pioneer, for he introduced into English prosody a new metre from Italy, blank verse (unrhymed decasyllabics, five stresses to the line). Unrhymed verse was a humanist ideal, for the Renaissance humanists aspired to emulate classical poets, and no Greek or Latin verse of the classical period used rhyme. In the half-century after Surrey, some humanist scholars not only eschewed rhyme but tried to reproduce in English prosody the quantitative system of scansion used in Greek and Latin poetry. In this system, syllables are 'long' or 'short' not according to stress but depending on whether the vowel in the syllable is long or short. A vowel preceding two consonants was always long, but the quantity of vowels not followed by two consonants had to be learnt: the first syllable of *monet* is short, the first syllable of *conor* is long.

Unfortunately, the advocates of quantity failed to understand that, although the metre is quantitative, Latin verse is also stressed:

the prosody of the hexameter consists of a fixed pattern of dactyls
(–∪∪) and spondees (– –), which might correspond to the actual
stresses of the words or might conflict with them. The fifth foot of
a hexameter is normally a dactyl, so the first long syllable also
carries the stress; but in the first four feet there may be either
correspondence or conflict. Thus in the line

> olli sic breviter fata est longaeva sacerdos

the last syllable of *breviter* is long before the two consonants rf, but
the syllable would not be stressed, whereas the first syllable of the
word is metrically short but also stressed. In Virgil's poetry espe-
cially, the variety of effects made possible by exploiting coincid-
ence and conflict between quantity and stress cannot be reproduced
in English.

The exponents of quantity followed the advice of Roger Ascham,
who taught the doctrine of literary imitation of classical writers,
and of Thomas Drant, who drew up rules for writing English
quantitative verse. Their crude and misguided efforts (so poor was
their ear that they actually supposed Surrey to have composed
quantitatively) produced an absurd prosody which totally fails to
approach the music of Virgil.

In 1602, when the vogue was over and the experiments aban-
doned, Thomas Campion wrote in his *Observations in the Art of
English Poesie* that 'heroical verse' (i.e. quantitative hexameters) had
often been attempted in English 'but with passing pitiful success'.
'Passing pitiful' is too kind a description of Richard Stanyhurst's
version of *Aeneid* I–IV, composed when the fashion was at its height
(1584). Here is a specimen:

> Dido the poore Princesse gauld with such destenye cutting,
> Crav's mortal passadge: too look toe the sky she repyneth.
> And toe put her purpose forward, this light toe relinquish,
> When she the gift sacrifice with the incense burned on altars
> (Grisly to be spoaken) thee moisture swartly was altred:
> And the wyne, in powring, lyke blood black sootish apeered.
> This too no creature, no, not to her sister is opned.

> Further in eke in the palaice a chapel fayre marbil abydeth,
> Vowd to her first husband, which cel shee woorshiped highlye.
> With whit lillye fleses, with garland greenish adorned:
> Heere to her full seeming she dyd hyre thee clamor of elfish
> Goast of her old husband, her furth to his company wafting,
> When the earth with thee shaads of night was darckly bemuffled.
> Also on thee turrets the skrich howle, lyke fetchliefe yfetled,
> Her burial roundel doth ruck, and cruncketh in howling.
> Sundry such od prophecyes, many such prognosticat omens,
> In foretyme coyned, theire threatnings terrible utterd.

Stanyhurst's text is almost impossible to read. The spelling is entirely unreformed, the language full of barbarisms (swartly, ruck, cruncketh). When the word 'to' is to be scanned as a long syllable it is printed as· 'too' or 'toe'; when 'the' is to be scanned as a long syllable it is printed as 'thee'. In line 13, the first 'the' is elided before 'earth', the second 'thee' is long: the line is meant to be scanned as four spondees with a dactyl in the fifth foot ($--/---/---/---/-\cup\cup/-\cup$). If ever a poet 'miswrote and mismetred' English, it was Stanyhurst. Thomas Warton said of him that 'it seems impossible that a man could have written in such a style without intending to burlesque . . . yet it is certain that Stanyhurst seriously meant to write heroic poetry'.

Of the other translators of Virgil who attempted quantitative hexameters, William Webbe, who included versions of the first two eclogues in his *Discourse of English Poetrie* (1586), is perhaps the least unsuccessful. Further discussion of this metre can be found in the letters of G(abriel) H(arvey) and E(dmund) S(penser) and in one of the glosses added by 'E.K.' to the May eclogue of Spenser's *Shepheards Calender*. The technique was revived in the twentieth century by Robert Bridges.

A far more successful and important translation, the first complete English-language *Aeneid*, is that of Thomas Phaer and Thomas Twyne. Phaer's version of Books I–VII appeared in 1558; he completed two and a half more books (1562); Twyne finished Book X, adding XI and XII in 1573 and Maffio Veggio's thirteenth book in

1584. Twyne revised the whole text for both the 1573 and the 1584 editions, so the translation should be credited to both poets (C. S. Lewis does not even mention Twyne in his *English Literature in the Sixteenth Century*). The metre is rhymed fourteeners, very natural to English and easy to read: the metre of two other famous Renaissance translations, Golding's version of Ovid's *Metamorphoses* (1565–7) and Chapman's *Iliad* (1598–1611). In the nineteenth century William Morris used the same metre for his *Aeneids*. Phaer–Twyne, though marred by occasional awkwardness of diction ('gothicisms'), has great strength and beauty, and remained the only complete English *Aeneid* until the middle of the next century, when John Ogilby made not one but two complete versions.

## The Seventeenth Century

Though Dryden sneered at Ogilby's versions, he was not above making use of them. In fact, he borrowed from many of his seventeenth-century predecessors. This was the century of the heroic couplet, which had become fashionable among the university wits of the 1590s (Donne's satires, for example). Latin verse satire and Latin epic both used the hexameter, so the heroic couplet, revived from Chaucer's time, conveniently offered itself as an appropriate instrument for epic as well as satire. It was used in 1605 by Joshua Sylvester for his translation of Du Bartas' epic *The Divine Weekes and Works*, by Thomas May in 1628 for his version of the *Georgics*, and for the rest of the century by most translators of Virgil (except for a few mavericks). If a number of writers use the rhyming couplet when translating the same text, certain key rhyme words will often reappear at the end of lines and a generic similarity from version to version will emerge. Dryden's Virgil may be described as a collaborative culmination of the efforts of his less gifted forerunners. In particular, he eradicated the widely used 'periphrastic' present tense ('does go', etc.). Waller's celebrated smoothness was partly the result of a too-free admission of the auxiliary verb, as Johnson points out in his *Life* of Waller. Elsewhere (in his *Life* of

Denham) Johnson attributes a famous remark to Prior: 'Denham and Waller improved our versification, and Dryden perfected it.' This perfection, however, (Johnson again) consisted largely of 'the art of concluding the sense in couplets, which has perhaps been with rather too much constancy pursued'.

It is perhaps improper to speak of plagiarism when considering Dryden's Virgil, but it is undeniable that his versions often coincide with those of his predecessors in phrase, rhyme and even line. Dryden is hard on Ogilby, whose labours, whatever their intrinsic merit, were on a monumental scale, but he is also hard on the various 'holiday authors', as he calls them, gentlemen amateurs who dabbled in bits of Virgil, especially the ever-popular fourth *Aeneid*. For some years before his own complete Virgil appeared (1697), Dryden edited a number of anthologies of translations from the classics. These 'poetical miscellanies', published by Jacob Tonson and continued into the next century after Dryden's death, included versions not only of portions of the *Aeneid* and the *Georgics* but also of the ten *Eclogues*, by different hands. Dryden contributed the Fourth Eclogue, but when his own complete version of all ten poems appeared it was evident that some phrases and lines from other men's work had found their way into his own. In one case, that of the Earl of Lauderdale, he acknowledged his indebtedness (see Appendix C).

For all its strengths, however, Dryden's Virgil has serious limitations. 'He has neither a tender heart nor a lofty sense of moral dignity,' wrote Wordsworth in a letter to Scott of 7 November 1805. Dryden's very strengths are sometimes a handicap. Eliot said of him, 'he states immensely: he suggests nothing'; and of all poets who ever wrote in any language Virgil is supremely the poet of suggestion, the poet of the subtext, the not quite articulated. As Conington pointed out, Virgil had 'a peculiar habit of hinting at two or three modes of expression while actually employing one'.

The seventeenth century (if we extend it by twenty years to include Pope's *Iliad*) is the golden age of English translation. Many of the poets who tried their hand at the practice also wrote about the theory of translation, none more fully than Dryden himself, in his preface to *Sylvae* (the second part of the poetical miscellanies, 1685) and in the long 'Dedication to the Aeneis', in which he formulates the famous principle that translation should be 'not so strait as metaphrase, nor so loose as paraphrase'. (For a comment by Denham on the art of translation, see Appendix B.) The poets of this period took their work seriously, and set out collective principles by which their successors may be judged.

## After Dryden

It might be supposed that Dryden had rendered superfluous any further attempts to translate Virgil into heroic couplets. But further attempts there were, throughout the eighteenth century and into the nineteenth. A survey of these efforts, with excerpts, will be found in a seminal essay on the English translators of Virgil (1861) by the great Victorian classical scholar John Conington. The poetic merit of these versions is limited, they are extremely monotonous if read at any length, and they add nothing to their predecessors in opening up Virgil to the modern reader. Pitt, Symmons and Sotheby not only had to follow Dryden in handling the couplet, but also had to follow an even greater master, Pope (one of whose early pastorals is included as an example of imitation rather than translation). Conington points out that to glance down a page of Pitt or Symmons is to see how circumscribed their work is by repeated pairs of conventional rhyme words: 'Tyre–fire, round–crowned, above–Jove, inspire–fire, toast–coast'. From these one can infer 'pretty well what the rest of the line is likely to have been'. The moral, says Conington, is that 'no one is likely to attain as a poetical translator the excellence which would be denied him as an original writer'. The converse, however, is not necessarily the case. Wordsworth made versions of several passages into heroic couplets, but it is doubtful if one could infer his greatness as an original poet from his translations.

While the eighteenth century continued to be dominated by the heroic couplet, blank verse, with Milton's great example behind them, attracted several writers, including Brady, Trapp, Hawkins and Beresford. None of their versions has sufficient distinction to demand representation. Cowper had translated the *Odyssey* into blank verse in 1792, but, as Conington observes, this translation 'established a case for blank verse as wielded by Cowper, not as wielded by Beresford'.

The eighteenth century saw a revival of interest in the *Georgics*, a text which inspired much of the poetry of rural retirement so popular during this period. Thomson's *Seasons* finds a place in this volume as an example of imitation rather than translation, and as a reminder that, just as only an original poet could breathe new life into the couplet after Dryden and Pope, so only an original poet could breathe new life into blank verse after Milton.

## The Nineteenth Century

During the Victorian period, several interesting metrical experiments in translating Virgil were made by writers who (though sometimes with rather odd results) genuinely tried to get away both from Dryden and from Milton. Towards the end of his 1861 essay Conington quotes from a translation by James Henry, a distinguished classical scholar who, like Conington himself, edited the Latin text of the *Aeneid*. Henry made two attempts at translating the *Aeneid*. In 1845 he published a version of Books I and II done into a curious blank verse, characterized by a frequently strong-stressed first syllable, considerable use of hypermetre (i.e. an eleventh syllable), inverted syntax, neologisms, archaisms and compounds. Some years later (1853) he published new versions of Books I–VI, and it is these to which Conington refers. He now used a short line with two stresses and varying rhythms, which Conington calls 'Pindaric', using the term in the sense in which English poets of the seventeenth and eighteenth centuries used it, to mean an ode supposedly in the manner of the Greek poet Pindar.

In 1866 Conington himself entered the field, with a translation of the whole *Aeneid* into the metre of Scott's *Marmion*, chosen primarily for its rapidity of movement. Rapidity was one of Arnold's criteria for translating Homer, but it may be doubted whether Virgil's hexameters share this characteristic. Latin has far more long syllables than Greek, and some of Virgil's finest and most moving poetry is very far from rapid. Here are two famous lines describing the souls of the dead awaiting passage across the river Styx:

> stabant orantes primi transmittere cursum,
> tendebantque manus ripae ulterioris amore.       (*Aeneid* VI, 313–14)

Here the long slow syllables, the repeated *–or* sound, the elision of *ripae*, suggest the yearning of the souls and (as William Empson noted in *Seven Types of Ambiguity*) the length of time they have been waiting. Here is Conington's version of these lines:

> Each in pathetic suppliance stands
> So may he first be ferried o'er,
> And stretches out his helpless hands
> In yearning for the further shore.

Compare the version of a modern translator, Robert Fitzgerald:

> There all stood begging to be first across
> And reached out longing hands to the far shore.

For an intelligent critique of Conington, and also of Dryden, we may turn to Sir Charles Bowen, an eminent lawyer, who published his version of the *Eclogues* and *Aeneid* I–VI in 1887. Like Gladstone's, Bowen's classical studies had to be fitted into his public duties, and his intention to complete the *Aeneid* and translate the *Georgics* was never realized. In his preface, he calls Dryden's Virgil 'scarcely more than a paraphrase', while of Conington's – the only other version he singles out for its literary merit – he says that the choice of the manner and metre of Scott 'inflicts upon the reader a shock from which it is not easy to recover . . . the sweet and solemn majesty of the ancient form is wholly gone'. He then argues that Virgil must be translated *lineally* – a view endorsed by most modern translators – and that blank verse, the couplet and the ballad-metre cannot do this. A longer line is required, and Bowen uses a rhymed pseudo-hexameter, six stresses to the line, but with the last syllable lopped off. He thus emends Coleridge's famous specimen hexameter

> In the hexameter rises the fountain's silvery column

into

> In the hexameter rises the fountain's silvery spray

which turns out very much like Browning's metre in 'Abt Vogler'.

A long line was also favoured by William Morris, who revived the rhymed fourteener used by Phaer–Twyne, in a version which makes the *Aeneid* sound more like an Anglo-Saxon poem than a translation of Virgil: archaisms like 'wend', together with the third-person singular verb in —eth and frequent compounds consisting of conjoined monosyllables (war-way, war-got, sword-lust, time-old, hard-heart) combine to create a powerful though highly mannered effect.

## The Twentieth Century

In 1905, Robert Bridges made a line-for-line version of *Aeneid* VI into quantitative hexameters, not attempted since the sixteenth century. This is an impressive piece of writing, despite certain eccentricities: the archaic third-person verb in —eth, the use of the ampersand and the apostrophe in such forms as 'hav'', and spellings like phrenzy, companyon, oblivyon. Bridges later incorporated some of these metrical and typographical innovations into his *Testament of Beauty* (1930).

There have been many new translations of Virgil in recent years – at least four versions of the *Aeneid*, for instance, in the last half-century. All face a common problem: what literary style to adopt, and what metrical system. Bridges shares with Morris a Victorian high seriousness of diction, even if it occasionally smacks of Gothic revival, and a sense of the value of a strict prosody. We have today no shared and common poetic discourse. There is a tendency to lapse into archaism (Day Lewis uses the word 'wend', also favoured by Morris) or into too easy forms of everyday speech with its attendant danger of perpetuating idioms current when the translator was at work – nothing dates more quickly than the latest phraseology. As to metre, most modern translators favour what L. P. Wilkinson, in the introduction to his Penguin edition of the *Georgics*, calls 'a loose, predominantly five-beat metre which often streamlines itself into blank verse but which admits of variations such as the "sprung rhythm" of Hopkins has made acceptable'. Line-by-line translation, a novelty in the nineteenth century, is now generally adopted. The aim of most modern translators has been to keep going what Patric Dickinson called 'the impulse of the narrative', even if some of the subtleties of the original are lost.

The bulk of this volume consists of straight translation, but a number of pieces have been included to illustrate the influence of Virgil on English poetry: Spenser's *Shepheards Calender*, Milton's 'Lycidas' and Thomson's *Seasons* provide examples of this influence. In our own time, Robert Lowell, W. H. Auden, V. Sackville-West and Allen Tate have written poems in which Virgil's presence is revived and revalued.

# CHRONOLOGY OF EVENTS
# IN VIRGIL'S LIFE

70 BC Virgil born near Mantua, in the province of Cisalpine Gaul, northern Italy.

65 Birth of Horace.

63 Birth of Octavian (afterwards Augustus).

49 Civil wars begin. Virgil moves south, to near Naples.

48 Julius Caesar defeats Pompey (Sextus Pompeius) at Pharsalus.

44 Julius Caesar assassinated.

43 Triumvirate of Antony, Octavian and Lepidus.

42 Caesarians Antony and Octavian defeat republicans Brutus and Cassius at Philippi.
Beginning of land confiscations for resettlement of civil war veterans.
Julius Caesar deified.

40 Virgil's Fourth ('Messianic') Eclogue written.

38–36 Octavian's wars with Pompey; defeat and death of Pompey.

37 Virgil completes the *Eclogues* and begins the *Georgics*.

31 Battle of Actium.

30 Suicide of Antony and Cleopatra.
Virgil begins the *Aeneid*.

29 Octavian celebrates triumphs.

27 Octavian assumes title of Augustus and establishes the Principate.

23 First three books of Horace's *Odes* published.

19 Virgil completes the *Aeneid*, but plans to spend a further three years revising it. Leaves for Greece, but is taken ill and dies at Brundisium (Brindisi). Buried near Puteoli (Pozzuoli) on road from Naples.

8 Death of Horace.

AD 14 Death of Augustus; accession of Tiberius.

# FURTHER READING

For those wishing to read Virgil in the original with the help of notes in English, the recommended texts are those edited by R. D. Williams (*Aeneid*, 1972, *Eclogues and Georgics*, 1979). These include helpful bibliographies and introductions. The works listed below are of particular relevance to the present anthology.

Colin Burrow, *Epic Romance* (1993).

John Chalker, *The English Georgic* (1969).

John Conington, 'The English Translators of Virgil', in *Miscellaneous Writings of John Conington*, ed. J. A. Symonds, vol. I (1872), pp. 137–97.

John Dryden, 'Dedication of the Aeneis', with other prose writings on Virgil, reprinted in *The Works of John Dryden*, vol. V, ed. W. Frost and V. A. Dearing (1987).

T. S. Eliot, 'What is a Classic?' (Address to the Virgil Society, 1944): reprinted in *On Poetry and Poets* (1957).

William Frost, 'Translating Virgil, Douglas to Dryden', in *Poetic Traditions of the English Renaissance*, ed. M. Mack and G. de F. Lord (1982). pp. 271–86.

K. W. Gransden, *Virgil: the Aeneid* ('Landmarks of World Literature', 1990).

T. W. Harrison, 'English Virgil: the Aeneid in the XVIII Century' (Philologica Pragensis, 1967).

D. E. Hill 'What Sort of Translation of Virgil Do We Need?' in *Virgil*, ed. I. McAuslan and P. Walcot (1990).

C. S. Lewis, *English Literature in the Sixteenth Century* (1954).

C. Martindale, ed., *Virgil and His Influence* (1954).

F. W. H. Myers, 'Virgil', in *Essays Classical* (1883, reprinted 1901), pp. 106–76.

L. Proudfoot, *Dryden's Aeneid and Its Seventeenth Century Predecessors* (1960).

D. West, *Virgil: the Aeneid. A New Prose Translation* (1991). The appendices include maps, a gazetteer and genealogical trees.

T. Ziolkowski, *Virgil and the Moderns* (1993).

# EDITOR'S NOTE

Apart from the *Eclogues*, Virgil's poetry consists of two large-scale works, 'through-composed' but arranged in 'books' of between 400 and 1,000 lines. It has therefore been necessary to include a few longer extracts from both the *Georgics* and the *Aeneid* in order to illustrate the poet's narrative and descriptive techniques. It has also seemed desirable to represent the seventeenth-century translators, many of whose versions have never been reprinted, as substantially as possible. A few celebrated passages, the death of Dido and the descent into the Underworld, for example, are represented by more than one version.

Line references to the Latin text in the headnotes are to the Oxford edition, edited by R. A. B. Mynors.

My principal debt in compiling this anthology is to the catalogues of the British Library, through which I was able to discover much early material. Most of this has been reprinted from the original editions, since no modern texts exist. I should also like to thank Professor Christopher Ricks, Mr Tony Harrison and Mr Paul Merchant for drawing to my attention material I might otherwise have missed. I am also greatly indebted to Esther Sidwell, who has saved me from many errors and inconsistencies.

K.W.G.

# A NOTE ON THE SPELLING
# OF 'VIRGIL' AND 'AENEID'

The poet's name in Latin is Publius Vergilius Maro. But after the fifth century the spelling Virgilius crept in: perhaps by analogy with *virga*, a wand, for Virgil had a popular reputation as a guide to the underworld, and Mercury, the conveyor of the souls of the dead, carried a wand; perhaps also by analogy with *virgo* (virgin): in his lifetime he was nicknamed 'Parthenias' (maidenly), and his Fourth Eclogue salutes the return to earth of the Virgin (Justice). This later spelling led to the English Virgil, established in the Middle Ages and generally accepted ever since, though a few writers continue to prefer Vergil, which has no real authority in English.

The name of Virgil's epic in Latin is *Aeneis*: since there are twelve books the correct title is *Aeneidos libri XII*, 'the twelve books of the *Aeneid*'. The English name is thus formed out of the Latin genitive; again, a misguided pedantry has led some translators to call the poem 'Aeneis', 'Aeneids', or 'Aeneados'.

# GEOFFREY CHAUCER
(*c.* 1343–1400)

## The Legend of Good Women, 958–1058 *The legend of Dido*

Aeneas' arrival in Carthage: an epitome rather than a translation of *Aeneid* I, 305–642. The poem is the first in English to make use of the decasyllabic ('heroic') couplet; see Introduction.

> So longe he saylede in the salte se
> Tyl in Libie unnethe aryvede he
> With shipes sevene and with no more navye;
> And glad was he to londe for to hye,
> So was he with the tempest al toshake.
> And whan that he the haven hadde ytake,
> He hadde a knyght, was called Achates,
> And hym of al his felawshipe he ches
> To gon with hym, the cuntre for t'espie.
> 10 He tok with hym no more companye,
> But forth they gon, and lafte his shipes ryde,
> His fere and he, withouten any gyde.
> So longe he walketh in this wildernesse,
> Til at the laste he mette an hunteresse.

---

**2** *unnethe*: with difficulty
**12** *fere*: companion

A bowe in hande and arwes hadde she;
Hire clothes cutted were unto the kne.
But she was yit the fayreste creature
That evere was yformed by Nature;
And Eneas and Achates she grette,
20  And thus she to hem spak whan she hem mette:
'Saw ye,' quod she, 'as ye han walked wyde,
Any of my sustren walke yow besyde
With any wilde bor or other best,
That they han hunted to, in this forest,
Ytukked up, with arwes in hire cas?'
'Nay, sothly, lady,' quod this Eneas;
'But by thy beaute, as it thynketh me,
Thow myghtest nevere erthly woman be,
But Phebus syster art thow, as I gesse.
30  And if so be that thow be a goddesse,
Have mercy on oure labour and oure wo.'
'I n'am no goddesse, sothly,' quod she tho;
'For maydens walken in this contre here,
With arwes and with bowe, in this manere.
This is the reyne of Libie there ye ben,
Of which that Dido lady is and queen' –
And shortly tolde hym al the occasyoun
Why Dido cam into that regioun,
Of which as now me lesteth nat to ryme;
40  It nedeth nat, it were but los of tyme.
For this is al and som, it was Venus,
His owene moder, that spak with him thus,
And to Cartage she bad he sholde hym dighte,
And vanyshed anon out of his syghte.

---

**22** *sustren*: sisters
**25** *ytukked up*: with skirt tucked up
**29** *Phebus syster*: Diana
**43** *dighte*: hasten

I coude folwe, word for word, Virgile,
But it wolde lasten al to longe while.
      This noble queen that cleped was Dido,
That whilom was the wif of Sytheo,
That fayrer was than is the bryghte sonne,
50  This noble toun of Cartage hath bigonne;
In which she regneth in so gret honour
That she was holden of alle queenes flour
Of gentillesse, of fredom, of beaute,
That wel was hym that myghte hire ones se;
Of kynges and of lordes so desyred
That al the world hire beaute hadde yfyred,
She stod so wel in every wightes grace.
      Whan Eneas was come unto that place,
Unto the mayster temple of al the toun
60  Ther Dido was in hire devocyoun,
Ful pryvyly his weye than hath he nome.
Whan he was in the large temple come,
I can nat seyn if that it be possible,
But Venus hadde hym maked invysible –
Thus seyth the bok, withouten any les.
And whan this Eneas and Achates
Hadden in this temple ben overal,
Thanne founde they, depeynted on a wal,
How Troye and al the lond destroyed was.
70  'Allas, that I was born!' quod Eneas;
'Thourghout the world oure shame is kid so wyde,
Now it is peynted upon every syde.
We, that weren in prosperite,
Been now desclandred, and in swich degre,
No lenger for to lyven I ne kepe.'
And with that word he brast out for to wepe

---

**48** *Sytheo*: Sychaeus
**65** *les*: lie
**74** *desclandred*: disgraced

So tenderly that routhe it was to sene.
This fresshe lady, of the cite queene,
Stod in the temple in hire estat real,
80  So rychely and ek so fayr withal,
So yong, so lusty, with hire eyen glade,
That, if that God, that hevene and erthe made,
Wolde han a love, for beaute and goodnesse,
And womanhod, and trouthe, and semelynesse,
Whom shulde he loven but this lady swete?
Ther nys no woman to hym half so mete.
Fortune, that hath the world in governaunce,
Hath sodeynly brought in so newe a chaunce
That nevere was ther yit so fremde a cas.
90  For al the companye of Eneas,
Which that he wende han loren in the se,
Aryved is nat fer from that cite;
For which the gretteste of his lordes some
By aventure ben to the cite come,
Unto that same temple, for to seke
The queene, and of hire socour to beseke,
Swich renoun was there sprongen of hire goodnesse.
And whan they hadden told al here distresse,
And al here tempest and here harde cas,
100 Unto the queen apeered Eneas,
And openly biknew that it was he.                    (*c.* 1372–80)

_____

**77** *routhe* (*ruth*): pity
**89** *fremde*: strange
**98–9** *here*: their

# GAVIN DOUGLAS (c. 1474–1522)

## The Second Buke of Eneados, chapter 9 [Aen. II. 506–59] *The death of Priam*

From Aeneas' narrative to Dido of his last hours in Troy. Douglas's *XIII Bukes of Eneados* (the 'thirteenth book' was added by the Italian humanist Maffio Veggio in the fifteenth century) was written in Scots about 1513 and first printed in 1553; it was the first complete verse translation of the poem made in Britain. The text here printed is that of D. F. C. Coldwell, edited from the MS in the library of Trinity College, Cambridge, for the Scottish Text Society, series 3, no.25 (1957). Cf. the version of the same passage by Surrey (below).

> Into this nixt cheptour ȝe may attend
> Of Priam, kyng of Troy, the fatale end.
>
> Peraventur of Priamus wald ȝe speir
> Quhou tyd the chance. Hys fait, gif ȝe lyst, heir:
> Quhen he the cite saw takyn and downbet,
> And of his palyce brokyn euery ȝet,
> Amyd the secret closettis eik hys fays,
> The auld grayth, al for nocht, to hym tays
> Hys hawbryk quhilk was lang furth of vsage,
> Set on his schulderis trymlyng than for age;
> A sword but help about hym beltis he
> 10  And ran towart hys fays, reddy to de.
> Amyd the closs, vnder the hevyn al bayr,
> Stude thar that tyme a mekil fair altare,
> Neyr quham thar grew a rycht ald lawrer tre

---

1 *speir*: ask
2 *Quhou tyd*: how went
7 *quhilk*: which
11 *closs*: court, close
13 *quham*: which

Bowand towart the altare a litill wie,
That with his schaddow the goddis dyd ourheld.
Hecuba thyddir with his childer for beild
Ran al invane and about the altare swarmys,
Brasand the godlyke ymage in thar armys,
As for the storm dowis flokkis togidder ilkane.

20    Bot quhen scho saw how Priamus has tane
His armour, so as thocht he had beyn ȝyng:
'Quhat fulych thocht, my wrachit spowss and kyng,
Movis the now syk wapynnys forto weld?
Quhidder hastis thou?' quod sche. 'Of na sik beld
Haue we now mystir, nor syk diffendouris as the,
The tyme is nocht ganand tharto we se,
In cace Hectour war present heir, my son,
He mycht nocht succur Troy, for it is won,
Quharfor I pray the syt doune and cum hydder

30    And lat this altare salue wss al togidder,
Or than atanys al heir lat ws de.'
Thus said scho and with sik sembland as mycht be
Hym towart hir has brocht, but ony threte,
And set the auld doune on the haly sete.
Bot lo, Polytes, ane of Priamus sonnys
Quhilk from the slauchter of Pyrrus away run is,
Throw wapynnys fleyng and his ennemyss all,
Be lang throwgangis and mony voyd hall;
Woundit he was, and come to seik reskew.

40    Ardently Pyrrus gan him fast persew,
With grondyn lance at hand so neir furthstrekit,

---

14 *Bowand*: bowing
16 *thyddir*: thither
19 *dowis*: doves; *ilkane*: each one
23 *syk wapynnys*: such weapons
24 *beld*: comfort, succour
26 *ganand*: suitable
31 *atanys*: at once; *lat ws de*: let us die
38 *throwgangis*: thoroughfares

Almaist the hed hym twichit and arekit,
Quhil at the last, quhen he is cummyn, I weyn,
Befor his faderis and his moderis eyn,
Smate hym down ded in thar sycht quhar he stude,
The gaist he ȝald with habundans of blude.
Priamus than, thocht he was halfdeill ded,
Mycht nocht conteyn his ire nor wordis of fed,
Bot cryis furth: 'For that cruell offens
50    And owtragyus fuyl hardy violens,
Gif thar be piete in the hevin abone
Quhilk takis heid to this at thou has done,
The goddis mot condyngly the forȝeld,
Eftir thi desert rendring sik gaynȝeld,
Causit me behald myne awyn child slane, allace,
And with hys blude fylit the faderis face.
Bot he quhamby thou fenys thi self byget,
Achil, was not to Priam sa hard set,
For he, of rycht and faith eschamyt eik,
60    Quhen that I come hym lawly tobeseik,
The ded body of Hector rendrit me,
And me convoyit hame to my cite.'
Thus sayand the ald waykly, but forss or dynt,
A dart dyd cast, quhilk with a pyk gan stynt
On his harness, and in the scheild dyd hyng
But ony harm or other dammagyng.
Quod Pyrrus, 'Sen always thou saist swa,
To Pellyus son, my fadir, thou most ga.
Beir hym this message, ramembir weil thou tell
70    Him al my warkis and dedis sa cruell —

---

**46** 'he yielded up the ghost'
**52** *at*: that
**53** *condyngly*: deservedly
**57** *quhamby*: by whom
**59** *eschamyt*: ashamed
**67** 'since that's the line you're taking'

Schaw Neoptolemus is degenerit cleyn.
Now salt thou de.' And with that word in teyn
The ald trymlyng towart the altare he drew,
That in the hait blude of his son, sched new,
Fundrit; and Pyrrus grippis hym by the hayr
With his left hand, and with the tother albayr
Drew furth his schynand swerd, quhilk in his syde
Festynnyt, and onto the hyltis dyd he hyde.
Of Priamus thus was the finale fait —
80    Fortone heir endit his gloryus estait,
Seand Ilion albyrn in fryis brown
And Troys wallis fall and tumlyt down.
That ryal prince, vmquhile our Asya
Apon sa feil pepil and realmys alswa
Ryngnyt in welth, now by the cost lyis ded
Bot as a stok and of hakkit his hed,
A corps but lyfe, renown or other fame,
Onknawyn of ony wight quhat was his name.    (1553)

---

**71** *Neoptolemus*: the other name of Pyrrhus, Achilles' son; *degenerit cleyn*: completely degenerate (spoken with scornful irony — cf. Surrey's version, below)
**81** *Seand*: seeing
**83** *vmquhile*: erstwhile
**84** *Apon sa feil pepil*: upon so many people
**85** *Ryngnyt*: reigning
**87** *but*: without

# SURREY, HENRY HOWARD, EARL OF (1516–47)

## Aeneid II, 654–729 [Aen. II. 506–58] *The death of Priam*

From Aeneas' narrative to Dido of his last hours in Troy. See the same passage in the only earlier version, that of Gavin Douglas (above), which Surrey certainly used. He translated only Books II and IV: Book IV was first printed in 1554, Book II (together with IV) in 1557, in *Tottels Miscellany*, from which the present text, ed. E. Jones (Clarendon Medieval and Tudor Texts, 1964), is taken.

These translations represent the earliest use in English of blank verse.

Parcase yow wold ask what was Priams fate.
When of his taken town he saw the chaunce,
And the gates of his palace beaten down,
His foes amid his secret chambers eke,
Th'old man in vaine did on his sholders then,
Trembling for age, his curace long disused,
His bootelesse swerd he girded him about,
And ran amid his foes ready to die.
    Amid the court under the heven all bare
10  A great altar there stood, by which there grew
An old laurel tree, bowing therunto,
Which with his shadow did embrace the gods.
Here Hecuba with her yong daughters all
About the altar swarmed were in vaine,
Like doves that flock together in the storme;
The statues of the gods embracing fast.
But when she saw Priam had taken there
His armure, like as though he had ben yong,
'What furious thought, my wretched spouse,' quod she,
20  'Did move thee now such wepons for to weld?
Why hastest thow? This time doth not require

Such succor, ne yet such defenders now;
No, though Hector my son were here againe.
Come hether; this altar shall save us all,
Or we shall dye together.' Thus she sayd.
Wherwith she drew him back to her, and set
The aged man down in the holy seat.
    But loe, Polites, one of Priams sons,
Escaped from the slaughter of Pyrrhus,
30   Comes fleing through the wepons of his foes,
Searching all wounded the long galleries
And the voyd courtes; whom Pyrrhus all in rage
Followed fast to reach a mortal wound,
And now in hand wellnere strikes with his spere.
Who fleing fourth till he came now in sight
Of his parentes, before their face fell down,
Yelding the ghost, with flowing streames of blood.
Priamus then, although he were half ded,
Might not kepe in his wrath, nor yet his words,
40   But cryeth out: 'For this thy wicked work,
And boldnesse eke such thing to enterprise,
If in the heavens any justice be
That of such things takes any care or kepe,
According thankes the gods may yeld to thee,
And send thee eke thy just deserved hyre,
That made me see the slaughter of my childe,
And with his blood defile the fathers face.
But he, by whom thow fainst thy self begot,
Achilles, was to Priam not so stern.
50   For loe, he tendring my most humble sute
The right and faith, my Hectors bloodlesse corps
Rendred for to be layd in sepulture,
And sent me to my kingdome home againe.'
Thus sayd the aged man, and therewithall

---

**48–53** The reference is to *Iliad* XXIV, in which Achilles handed back
Hector's body to Priam.

Forcelesse he cast his weake unweldy dart,
Which, repulst from the brasse where it gave dint,
Without sound hong vainly in the shieldes bosse.
Quod Pyrrhus: 'Then thow shalt this thing report.
On message to Pelide my father go.
60    Shew unto him my cruel dedes, and how
Neoptolem is swarved out of kinde.
Now shalt thow dye,' quod he. And with that word
At the altar him trembling gan he draw
Wallowing through the blodshed of his son;
And his left hand all clasped in his heare,
With his right arme drewe fourth his shining sword,
Which in his side he thrust up to the hilts.
Of Priamus this was the fatal fine,
The wofull end that was alotted him.
70    When he had seen his palace all on flame,
With ruine of his Troyan turrets eke,
That royal prince of Asie, which of late
Reignd over so many peoples and realmes,
Like a great stock now lieth on the shore;
His hed and sholders parted ben in twaine,
A body now without renome and fame.                    (1557)

---

**59** *Pelide*(s): Achilles (son of Peleus)
**61** *Neoptolem*(us): alternative name of Pyrrhus. The line is spoken with bitter
scorn: 'tell my father that his son has abandoned his ancestral virtue'. Douglas
keeps closer to the Latin *degenerem*.

# EDMUND SPENSER (1552–99)

## The Shepheardes Calender, June *The June Eclogue*

An imitation of Virgil, full of allusions to the *Eclogues*: pastoral content and discontent, the art of song, lost love, the lament for a dead mastersinger. As in Virgil, the 'shepherds' are really poets: Colin is Spenser in the same way as Menalcas in Eclogue IX is Virgil. See Appendix A.

> *This Æglogue is wholly vowed to the complayning of Colins ill successe in his loue. For being (as is aforesaid) enamoured of a Country lasse Rosalind, and hauing (as seemeth) founde place in her heart, he lamenteth to his deare frend Hobbinoll, that he is nowe forsaken vnfaithfully, and in his steede Menalcas, another shepheard, receiued disloyally. And this is the whole Argument of this Æglogue.*

HOBBINOL    COLIN CLOVTE
Lo *Colin*, here the place, whose pleasaunt syte
From other shades hath weand my wandring mynde.
Tell me, what wants me here, to worke delyte?
The simple ayre, the gentle warbling wynde,   .
So calme, so coole, as no where else I fynde:
The grassye ground with daintye Daysies dight,
The Bramble bush, where Byrds of euery kynde
To the waters fall their tunes attemper right.

COLLIN
O happy *Hobbinoll*, I blesse thy state,
10    That Paradise hast found, whych *Adam* lost.
Here wander may thy flock early or late,
Withouten dreade of Wolues to bene ytost:
Thy louely layes here mayst thou freely boste.

But I vnhappy man, whom cruell fate,
And angry Gods pursue from coste to coste,
Can nowhere fynd, to shroude my lucklesse pate.

HOBBINOLL

Then if by me thou list aduised be,
Forsake the soyle, that so doth the bewitch:
Leaue me those hilles, where harbrough nis to see,
20  Nor holybush, nor brere, nor winding witche:
And to the dales resort, where shepheards ritch,
And fruictfull flocks bene euery where to see.
Here no night Rauens lodge more black then pitche,
Nor eluish ghosts, nor gastly owles doe flee.

But frendly Faeries, met with many Graces,
And lightfote Nymphes can chace the lingring night,
With Heydeguyes, and trimly trodden traces,
Whilst systers nyne, which dwell on Parnasse hight,
Doe make them musick, for their more delight:
30  And Pan himselfe to kisse their christall faces,
Will pype and daunce, when Phœbe shineth bright:
Such pierlesse pleasures haue we in these places.

COLLIN

And I, whylst youth, and course of carelesse yeeres
Did let me walke withouten lincks of loue,
In such delights did ioy amongst my peeres:
But ryper age such pleasures doth reproue,
My fancye eke from former follies moue
To stayed steps: for time in passing weares
(As garments doen, which wexen old aboue)
40  And draweth newe delightes with hoary heares.

---

**27** *Heydeguyes*: country dances

Tho couth I sing of loue, and tune my pype
Vnto my plaintiue pleas in verses made:
Tho would I seeke for Queene apples vnrype,
To giue my Rosalind, and in Sommer shade
Dight gaudy Girlonds, was my comen trade,
To crowne her golden locks, but yeeres more rype,
And losse of her, whose loue as lyfe I wayd,
Those weary wanton toyes away dyd wype.

HOBBINOLL

Colin, to heare thy rymes and roundelayes,
50   Which thou were wont on wastfull hylls to singe,
I more delight, then larke in Sommer dayes:
Whose Echo made the neyghbour groues to ring,
And taught the byrds, which in the lower spring
Did shroude in shady leaues from sonny rayes,
Frame to thy songe their chereful cheriping,
Or hold theyr peace, for shame of thy swete layes.

I sawe Calliope wyth Muses moe,
Soone as thy oaten pype began to sound,
Theyr yuory Luyts and Tamburins forgoe:
60   And from the fountaine, where they sat around,
Renne after hastely thy siluer sound.
But when they came, where thou thy skill didst showe,
They drewe abacke, as halfe with shame confound,
Shepheard to see, them in theyr art outgoe.

COLLIN

Of Muses Hobbinol, I conne no skill:
For they bene daughters of the hyghest Ioue,
And holden scorne of homely shepheards quill.
For sith I heard, that Pan with Phœbus stroue,

---

**43** *Queene apples vnrype*: fresh quinces (cf. Virgil, Eclogue II, 52)

Which him to much rebuke and Daunger droue:
70   I neuer lyst presume to Parnasse hyll,
But pyping lowe in shade of lowly groue,
I play to please my selfe, all be it ill.

Nought weigh I, who my song doth prayse or blame,
Ne striue to winne renowne, or passe the rest:
With shepheard sittes not, followe flying fame:
But feede his flocke in fields, where falls hem best.
I wote my rymes bene rough, and rudely drest:
The fytter they, my carefull case to frame:
Enough is me to paint out my vnrest,
80   And poore my piteous plaints out in the same.

The God of shepheards Tityrus is dead,
Who taught me homely, as I can, to make.
He, whilst he liued, was the soueraigne head
Of shepheards all, that bene with loue ytake:
Well couth he wayle hys Woes, and lightly slake
The flames, which loue within his heart had bredd,
And tell vs mery tales, to keepe vs wake,
The while our sheepe about vs safely fedde.

Nowe dead he is, and lyeth wrapt in lead,
90   (O why should death on hym such outrage showe?)
And all hys passing skil with him is fledde,
The fame whereof doth dayly greater growe.
But if on me some little drops would flowe,
Of that the spring was in his learned hedde,
I soone would learne these woods, to wayle my woe,
And teache the trees, their trickling teares to shedde.

---

**71** *lowe, lowly*: key words of Renaissance pastoral; cf. 82, 'homely'.
**81** *Tityrus*: Chaucer

Then should my plaints, causd of discurtesee,
As messengers of all my painfull plight,
Flye to my loue, where euer that she bee,
100 And pierce her heart with poynt of worthy wight:
As shee deserues, that wrought so deadly spight.
And thou Menalcas, that by trecheree
Didst vnderfong my lasse, to wexe so light,
Shouldest well be knowne for such thy villanee.

But since I am not, as I wish I were,
Ye gentle shepheards, which your flocks do feede,
Whether on hylls, or dales, or other where,
Beare witnesse all of thys so wicked deede:
And tell the lasse, whose flowre is woxe a weede,
110 And faultlesse fayth, is turned to faithlesse fere,
That she the truest shepheards hart made bleede,
That lyues on earth, and loued her most dere.

HOBBINOL

O carefull Colin, I lament thy case,
Thy teares would make the hardest flint to flowe.
Ah faithlesse Rosalind, and voide of grace,
That art the roote of all this ruthfull woe.
But now is time, I gesse, homeward to goe:
Then ryse ye blessed flocks, and home apace,
Least night with stealing steppes doe you forsloe,
120 And wett your tender Lambes, that by you trace.

Colins Embleme
*Gia speme spenta.* (1579)

---

103 *vnderfong*: deceive
117–20 For the formal ending, cf. the close of Virgil, Eclogue X.

# EDMUND SPENSER

## The Shepheardes Calender, November, 173–210
### The apotheosis of Dido

Only Dido's name is from the *Aeneid*: the poem is an imitation of
the apotheosis of the shepherd Daphnis in Virgil, Eclogue VI, 56–80.
Spenser's poem, like Virgil's, begins with a lament for the dead
shepherd, mourned by his companions and by the Muses, and then
changes to a celebration of his deification. This formal structure
recurs in Milton's 'Lycidas' and in many later pastoral elegies.

The passage juxtaposes Christian and pagan imagery in the usual
Renaissance humanist style.

> Why wayle we then? why weary we the Gods with playnts,
> As if some euill were to her betight?
> She raignes a goddesse now emong the saintes,
> That whilome was the saynt of shepheards light:
> And is enstalled nowe in heauens hight.
> > I see thee blessed soule, I see,
> > Walke in Elisian fieldes so free.
> > > O happy herse,
> Might I once come to thee (O that I might)
> > > O ioyfull verse.

10

> Vnwise and wretched men to weete whats good or ill,
> We deeme of Death as doome of ill desert:
> But knewe we fooles, what it vs bringes vntil,
> Dye would we dayly, once it to expert.
> No daunger there the shepheard can astert:
> > Fayre fieldes and pleasaunt layes there bene,
> > The fieldes ay fresh, the grasse ay greene:
> > > O happy herse,

---

**14** *expert*: experience
**15** *astert*: befall

Make hast ye shepheards, thether to reuert,
20      O ioyfull verse.

Dido is gone afore (whose turne shall be the next?)
There liues shee with the blessed Gods in blisse,
There drincks she Nectar with Ambrosia mixt,
And ioyes enioyes, that mortall men doe misse.
The honor now of highest gods she is,
    That whilome was poore shepheards pryde,
    While here on earth she did abyde.
        O happy herse,
Ceasse now my song, my woe now wasted is.
30      O ioyfull verse.

THENOT
Ay francke shepheard, how bene thy verses meint
With doolful pleasaunce, so as I ne wotte,
Whether reioyce or weepe for great constrainte?
Thyne be the cossette, well hast thow it gotte.
Vp Colin vp, ynough thou morned hast,
Now gynnes to mizzle, hye we homeward fast.

Colins Embleme
*La mort ny mord.*                    (1579)

# THOMAS PHAER (*c.* 1510–60) and
# THOMAS TWYNE (1543–1613)

## The Whole xii Bookes of the Aeneidos of Virgill, V, 891–927 [Aen. V. 835–71] and VI, 673–789 [Aen. VI. 637–751] *The death of Palinurus* and *Aeneas and Anchises in the Elysian Fields*

From the first complete translation of the *Aeneid* into English (1584): printed from the edition by Stephen Lally (1987). For further details see Introduction, pp. xxiii–xxiv.

On the last lap of the voyage to Italy, Aeneas' pilot, Palinurus, fell overboard mysteriously and was drowned, thus fulfilling Neptune's prophecy that all but one of the surviving Trojans would land safely in Italy. This haunting episode is the subject of a modern study by Cyril Connolly, *The Unquiet Grave* (1984).

In the Elysian Fields (second extract), Aeneas is greeted by his father, who describes the soul's journey after death and expounds the principle of 'Universal Mind': a celebrated passage in which Virgil drew on Pythagorean, Platonic and Stoic philosophy.

*Palinure his principall pylot*

And now from heauen ye drowping night her mid course
                                                          nere had past
And folkes in slumber sweete, their wery limmes on rest had
                                                          cast,
And Mariners had layd them selues on hatches hard of bars:
Whan lightinge swift, from skies the God of sleape did fall
                                                          from stars,
And brake the darke of night, with glimsing shade of fayned
                                                          beames.
To thee (O Palinure) and brought to thee right heauy
                                                          dreames,

Without desert, and on the pup full hie his seate did take,
Resembling Phorbas face, and vnto him these wordes he
                                                    spake.
Freend Palinure, lo how the tydes them selues conueys the
                                                    fleete.
10   This gale by measure blowes: an houre of rest to take is
                                                    meete.
Lay downe thy head, and steale thy painfull eyes one nap of
                                                    sleepe,
I will for thee my selfe supply thy rowme thy helme to keepe.
Whom aunswerd Palinure, skant lifting eyes for slumber
                                                    deepe.
Know I not yet my seas? what? thinkst thou mee so small of
                                                    wit,
To trust this fawning face? shall I my lorde and prince
                                                    commit,
To this inconstant beast? should I beleeuve that monster
                                                    wilde?
So oft as I with flattring seas, and skies haue ben begilde?
Such things he spake, and holding hard at helme he cleaued
                                                    fast,
And still did serue the streames, and still on stars his eyes did
                                                    cast.
20   Behold, the God on him a dropping braunch of Lymbo pyt
With deadly sleeping dewe, on both his temples dashing
                                                    smyt.
And struggling to resist, his swimming eyes with sleepe
                                                    opprest,
Skant first resolued were his weery limmes with sodeyn rest.
And leaning noddid lowe: whan half the pup with him he
                                                    drew,
And rother, helme, and all, in myds of seas he falling threw

---

7, 24 *pup*: poop
8 *Phorbas*: presumably one of the crew
25 *rother*: rudder

Quite hedlong ouer bourd, and calling oft his mates in vaine.
The God than toke his winges, and thin in winde he went
                                                        againe.
Yet nerethelesse therfore, with safe conduct their fleete did
                                                        pas,
And careles ronnes their course, as god Neptunes promise
                                                        was.
30   And now they entring were the straytes, Sirenes rockes that
                                                        hight,
A parlous place sometime, and yet with bones of people
                                                        whight.
Than breaking broad the floods, the saltsea stones full hoarce
                                                        did sound,
Whan lord Aeneas felt his ship to stray and maister dround.
And toke himselfe the giding than therof in seas by night,
Lamenting much in minde his freends mischaunce and heauy
                                                        plight.
O Palinure, that flattring seas and skies to much didst trust,
All naked on some straungy sand onburied lye thou must.

*Description of Paradise*

These things so done, and all the goddesse gift fulfild at last:
Into the gladsome feeldes they come, where arbers sweete
                                                        and greene,
And blessed seates of soules, and pleasant woods and groues
                                                        are sèene.
A fresher feeld of aier whom larger light doth ouerstrow,
And purer breath, their priuat sonne, their priuat stars they
                                                        know.
Some to disport them selues there sondry maistries tried on
                                                        grasse.
And some their gambolds plaid, and some on sand there
                                                        wrastling was.
Some frisking shake their feete, & measures tread & rimes
                                                        they sowne.

And Orpheus among them stands, as priest in trayling gowne,
10   And twancling makes them tune, with notes of musike
                                               seuerall seuen,
And now with Yuery quill, now strings he strikes with
                                               fingers euen.
There were the Troyan lords, and antike stocke of noble race,
Most prudent princes strong, and borne in yeres of better
                                               grace.
Both Ilus, and Assaracus, and founder first of Troy.
King Dardan, at their armour weedes he wondred much with
                                               ioy.
Their speares beside them stand, their charets strong are set
                                               on ground,
Their comly coursing steedes along the launds do feede
                                               vnbound.
What minds, what loue they had, to deeds of arms what life
                                               they drew,
Or what delite in steedes: the same them dead doth now
                                               pursue.
20   Another sort he seeth, with hand in hand where gras doth
                                               spring,
That feasting feede them selues, and heaue and how for joy
                                               they singe.
Among the Laurell woods, and smelling floures of arbers
                                               sweete,
Where bubbling soft with sound the riuer fresh doth by them
                                               fleet,
There such as for their contreys loue while liues in them did
                                               last
In battel suffred wounds, or priestes that godly were and
                                               chast,
Or prophets pure of life, and worthy things to men did preach:
Or to adorne mans mortall life did science goodly teache:
Their heads are compas knit with garlond floures right fresh
                                               of hewe,
To whom than Sibly spake, as round about her fast they drew,

30  Onto Musaeus first, for he inclosed is in throng
    With numbers great of soules, and him they keepe alwaies
                                              among,
    Bresthigh aboue them all, and all to him their heads incline.
    Declare (quoth she) you blessed soules, and thou priest most
                                              diuine,
    What place Anchises hath? where shal we find him? for his
                                              sake
    We be come here, and passed haue the floods of Limbo lake.
    Than vnto her the sacred priest with wordes full gentle
                                              spake.
    No man hath certen house, but in these shadowes broad we
                                              dwell,
    In beds of riuer bankes, and medowes new that sweetely
                                              smell.
    But you, if such desire you haue, passe ouer yonder downes,
40  My selfe shall be your gide by easie path into those bownes.
    He said, and went before them both and fieldes ful bright
                                              that shynd
    He shewd them from aboue, and all the downes they left
                                              behind.
        Anchises prince, that time in pleasant vale surueying was
    The soules included there that to the world againe should
                                              passe.
    And reckned all his race, and childers childerns line he told,
    And kest their destnies all, and liues, and lawes, and manhods
                                              bold.
    He whan against him there Aeneas comming first beheld,
    As he did walke in grasse, his hands to heauen for ioy vp
                                              held,
    With tricling teares on cheekes, & thus his voyce from him
                                              did yeld.
50      And art thou comen at last, long looked for, my son so
                                              deere?

---

**46** *kest:* cast, forecast

Thy vertue ouercame this passage hard, and now so cleere,
Do I behold thy face? with rendring speech to speech of
thine?
So verily mee thought, and in my minde I did deuine
Acompting still the times, nor mee my carcke hath not
begilde.
What contreys thee (my son) what combrous seas? what
nations wilde
Turmoyled with daungers all, thee scaped now do I receiue?
How sore affraid I was, lest Lybie lands should thee deceiue?
He therunto: Thy ghost O father sweet, thy greeuous ghost,
Perturbing in my dremes hath me compeld to see this coast.
60   On Tirrhen shore my nauy stands at seas, now let vs ioyne
Good father hand in hand, now thee from mee do not
purloyne.
Thus talked he with teares.
Three times about his necke his armes he would haue set, and
thries
In vaine his likenes fast he helde, for through his hands he
flies
Like winde, vngropable, or dreames that men most swift
espies.
   This while Aeneas seeth a croked vale, and secret wood,
And shrubs of sounding trees, and fleeting through them
Lethee flood,
With sleeping sound, that by those pleasant dwellings softly
ran:
And peoples thicke on euery side that no man number can.
70   As bees in medowes fresh, (whom somer sun doth shining
warme)
Assembling fall on floures, and Lilies white about they
swarme,
With huzzing feruent noyse, that euery feeld of murmour
ringes.
Aeneas with that sight amasid stood, and of those things
The causes all did axe, what flood it is, so dull that glides?

And what those peoples ben, that fill so thicke those water
                                            sides?
Anchises than to him. These soules (quoth he) that bodies
                                            new
Must yet againe receiue, and limmes eftsones with life endue,
Here at this Lethee flood they dwell, and from this water
                                          brincke
These liquors quenching cares, & long forgetful draughts
                                      they drink,
80    That of their liues, and former labours past, they neuer
                                        thinke.
    These things to thee, full trew I shall set forth before thine
                                        eyes,
And shew thee all our stocke, of thee and mee that shall arise,
That more thou maist reioyce Italia land to finde at last.
O father, is it true? may soules that ones this world hath past
And blessed ben in ioy, to bodies dull againe remoue?
What meane they so? why wretched worldly light do they so
                                        loue?
I will declare forsooth, nor long (my son) I will thee holde,
Anchises aunswer made, and all in order did vnfolde.
    First heauen and earth, and of the seas that flittring feeldes &
                                        fines,
90    These glorious stars, this glistring globe of moone so bright
                                      that shines,
One liuely soule there is, that feedes them all with breath of
                                        loue,
One mind through al these members mixt this mighty masse
                                      doth moue.
From thence mankinde, & beasts, and liues of foules in aier
                                      that flies,
And all what marblefaced seas conteines of monstrous fries,
The chafing fier among them all there sits, and heauenly
                                      springes
Within their seedes, if bodies noisom them not backward
                                      bringes.

But lompe of liueles earth, and mortall members make them
dull.

This causeth them, of lust, feare, griefe and ioy, to be so full.

Nor closed so in darke, can they regard their heauenly kinde,

100    Nor carcas foule of flesh, and dongeon vile of prison blinde.

Moreouer, whan their end of life, and light them doth
forsake:

Yet can they not their sinnes nor sorowes all (poore soules)
of shake.

Nor all contagions fleshly, from them voides, but must of
neede

Much things congendred long, by wondrous meanes at last
outspreed.

Therfore they plaged ben, and for their former fautes and
sinnes

Their sondry paines they bide, some hie in ayer doth hang on
pinnes.

Some fleeting ben in floods, and deepe in gulfes them selues
they tier

Till sinnes away be washt, or clensed cleere with purging fier.

Eche one of vs our penaunce here abides, than sent we bee

110    To Paradise at last, we few these fieldes of ioy do see:

Till compas long of time, by perfit course, hath purged
quight

Our former cloddrid spots, and pure hath left our ghostly
spright,

And sences pure of soule, and simple sparkes of heauenly
light.

Than all, whan they a thousand yeres that wheele haue turnd
about,

To drinke of Lethee flood, by clusters great, God calles them
out.

That there forgetting all their former liues, and former sin,

The mortall world afresh, in bodies new they may begin.

(1584)

# WILLIAM WEBBE (fl. 1568–91)

## Eclogue I [Ecl. I]

Included, with Eclogue II, in his *Discourse of English Poetrie* (1586) to illustrate his somewhat confused theories of prosody. His quantitative hexameters may be compared with those of Stanyhurst (see Introduction).

The First Eclogue, like the Ninth, deals with the land-confiscations which followed the battle of Philippi (see Introduction).

MELIBAEUS

Tityrus, happilie thou lyste tumbling under a beech tree,
All in a fine oate pipe these sweete songs lustilie chaunting:
We, poore soules, goe to wracke, and from these coastes be
                                                        remooved,
And fro our pastures sweete: thou Tityr, at ease in a shade
                                                        plott,
Makst thick groves to resound with songs of brave Amarillis.

TITYRUS

O Melibaeus, he was no man but a god who releevde me:
Ever he shalbe my God: from this same Sheepcot his alters
Never a tender lamb shall want, with blood to bedew them.
This good gift did he give, to my steeres thus freelie to
                                                        wander,
10  And to myselfe (thou seest) on pipe to resound what I listed.

MELIBAEUS

Grutch thee sure I doo not, but this thing makes me to
                                                        wonder,
Whence comes all this adoo: with grievous paine not a little

---

6–7 *The god is Octavian.*

Can I remove my Goates: here, Tityre, skant get I forward
Poore olde crone, two twins at a clappe i'th' boysterous has
                                                        ills
Left she behind, best hope i' my flock laid hard on a bare
                                                        stone.
Had not a luckless lotte possest our mindes, I remember
Warnings oft fro the blast-burnt oake we saw to be sent us.
Oft did a left hand crow foretell these things in her hull tree,
But this God let us heare what he was, good Tityre tell me.

TITYRUS

20   That same Cittie so brave which Rome was wont to be
                                                        called,
Fool did I think to be like this of ours, where we to the
                                                        pastures
Wonted were to remove from dammes our pretty Cattell.
Thus did I thinke young whelpes, and Kids to be like to the
                                                        mothers,
Thus did I wont compare manie great things with many
                                                        little.
But this above all towns as loftily mounteth her high head,  ·
As by the lowe base shrubbes tall Cypresse shooteth above
                                                        them.

MELIBAEUS

And what did thee move that needes thou must go to see
                                                        Rome?

TITYRUS

Freedome: which though late, yet once lookt backe to my
                                                        pore state,
After time when haires from my beard did ginne to be
                                                        whitish:

---

**18** *hull*: hollow

30 Yet lookt back at last and found me out after a long time.
When Amarill was once obtainde, Galatea departed:
For (for I will confesse) whilst as Galatea did hold mee,
Hope did I not for freedome, and care had I none to my
cattell.
Though manie faire young beastes our folde for the aulters
aforded
And manie cheeses good fro my presse were sent to the
Cittie:
Seldome times did I bring anie store of pence fro the markett.

MELIBAEUS
O Amarill, wherefore to thy Gods (very much did I
mervaile)
Heavilie thou didst praie: ripe fruites ungathered all still;
Tityrus is not at home: these Pyne trees, Tityre, mist thee.
40 Fountaines longd for thee: these hedgrowes wished thy return
home.

TITYRUS
What was then to be doone? from bondage could not I wind
out:
Neither I could have found such gentle Gods anywhere els.
There did I see (Meliboee) that youth whose hestes I by
course still.
Fortnights whole to observe on the Altars sure will I not
faile.
Thus did he gentlie graunt to my sute when first I
demaunded.
Keepe your heardes poore slaves as erst, let bulles to the
makes still.

43 *by course still*: ever steer by
46 *makes*: mates

MELIBAEUS

Happy olde man, then thou shalt have thy farme to remaine
                                                          still,
Large and large to thyselfe, others naught but stony gravell:
And foule slymie rush wherewith their lees be besprinkled.
50  Here no unwoonted foode shall grieve young theaves who be
                                                          laded,
Nor the infections foule of neighbours flocks shall annoie
                                                          them.
Happie old man! In shadowy banks and coole pretty places
Here by the quainted floodes and springs most holie
                                                          remaining,
Here these quicksets fresh which lands sever out fro thy
                                                          neighbors,
And greene willow rowes which Hiblea bees do rejoice in,
Oft fine whistring noise, shall bring sweete sleepe to thy
                                                          sences.
Under a Rock side here will proyner chaunt merrie ditties,
Neither on highe Elme trees, thy belovde Doves loftilie
                                                          sitting,
Nor prettie Turtles trim will cease to croake with a good
                                                          cheere.

TITYRUS

60  First, therefore swift buckes shall flie for foode to the skies
                                                          ward,
And from fish withdrawn broade seas themselves shal avoid
                                                          hence:
First, (both borders broke) Araris shall run to the Parthanes,

---

54 *quicksets*: sapling hedges    57 *proyner*: pruner
60–64 The figure is called 'adunaton' (impossibility): 'sooner shall deer
pasture in the sky, the sea empty its fish on to the shore, and the rivers Tigris
and Araris leave their courses than I shall forget his face.'

And likewise Tygris shall againe runne backe to the
                                              Germanes,
Ere his countnaunce sweete shall slippe once out from my
                                              hartroote.

MELIBAEUS
We poor soules must soone to the land cald Affrica packe
                                              hence,
Some to the farre Scythia, and some must to the swift flood
                                              Oaxis.
Some to Britannia coastes quite parted farre fro the whole
                                              world.
Oh these pastures pure shall I nere more chance to behold
                                              yee?
And our cottage poore with warme turves coverd about
                                              trim.
70  Oh these trim tilde landes, shall a recklesse souldier have
                                              them?
And shall a Barbarian have this croppe? see what a mischiefe
Discord vile hath araisde? for whom was our labour all
                                              tooke?
Now Meliboee ingraft pearie stocks, sette vines in an order.
Now goe (my brave flocke once that were) O now go my
                                              kidlings.
Never againe shall I now in a greene bowre sweetelie reposed
See ye in queachie briers farre aloofe clambring on a high hill.
Now shall I sing no Jygges, nor whilst I doo fall to my
                                              junkets
Shall ye my Goates cropping sweete flowers and leaves sit
                                              about me.

---

**62** *Araris*: the river Saône
**66** *Oaxis*: perhaps the river Oxus

TITYRUS

Yet thou maist tarry here, and keepe me companie this night,
80   All on a leavie couch: good Apples ripe doo I not lacke,
Chestnutts sweete good store, and plentie of curddes will I set
                                                                thee.
Marke i' the Towne how chimnie tops do beginne to be
                                                        smoaking,
And fro the Mountaines high how shaddowes grow to be
                                                        larger. (1586)


# ABRAHAM FLEMING (c. 1522–1607)

## [Ecl.V. 56–90] *The apotheosis of Daphnis*

This pastoral elegy was often imitated, e.g. by Spenser and Milton.
Fleming made two versions of the *Eclogues*: the first (1575) used
rhymed fourteeners; the second (1589), from which this text is
taken, used the same metre, but unrhymed, and introduced into the
text various explanatory glosses, placed in square brackets.

MENALCAS

White Daphnis wondreth at the light unwonted of Olympus,
And underfoot doth see the clouds and stars that shine
                                                        beneath,
And therefore pleasure doth possess the glad and joyful
                                                        woods,
And other country grounds beside, and Pan and shepherds
                                                        too,
And those same gyrls the Dryades [which keep among the okes].
The woolf deviseth not ne thinks on snares for sillie beasts,
Ne trains and nets devise deceit for [stags and running] harts,

---

**79–83** The pastoral invitation reconciles the tensions of the dialogue and
brings the poem to an 'Arcadian' close.

Good Daphnis loveth quietness [he loveth rest and peace]:
The hills unshorne lift up for joy their voices to the stars,
10   The rocks themselves, the very groves, [for joy] sound out
their songs,
A god is Daphnis [doubtless] he, O Menalc, is a god.
O Daphnis, o be good and kind and gracious unto thine;
Behold four altars, two for thee O Daphnis, and for Phoebe
Two other altars I will dresse and readie make for thee;
Yerely two pots both foming [full] of new milk [to the brim],
And two kans full of good fat oile; and being merry I
Will make thee bankets first of all, with much wine
[thereunto],
Before the fire if it be cold, if hot then in the shade,
And I will pour out quaffing cups of malmsey wine [which
are]
20   New [strange and passing pleasant drinks] like ippocrasse in
taste.

Damet and Aegon he of Creet shall sing songs unto me,
Alphesibey shall counterfeit the dancing satyrs too;
These [duties] ever shall be done to thee [for honors sake]:
And when we shall restore and pay the nymphs our woonted
vowes,
And when we shall devoutly view and go about the fields,
While boars shall love the tops of hills, and fish the rivers
[streames],
While bees shall feed of thyme and grashoppers of [heavenly]
dew,
Thye honor, name and praises shall for evermore remaine.
To thee shall husbandmen [and all that dwell in countrie soile]
30   Make vowes, as unto Bacchus and to Ceres [they do use],
And thou shalt charge them with their vowes [in binding
them to pay].

---

**20** *ippocrasse* (variously spelt with or without an h): a cordial wine flavoured
with spices; the Latin is *Ariusia vina* (Chian wine)
**27–8** 'as long as the natural order of things lasts'. The reassertion of this order
is part of the celebration of Daphnis' apotheosis.

MOPSUS

What gifts, what gifts for such a song shall I bestow on thee?
For neither doth the blast of sowtherne wind whenas it
comes,
Nor watershores and banks [be dasht] and beaten with the
floods,
Nor streames which downward run among the vallies full of
stones,
So much delight and please me [as the song which thou hast
sung].

MENALCAS

We will bestow upon thee first this brittle pipe; this pipe
Taught us 'the shepherd Corydon did love Alexis faire',
The same taught us 'whose beasts are these, are they Melib's
or no?'

MOPSUS

40  But Menalc, take thou here my shepherd's staff, which
Antigen
When oft he urged the fame of me, yet had it not away,
(And yet at that time Antigen was worthy to be loved),
My trim fair staff with seven knots and [shepherds] hook of
brass. (1589)

---

38-9 Quotations from the opening lines of Virgil's Second and Third Eclogues.

# EDMUND SPENSER (1552–99)

## The Faerie Queene, III, ix, stanzas 32–46

An epitomized version, in the romance mode, of the entertainment
given by Dido to Aeneas in which she learns of the fate of Troy.

Now when of meats and drinks they had their fill,
    Purpose was moued by that gentle Dame,
    Vnto those knights aduenturous, to tell
    Of deeds of armes, which vnto them became,
    And euery one his kindred, and his name.
    Then Paridell, in whom a kindly pryde
    Of gracious speach, and skill his words to frame
    Abounded, being glad of so fit tyde
Him to commend to her, thus spake, of all well eyde.

10 Troy, that art now nought, but an idle name,
    And in thine ashes buried low dost lie,
    Though whilome far much greater then thy fame,
    Before that angry Gods, and cruell skye
    Vpon thee heapt a direfull destinie,
    What boots it boast thy glorious descent,
    And fetch from heauen thy great Genealogie,
    Sith all thy worthy prayses being blent,
Their of-spring hath embaste, and later glory shent.

Most famous Worthy of the world, by whome
20     That warre was kindled, which did Troy inflame,
    And stately towres of Ilion whilome
    Brought vnto balefull ruine, was by name
    Sir Paris far renowmd through noble fame,
    Who through great prowesse and bold hardinesse,
    From Lacedæmon fetcht the fairest Dame,
    That euer Greece did boast, or knight possesse,
Whom Venus to him gaue for meed of worthinesse.

Faire Helene, flowre of beautie excellent,
　　And girlond of the mighty Conquerours,
30　　That madest many Ladies deare lament
　　The heauie losse of their braue Paramours,
　　Which they far off beheld from Troian toures,
　　And saw the fieldes of faire Scamander strowne
　　With carcases of noble warrioures,
　　Whose fruitlesse liues were vnder furrow sowne,
And Xanthus sandy bankes with bloud all ouerflowne.

From him my linage I deriue aright,
　　Who long before the ten yeares siege of Troy,
　　Whiles yet on Ida he a shepheard hight,
40　　On faire Oenone got a louely boy,
　　Whom for remembraunce of her passed ioy,
　　She of his Father Parius did name;
　　Who, after Greekes did Priams realme destroy,
　　Gathred the Troian reliques sau'd from flame,
And with them sayling thence, to th'Isle of Paros came.

That was by him cald Paros, which before
　　Hight Nausa, there he many yeares did raine,
　　And built Nausicle by the Pontick shore,
　　The which he dying left next in remaine
50　　To Paridas his sonne.
　　From whom I Paridell by kin descend;
　　But for faire Ladies loue, and glories gaine,
　　My natiue soile haue left, my dayes to spend
In sewing deeds of armes, my liues and labours end.

Whenas the noble Britomart heard tell
　　Of Troian warres, and Priams Citie sackt,
　　The ruefull story of Sir Paridell,

---

**33.36** *Scamander* and *Xanthus*: rivers of Troy

She was empassiond at that piteous act,
With zelous enuy of Greekes cruell fact,
60       Against that nation, from whose race of old
She heard, that she was lineally extract:
For noble Britons sprong from Troians bold,
And Troynouant was built of old Troyes ashes cold.

Then sighing soft awhile, at last she thus:
O lamentable fall of famous towne,
Which raignd so many yeares victorious,
And of all Asie bore the soueraigne crowne,
In one sad night consumd, and throwen downe:
What stony hart, that heares thy haplesse fate,
70       Is not empierst with deepe compassiowne,
And makes ensample of mans wretched state,
That floures so fresh at morne, and fades at euening late?

Behold, Sir, how your pitifull complaint
Hath found another partner of your payne:
For nothing may impresse so deare constraint,
As countries cause, and commune foes disdayne.
But if it should not grieue you, backe agayne
To turne your course, I would to heare desyre,
What to Aeneas fell; sith that men sayne
80       He was not in the Cities wofull fyre
Consum'd, but did him selfe to safetie retyre.

Anchyses sonne begot of Venus faire,
(Said he,) out of the flames for safegard fled,
And with a remnant did to sea repaire,
Where he through fatall errour long was led
Full many yeares, and weetlesse wandered

---

**59** *fact*: deed
**62–3** The legend that the Britons were descended from a Trojan improbably
named Brutus was invented in the Middle Ages.

From shore to shore, emongst the Lybicke sands,
Ere rest he found. Much there he suffered,
And many perils past in forreine lands,
90   To saue his people sad from victours vengefull hands.

At last in Latium he did arriue,
    Where he with cruell warre was entertaind
    Of th'inland folke, which sought him backe to driue,
    Till he with old Latinus was constraind,
    To contract wedlock: (so the fates ordaind.)
    Wedlock contract in bloud, and eke in blood
    Accomplished, that many deare complaind:
    The riuall slaine, the victour through the flood
Escapęd hardly, hardly praisd his wedlock good.

100   Yet after all, he victour did suruiue,
    And with Latinus did the kingdome part.
    But after, when both nations gan to striue,
    Into their names the title to conuart,
    His sonne Iülus did from thence depart,
    With all the warlike youth of Troians bloud,
    And in long Alba plast his throne apart,
    Where faire it florished, and long time stoud,
Till Romulus renewing it, to Rome remoud.

There there (said Britomart) a fresh appeard
110   The glory of the later world to spring,
    And Troy againe out of her dust was reard,
    To sit in second seat of soueraigne king,
    Of all the world vnder her gouerning.
    But a third kingdome yet is to arise,
    Out of the Troians scattered of-spring,
    That in all glory and great enterprise,
Both first and second Troy shall dare to equalise.

It Troynouant is hight, that with the waues
  Of wealthy Thamis washed is along,
120   Vpon whose stubborne neck, whereat he raues
  With roring rage, and sore him selfe does throng,
  That all men feare to tempt his billowes strong,
  She fastned hath her foot, which standes so hy,
  That it a wonder of the world is song
  In forreine landes, and all which passen by,
Beholding it from far, do thinke it threates the skye.

The Troian Brute did first that Citie found,
  And Hygate made the meare thereof by West,
  And Ouert gate by North: that is the bound
130   Toward the land; two riuers bound the rest.
  So huge a scope at first him seemed best,
  To be the compasse of his kingdomes seat:
  So huge a mind could not in lesser rest,
  Ne in small meares containe his glory great,
That Albion had conquered first by warlike feat.            (1590)


# CHRISTOPHER MARLOWE
(1564–93)

Dido, Queen of Carthage, V, i, 83–192 *The departure of Aeneas*

First printed 1594: the present text is from the edition of H. J.
Oliver (1968). Lines 54–8 quote directly from *Aeneid* IV, 317–19,
360–61. Marlowe's Aeneas departs abruptly, doubtless to increase
the audience's sympathy for Dido.

  *Dido.* [*Aside*] I fear I saw Aeneas' little son
    Led by Achates to the Trojan fleet:
    If it be so, his father means to fly.
    But here he is; now, Dido, try thy wit.

[*To Aeneas*] Aeneas, wherefore go thy men aboard?
Why are thy ships new-rigg'd? Or to what end,
Launch'd from the haven, lie they in the road?
Pardon me though I ask; love makes me ask.

*Aen.* O pardon me if I resolve thee why!
10     Aeneas will not feign with his dear love.
I must from hence: this day swift Mercury,
When I was laying a platform for these walls,
Sent from his father Jove, appear'd to me
And in his name rebuk'd me bitterly
For lingering here, neglecting Italy.

*Dido.* But yet Aeneas will not leave his love.

*Aen.* I am commanded by immortal Jove
To leave this town and pass to Italy,
And therefore must of force.

20 *Dido.* These words proceed not from Aeneas' heart.

*Aen.* Not from my heart, for I can hardly go,
And yet I may not stay; Dido, farewell!

*Dido.* 'Farewell'! Is this the mends for Dido's love?
Do Trojans use to quit their lovers thus?
Fare well may Dido, so Aeneas stay;
I die if my Aeneas say 'farewell'.

*Aen.* Then let me go and never say 'farewell'.

*Dido.* 'Let me go'; 'farewell'; 'I must from hence':
These words are poison to poor Dido's soul.
30     O speak like my Aeneas, like my love!
Why look'st thou toward the sea? The time hath been
When Dido's beauty chain'd thine eyes to her.
Am I less fair than when thou sawest me first?
O then, Aeneas, 'tis for grief of thee!
Say thou wilt stay in Carthage with thy Queen,
And Dido's beauty will return again.
Aeneas, say, how canst thou take thy leave?
Wilt thou kiss Dido? O, thy lips have sworn
To stay with Dido! Canst thou take her hand?
40     Thy hand and mine have plighted mutual faith!

      Therefore, unkind Aeneas, must thou say,
      'Then let me go and never say "farewell"'?
*Aen.* O Queen of Carthage, wert thou ugly-black,
      Aeneas could not choose but hold thee dear;
      Yet must he not gainsay the Gods' behest.
*Dido.* The Gods? What Gods be those that seek my death?
      Wherein have I offended Jupiter
      That he should take Aeneas from mine arms?
      O no, the Gods weigh not what lovers do:
50     It is Aeneas calls Aeneas hence;
      And woeful Dido, by these blubber'd cheeks,
      By this right hand, and by our spousal rites,
      Desires Aeneas to remain with her:
      *Si bene quid de te merui, fuit aut tibi quidquam*
      *Dulce meum, miserere domus labentis: & istam*
      *Oro, si quis adhuc precibus locus, exue mentem.*
*Aen. Desine meque tuis incendere teque querelis,*
      *Italiam non sponte sequor.*
*Dido.* Hast thou forgot how many neighbour kings
60     Were up in arms, for making thee my love?
      How Carthage did rebel, Iarbas storm,
      And all the world calls me a second Helen,
      For being entangled by a stranger's looks?
      So thou wouldst prove as true as Paris did,
      Would, as fair Troy was, Carthage might be sack'd,
      And I be call'd a second Helena!
      Had I a son by thee, the grief were less,
      That I might see Aeneas in his face:
      Now if thou goest, what canst thou leave behind
70     But rather will augment than ease my woe?
*Aen.* In vain, my love, thou spend'st thy fainting breath:
      If words might move me, I were overcome.
*Dido.* And wilt thou not be mov'd with Dido's words?
      Thy mother was no Goddess, perjur'd man,
      Nor Dardanus the author of thy stock;
      But thou art sprung from Scythian Caucasus,

And tigers of Hyrcania gave thee suck.
Ah foolish Dido to forbear this long!
Wast thou not wrack'd upon this Libyan shore
And camest to Dido like a fisher swain?
Repair'd not I thy ships, made thee a king,
And all thy needy followers noblemen?
O serpent that came creeping from the shore
And I for pity harbour'd in my bosom,
Wilt thou now slay me with thy venomed sting,
And hiss at Dido for preserving thee?
Go, go, and spare not; seek out Italy;
I hope that that which love forbids me do
The rocks and sea-gulfs will perform at large
And thou shalt perish in the billows' ways,
To whom poor Dido doth bequeath revenge.
Ay, traitor, and the waves shall cast thee up,
Where thou and false Achates first set foot;
Which if it chance, I'll give ye burial,
And weep upon your lifeless carcases,
Though thou nor he will pity me a whit.
Why starest thou in my face? If thou wilt stay,
Leap in mine arms: mine arms are open wide.
If not, turn from me, and I'll turn from thee;
For though thou hast the heart to say farewell,
I have not power to stay thee.          [*Exit* AENEAS.]
                                  Is he gone?
Ay, but he'll come again, he cannot go,
He loves me too too well to serve me so.
Yet he that in my sight would not relent
Will, being absent, be obdurate still.
By this is he got to the water-side;
And see, the sailors take him by the hand,
But he shrinks back, and now, rememb'ring me,
Returns amain: welcome, welcome, my love!
But where's Aeneas? Ah, he's gone, he's gone!          (1594)

# CHRISTOPHER MARLOWE

## The Passionate Sheepheard to His Love

First printed in a four-stanza version in *The Passionate Pilgrim* (1599); the text here printed first appeared in the anthology *Englands Helicon* (1600). The poem is an imitation of Corydon's pastoral invitation in Virgil, Eclogue II.

> Come live with mee, and be my love,
> And we will all the pleasures prove,
> That Vallies, groves, hills and fieldes,
> Woods, or steepie mountaine yeeldes.
>
> And wee will sit upon the Rocks,
> Seeing the Sheepheards feede theyr flocks,
> By shallow Rivers, to whose falls,
> Melodious byrds sing Madrigalls.
>
> And I will make thee beds of Roses,
> And a thousand fragrant poesies,
> A cap of flowers, and a kirtle,
> Imbroydred all with leaves of Mirtle.
>
> A gowne made of the finest wooll,
> Which from our pretty Lambes we pull,
> Fayre lined slippers for the cold:
> With buckles of the purest gold.
>
> A belt of straw, and Ivie buds,
> With Corall clasps and Amber studs,
> And if these pleasures may thee move,
> Come live with mee, and be my love.

The Sheepheards Swaines shall daunce & sing,
For thy delight each May-morning,
If these delights thy minde may move;
Then live with mee, and be my love.                    (1600)


# SIR JOHN HARINGTON
(1561–1612)

## The Sixth Book of Virgil's Aeneid, stanzas 41–64
[Aen.VI. 264–439] *The descent into the underworld*

Harington's version of *Aeneid* VI in *ottava rima* was made in 1604
and first published in 1991 by S. Cauchi from Turnbull Add. MS.
23 in the Berkshire Record Office, Reading. The MS comprises a
translation and commentary in Harington's autograph with a scribe's
transcription of the Latin text.

> Yee gods of sowls in Darknes deep that dwell
> Thow Phlegeton, and Chaos voyd of lyght
> grawnt with your favors leave to mee to tell
> things hard thowgh hid in deeps from mortall syght.
> They March amidd the regions dark of hell
> And Plutoes kingdoms of eternall night
>     as dull as winter nights with vs or duller
>     that show some shapes, but yet can Iudg no culler.
>
> At th'vtter Porch and evn in Orcus Iaws
> 10  sat sorrows sad, and sharp revenging care,
> fears, filthy want, and famin foe to laws
> In fearfull shapes, and death that none doth spare,
> Deaths Cosen Sleep, Ioys sprung on evill cawse,

---

**9** *vtter*: outermost

to which moste Crewell warrs an obiect are,
 with pale deseases, payns that ever rage
 and that that kills withowt diseases, age.

Thear sat the Eumenides in Iron chayrs,
thear raging discord that in bloody bands
tyes vp the vypers her decheavled hayrs:
20 Amid all thease a myghty ellm thear stands
to shade of which each ydle dream repayrs
and lurke in leavs in nomber as the sands,
 No words can well expresse, no language consters
 the sundry fowrms of thease same ydell monsters.

Centawrs mishapen, Scillas doble shapes,
And Bryareus with working hands one hundred,
Thear Lernas roring lyon hugely gapes,
Chimeras ghastly flames, and greatly wondred,
Harpias, gorgons, tygers, wolvs, and apes,
30 from which Eneas seeking to bee sunderd,
 with naked sword in hand wold them invade
 save that his guyde did otherwyse perswade.

She showd him by a playn and short discowrse
those all wear fansyes voyd of substance quyte,
This past they followd on with speedy cowrse,
the way to tartar waters leading ryght,
Height Acheron, whose ever swelling sowrse
Casts sands on blacke cocytus Day & nyght.
 whear cruell Caron keeps the fatall whery,
40 a sowr old syre, still angry never mery.

Gray locks hee had and flaming eys, his boat
with ore somtyme hee guyds, somtyme with sayle,

---

**23** *consters*: construes

his garment was a bare yll favord coat,
Thowgh struck in yeers, yeers made not strength to fayle.
To this streams banks, great swarms of sowls did float
and sewd to passe, yet cowld not all prevayle
    Men, women, babes, great Lords, and lytle boys
    slayn in theyr parents syghts, theyr parents Ioys.

As thicke as leavs do fall in awtum frost,
50  as thicke as lytle byrds in flocks do flye,
whom winters cold, makes seeke a warmer coast,
so stood the sowls that did for passage cry,
The sullen syre admitts not evry ghost,
but vnto dyvers passage doth deny;
    Eneas calls his guyd demawnding her,
    the cawse of that confused noyse and sterr.

O virgin chaste, sayd hee, the cawse delyver,
of this concowrse of sowls, and what's the matter,
why all make equall suyt to passe the ryver?
60  and why are some forbidden near the latter?
Then spake Apollos faythfull awnswer gever,
Anchyses sonne thow heavn-born wyght; the water
    thow see'st, Cocytus ys the stigian lake,
    whose name ye Godds in vayn dare never take.

All thease are sowls whose corses are vnbery'd,
the shipman Caron ẙs whose ayd they crave.
all those that passe are soche as are enterred,
For yf theyr carcase bee not layd in grave,
they wander heer and thear, till having erred
70  one hundred yeers, then leave to passe they have.
    Till then by fates decrees yt ys forbidden,
    and they that prease to passe are sharply chidden.

---

55 *his guyd*: the Sibyl, prophetess of Apollo
69 *erred*: wandered (Latin *errare*)

Eneas sadly mused in his mynde,
and tooke compassyon of theyr greevows case,
Thear Orons with Lewcaspis hee did fynde,
that led the Lycian fleet, who by disgrace
In Lybian seas wear drownd by raging wynde,
hee fownd eake Palinurus in the place,
   who whyle hee sat observing starrs at ease,
80   by hard mishap fell hedlong in the seas.

Him, when in shaddow darke and place obscure,
he had by certayn observacions fownd,
what god bereavd vs thee o Palynure?
declare (sayd hee) how hapt yow to be drownd?
for Phebus sayings otherwyse most sewr,
did fayle in this, that thow Italyan grownd,
   showldst savely towch, and now to drown yee sleeping,
   was this great god Appollos promis keepinge?

No; Phebus did not fayle, (thus hee replyes,)
90   O troian Prince, nor any god mee drown,
But whyle I gaz'd to moche on starrs & skyes
The steer did slippe, and that and I fell down,
I swear by foming seas, I then did pryze
More then my lyfe, your safty and your crown,
   Least that your ship of Master spoyld & rother
   Miscarry myght by one mishappe or other.

---

75 Orons (Orontes) was drowned in the storm which wrecked most of
Aeneas' fleet in Book I. Leucaspis is not mentioned elsewhere in the poem.
78 Palinurus, Aeneas' helmsman, was drowned in Book V.
95 *rother*: rudder

Three stormy nights by tempests I was borne,
In surging waves of water sallt and cold,
at length the fowrth, full early in the morne
100 I did aloofe Italyan land behold.
I swam to shore, but thear a sharper storme
I met: whyle nummed hands on rocks tooke hold,
 the barbarows peeple tooke mee for a pray,
  and cloggd with heavy cloths they did mee slay.

And now my corse, in waves and wyndes ys tost
But oh deer Sir by heavns I yow implore,
by that pure lyght, by your deer fathers ghoste,
by sweet Iulus hopes still growing more,
free mee from owt this place, or bee at cost
110 to bury mee, and search velynus shore,
 Or yf yowr mother some new means have tawght yow
  for sewr some means devyne have hether browght yow.

Nor durst yow ellse adventer ore this lake,
except with heavnly favor yow wear blest
help mee to bee transported for your sake
that at the least my sowle may take some rest.
to this, the prophetesse doth awnswer make
O Pallinure how dare yow this request?
 To passe thease banks vnbid? oh humor strawnge,
120  No. never thinke the fates with prayr to chawnge.

Yet take (sayth shee) this comfort of your case
that all the towns and cittyes neer abowt
shall so bee skard with visyons in the place,
to forse them seeke your bones, and fynde them owt,
and thear a toomb that no tyme shall deface,

---

110 *velynus shore*: the harbour of Velia in Lucania

to make, and celebrat with rytes devowt.
   this made him paciently his payns endewr,
   the place ys to this day nam'd Palynure.

So marcht Eneas forward with his guyde
130  amid the wood, and make all hast they may
But when the sturdy ferryman espyde,
a man in arms, foorthwith hee bad him stay,
and rewdly, and abruptly thus hee cryde,
Hoe, sirrha, yow, that armed come this way,
   tell why yow hether come? and what's your arrant?
   men lyving to transport, wee have no warrant.

Nor was't with my goodwill that Hercles went
or Theseus and Perithous Past this lake,
thowgh valyent men, and of Dyvyne descent,
140  the fyrst of thease the three mowth dog did take,
with myghty strength, evn from god Plutus tent,
and bownd and cawsd the Crewell curre to quake.
   thease wold have slockt owr mistres from owr prince
   a thinge that bred vs moche suspicion since.

Then thus th' Amphrisyan Prophetesse replyde,
nor forse, nor frawd ys heer nor any yll
owr weapons all boad peace; your dog vntyde
may stay for vs, and bark at shaddows still,
Proserpin in her vnkles howse may byde,
150  and keep her selfe vnspotted, yf she will.
   This prince for arms, and pyety renownd,
   goes to his fathers ghoste heer vnder grownd.

---

**135** *arrant*: errand
**145** *th' Amphrisyan Prophetesse*: periphrasis for the Sibyl, in the learned Alexandrian manner often affected by Virgil.
**147** *your dog*: Cerberus
**149** *Proserpin*: Jupiter's daughter by Ceres; Pluto was her uncle. She had to spend half of every year in the underworld.

But yf yow can dispyse and set at nowght
so great a pyetye and of soch renown,
yet looke on this, the bow then owt shee browght,
which she before had hidden with her gown:
The fatall brawnch appeasd his peevish thowght,
and wondring at the guift hee seast to frown,
   nor now disputing or repyning more,
160   he shovs his barke apace vnto the shore.

Then presently hee cleereth all the banks
and drave away the sowls that sat thearon,
with fury great disturbing all theyr ranks,
and (save the two fornam'd) admitting none
But this vnwonted wayght so sprung the planks,
of that pitcht rotten boat, yt leakt anon.
   At last vppon the slymy banks & yellow
   hee landeth safe Sibilla and her fellow.

Fell Cerberus, with treple sownding chopps
170   and barking lowd ore all the region Rings,
But when she gave him honny-charmed sopps,
evn as hee reard his brissles, vypers stings,
his thre-fold throat she fills and mowths she stopps,
and with that medcin him a sleep she brings.
   The cur lyes snorting all a long his den,
   And thus Eneas wan that passage then.

Now past the flood, whear very few return,
evn on that passage entry hee myght heer,
the wofull cryes of children that did mowrn,
180   Babes drawn from nurses duggs, and mothers deer,
and sent to hastend death by some yll towrn,

---

155 *the bow*: the Golden Bough, the talisman with which a living soul might pass into the underworld
164 *the two fornam'd*: Aeneas and the Sibyl

Next thease, wear men condemnd, yt had been cleer
  Nor wear they rashly sent vnto thease places,
  But Minos made enquyry of theyr cases.

Hee makes by sylent Iewryes inquisycion
of all theyr crymes, both whear, & when, and how.
Theyr place was next, that for some bad suspicion
have killd them selvs: how glad wowld they bee now
with poverty, or any base condicion,
190   to towrn to lyfe yf fates wold yt allow.
      but heer they ly, in Lothsome prison bownd,
      whear Stix with nynefold streams doth them surrownd.

                              (1604; first published 1991)


# THOMAS MAY (1595–1658)

## Georgicon IV, 1–254 [Georg. IV. 1–227] *On bees*

In depicting bees as social creatures with their own share of the
divine spark, Virgil illustrates once more the pantheistic view of the
world which dominates the entire poem.

Aeriall Honey next, a gift divine
Ile sing; Mecaenas, grace this piece of mine.
Admired spectacles of Creatures small,
Their valiant Captaines, and in order all
Their Nations, Manners, Studies, People, Fight,
I will describe; nor think the Glory slight,
Though slight the Subject be, to him, whom ere
Th'invokes gods, and pleas'd Apollo heare.

---

**184** *Minos*: a judge of the dead
**1** Honey was the gift of the gods in the Golden Age (cf. Eclogue IV, 30).
**2** Each book of the *Georgics* is dedicated to Maecenas.

First for your Hives a fitting station finde
10  Shelter'd from windes rough violence, for winde
Hinders their carriage; let no Sheep there play,
Nor frisking Kids the flowery meadowes lay,
Nor wanton Heifers neare the hiving place
Strike off the dew, nor tread the springing grasse.
Let speckled Lizzards thence be far away,
The Woodpeckers, and other Birds of prey,
And Progne marked on her stained breast
With bloody hands; for she to feed her nest
Seizes the flying Bees, and thither brings
20  As sweetest food; but near pure Chrystall springs
Green mossie fountaines stil your Bee-hives place,
And streames that glide along the Verdant grasse,
Shaded with palms, or spreading olive-trees:
That when new kings draw out their swarming bees
And from their combes dismiss'd in spring they play,
The neighboring banks may then invite their stay,
Cooling their heat, and trees so near the hive
A green and shady coverture may give.
Into the poole, whether it stand or flow,
30  Great stones across and willow branches throw
As bridges for the Bees to stand upon,
And spread their wings against the summer sun,
When strong Eastwindes by chance have scatter'd them
In coming home, or drown'd them in the streame.
Let beds of Violets, and wild Betony,
Green Cinnamon, and fragrant Savory
Grow round about the spring. But whether you
To make your hives, trees barkes together sow,
Or hives of limber Osyars woven get,
40  Make the mouth narrow, lest the summers heat

---

**17** Progne (Procne) murdered her son and was turned into a swallow, bearing the signs of murder on her breast.

Dissolve the honey, or cold winter freeze;
For both extreames alike annoy the Bees.
Nor is't in vain that they with all their powers
Daube up each chinck with waxe, & fil with flowers
Each breathing hole, and to that end prepare
A glew more clammy than all birdlime farre,
And Phrygian Ida's pitch; and under ground
(If fame speak truly) Bees have oft been found
Breeding in digged caves, and oft been known
50   In holes of trees, and hollow pumice stone.
But daube thou up the chinky hives with clay
To keep them warme, and leaves above them lay.
Neere to the hives let no deep waters flow,
Nor crabs be drest, nor poisonous yew-trees grow;
Or where mud standing stinkes, or ecchos bound
From hollow rocks with their reflected sound.
But when bright *Sol* hath banish'd Winter chas'd
Under the earth, and Summer light hath grac'd
The sky againe; over the fields, and woods
60   They wander straight, lightly the brinkes of floods
They sip, and tast the purple flowers; from thence
(What sweetnesse ere it be that stir their sence)
Care for their brood and progeny they take;
Thence work their waxe, and hony clammy make.
Then when dismiss'd their hives, up to the sky
In Summer ayre thou seest them swarming fly,
Wondring to view dark clouds driven by the wind.
Then mark them well, they go sweet streames to find
And leavie bowers; upon this place do thou
70   Base honey-suckles, and beaten mill-foile strow;
And roundabout let tinckling brasse resound;
Their farther progresse this charmd place will bound.
There they will make their stand, or else desire

---

**47** Refers to the pitch-pines which grew on Mount Ida near Troy.

Back to their own known lodgings to retire.
But if they chance to sally out to wars
(As oft two kings have caused mortall jars)
The common Bees affections straight are found,
And trembling hearts to fight; that martiall sound
Of brasse checks their delay, and then a voice
80    Is heard resembling trumpets winding noise.
Then straight they muster, spread their glittering wings,
And with their beaks whet their dead-doing stings.
Then to the standard royall all repaire
About their king, and loudly buzzing dare
Their foes t'appeare; in weather clear, and faire
They sally forth: their battels joyne i' th' ayre.
The Welkin's fill'd with noise; they grapple all,
And grappling so in clusters head long fall;
Haile from the winters sky fals not so fast,
90    Nor shaken oakes so thick do shed their mast.
In midst of th'armies with bright glorious wings,
And mighty spirits fly the daring kings
(Though bodies small) resolved not to yeeld,
Till one side vanquisht have forsooke the field.
Wouldst thou this fight, and furious heate allay?
A little dust thrown up will part the fray.
    But when both kings drawn home from battel be,
Kill him that seemes the worst, lest thriftlesse he
Do hurt, and let the other reigne alone.
100    For of two sorts they are, one fairely knowne
By glittering specks of gold, and scales of bright
But ruddy hue. This fairest to the sight
Is best: by sloth the other's nasty growne,
And hangs his large unweildy belly downe.
Different, as are the kings, the subjects are.

---

**75–96** Famous example of mock-heroic; the last two lines are almost Swiftian
in their abrupt bathos.

Some foule and filthy, like the traveller,
That comes from dusty waies, and dirt doth spit
From his dry throate; the other gold-like bright,
With well proportion'd spots his limbes are deckt.
110   This is the better broode; from these expect
Honey at certaine seasons of the yeare
Most sweet, and yet not sweet alone, but cleare,
And such as Bacchus hardnesse will allay.
But when in th' aire the swarmes at randome play,
Scorning their combes, forsaking their cold hive,
Dost thou from this vaine sport desire to drive
Their wandring thoughts? not toilsome is the pains,
Clip but the princes wings; whilst he remaines
Within, no common Bee will dare to make
120   High flight, nor th' ensignes from the campe to take.
Let Saffron gardens odoriferous,
Which th'image of Lampsacian Priapus
Guards with his hooke of willow to affright
Both Theeves, and hurtful Fowles, the Bees invite.
Let him himselfe, which feares his Bees to want,
Bring Thyme, & Pines down from the hills, to plant,
Wearing his hands with labour hard, and round
Bestow a friendly watering on the ground.
      And did I not now neere my labours end
130   Strike saile, and hasting to the harbour tend,
Perchance how fruitfull gardens may be drest
I'd teach, and sing of twice rose-bearing Pest:

---

**122** Priapus was the rural deity who protected gardens; he was said to have come from Lampsacus in the Hellespont. The Latin has '*Hellespontiaci*' not '*Lampsacii*'.

**129–130** Naval metaphor for the poet's journey through his task.

**129–165** A famous passage: Virgil makes a passing reference (the figure called praeteritio) to gardens, regretting that he has no room to develop this subject. The portrait of the poor, proud and self-sufficient smallholder may be compared with the praise of the Italian farmer in *Georgics* II.

**132** Pest (Paestum) was famous for its twice-flowering roses.

How Succory by waters prospers well,
On grasse how bending Cucumbers do swell,
And bankes of Persley greene: besides to show
How the late-blooming Daffodils do grow
I would not faile, and twigs of Beares-foot show,
Shore-loving Myrtles, and pale Ivie too.
For where Tarentum's lofty Turrets stand,
140   Where slow Galesus soakes the fallow Land,
I saw an old Cilician, who possest
Few akers of neglected ground undrest,
Not fit to pasture beasts, nor vines to beare:
Yet he among the bushes here, and there
Gathering few pot-hearbs, vervaine, lilies white,
And wholesome poppey, in his mind's delight
Equall'd the wealth of Kings, and comming still
Late home at night, with meat unbought, did fill
His laden board; he gather'd first of all
150   Roses in spring, and apples in the fall.
And when sad winter with extreamest cold
Crack'd even the stones, & course of floods did hold
With bridling ice, he then pluck'd leaves of soft
Beares-foot, and check'd the springs delayings oft,
And Zephyres sloath. He therefore first was found
With fruitfull Bees, and swarmes still to abound,
And froathy honey from the combes could squeeze.
He still had fruitful vines, and linden trees.
And for each blossome, which first cloath'd the tree
160   An apple ripe in Autumne gather'd he.
He could to order old grown Elmes transpose.
Old peare trees hard, & black thorne bearing sloes,
The plaine tree too, that drinking shade bestowes.
But too much straighten'd, I must now forsake
This taske for others afterward to take.

---

**139–41** The Cilicians lived in Asia Minor; perhaps this old man had settled in
South Italy (Tarentum is the modern Taranto).

And now Ile show those natures, which on Bees
Great *Jove* himselfe bestow'd: for what strange fees,
Following a tinckling noise, and brazen ring
In Cretan caves they nourish'd heavens high King.
170 Bees only live in common-wealths, and Bees
Only in common hold their progenies:
Live by lawes constant, and their own abodes
Certainly know, and certain houshold gods;
And mindfull of ensuing winter, they
Labour in summer, and in publike lay
Up their provision. Some for gathering food
Are by the states commission sent abroad
To labour in the fields: some still at home
Lay the foundations of the honey combe
180 Of glue, tree-gumme, and faire Narcissus reare:
Then to the top they fasten everywhere
Their clammy waxe: care for their brood some take
(The nation's hope): some purest honey make,
Till th' honey combe with clearest nectar swels.
Some lot appoints to stand as centinels,
And to foresee the showres, and stormes to come
They watch by turns: those that come laden home
Some ease: or joyning all their strengths in one
Far from the hive they chase the lazie Drone.
190 To work they fall: their fragrant honeyes hold
A sent of Thyme; as when the Cyclops mould
Jove's thunder from th'hard-yeelding masse in hast,
Some take and pay againe the windy blast

---

**166–9** As a baby Jupiter was hidden by his mother in a cave on Mount Dicte
in Crete (still shown to visitors) to save him from his father Saturn, whom he
was destined to supplant. The baby's cries were drowned by the cymbals of
the Curetes (local semi-divine beings), which attracted bees to the cave,
where they nourished the baby god.
**191–2** A mock-heroic simile: the Cyclopes were giants localized under Mount
Etna, where they plied their trade as smiths to the gods.
**193** *take and pay againe*: the Latin means that they suck in and blow out air
with their bellows.

From bull-hide bellowes: others in the lakes
Do quench the hizzing irons; Aetna shakes
With weight of anviles, whilst their armes so stronge
In order strike, and with hard–holding tongs
The iron turne; such inbred thrifty care
(If little things with great we may compare)
200    Each in his function Bees of Athens take.
The elder keep within the townes, and make
Daedalian fabricks to adorne the combe;
But late returne the younger weary home
Their thighes laden with Thyme: they feed upon
Wildings, greene Willowes, Saffron, Cinnamon,
Pale Hyacinths and fruitfull Linden trees.
One time of work, and rest have all the Bees.
Forth in the morn they goe, and when late night
Bids them leave gathering, home they take their flight
210    And there refresh their bodies; then a sound
And buzzing's heard about th'hives confines round.
But when they all are lodg'd in silence deep
They rest, their weary Senses charm'd by sleep.
Nor stray they far when clouds orecast the skyes,
Nor trust the weather when Eastwindes arise.
But neare their Cities short excursions make,
And safely water, or small pebbles take
(As in rough seas with sand the Vessels light
Ballast themselves) to poize their wandering flight.
220    But at that wondrous way you must admire
By which Bees breede: they feele not Venus fire,
Nor are dissolv'd in lust, nor yet endure
The paines of childing travell: but from pure
Sweet flowers, & Herbs their progeny they bring
Home in their mouths. They all elect their king

---

**200** The bees of Mount Hymettus near Athens were proverbial for fine honey.

And little nobles; their wax mansions
And courts they build; & oft 'gainst hardest stones
They fret their wings, and spoile them as they fly,
And gladly under their sweet burthens dy:
230  So great's their love of flowers, ambition too
They have of making Honey. Therefore though
Their lives be short (as not above the space
Of seven yeares) yet their immortall race
Remaines; the fortunes of their houses hold;
For many yeares are grand-sires' grand-sires told.
Besides not Aegypt, nor rich Lydia more,
Nor Medes, nor Parthians do their kings adore;
Whilst he's alive, in concord all obey;
But when he dyes, all leagues are broke, and they
240  Themselves destroy their gathered food at home,
And rend the fabrick of their honey combe.
'Tis he preserves their workes; him all admire,
And guard his person with a strong desire:
They carry him, for him they hazzard death,
And think in war they nobly lose their breath.
Noting these signs, and tokens, some define
The Bees partakers of a soule divine,
And heavenly spirit; for the godhead is
Diffus'd through earth, through seas, & lofty skies.
250  From hence all beasts, men, cattle, all that live,
All that are borne their subtle soules receive.
Hither againe they are restor'd, not dy,
But when dissolv'd, returne, and gladly fly
Up to the stars; in heaven above they live.                    (1628)

---

**246–54** Virgil's pantheistic belief that the divine is present in all living things
is developed more fully in Anchises' famous speech on the soul's immortality
(*Aeneid* VI, 724–51).

# GEORGE SANDYS (1578–1644)

[Aen. I. 94–101, 198–207, 415–502] *Aeneas, shipwrecked on his way to Italy, wishes he had died at Troy; later, cast ashore on the coast of Libya, he encourages his men; accompanied by Achates, and made invisible by Venus, he reaches Carthage and enters Juno's temple, where he sees pictures of the Trojan war*

Sandys's version of *Aeneid* I was first printed as an Appendix to his translation of Ovid's *Metamorphoses* (1632) under the title 'An Essay to the Translation of Virgil's Aeneis'. This text is printed from the second edition of 1640. Sandys's version is notable for its extensive use of enjambment, which breaks up the couplets more freely than his successors did.

'Thrice happy you, who in your parents' sight
Before Troy fell in honourable fight!
O Diomed, of Greeks the most renoun'd,
Why could not thy strong hand this life confound
In Phrygian fields? Where great Sarpedon, where
Brave Hector fell by fierce Achilles' speare:
Where Simois in his tainted streames o'erwhelmes
So many worthies, heapes of shields and helms.'

\*

'O Mates (for we to sorrowes are inur'd),
10  O you who greater mischiefs have indur'd,
God also will impose an end to these.
You rabid Scylla, rocks-enraging seas,
And dire Cyclopian cliffes have seen, and past;
Raise up your spirits, from your bosomes cast
Dejecting feare. The memory of these

---

5 Sandys keeps closely to the rhythm of the Latin, which Dryden ignores.
11 Sandys is very close to the Latin (*deus dabit his quoque finem*).

Perhaps in future times as much may please.
Through various fortunes, dangers more than great,
We Latium seeke; where Fates a quiet seat
For us intend; there shall we Ilium raise:
20   Be bold: yourselves preserve for better dayes.'

*

Meanwhile they both the trodden path pursue
And from a hill the neighbouring Citie view,
That ample pile (a village late) they then
Admire: the gates, the streets, and noise of men.
The Tyrians ply their tasks: some bulwarks rear,
Strong walls extend and stones or roule or beare:
Some seats for houses choose; some laws project,
Grave magistrates and senators elect.
Here these an ample haven dig; there they
30   For loftie Theaters foundations lay.
Others in quarries mighty Pillars hew,
To grace the spectacles that should ensue.
    Industrious bees so in the prime of May
By sunshine through the flowery meadows stray,
When they produce their young, or store their hive
With liquid honey, or in cabins stive
That pleasant nectar, when they take the loads
Which others bring, or chase from their abodes
The lazy drone; the honey redolent
40   With flowers of thyme; all hot on labour bent.
    'O happy you whose citie thus aspires!'
Aeneas said, 'and her high roofs admires.'
With that (o wonderful!) wrapt in a cloud
Invisible he mingles with the crowd.
A shady grove amidst the Citie stood:
Here Tyrians erst, when by the raging flood

---

**36** *stive*: enclose

And furious tempest on those borders thrown,
Digg'd up a horse's head, by Juno shown,
Which never-failing plenty did foretell,
50   And that they should in glorious arms excell.
Here Tyrian Dido Juno's temple plac'd,
In offerings rich, by her fair statue grac'd:
The staires of brass, the beames with brass were bound,
The brazen doors on grinding hinges sound.
The sights within this sumptuous Fane his fear
Did first asswage; and first Aeneas here
Durst hope for safety, his sad spirits rais'd:
For as on all those rarities he gaz'd
(The Queen expecting) their felicities
60   And emulous arts admiring, he his eyes
Now fixt on Ilium's fatal fights, through all
The world divulg'd: the Grecian general,
Old Priam sees and stern Aeacides
Cruel to both. Struck with such sights as these
To Achates said: 'what place, what region,
So distant where our labours are unknown!
Lo, Priamus! here vertue hath her meed,
And our misfortunes human pittie breed.
This fame may help procure; suppress thy dread.'
70   This said, his thoughts upon the picture fed;
His heart with sighs, his eyes with rivers fraught;
For now he sees how they at Ilium fought.
Here fled the Greeks, the Troian youth pursue;
Bright-helmed Achilles there the Phrygians slew.
Not far off Rhesus' white pavilion stood
By cruel Diomed through streams of blood.
In dead of night surpriz'd, who bare away

---

59 *The Queen expecting*: awaiting the Queen
63 *Aeacides*: Achilles (descended from Aeacus). Virgil does not use the form
here, but he does use it above (Sandys, line 6) where Sandys has Achilles.

His horses to the Grecian camp, e'er they
Of Xanthus drank, or of Troy's pastures fed.
80 Here Troilus disarmed and wounded fled,
Poor boy, too weak to match Achilles' force;
Cast from his chariot by his frighted horse
Yet holds the reines; his neack and tresses trail'd
On purpled earth, his spear the dust engrail'd.
Now with a robe the Ilian dames repaire
To partial Pallas' Fane with flowing haire,
While they their bosoms beat, and sue for grace:
The angry goddess turns away her face.
About Troy's wall thrice Hector uncontroll'd
90 Achilles drags, and sells his corse for gold.
Deep groans and signs Aeneas' heart oppresse,
When he beheld th' insulting foe possesse
The body, armes and chariot of his friend,
While Priam's knees to proud Achilles bend.
Then sees himself amidst those stern alarms,
The eastern squadrons and black Memnon's armes;
With Amazonian troops and moon-like shields
Penthesilea scoures the trampled fields;
Her seared breast bound with a golden bend:
100 Bold maid that durst with men in armes contend.
    While he these wonders sees, while yet amaz'd
Dardan Aeneas on each object gaz'd,
Fair-featured Dido, with a goodly train
Of gallant courtiers enter'd Juno's Fane.
As when Diana, prest to revels, crowns
Eurotus' banks or Cynthus' loftie downs;
A thousand mountain nymphs about her throng:

---

80–84 The story of Troilus is not in Homer.
85–8 See *Iliad* VI, 269–311.
89–93 See *Iliad* XXIII–XXIV.
96–100 These episodes of the Trojan war are post-Homeric.

She with her quiver on her shoulder hung,
Marching in state, surmounteth all the rest,
110 And fills with joy Latona's silent breast.                    (1632)


# JOHN MILTON (1608–74)

## Lycidas

'Lycidas' is a pastoral elegy for the poet Edward King. Much of its
inspiration and imagery is from Virgil's last eclogue, the lament for
Gallus. The concluding apotheosis echoes the end of Eclogue V (the
apotheosis of Daphnis).

> *In this Monody the Author bewails a learned Friend, unfortunatly*
> *drown'd in his Passage from Chester on the Irish Seas, 1637. And*
> *by occasion foretels the ruine of our corrupted Clergy then in their*
> *height.*

Yet once more, O ye Laurels, and once more
Ye Myrtles brown, with Ivy never-fear,
I com to pluck your Berries harsh and crude,
And with forc'd fingers rude,
Shatter your leaves before the mellowing year.
Bitter constraint, and sad occasion dear,
Compels me to disturb your season due:
For Lycidas is dead, dead ere his prime
Young Lycidas, and hath not left his peer:
10 Who would not sing for Lycidas? he knew
Himself to sing, and build the lofty rhyme.

---

**110** *Latona*: Juno
**1–2** Cf. Eclogue X, 13.
**10** Cf. Eclogue X, 3: '*neget quid carmina Gallo?*'

He must not flote upon his watry bear
Unwept, and welter to the parching wind,
Without the meed of som melodious tear.
   Begin then, Sisters of the sacred well,
That from beneath the seat of Jove doth spring,
Begin, and somwhat loudly sweep the string.
Hence with denial vain, and coy excuse,
So may som gentle Muse
20 With lucky words favour my destin'd Urn,
And as he passes turn,
And bid fair peace be to my sable shrowd.
For we were nurst upon the self-same hill,
Fed the same flock, by fountain, shade, and rill.
   Together both, ere the high Lawns appear'd
Under the opening eye-lids of the morn,
We drove a field, and both together heard
What time the Gray-fly winds her sultry horn,
Batt'ning our flocks with the fresh dews of night,
30 Oft till the Star that rose, at Ev'ning, bright
Toward Heav'ns descent had slop'd his westering wheel.
Mean while the Rural ditties were not mute,
Temper'd to th'Oaten Flute,
Rough Satyrs danc'd, and Fauns with clov'n heel,
From the glad sound would not be absent long,
And old Damætas lov'd to hear our song.
   But O the heavy change, now thou art gon,
Now thou art gon, and never must return!
Thee Shepherd, thee the Woods, and desert Caves,
40 With wilde Thyme and the gadding Vine o'regrown,
And all their echoes mourn.
The Willows, and the Hazle Copses green,
Shall now no more be seen,
Fanning their joyous Leaves to thy soft layes.
As killing as the Canker to the Rose,
Or Taint-worm to the weanling Herds that graze,

Or Frost to Flowers, that their gay wardrop wear,
When first the White thorn blows; .
Such, Lycidas, thy loss to Shepherds ear.
50     Where were ye Nymphs when the remorseless deep
Clos'd o're the head of your lov'd Lycidas?
For neither were ye playing on the steep,
Where your old Bards, the famous Druids ly,
Nor on the shaggy top of Mona high,
Nor yet where Deva spreads her wisard stream:
Ay me, I fondly dream!
Had ye bin there – for what could that have don?
What could the Muse her self that Orpheus bore,
The Muse her self, for her inchanting son
60     Whom Universal nature did lament,
When by the rout that made the hideous roar,
His goary visage down the stream was sent,
Down the swift Hebrus to the Lesbian shore.
     Alas! What boots it with uncessant care
To tend the homely slighted Shepherds trade,
And strictly meditate the thankles Muse,
Were it not better don as others use,
To sport with Amaryllis in the shade,
Or with the tangles of Neæra's hair?
70     Fame is the spur that the clear spirit doth raise
(That last infirmity of Noble mind)
To scorn delights, and live laborious dayes;
But the fair Guerdon when we hope to find,
And think to burst out into sudden blaze,
Comes the blind Fury with th'abhorred shears,
And slits the thin-spun life. But not the praise,
Phœbus repli'd, and touch'd my trembling ears;
Fame is no plant that grows on mortal soil,

---

**50ff**. Cf. Eclogue X, 9–12.
**58ff**. *Orpheus*: cf. *Georgics* IV, 523–5.
**77** Cf. Eclogue VI, 3–4.

Nor in the glistering foil
80  Set off to th'world, nor in broad rumour lies,
But lives and spreds aloft by those pure eyes,
And perfet witnes of all-judging Jove;
As he pronounces lastly on each deed,
Of so much fame in Heav'n expect thy meed.
    O Fountain Arethuse, and thou honour'd floud,
Smooth-sliding Mincius, crown'd with vocall reeds,
That strain I heard was of a higher mood:
But now my Oate proceeds,
And listens to the Herald of the Sea
90  That came in Neptune's plea,
He ask'd the Waves, and ask'd the Fellon winds,
What hard mishap hath doom'd this gentle swain?
And question'd every gust of rugged wings
That blows from off each beaked Promontory,
They knew not of his story,
And sage Hippotades their answer brings,
That not a blast was from his dungeon stray'd,
The Ayr was calm, and on the level brine,
Sleek Panope with all her sisters play'd.
100  It was that fatall and perfidious Bark
Built in th'eclipse, and rigg'd with curses dark,
That sunk so low that sacred head of thine.
    Next Camus, reverend Sire, went footing slow,
His Mantle hairy, and his Bonnet sedge,
Inwrought with figures dim, and on the edge
Like to that sanguine flower inscrib'd with woe.
Ah! Who hath reft (quoth he) my dearest pledge?
Last came, and last did go,
The Pilot of the Galilean lake,
110  Two massy Keyes he bore of metals twain,

---

85–6 *Arethuse*: cf. Eclogue X, 1; *Mincius*: cf. Eclogue VII, 12–13.
106 Hyacinth: cf. Eclogue III, 106.

(The Golden opes, the Iron shuts amain)
He shook his Miter'd locks, and stern bespake,
How well could I have spar'd for thee young swain.
Anow of such as for their bellies sake,
Creep and intrude, and climb into the fold?
Of other care they little reck'ning make,
Then how to scramble at the shearers feast,
And shove away the worthy bidden guest.
Blind mouthes! that scarce themselves know how to hold
120    A Sheep-hook, or have learn'd ought els the least
That to the faithfull Herdmans art belongs!
What recks it them? What need they? They are sped;
And when they list, their lean and flashy songs
Grate on their scrannel Pipes of wretched straw,
The hungry Sheep look up, and are not fed,
But swoln with wind, and the rank mist they draw,
Rot inwardly, and foul contagion spread:
Besides what the grim Woolf with privy paw
Daily devours apace, and nothing sed,
130    But that two-handed engine at the door,
Stands ready to smite once, and smite no more.
    Return Alpheus, the dread voice is past,
That shrunk thy streams; Return Sicilian Muse,
And call the Vales, and bid them hither cast
Their Bels, and Flourets of a thousand hues.
Ye valleys low where the milde whispers use,
Of shades and wanton winds, and gushing brooks,
On whose fresh lap the swart Star sparely looks,
Throw hither all your quaint enameld eyes,
140    That on the green terf suck the honied showres,
And purple all the ground with vernal flowres.
Bring the rathe Primrose that forsaken dies.

---

**132** Milton returns to the world of pastoral after a satirical digression on the
state of the real world.

The tufted Crow-toe, and pale Gessamine,
The white Pink, and the Pansie freakt with jeat,
The glowing Violet.
The Musk-rose, and the well attir'd Woodbine,
With Cowslips wan that hang the pensive hed,
And every flower that sad embroidery wears:
Bid Amaranthus all his beauty shed,
150  And Daffadillies fill their cups with tears,
To strew the Laureat Herse where Lycid lies.
For so to interpose a little ease,
Let our frail thoughts dally with false surmise.
Ay me! Whilst thee the shores, and sounding Seas
  ·Wash far away, where ere thy bones are hurld,
Whether beyond the stormy Hebrides,
Where thou perhaps under the whelming tide
Visit'st the bottom of the monstrous world;
Or whether thou to our moist vows deny'd,
160  Sleep'st by the fable of Bellerus old,
Where the great vision of the guarded Mount
Looks toward Namancos and Bayona's hold;
Look homeward Angel now, and melt with ruth.
And, O ye Dolphins, waft the haples youth.

     Weep no more, woful Shepherds weep no more,
For Lycidas your sorrow is not dead,
Sunk though he be beneath the watry floar,
So sinks the day-star in the Ocean bed,
And yet anon repairs his drooping head,
170  And tricks his beams, and with new spangled Ore,
Flames in the forehead of the morning sky:
So Lycidas sunk low, but mounted high,
Through the dear might of him that walk'd the waves
Where other groves, and other streams along,
With Nectar pure his oozy Lock's he laves,

---

**168–70** For the simile, cf. *Aeneid* VIII, 589–91.

And hears the unexpressive nuptiall Song,
In the blest Kingdoms meek of joy and love.
There entertain him all the Saints above,
In solemn troops, and sweet Societies
180 That sing, and singing in their glory move,
And wipe the tears for ever from his eyes.
Now Lycidas the Shepherds weep no more;
Hence forth thou art the Genius of the shore,
In thy large recompense, and shalt be good
To all that wander in that perilous flood.
    Thus sang the uncouth Swain to th'Okes and rills;
While the still morn went out with Sandals gray,
He touch'd the tender stops of various Quills,
With eager thought warbling his Dorick lay:
190 And now the Sun had stretch'd out all the hills,
And now was dropt into the Western bay;
At last he rose, and twitch'd his Mantle blew:
To morrow to fresh Woods, and Pastures new.          (1637)


# ROBERT HERRICK (1591–1674)

## A Pastorall Sung to the King: Montano, Silvio, and Mirtillo, Shepheards

From *Hesperides* (1648). The poem contains echoes of several of
Virgil's Eclogues. The figure of the disconsolate lover passed into
English pastoral through Spenser's *Shepheardes Calender*.

*Mon.* Bad are the times. *Sil.* And wors then they are we.
*Mon.* Troth, bad are both; worse fruit, and ill the tree:
The feast of Shepheards fail. *Sil.* None crowns the cup

---

**184** Cf. Eclogue V, 65: '*sis bonus o felixque tuis*'.

Of Wassaile now, or sets the quintell up:
And He, who us'd to leade the Country-round,
Youthfull Mirtillo, Here he comes, Grief drownd.
*Ambo.* Lets cheer him up. *Sil.* Behold him weeping ripe.
*Mirt.* Ah! Amarillis, farewell mirth and pipe;
Since thou art gone, no more I mean to play,
10    To these smooth Lawns, my mirthfull Roundelay.
Dear Amarillis! *Mon.* Hark! *Sil.* mark: *Mir.* this earth grew
                                                    sweet
Where, Amarillis, Thou didst set thy feet.
*Ambo.* Poor pittied youth! *Mir.* And here the breth of kine
And sheep, grew more sweet, by that breth of Thine.
This flock of wooll, and this rich lock of hair,
This ball of Cow-slips, these she gave me here.
*Sil.* Words sweet as Love it self. Montano, Hark.
*Mirt.* This way she came, and this way too she went;
How each thing smells divinely redolent!
20    Like to a field of beans, when newly blown;
Or like a medow being lately mown.
*Mont.* A sweet-sad passion. –
*Mirt.* In dewie-mornings when she came this way,
Sweet Bents wode bow, to give my Love the day:
And when at night, she folded had her sheep,
Daysies wo'd shut, and closing, sigh and weep.
Besides (Ai me!) since she went hence to dwell,
The voices Daughter nea'r spake syllable.
But she is gone. *Sil.* Mirtillo, tell us whether.
30    *Mirt.* Where she and I shall never meet together.
*Mont.* Fore-fend it Pan, and Pales do thou please
To give an end: *Mir.* To what? *Sil.* such griefs as these.
*Mirt.* Never, O never! Still I may endure
The wound I suffer, never find a cure.

---

4 *quintell* (quintain): a kind of tilting game popular at country festivals
24 *Bents*: reeds
31 *Pales*: tutelary deity of flocks and herds; cf. Eclogue III, 35.

*Mont.* Love for thy sake will bring her to these hills
And dales again: *Mir.* No I will languish still;
And all the while my part shall be to weepe;
And with my sighs, call home my bleating sheep:
And in the Rind of every comely tree
40  Ile carve thy name, and in that name kisse thee:
*Mont.* Set with the Sunne, thy woes: *Sil.* The day grows old:
And time it is our full-fed flocks to fold.

*Chor.* The shades grow great; but greater growes our sorrow,
                    But lets go steepe
                    Our eyes in sleepe;
                    And meet to weepe
                    To morrow.                              (1648)

---

**39–40** Cf. Eclogue X, 53.
**41–3** Cf. Eclogue I, 82–3.

# JOHN OGILBY (1600–1676)

[Aen. VI. 264–330] *The descent into the underworld*

Ogilby made the first English translation of the complete works of
Virgil, a feat not repeated until Dryden, who belittled Ogilby but
certainly consulted him. In fact, Ogilby made not one but two
versions of Virgil: the first (1649) continued to be reprinted even
after the second (1654) appeared. The two texts are quite different,
as a comparison of the same passage printed here from both texts
will show; the later version does not always improve on the earlier.
Cf. also Dryden's version of the same passage.

> You gods who souls command, and silent ghosts,
> Phlegeton, Chaos, night's vast dismall coasts,
> Grant I declare things heard, by your aid shew
> What earth and darkness long hath hid below.
>     Obscur'd through shades and wofull night they past
> Through Pluto's empty courts and kingdoms waste;
> As through dark woods when a new moon displaid
> Pale beams, and Jove the sky hides with a shade,
> And black night colour did from things compell,
> 10     Just at the door, before the gates of hell,
> Sorrow repos'd, with her revenging rage,
> Pale sicknesses and discontented age;
> Fear, with dire famine and base poverty,
> Labour and death, shapes terrible to see.
> Then sleep allied to death and fond joys are
> Placed on the other side, with deadly war,
> On iron beds. Furies and discord sit,
> Their viperous hair with bloody fillets knit.
> Here a dark elm did ancient boughs display,
> 20     The seat (as they report) where vain dreams lay,
> And stuck to every leaf: then a huge brood
> Of various monsters, biformed Scylla stood,

And centaurs in the porch; with hundred hands
Briareus and the Lernian Hydra stands,
Chimera hissing loud, and arm'd with fire,
The triple shade, Gorgons and harpies dire.
    Aeneas draws, then struck with sudden fear
Opposing the sharp point, to them drew near,
But that his learn'd companion him perswades
30  They were but fleeting forms and empty shades,
In vain he had attempted ghosts to wound.
Hence led the way to th' Acherontick sound,
With a vast gulph here whirlpits vext with mud
Boyling casts sands up from the Stygian flood.
    Charon the horrid ferryman these deeps
(With dreadful squallidness) and river keeps.
His untrimmed cheeks were rough with hoary hair,
Knotty his beard, his fiery eyes did stare;
Ty'd on his shoulders hung a sordid coat;
40  He trims his sails, drives with a pole his boat,
And in his rusty bark wafts passengers.
The god was youthful still, though struck in years.
    Here all the scattered throngs rush to these coasts,
Men, women, came, and valiant heroes' ghosts,
Depriv'd of life, boys, virgins, young men here
Before their parents laid upon the bier.
As in first cold of autumn from the trees
The leaves fall thick, or to the shore from seas
The birds repair in flocks, when early frosts
50  Drive them from water unto warmer coasts,
They stand, and first for passages implore,
Their hands lift up, longing for th' other shore.
But the grim wafter these, now them, receives,
But others far off on the sand he leaves.

---

47–50 This famous simile was imitated by Dante (*Inferno* III, 112–20).
Ogilby's second version seems inferior to his first.

Aeneas, wondering at the tumult, said:
'Wherefore this concourse to the stream, O maid?
Say what these souls require, why those the shores
Forsake, and others billows rowl with oars.'
Brief th' aged Priestess thus to him replies:
60  'Anchises' son, sure stock of deities,
Thou Styx, Cocytus view'st; by this to swear
And to deceive the power, the gods do fear.
All those sad troops thou seest are not interred:
That Charon – those he wafts are sepulchred.
Until their bones in quiet rest, before
None pass these hoarse waves to the horrid shore.
A hundred years to wander here they're bound,
Permitted then to pass the Stygian sound.'          (1649)

*

You gods, that souls and silent shades command,
Hell, Chaos, and that miserable land,
Grant that I may discover under ground,
Wonders, in deep and utter darkness drown'd.
      Through solitary night, through shades they go,
Through Pluto's empty courts, and seats of woe.
Like one in woods that glimmering beams receives,
The new moon sprinkles through disturbed leaves,
When Jove hides heaven in clouds, and sullen night
10  Makes no distinction betwixt black and white.
      Just in the gates, and horrid jaws of hell
Sorrow, and fear, and pale diseases dwell;
Revenging cares, and discontented Age,
Invincible Necessity, and Rage;
Labour and Death, and Sleep to death akin;
Then all the false delights of deadly sin,

---

63–8 The belief that the unburied soul cannot cross the river Styx into Hades
is first found in Homer, *Iliad* XXIII (the ghost of Patroclus appears to
Achilles begging for burial).

Terrible forms, Discord and bloody wars
On th' other side lay, broaching still new jars;
The furies there their iron couches found,
20   Their viperous hair with bloody ribbands bound.
    Just in the midst an ancient elm displaid
Extended branches, with a gloomy shade,
Where idle dreams repose (as stories tell)
And under every leaf in clusters dwell.
Then several kinds of monstrous shapes appear:
There Scylla stood, the Centaurs stabled there;
Briareus, fencing with a hundred hands,
By Lernian Hydra, fiercely hissing, stands,
Gorgons, and Harpies belching dreadfull flame,
30   Chimera up with triple Geryon came.
    Aeneas draws, surpriz'd with sudden fear,
Offering the dreadful point to them drew near;
But that his learn'd Associate him perswades
They were but fleeting and fantastick shades,
In vain he had attempted ghosts to wound.
Hence led the way to th' Acherontick sound:
With a vast gulph here whirlpits vext with mud
Cast boyling sands up from the Stygian flood.
    The ferryman of Hell, foul Charon, keeps
40   These horrid waters and infernal deeps;
His untrimm'd cheeks are rough with hoary hair,
Elf-locked his beard, his fiery eyes do stare;
Ty'd o'er his shoulders hangs a sordid coat;
Whose pole and sails drive on his crazy boat
Laden with passengers; though old, the god
Is youthful still, his veins still full of blood.
To these sad banks old, young, both rich and poor,
Haste in confused throngs; upon this shore
Matrons and men, lamenting babes remain
50   'Mongst valiant kings in bloody battle slain,
With beauteous virgins and brave youth, that were
Laid in their parents' presence on the bier.

No thicker leaves in woods thou mayst behold
Fall from their trees, nipt with autumnal cold;
No thicker fowl from th' Ocean flock, whom frosts
From winter-quarters drive to warmer coasts.
With rear'd-up hands they earnestly implore
For transportation to the farther shore.
But churlish Charon culls his freight, then beats
60    The rest, lamenting, to remoter seats.
Here Prince Aeneas, much admiring, spake:
'What means these concourse, virgin, to the lake?
What would these souls? Why leave they thus these shores?
Why those rowl sable waves with yielding oars?'
Then thus the long-lived priestess straight replyes:
'Anchises' son, and sprung from deities,
Thou Styx behold'st and deep Cocytus now,
By which gods swearing dare not break their vow.
Those wofull souls thou seest are not interr'd;
70    That's Charon – those he wafts are sepulchred.
None are transported o're these horrid waves
Untill their bones find quiet in their graves.
A hundred years they on these shores remain,
At last their long-expected passage gain.'          (1654)


# JOHN OGILBY

[Georg. I. 125–59] *The end of the Golden Age*

See Introduction, p. xii.

Before Jove's time, no Tiller vext the grounds,
Inclos'd his own or limits others' bounds.
All common was, and of her own accord
The earth full plenty freely did afford.

He to foul Serpents deadly poison gave,
Commanded Wolves to prey, and Seas to rave.
Robb'd leaves of Honey, fire conceal'd, and Wine,
Which ran before in Rivers, did confine;
That various Arts by study might be wrought
10   Up to their hight, and Corn in furrow sought,
And Mortals should from Veins of flint strike fire.
Then Rivers first did Alder Boats admire;
Then Sailors nam'd and number'd every Star,
And knew what all the Constellations were;
The snares for Beasts, and lime for Birds was found,
And how Dogs should the mighty woods surround;
This, strikes broad Rivers with his casting Net,
That, fishing lines draws from the Ocean wet.
Then Steel and grating saws were first receiv'd:
20   Before, soft wedges easie Timber cleav'd.
    Then Arts began, fierce toyl through all things breaks,
And urgent want strange projects undertakes.
First, Ceres Mortals taught to plough the ground,
When Akorns scarce in sacred Groves were found,
And Dodon mast deni'd; then swains did toyl
Lest smutting mildews golden ears should soyl,
And the base Thistle over all aspire;
The corn decaies, whole Groves of armed Brier
And Burs arise, and o'er a glorious land
30   Pernitious Darnel and wild Oats command.
Unless with Rakes thou daily break'st the grounds,
And Birds affright'st with terrifying sounds,

---

5–8 According to this version of the myth, when the Golden Age ended Jove (Jupiter) removed from man the gifts of honey, wine and fire, which had to be rediscovered.
23 *Ceres*: goddess of corn
25 *Dodon*: the sacred grove of Zeus (the Roman Jupiter) was famous for its oak trees; *mast*: food made out of acorns, more suitable for swine than men (cf. 36)

Cut'st spreading Weeds which shade thy golden grain,
And supplication mak'st with vows for rain,
Thou shalt in vain see others' great increase
When shaken Oke thy hunger must appease.                (1654)


# SIR JOHN DENHAM (1615–69)

## The Destruction of Troy, 496–549 [Aen. II. 506–58]
### The death of Priam

A revised text of an earlier attempt, published 1656. Printed from
the 1668 edition of his *Poems and Translations*, ed. T. H. Banks, *The
Poetical Works of Sir John Denham*, 2nd edition, 1969. See also the
earlier versions of this passage by Douglas and Surrey. Dryden
consulted Denham's version: the final line appears unchanged in his
translation, while other lines are only slightly rephrased. For
Denham's views on the theory of translation see Appendix B.

Now Priams fate perhaps you may enquire,
Seeing his Empire lost, his Troy on fire,
And his own Palace by the Greeks possest,
Arms, long disus'd, his trembling limbs invest;
Thus on his foes he throws himself alone,
Not for their Fate, but to provoke his own:
There stood an Altar open to the view
Of Heaven, near which an aged Lawrel grew,
Whose shady arms the houshold Gods embrac'd;
10   Before whose feet the Queen her self had cast,
With all her daughters, and the Trojan wives
As Doves whom an approaching tempest drives
And frights into one flock; But having spy'd
Old Priam clad in youthful Arms, she cry'd,
Alas my wretched husband, what pretence
To bear those Arms, and in them what defence?
Such aid such times require not, when again

If Hector were alive, he liv'd in vain;
Or here We shall a Sanctuary find,
20    Or as in life, we shall in death be joyn'd.
Then weeping, with kind force held & embrac'd
And on the sacred seat the King she plac'd;
Mean while Polites one of Priams sons
Flying the rage of bloudy Pyrrhus, runs
Through foes & swords, & ranges all the Court
And empty Galleries, amaz'd and hurt,
Pyrrhus pursues him, now oretakes, now kills,
And his last blood in Priams presence spills.
The King (though him so many deaths inclose)
30    Nor fear, nor grief, but Indignation shows;
The Gods requite thee (if within the care
Of those above th' affairs of mortals are)
Whose fury on the son but lost had been,
Had not his Parents Eyes his murder seen:
Not That Achilles (whom thou feign'st to be
Thy Father) so inhumane was to me;
He blusht, when I the rights of Arms implor'd;
To me my Hector, me to Troy restor'd:
This said, his feeble Arm a Javelin flung,
40    Which on the sounding shield, scarce entring, rung.
Then Pyrrhus; go a messenger to Hell
Of my black deeds, and to my Father tell
The Acts of his degenerate Race. So through
His Sons warm bloud, the trembling King he drew
To th' Altar; in his hair one hand he wreaths;
His sword, the other in his bosom sheaths.
Thus fell the King, who yet surviv'd the State,
With such a signal and peculiar Fate.
Under so vast a ruine not a Grave,
50    Nor in such flames a funeral fire to have:
He, whom such Titles swell'd, such Power made proud
To whom the Scepters of all Asia bow'd,
On the cold earth lies th' unregarded King,
A headless Carkass, and a nameless Thing.          (1656, 1668)

# SIDNEY GODOLPHIN (1610–43)

## The Passion of Dido for Aeneas: Translated out of the Fourth Book of Virgil, 1–182 [Aen. IV. 1–172]

Godolphin's easy and lucid style created a new standard in the translation of Virgil. Denham, Lauderdale and Dryden were all influenced by him. He did not live to complete his version of Book IV; a passage of 134 lines was added by Edmund Waller.

Mean while the Queen fanning a secret fire,
In her own breast revolves her deepe Desire.
She oft reflects upon the princely grace
Of great Æneas, and that noble race
From whence he springs; her wounded fancy feeds
On his discourse, his high Heroick deeds,
His words his looks, her waking thoughts imploy,
And when she sleepes, she sees him with more joy,
But seldome sleeps: For when the shades of night
10   Had left their Empire to the rising Light,
Folding her Sister in her armes, she sayes,
What unacquainted thoughts, what dreams are these?
How great a Guest within our walls we hold,
How wise in Counsell, and in Armes how bold?
The mortall seed of man acknowledge feare
But this brave Prince his equall mind doth beare
Above all Chance. Did not my changelesse vow
And mine owne will engage me to allow
No other Love; my first Affection dead
20   And with the Soul of my Sichæus fled:
Were not all joyes growne tastlesse, and the name
Of Love offensive, since I lost that flame;
I might perhaps indulge this one desire.
For, Anna, I confesse since funerall fire
Embrac'd Sichæus, this first beame of Light
Hath offered comfort to so dark a night,

Unwonted motions in my thoughts retriv'd,
I find and feel the brand of care reviv'd.
But may the earth, while yet alive, devoure
30  This haplesse frame, and Jove his thunder poure
Upon my head, and sink me to that shade
That silent deep, whence no returne is made:
Before I doe those sacred Knots unty,
Which bind me to so deare a memory.
He first unto my soul this ardor gave,
And may he hold it in his quiet grave,
This said, she weeps afresh. Anna replyes,
O Chiefly Lov'd and Dearer then mine eyes,
Sad and alone for ever wil you wast
40  Your verdant youth, nor natures bounties taste
In their due season? think you that the dead
In their cold urns welcome the tears we shead?
What though no prayrs have yet had power to move
Your thoughts to entertain a second love;
Yet will you now with your own heart contest?
Nor give admittance to a pleasing guest?
Consider where this new Plantation lyes,
And amidst whom these walls of Carthage rise:
Here the Getulians, fierce Numidians there,
50  On either side engage your watchfull fear.
Propitious Heavens, it seems, and Juno lead
These Trojans here with so desir'd an aid:
This match will mixe your fortunes and advance
The Tyrian State above all force or chance.
Invoke the powers above, with soft delay
Engage the Dardan Prince to longer stay:
Till the swoln Seas and winds their fury spend,
And Calmer Gales his purposes attend.
      This speech revives the Courage of the Dame
60  And through her burning veines dilates the flame.
First to the holy temple they repaire
And seek indulgence from above by praire:

Law-giving Ceres, Phœbus they invoke,
But above all do Venus Altars smoke
Propitious to the bands of Love; the Queen
With her own hands, the Heifer's horns between,
Poures the full bowls, or midst the sacrifice
Intentive walkes, as the rich Odours rise
Fresh gifts she brings, and with a thoughtfull brain
70  Surveyes the panting Livers of the slain;
Blind prophesies, Vain Altars, bootlesse Prayer
How little help they? while so neer a care
Presses the Queen and mingled with her bloud
Spreads secret poyson through the purple floud.
The Haplesse Dido is enrag'd by love;
And with uncertain thoughts doth wildly move:
    So when a Shepheards roving Arrows find
And pierce (to him unknown) some careless Hind
She flyes through woods and seeks the streames opprest
80  The deadly Arrow rankles in her breast.
Now to the Walls she leads her Trojan Chief,
And with this food she entertain'd her grief
Shews the Sidonian-wealth, and, as she speaks,
Her own discourse by care diverted breaks;
The evening closes with another feast
And there again sh'invites the princely Guest
To tell his dangers past, and there again
She drinks together deeper Love and Pain.
    But when the Prince (night's darker ensign spread,
90  And sleepy dew upon all Mortalls shed)
Doth bid farewell, she waking there alone
Deserted mourns that her Dear Guest is gone;
Or keeps Ascanius in her Armes, to prove
If likenesse can delude her restlesse Love.
Mean while her stately structures slowly rise,
Halfe-finisht Carthage rude and broken lyes.
That high design, to heaven exalted frame,
Confus'd appears, and like a ruine lame.

Which when survey'd by Juno from above
100   And that the Queen neglects her fame for love;
Approaching Venus, thus Saturnia sayes:
What ample Trophies, never-dying prayse,
To you and to your Cupid will be paid?
That two such Gods one woman have betray'd.
I know with what designe you us'd this Art
Planting Æneas thus in Dido's heart,
Suspecting least these walls of Ours might prove
Faithlesse to him if not secur'd by Love.
But shall this partiall quarrell never cease?
110   May we not now fixe on eternall peace?
Fair Dido loves and feels your golden Dart;
Give but like ardoux to Æneas Heart,
And we wil rule this State with equall power,
And give the Trojan Carthage for a Dower.
Venus replyes (seeing the wife of Jove
To crosse the height of Roman greatnesse strove
With this deceit), What madnesse can refuse
Friendship with you where you a friendship chuse?
But whether Jove will favour this designe
120   And the great people in one Empire joyn;
This in your prayers, who are his wife, doth lye.
      Juno returns; Impose this taske on me,
For what is now in hand let this suffice.
The Trojan Prince with his unhappy prize
The wounded Queen, to chase the flying Dear
Soon as the beams of Morning-light appeare
Hyes to the Fields; there, on the goodly traine
A darkning shower I'le pour of hayl and raine,

---

**101** *Saturnia*: Juno. In her hatred for the Trojans, she plots to detain Aeneas at Carthage and thereby delay his mission to Italy. Venus, knowing that Jupiter will never agree to this plan, pretends to fall in with it, thereby helping to deceive Dido into assuming that Aeneas' love for her will be permanent.

Shake heaven with thunder, while the pale troop ride
130  Disperst with fear and lost without a guide:
One Cave in her dark bosome shall afford
Shelter to Dido and the Trojan Lord,
And if, as I, propitious to their love
You shine; this shall their Hymeneall prove;
All rites shall here be done. Venus with smiles
Consents, but laughs within, at Juno's wiles.

The morning come, early at light's first ray
The gallant youth rise with the chearfull day:
Sharp Javelins in their hands, their Coursers by
140  They walke amidst the hound's impatient Cry:
Neerer the gates the Tyrian Peers attend,
And waite the Queen now ready to descend.
Her prouder Steed as fill'd with high disdain
Stamps the dull Earth, & Chawes the frothy Reine.
Mounted at last, her golden Quiver on
Ty'd up with gold, her Hair which gold-like shone,
Her purple garment, claspt with gold, in head
Of her fair troop, the brighter Queen doth lead
With these the Trojans, and their great Chief close
150  As one fair stream into another flows.
He like Apollo in his light and heat
When he returnes unto his Native seat
Of Delos, and fresh verdure doth restore
Forsaking Xanthus and the Lycian shore
Thus he on Cynthus tops, his own retreat
Securely walkes, thus welcome and thus great
The Dryopeans and the Cretans by,
So doth his quiver clash; not lesse then he
Æneas shines, like beauty's in his face
160  And in his motions like attractive grace.

---

**137** The celebrated 'royal hunt and storm' in which the goddesses' plot is consummated.

While thus they climb the pathless hills, the cry
Pursues the fearfull heards which headlong fly
Down to the vales, and on the boundlesse plain
A longer chase in view of all maintain.
    But glad Ascanius spurrs his willing horse
Now these, now those, out-passing in the Course.
He wishes some incensed Bore his prey,
Or Lyon from the Hills would Cross his way.
    Mean while the gathering Clouds obscure the Pole,
170 They flash out lightning and in Thunder roule:
A bitter storme succeeds, the troops divide
And ore the Hills disperst to Coverts ride.
One Cave in her dark bosome doth afford
Shelter to Dido and the Trojan Lord.
Heaven shines with fire, earth shakes at this success
The Conscious air is fill'd with Prodigies.
    This was the hour, which gave the fatall blow,
The pregnant spring of all succeeding woe.
Tender respects no more have power to move
180 The haplesse Queen, no more she hides her love,
But doth hir Crime express with Hymens name,
And lives expos'd a Theame to various fame.        (1658)

---

175-8 Imitated by Milton to describe Nature's reaction to the eating of the
apple by Eve, *Paradise Lost* IX, 782-4: 'Earth felt the wound, and Nature
from her seat/Sighing through all her works gave signs of woe/That all was
lost.'

# JAMES HARRINGTON (1611–77)

## Eclogue IX [Ecl. IX]

Printed from *An Essay upon Two of Virgil's Eclogues and Two Books of his Aeneis* (1658). The situation in the poem recalls that in Eclogue I (see Introduction). The poet Menalcas has been dispossessed of his land and the two shepherds, meeting on the road, wistfully recall fragments of his verse, lamenting the fact that song, like farming, has become a casualty of war. The fragments here italicized recall passages from Virgil's other eclogues.

> *By Meris in this Eclogue is to be understood Virgil's shepherd or Baylif, who carries a present of kids to mollify the centurion Arius; by Menalcas is meant Virgil himself, some of whose verses Meris is wooed by Lycidas to repeat.* [Translator's headnote]

LYCIDAS
Whither away good Meris, to the town?

MERIS
O Lycidas, the like was never known!
We live to see a guest come in a doors
And say, 'my friends, this house, these fields, are ours;
I pray, depart!' Nay, and for this (because
Fortune will have obedience to her laws)
Must I these kids unto his worship bear
But shall not say, 'much good may do you, sir'.

LYCIDAS
There was a speech methinks that since among
10  The gallant courtiers your Menalcas sung,
They left him all his goodly fields that reach
Down from the hills to the bald-pated beech.

MERIS

Why, so they talked indeed; but songs and loves
Are unto soldiers as to eagles doves.
Neither your Meris nor Menalcas now
Had been alive, had the auspicious crow
Out of her hollow roost not stood my friend
And warned me that I should no more contend.

LYCIDAS

Is there such wickedness! in thee alone,
20   Menalcas, all our melody had gone.
Who should have sung the nymphs? our springs with bowers
Have clouded, or have starred our fields with flowers?
Who ere made verse like that I stole from thee
When thou to Amaryllis stol'st from me!
*Feed, Tityrus, the flock till I return,*
*I go not far, and drive 'em to the bourn,*
*But driving make me not more haste than speed,*
*The goat is parlous with the horn, take heed.*

MERIS

What then were those to Varus set by yours:
30   *Varus thy name [if Mantua be ours,*
*Mantua whose guilt is that he is too near*
*Cremona] swans unto the sky shall bear.*

LYCIDAS

As thou dost hope thy swarm shall scape the Ew,
Or that the honeysuckle shall indue
The strutting udders of thy cows, begin,
If thou hast any more, for I am in;

---

**28** *parlous*: perilous
**30** *Varus*: a land commissioner who may have been responsible for disposing
of land in Mantua, the poet's home town. Land in Cremona, sixty kilometres
distant, may perhaps have already been fully allocated.
**33** *Ew*: the yew tree, which gave honey a bitter flavour.

Me have the sisters made a poet too,
And this our swains throughout the fields avow;
But I believe them not: such strains as these
40   To Varus or the Muses' swans were geese.


MERIS

I am upon it, and if I can bring
It well to mind, a noble air shall sing.
*Come, fairest Galatea, come away.*
*What sport is there for me where Delphins play?*
*The purple spring here scatters on the shores*
*Of creeping rivlets, his delicious stores.*
*The poplar with the vine hath joyning made*
*Us party-coloured bowers and cooling shade.*
*Come, lovely sea-nymph, from the furrowed deep,*
50   *And let the shores thy flock of billows keep.*


LYCIDAS

Now, that at which the sky grew clear as curds
Last night – I have the tune, what are the words?


MERIS

*Why heedst thou Daphnis' antiquated signs?*
*Behold, the star of heav'n-born Caesar shines,*
*Whose month bestows upon the gods of bread*
*And wine, the ruby crown and golden head.*
*Engraft thine apples, Daphnis, and thy pears,*
*The harvest shall descend upon thine heirs.*
You should have more, but all is gone with time:
60   I could have brought the sun to bed in rime:

---

**43ff.** The song to Galatea is a well-known pastoral theme from Theocritus;
cf. Eclogue II, 45.
**55–6** *the gods of bread/And wine*: Ceres and Bacchus
**58** Cf. Eclogue I, 73.

Now me my verses and my voice forsake,
The wolf hath seen me first. But this way make
You merry, till Menalcas come, and feast
Upon our flow'ry carpets with the rest.

LYCIDAS
Ah, thou by these hast but my flame increast.
The air to hearken has his murmur ceast.
The silent wave his roughness at thy feet
Hath laid as smooth as glass. That we are yet
But half our way, Bianor's tomb now shows;
70    Here, where the shepherds cut him verdant boughs,
Here, Meris, let us sing, thy kids here lay,
We shall be time enough at Mantua.
Or if the moist surprise of night we fear,
Sing as we go, and I the kids will bear.

MERIS
Good Lycidas, be said; if we first bring
Our work about, we shall have time to sing.                (1658)

---

**75** *said*: gainsaid

# SIR RICHARD FANSHAWE
(1608–66)

[Aen. IV. 450–585] *Aeneas' departure from Carthage*

From *The Fourth Book of Virgil's Aeneis, on the Loves of Dido and Aeneas* (1664). Apart from Sir John Harington, who used *ottava rima*, Fanshawe is the only seventeenth-century translator of Virgil who eschewed the heroic couplet: his Spenserian stanzas were consequently ignored by Dryden.

Then doth unhappy Dido, given ore
   By her last hope, desire to die. The light
   Is irksom to her eys. To confirm more
   Her purpose to imbrace eternal night,
   Placing on th' Incense-burning Altars bright
   Her gifts, the holy water she beheld
   Converted to black ink (portentous sight!)
   And the pour'd wine to roaping blood congeal'd;
This thing to none, not to her sister, she reveal'd.

10  A Marble Fane too in the house she had
   Where lay her first Lords ashes, kept among
   Her most adored Reliques; 'twas with sad
   Dark Yew-tree, and the whitest fleeces hung.
   Hence in the night she heard her husbands tongue,
   Call her, she thought. And oft the boading Owl
   Alone on the house top harsh dirges sung,
   And with long noats quav'rd a doleful howl,
Besides old Prophesies, which terrifie her soul.

   Cruel Æneas ev'n her sleeps torments:
20   And still she dreams she's wandring all alone
   Through a long way with steep and dark descents,
   Calling her Tyrians in a Land, where none,
   But some pain'd Ghost Eccho's her with a groane.

As when mad Pentheus troops of Furies fright,
Who sees a twofold Thebes, and double Sunne:
Or when Orestes flyes his Mothers sight,
Hunting his bloody track with Hel-hounds by torchlight.

Sunke then with grief, possest with furies, bent
On death, she plots the meanes, and in her Eye
30    A feign'd hope springing, hiding her intent
Accosts sad Anne. Partake thy sisters Joy,
I've found a way to make him burne as I,
Or turne me cold like him. Neere Phœbus set
At the lands end doth Æthiopia lye,
Where on great Atlas necke, the Heav'n thick set
With glorious Diamond-starres hangs like a Carkanet.

Of a great Sorceresse I have been told
There borne, who did th' Hesperian Temple keepe,
The Dragon fed, and sacred fruit of Gold
40    Watcht on the tree which she for dew did steepe
In Honey, and moist Poppy causing sleepe.
Shee undertakes to cure the Love-sick breast,
And whom shee list to plunge in Love as deepe,
The waters course in Rivers to arrest,
And call down stars from Heav'n, and cal up ghosts from rest.

Under her tread thou shalt perceive Earth groane,
And Oakes skip from the hills; I sweare to thee
(Calling the Gods to record, and thine own
Sweet head) that forc't to these black Arts I flee.
50    Thou on some Tow'r a stack build secretly,

---

**24-7** The double simile compares Dido with two Greek tragic heroes:
Pentheus, driven mad by the god Dionysus so that he sees double, and
Orestes, pursued by the ghost of his mother Clytemnestra and by the Furies.
**36** *Carkanet*: a necklace
**37ff.** Dido's recourse to magic recalls another Greek tragic figure, Medea.

Lay on it the mans cloathes, and sword which lyes
Within, and, that which prov'd a grave to me,
My Wedding Bed. So doth the Witch advise,
Ev'n that I blot out all the traytors memories.

This said, grew pale. Yet thinks not Anne that shee
With these new Rites her funerall doth shade,
Nor fears such Monsters, or worse extasie
Then at Sycheus death; Therefore obay'd.
But Dido, a great Pile of wood being made
60      The place with flowr's and fatäl Cypresse crown'd,
Thereon his cloaths and sword bequeathed laid,
His Picture on the Bed, the mystick ground
Known only to her selfe. Altars are placed round.

With haire dispread like a black falling storme,
Th'Inchantress thunders out three hundred names,
Orchus, and Chaos, Hecate-triforme,
Which Virgin Dian's triple-pow'r enseames,
She sprinkled, too, Avernus fabulous streames:
And hearts were sought for, sprouting forth ripe Bane,
70      With brazen sickles, cropt in the Moones beames,
And puld from new born Colt, that lumpe, which, ta'ne
From the Dams mouth, no love t'her issue doth remain.

Her self in a loose vest, one foot unshod,
With meale in pious hands neer th' Altar drew,
Witnesse ye guilty starres and every God
(Saith she) I'm forc't to dye. Invokes them too
Who care of Lovers take (if any doe)
Unequally. 'Twas night, and conqu'ring sleepe,

---

**67** Diana was the moon, the huntress and (in the underworld) Hecate, the
three-faced goddess associated with witchcraft and ghosts.
*enseames*: incorporates

With weari'd bodies the whole earth did strew;
80     When woods are quiet, and the cruell deep
When stars are half way down, when fields stil silence keep,

And beasts and painted Birds, which liquid Springs
    Inhabit, or which bushy Lands containe,
    Nuzling their cares beneath sleepes downy wings,
    Do bury the past dayes forgotten paine;
    All but the haplesse Queen, she doth refraine
    From rest, nor takes it at her eyes or heart.
    After long seeming dead, Love rose againe
    And fought with wrath, as when two Tydes do thwart,
90  Whilst thus her big thoughts roll & wallow to each part.

What shall I do? Shall I a suiter be
    To my old suitors, scorned by the new,
    And wooe those Kings so oft despis'd by me?
    What then? Shall I the Ilian Fleet pursue,
    And share all this mans fates? Yes, he doth shew
    Such sence of my first aides: Or say I wou'd,
    Whom he hath mockt, will not his proud ships too
    Reject? Ah foole, by whom the perjur'd brood
Of false Laomedon is not yet understood!

100  Grant they'd admit me, shall I flye alone
    With Mariners? Or chace him with the power
    Oth' emptyed Towne, and servants of mine own,
    And whom I scare from Tyre by the roots up tore,
    Compell to plough the horrid Seas once more?
    No, dye as thou deserv'st, cure woes with woe.

---

**99** Laomedon, an early king of Troy, cheated the gods of the payment he had promised them for building the walls of Troy. His perfidy, and its consequences for the Trojans, is a recurring theme of the *Aeneid*.

Thou syster, first, when I my teares did showre
To quench these rising flames, thou dids't them blow,
And out of cruel pity soldst me to the Foe.

Why might not I (alas) have mourn'd away
110    My widdow'd youth as well as Turtles do?
Nor twice have made my self misfortunes prey,
Or to Sicheus ashes prov'd untrue?
These words with sighs out of her bosome flew.
Æneas slept aboord, all things prepared.
To whom again Joves sonne with the same hiew
Divine, so silver-voyc'd, so golden hayr'd,
So straight and lovely shap't, thus rowsing him appear'd.

O Goddesse born, now dost thou sleepe? nor know
How many dangers watch to compasse thee?
120    Nor hear this good wind whispering thee to go?
Purpos'd to dye, great plots and dire broods she,
Who boyles with rage like a high going Sea.
Flye whilst thou maist flye. If the morning finde
Thee napping here, the Sea will cover'd be
With Ships, the shoare with flames: Fly with the wind,
Trust that, but do not trust a womans fickle mind.

This said, he mixt himself with night: But then
Æneas at these visions sore agast,
Starts out of sleepe, and cryes, up, up, O men,
130    Hoyse up your Sayles, flye to your Oares, row fast;
Behold a God from Heav'n again bids haste,
Cutting the wreathed Cable. O, who ere
We follow thee, obey'd as late thou wast
Most gladly. Aide what thou commandst, and steere
With prosp'rous stars bespoke as thou fly'st through their
sphere.

---

112 *Sicheus*: Dido's late husband
115 *Joves sonne*: Mercury, messenger of the gods

This said, whipt out his Lightning Sword, and strooke
   The fastning ropes. Like zeale his patterne bred
   In all. They snatcht, they ran, the shoares for sook,
   Their Sayles like wings over the waves were spread;
140     They comb'd with Oares gray Neptunes curled head.
   And now Aurora scattered rosie light
   Upon the Earth from Tythons purple bed.
   Whom Dido, having scoured all the night,
Discover'd from the Watch-Tower by her Ensignes white.

                                    (1664)

# ABRAHAM COWLEY (1618–67)

## A Translation out of Virgil [Georg. II. 458–540]
### In praise of rural life

From 'Several Discourses by way of Essays in Verse and Prose';
printed from the 1668 edition of the poet's works. The most famous
passage in the Georgics; later imitated by Thomson in The Seasons.

   Oh happy, (if his happiness he knows)
   The Countrey Swain! on whom kind Heav'n bestows
   At home all Riches that wise Nature needs;
   Whom the just Earth with easie plenty feeds.
   'Tis true, no morning Tide of Clients comes,
   And fills the painted Channels of his rooms,
   Adoring the rich Figures as they pass,
   In Tapstry wrought, or cut in living Brass;
   Nor is his Wooll superfluously Dy'd
10     With the dear poison of Assyrian pride;
   Nor do Arabian Perfumes vainly spoil
   The Native Life, and sweetness of his Oil.
   Instead of these, his calm and harmless life
   Free from th' allarms of fear, and storms of strife,

Does with substantial blessedness abound,
And the soft wings of Peace cover him round:
Through Artless Grots the murm'ring water glide;
Thick Trees both against Heat and Cold provide,
From whence the Birds salute him; and his ground
20  With lowing Herds, and bleating Sheep does sound;
And all the Rivers, and the Forrests nigh,
Both Food and Game, and Exercise supply.
Here a well hard'ned active youth we see,
Taught the great Art of chearful Povertie.
Here, in this place alone, there still do shine
Some streaks of Love both Humane and Divine:
From hence Astrea took her flight, and here
Still her last Footsteps upon Earth appear.
'Tis true, the first desire which does controul
30  All the inferior wheels that move thy soul,
Is, that the Muse me her High-Priest would make;
Into her Holy Scenes of Myst'ry take,
And open there to my minds purged Eye
Those wonders which to Sense the gods deny;
How in the Moon such change of shapes is found;
The Moon, the changing Worlds eternal bound.
What shakes the solid Earth, what strong disease
Dares trouble the fair Centre's antient ease;
What makes the Sea Retreat, and what Advance;
40  *Varieties too regular for chance.*
What drives the Chariot on of Winters light,
And stops the lazy Waggon of the night.
But if my dull and frozen Blood deny
To send forth th' Sp'rits that raise a Soul so high;
In the next place let Woods and Rivers be
My quiet, though unglorious destinie.
In Life's cool vale let my low Scene be laid;
Cover me, gods, with Tempe's thickest shade.
Happy the man, I grant, thrice happy he,
50  Who can through gross effects their causes see:

Whose courage from the Deeps of knowledge springs,
Nor vainly fears inevitable things;
But does his walk of Virtue calmly go,
Through all th'Alarms of Death and Hell below.
Happy! but next such Conqu'rors happy they,
Whose humble Life lies not in Fortunes way.
They unconcern'd from their safe distant seat
Behold the Rods and Scepters of the Great.
The quarrels of the Mighty without fear,
60   And the descent of forreign Troops they hear.
Nor can ev'n Rome their steady course misguide,
With all the lustre of her per'shing pride,
Them never yet did strife or av'rice draw,
Into the noisy Markets of the Law,
The Camps of Gowned War, nor do they live
By rules or forms that many mad-men give.
Duty for Natures bounty they repay.
And her sole Laws religiously obey.
    Some with bold Labour plough the faithless main,
70   Some rougher storms in Princes Courts sustain.
Some swell up their slight Sails with pop'lar Fame,
Charm'd with the foolish whistlings of a Name.
Some their vain Wealth to Earth again commit;
With endless cares, some brooding o'r it sit.
Countrey and Friends are by some wretches sold,
To lye on Tyrian Beds, and drink in Gold;
No price too high for profit can be shown;
Not Brothers Blood, nor hazards of their own.
Around the World in search of it they roam,
80   It makes ev'n their Antipodes their home.
Mean while the prudent Husbandman is found,
In mutual Duties driving with his ground,
And halfe the year he care of that does take,
That half the year grateful returns does make.
Each fertile month does some new gifts present,
And with new work his industry content.

This, the young Lamb, that the soft Fleece doth yield,
This, loads with Hay, and that, with Corn, the Field:
All sorts of Fruit crown the rich Autumn's pride:
90    And on a swelling Hill's warm stony side,
The pow'rful Princely purple of the Vine,
Twice dy'd with the redoubled Sun, does shine.
In th'Evening to a fair ensuing day,
With joy he sees his Flocks and Kids to play;
And loaded Kyne about his Cottage stand,
Inviting with known sound the Milkers hand;
And when from wholsome labour he doth come,
With wishes to be there, and wish'd for home,
He meets at door the softest humane blisses,
100   His chaste Wives welcome, and dear Childrens kisses.
When any Rural Holy-days invite
His Genius forth to innocent delight,
On Earths fair Bed beneath some Sacred shade,
Amidst his equal friends carelesly laid,
He sings thee Bacchus Patron of the Vine,
The Beechen Bowl foams with a flood of Wine,
Not to the loss of reason or of strength:
To active games and manly sport at length
Their mirth ascends, and with fill'd veins they see,
110   Who can the best at better Tryals be.
Such was the Life the prudent Sabins chose,
From such the old Hetrurian Virtue rose.
Such, Remus and the god his Brother led,
From such firm footing Rome grew th' Worlds head.
Such was the Life that ev'n till now does raise
The honour of poor Saturns Golden days:
Before Men born of Earth and buried there,
Let in the Sea their mortal fate to share.
Before new ways of perishing were sought,
120   Before unskilful Death on Anvils wrought.
Before those Beasts which humane Life sustain
By Men, unless to the gods use, were slain.        (1668)

# SIR JOHN DENHAM (1615–69)

## The Passion of Dido, 161–end [Aen. IV. 584–705]

From 'The Passion of Dido', written about 1653, published 1668. Denham omits several passages from Virgil's text, including the summoning of the nurse by Dido to fetch her sister (630–44 in the Latin); the conclusion (665–705) is cut to twenty-seven lines.

> Aurora now had left Tithonus bed,
> And o're the world her blushing Raies did spread;
> The Queen beheld as soon as day appear'd,
> The Navy under Sail, the Haven clear'd;
> Thrice with her hand her Naked Breast she knocks,
> And from her forehead tears her Golden Locks.
> O Jove, she cry'd, and shall he thus delude
> Me and my Realm! why is he not pursu'd?
> Arm, Arm, she cry'd, and let our Tyrians board
> With ours his Fleet, and carry Fire and Sword;
> Leave nothing unattempted to destroy
> That perjur'd Race, then let us dye with joy;
> What if the event of War uncertain were,
> Nor death, nor danger, can the desperate fear?
> But oh too late! this thing I should have done,
> Behold the Faith of him who sav'd from fire
> His honour'd houshold gods, his Aged Sire
> His Pious shoulders from Troy's Flames did bear;
> Why did I not his Carcase piece-meal tear
> And cast it in the Sea? why not destroy
> All his Companions and beloved Boy
> Ascanius? and his tender limbs have drest,
> And made the Father on the Son to Feast?
> Thou Sun, whose lustre all things here below
> Surveys; and Juno conscious of my woe;
> Revengeful Furies, and Queen Hecate,
> Receive and grant my prayer! if he the Sea
> Must needs escape, and reach th' Ausonian land,

10

20

If Jove decree it, Jove's decree must stand;
30  When landed, may he be with arms opprest
By his rebelling people; be distrest
By exile from his Country, be divorc'd
From young Ascanius sight, and be enforc'd
To implore Forrein aids, and lose his Friends
By violent and undeserved ends:
When to conditions of unequal Peace
He shall submit, then may he not possess
Kingdom nor Life, and find his Funeral
I' th' Sands, when he before his day shall fall:
40  And ye oh Tyrians with immortal hate
Pursue his race, this service dedicate
To my deplored ashes; let there be
'Twixt us and them no League nor Amity;
May from my bones a new Achilles rise,
That shall infest the Trojan Colonies
With Fire, and Sword, and Famine, when at length
Time to our great attempts contributes strength;
Our Seas, our Shores, our Armies theirs oppose,
And may our Children be for ever Foes.
50  A ghastly paleness deaths approach portends,
Then trembling she the fatal pile ascends;
Viewing the Trojan relicks, she unsheath'd
Æneas Sword, not for that use bequeath'd:
Then on the guilty bed she gently lays
Her self, and softly thus lamenting prays:
Dear Reliques whilst that Gods and Fates gave leave,
Free me from care, and my glad soul receive;
That date which fortune gave I now must end,
And to the shades a noble Ghost descend;
60  Sichœus blood by his false Brother spilt,
I have reveng'd, and a proud City built;
Happy, alas! too happy I had liv'd,
Had not the Trojan on my Coast arriv'd;
But shall I dye without revenge? yet dye,
Thus, thus with joy to thy Sichœus flye.

My conscious Foe my Funeral fire shall view
From Sea, and may that Omen him pursue.
Her fainting hand let fall the Sword besmear'd
With blood, and then the Mortal wound appear'd;
70  Through all the Court the fright and clamours rise,
Which the whole City fills with fears and cries,
As loud as if her Carthage, or old Tyre
The Foe had entred, and had set on Fire:
Amazed Anne with speed ascends the stairs,
And in her arms her dying Sister rears:
Did you for this, your self, and me beguile
For such an end did I erect this Pile?
Did you so much despise me, in this Fate
My self with you not to associate?
80  Your self and me, alas! this fatal wound
The Senate, and the People, doth confound.
I'le wash her Wound with Tears, and at her Death,
My Lips from hers shall draw her parting Breath.
Then with her Vest the Wound she wipes and dries;
Thrice with her Arm the Queen attempts to rise,
But her strength failing, falls into a swound,
Life's last efforts yet striving with her Wound;
Thrice on her Bed she turns, with wandring sight
Seeking, she groans when she beheld the light;
90  Then Juno pitying her disastrous Fate,
Sends Iris down, her Pangs to Mitigate,
(Since if we fall before th' appointed day,
Nature and Death continue long their Fray)
Iris Descends; This Fatal lock (says she)
To Pluto I bequeath, and set thee free,
Then clips her Hair, cold Numness strait bereaves
Her Corps of sense, and th' Ayr her Soul receives.          (1668)

---

**94–7** In some lines cut by Denham, Virgil explains that, because Dido's death
was not fated, Proserpine had not cut the lock from her hair which would
release her soul into the underworld. Iris now performs this rite.

# CHARLES COTTON (1630–87)

## Scarronides: or Virgile Travestie. A mock poem in imitation of the fourth book of Virgil's Aeneis in English burlesque (extract)

This extract is printed from the revised edition of 1670. A 'deflation-ary' parody, in which Virgil's gods and heroes speak and act in a low-life style. The metre also deflates the heroic couplet by remov-ing one foot: the resulting octosyllabics, with extravagant rhyme scheme, are called 'hudibrastic', after Samuel Butler's satire *Hudibras*.

'Twas now the time when candles are
Repriev'd by the Extinguisher;
When every thing to sleep down lies,
Dogs in their kennels, Hogs in sties,
And men and women rest their heads
And heels, in Flocks, or Feather-beds.
Now Men, and Fishes, Birds, and Beast,
And everything was laid to rest;
All but the woeful Queen (alas!)
10   Who now was brought unto that pass,
What with her love and what with spite,
She could not sleep a wink all night.
Her stomach now was piping hot,
It boyl'd and bubbled like a Pot,
And did so strong a wambling keep,
She fitter was to spew then sleep.
   Have you not seen an Animal
Yclep't an Horse, when in his stall,
The Botts, that terrible disease,
20   Doth on his tender bowels seize,
What groans he fetches and what pranks
He rowling plays upon the planks?

So Dido crost in her amours,
Tumbled away her sleeping hours.
Now on her back, and in such fashion,
As if she lay for consolation;
Now on her belly, now her side,
All postures, and all ways she try'd;
But all in vain, nothing would do,
30  Her heart was so opprest with wo,
And love within her did so rumble
She could do nought but toss and tumble:
At last, in midst of agitation,
She thus brake out into a passion;
'Which way poor Dido should thou turn thee,
While cruel love doth thus heart-burn thee?
Thou hast of hope not one poor spark left,
Th'ast brought thy Hogs to a fair Market.
Not one poor dram of Consolation,
40  O woman vile in desperation!
What shall I do in this condition
To keep me from the World's derision?
Shall I invite to be my spouse,
Someone I have forbid my house?
Some saucie, proud, New-Indian Jack,
And humbly beg of him to take
Aeneas' leavings, or like Trull here,
Run away basely with this Sculler.
Or shall I raise the Town in swarms
50  And bring him back by force of Arms!
Alas, I fear it is no boot!
Foul means will never bring him to't,
No, no, I'll die! this Halter yet,
When all trades fail, shall do the Feat.
Ah, sister, sister! hadst not thou
Play'd Mistress Quicklie's office so,
And sooth'd me up till I grew jolly,
I never had committed folly:

No, had I made the least resistance,
60    And kept the saucie Knave at distance,
I might have used him as I list,
And ne'r been brought to had-I-wist.'
    Thus lay the wretched Queen debating,
Nan, Fortune and her Lover rating.
Whilst he Drum-ful with his potation,
Ne'r dreaming on the doleful passion
He had most vilely left his drab in,
Lay drunk and snoring in his cabin.
But Mercury, though he slept profoundly,
70    Made bold to beat up's quarters roundly,
And thus 'gan rattle him: 'Thou lousie,
Mangie, careless, drunken, drowsie
Coxcomb! how oft must I be sent
Hither from Jove to complement
Your worship to a reverent care
Of the young Bastard here, your heir?
Whilst fast thou ly'st tipled, or tipling;
Nor car'st what danger the poor stripling
Lies open to. Y'had best snore on,
80    Some body will be here anon:
Take t'other nap, Do, till the Queen come,
She'll reckon with you for your income,
She'll rowse ye, 'faith! And (Goodman Letcher)
'Tis ten to one, with a good stretcher
About your ears; therefore my loving
Acquaintance, you were best be moving.
Upon my word, th' advice is wholsome,
Stay not until that angry soul come:
For if thou dost, mark what I say,
90    And be'st not gone before't be day,
If Carthage be n't about your ears

---

**62** *had-I-wist*: vain regret (literally 'if only I'd known')

As soon as ever day appears,
And do not thrash you back and side,
Far worse than Agamemnon did,
Those of your woman-stealing rabble –
Give me but sixpence, if thou'rt able,
And (here's my hand, I do not sport)
I'll give thee twenty shillings for't.'
    Thus having said, away he flies,
100  Ere Toss-pot could unglue his eyes,
Which were so cemented in that case,
The Page was got as far as Atlas
Back on his way, ere he could free 'um
From gowl and matter fit to see him:
And having streak'd and yawn'd awhile,
Snorted and kept that usual coil
That Drunkards use in suchlike cases,
And made some dozen Devil's faces,
At last he got his eyes unglued
110  Into a pretty magnitude.
He star'd about to spy the Vision
Had giv'n that courteous admonition:
But 'twas so dark, as well it might,
Being 'twixt twelve and one at night,
That had the nimble Courier
In kindness staid his leisure there,
Though clad in Falstaff's Kendal-Green,
He could not possibly be seen.
    Aeneas troubled herewithal,
120  Seeing he could not see at all,
Starts from the tilt where he had lain
And calls upon his Mates amain:
'Rise sirs, (quoth he) and look about ye,

---

**102** *Atlas*: the upholder of the universe. Mercury passes him on his flight to earth in *Aeneid* IV, 246–51.

I've had from Jove another how d'ye;
His man was here, and calls to go still,
His sweaty pumps are in my nose still.
He swears and offers to lay odds on't,
And if he say't, I'll lay my [cods] on't,
That if we do not leave the Dock
130 And get us hence by four o'clock,
We shall be murder'd if we were
Ten times as many as we are.
Therefore I think it not amiss for's
To launch, for there are rods in piss for's.
Let us but ply our oars like tall men,
Till we but got clear out of all ken,
Then if they have a mind to lace us,
Let Carthage, if they can, come trace us.
And thou, O Jove, top of my kin!
140 Who hitherto so kind hath been,
If now thou stick and do not fail's,
Let Dido whistle in our tails.'     (1670)

# JOHN CARYLL (1625–1711)

## Eclogue I [Ecl. I]

Printed from *Miscellany Poems: The First Part* (1684), which contains translations of all the Eclogues by various hands. Dryden contributed IV and IX, but he also made considerable use of Caryll's version in his complete Virgil: Caryll's lines 32, 35, 36, 69, 94–7 and 105–8 all reappear verbatim in Dryden, and there are other similarities.

For the background to this poem, see the note to Webbe's version.

MELIBEUS
> In peaceful Shades, which aged Oaks diffuse,
> You, Tityrus, enjoy your rural Muse;
> We leave our home and (once) our pleasant fields;
> The native swain to rude Intruders yields,
> While you in Songs your happy Love proclaim,
> And every Grove learn Amarillis' name.

TITYRUS
> A god (to me he always shall be so)
> O Melibeus! did this Grace bestow!
> The choicest Lamb which in my Flock does feed
10 > Shall each new Moon upon his Altar bleed:
> He every Blessing on his Creatures brings;
> By him the Herd does graze, by him the Herdsman sings.

MELIBEUS
> I envy not, but I admire your Fate,
> Which thus exempts you from our wretched State.
> Look on my Goats that browze, my Kids that play:
> Driven hence myself, these I must drive away.
> And this poor Mother of a new-fall'n Pair
> (The Herd's chief Hope, alas, but my Despair!)

Has left 'em in yond Brakes, beside the way,
20   Expos'd to every Beast and Bird of prey.
Had not some angry Planet struck me blind,
This dire Calamity I had divin'd:
'Twas oft foretold me by Heav'ns loudest voice,
Rending our tallest Oaks with dismal Noise:
Ravens spoke too, though in a lower tone,
And long from hollow Tree were heard to groan.
But say: what God has Tityrus reliev'd?

TITYRUS

The place call'd Rome, I foolishly believ'd,
Was like our Mantua, where on market-days
30   We drive our well-fed Lambs (the Shepherds praise;)
So Whelps (I knew), so Kids, their Dams express,
And so the great I measur'd by the less.
But other Towns when you to her compare,
They creeping Shrubs to the tall Cypress are.

MELIBEUS

What great occasion call'd you hence to Rome?

TITYRUS

Freedom, which came at last, though slow to come:
She came not till cold Winter did begin,
And age some Snow had sprinkled on my Chin:
Not then, till Galatea I forsook
40   For Amarillis, daign'd on me to look.
No hope for Liberty, I must confess,
No hope, nor care of Wealth, did me possess
Whilst I with Galatea did remain.
For though my Flock her Altars did maintain,
Though often I had made my cheese-press groan,
Largely to furnish our ungrateful Town,
Yet still with empty Hands I trotted home.

---

**29** *Mantua*: Virgil's home town (not named in the Latin text)

MELIBEUS

I wonder'd, Galatea! whence should come
Thy sad complaints to heav'n, and why so long
50   Ungathered on their Trees thy Apples hung?
Absent was Tityrus! Thee every Dale,
Mountain and Spring, thee every Tree did call!

TITYRUS

What should I do? I could not here be free,
And only in that place could hope to see
A God propitious to my Liberty.
There I the Heavenly Youth did first behold,
Whose monthly Feast while solemnly I hold,
My loaded Altars never shall be cold.
He heard my Prayers: 'Go home (he cry'd) and feed
60   In peace your Herd, let forth your Bulls for breed.'

MELIBEUS

Happy old Man! Thy farm untoucht remains,
And large enough, though it may ask thy pains
To clear the Stones and Rushes cure by Drains.
Thy teeming Ewes will no strange Pastures try,
Nor murrain fear from tainted Company.
Thrice happy Swain! guarded from Sirian beams,
By sacred Springs and long-acquainted Streams.
Look on that bordering Fence, whose Osier trees
Are fraught with Flowers, whose Flowers are fraught with
Bees:
70   How with their drowsie tone, the whistling Air
(Your sleep to tempt) a consort does prepare.
At further distance, but with stronger Lungs
The Wood-man joyns with these his rustick Songs:
Stock-Doves and murmuring turtles tune their Throat,
Those in a hoarser, these a softer Note.

---

**71** *consort*: a concert of music

TITYRUS

Therefore the Land and Sea shall Dwellers change,
Fish on dry Ground, Stags shall on Water range,
The Parthians shall commute their bounds with Francs,
Those shall on Soan, these drink on Tygris' Banks,
80   Ere I his God-like Image from my Heart
Suffer with black Ingratitude to part.

MELIBEUS

But we must roam to parts remote, unknown,
Under the Torrid and the Frigid Zone:
These frozen Scythia, and parcht Affrick those;
Cretan Oaxis others must inclose:
Some 'mongst the utmost Britains are confin'd
Doom'd to an Isle from all the World disjoyn'd.
Ah! must I never more my Country see,
But in strange Lands an endless Exile be?
90   Is my eternal Banishment decreed
From my poor Cottage, rear'd with turf and reed?
Must impious Soldiers all these grounds possess,
My Fields of standing corn, my fertile Leyes?
Did I for these Barbarians plow and sow?
What dire effects from civil Discord flow!
Graft Pears (O Melibeus!), plant the Vine!
The Fruit shall others' be, the Labour thine.
Farewell my Goats! a happy Herd, when mine!
No more shall I, in the refreshing Shade
100   Of verdant Grottoes, by kind Nature made,
Behold you climbing on the Mountain top,
The flow'ry Thyme and fragrant Shrubs to crop.
I part with ev'ry Joy, parting from you;
Then farewell all the World! Verses and Pipe, adieu!

---

76–81 The rhetorical figure called 'adunaton' (or impossibility).
79 *Soan*: Saône
85 *Oaxis*: perhaps the river Oxus
93 *Leyes*: meadows

TITYRUS
At least this Night with me forget your Care,
Chestnuts and well-prest Cheese shall be your fare;
For now the Mountain a long Shade extends,
And curling Smoke from village tops ascends.          (1684)


# THOMAS CREECH (1659–1700)

## Eclogue II [Ecl. II]

Printed from *Miscellany Poems: The First Part* (1684). An elegiac
monologue in which the shepherd Corydon expresses his unrequited
love for Alexis. The famous 'pastoral invitation' at 34ff. was often
imitated, for example by Marlowe in 'The Passionate Sheepheard to
His Love'.

    Young Corydon (hard Fate) an humble swain
    Alexis loved, the joy of all the plain,
    He loved, but could not hope for love again.
    Yet every day through groves he walked alone,
    And vainly told the hills and woods his moan.
    'Cruel Alexis! can't my verses move!
    Hast thou not pity? must I die for love?
       Just now the flocks pursue the shades and cool,
    And every lizard creeps into his hole.
10  Brown Thestylis the weary reapers seeks,
    And brings their meat, their onions and their leeks:
    And whilst I trace thy steps in every tree
    And every bush, poor insects sigh with me.
    And had it not been better to have borne
    The peevish Amaryllis' frowns and scorn,
    Or else Menalcas', than this deep despair?
    Though he was black, and thou art lovely fair!
    Ah charming beauty! 'tis a fading grace,

Trust not too much, sweet youth, to that fair face:
20  Things are not always used that please the sight,
    We gather black berries when we scorn the white.
    Thou dost despise me, thou dost scorn my flame,
    Yet dost not know me, nor how rich I am:
    A thousand tender lambs, a thousand kine,
    A thousand goats I feed, and all are mine:
    My dairy's full, and my large herd affords,
    Summer and winter, cream and milk and curds.
    I pipe as well as when through Theban plains
    Amphion fed his flocks, or charmed the swains;
30  Nor is my face so mean: I lately stood
    And viewed my figure in the quiet flood,
    And think myself, though it were judged by you,
    As fair as Daphnis, if that glass be true.
    Oh that with me the humble plains would please,
    The quiet fields and lowly cottages!
    Oh that with me you'd live and hunt the hare,
    Or drive the kids, or spread the following snare!
    Then you and I would sing like Pan in shady groves,
    Pan taught us pipes and Pan our art approves:
40  Pan both the sheep and harmless shepherd loves.
    Nor must you think the pipe too mean for you,
    To learn to pipe, what won't Amyntas do:
    I have a pipe, well-seasoned, brown and try'd,
    Which good Dametas left me when he died.
    He said, here, take it, for a legacy,
    Thou art my second, it belongs to thee,
    He said, and dull Amyntas envied me.
    Besides, I found two wanton kids at play
    In yonder vale, and those I brought away,
50  Young sportive creatures, and of spotted hue,
    Which suckle twice a day, I keep for you.
    These Thestylis hath begged, and begged in vain,

---

**28-9** The magical power of Amphion's music, like Orpheus', was proverbial.

But now they're hers, since you my gifts disdain.
　Come, lovely boy, the nymphs their baskets fill,
With poppy, violet and daffodil,
The rose, and thousand other fragrant flowers,
To please thy senses in thy softest hours.
These Nais gathers to delight my boy;
Come dear Alexis, be no longer coy.
60　I'll seek for chesnuts too in every grove,
Such as my Amaryllis used to love.
The glossy plums and juicy pears I'll bring,
Delightful all, and many a pretty thing.
The laurel and the neighbouring myrtle tree,
Confus'dly planted 'cause they both agree,
And prove more sweet, shall send their boughs to thee.
　Ah Corydon! thou art a foolish swain
And coy Alexis doth thy gifts disdain,
Or if gifts could prevail, if gifts could woo,
70　Iolas can present him more than you.
What doth the madman mean? He idly brings
Storms on his flowers and boars into his springs.
Ah, whom dost thou avoid? whom fly? the gods
And charming Paris too, have lived in woods.
Let Pallas, she whose art first raised a town,
Live there, let us delight in woods alone.
The boar, the wolf, the wolf the kid pursues,
The kid her thyme, as fast as t'others do's,
Alexis Corydon, and him alone.
80　Each hath his game, and each pursues his own.
Look how the wearied ox brings home the plow,
The sun declines, and shades are doubled now:

---

58 *Nais*: a nymph
74 Paris was brought up as a shepherd boy on Mt Ida.
75 Pallas Athene, one of whose Greek titles was 'keeper of the city'. In the famous beauty contest between the three goddesses, Paris rejected her in favour of Aphrodite.

And yet my passion nor my cares remove,
Love burns me still, what flame so fierce as love!
Ah, Corydon, what fury's this of thine!
On yonder elm there hangs thy half-pruned vine:
Come, rather mind thy useful work, prepare
Thy harvest baskets and make those thy care.
Come, mind thy plow, and thou shalt quickly find
90   Another, if Alexis prove unkind.'                    (1684)


# RICHARD DUKE (c. 1659–1711)

[Ecl. V. 56–90] *The apotheosis of Daphnis*

Printed from *Miscellany Poems: The First Part* (1684). Cf. the same
passage in Fleming's version.

MENALCAS
Daphnis now wondering at the glorious show,
Through heaven's bright pavement does triumphant go,
And sees the moving clouds, and the fixt stars below.
Therefore new joys make glad the woods, the plains,
Pan and the Dryads, and the cheerful swains.
The wolf no ambush for the flock does lay,
No cheating nets the harmless deer betray,
Daphnis a general peace commands, and nature does obey.
Hark! the glad mountains raise to heaven their voice!
10   Hark! the hard rocks in mystic tunes rejoice!
Hark! through the thickets wondrous songs resound,
A god! a god! Menalcas, he is crown'd!
O be propitious! O be good to thine!
See! here four hallowed altars we design,
To Daphnis two, to Phoebus two we raise,
To pay the yearly tribute of our praise.

Sacred to thee they each returning year
Two bowls of milk and two of oil shall bear:
Feasts I'll ordain, and to thy deathless praise
20  Thy votaries exalted thoughts to raise,
Rich Chian wines shall in full goblets flow,
And give a taste of nectar here below.
Dametas shall with Lictian Argon join,
To celebrate with songs the rites divine.
Alphesiboeus with a reeling gait
Shall the wild satyrs dancing imitate.
When to the nymphs we vows and offerings pay,
When we with solemn rites our fields survey,
These honours ever shall be thine; the boar
30  Shall in the fields and hills delight no more,
No more in streams the fish, in flowers the bee,
E'er, Daphnis, we forget our songs to thee.
Offerings to thee the shepherds every year
Shall, as to Bacchus and to Ceres, bear.
To thee as to those gods shall vows be made,
And vengeance wait on those, by whom they are not paid.

MOPSUS

What present worth thy verse can Mopsus find?
Not the soft whispers of the southern wind
So much delight my ear, or charm my mind,
40  Not sounding shores beat by the murmuring tide,
Nor rivers that through stony valleys glide.

MENALCAS

First you this pipe shall take: and 'tis the same
That played poor Corydon's unhappy flame:
The same that taught me Meliboeus' sheep.

---

**43–4** Oblique references to the Second (Corydon) and Third (Meliboeus) Eclogues.

MOPSUS

You then shall for my sake this sheephook keep,
Adorned with brass, which I have oft denied
To young Antigenes in his beauty's pride.
And who could think he then in vain could sue?
Yet him I would deny, and freely give it you.          (1684)


# SIR WILLIAM TEMPLE (1628–99)

## Eclogue X [Ecl. X]

'Eclogue X. Translated, or rather imitated, in the year 1666', and
printed, unattributed, in *Miscellany Poems: The First Part* (1684).

Perhaps the most influential of Virgil's pastorals (e.g., on Milton's
'Lycidas'). Gallus was a soldier, statesman and love poet (his elegies do
not survive). His dying lament may be compared with the less
serious 'complaint' of Corydon in Eclogue II. Macaulay thought
these two eclogues the best of all Virgil's compositions.

Temple has omitted the eight-line 'coda' in which Virgil 'signs
off' as a pastoral poet: for a translation, see the version by Sir C.
Bowen.

One labour more, O Arethusa, yield,
Before I leave the shepherds and the field.
Some verses to my Gallus ere we part,
Such as may one day break Lycoris' heart,
As she did his; who can refuse a song,
To one that loved so well and died so young!
So mayst thou thy beloved Alpheus please,

---

**1** *Arethusa*: a sea-nymph who, while bathing in the Arcadian river Alpheus,
was pursued by the river-god and turned into a fountain near Syracuse in
Sicily.
**6** Temple has added this line; Virgil says merely 'Gallo' (to Gallus).

When thou creep'st under the Sicanian seas.
Begin, and sing Gallus' unhappy fires,
10  Whilst yonder goat to yonder branch aspires,
Out of his reach. We sing not to the deaf;
An answer comes from every trembling leaf.
    What woods, what forests, had enticed your stay?
Ye Naiades, why came ye not away?
When Gallus died by an unworthy flame,
Parnassus knew, and lov'd too well his name
To stop your course; nor could your hasty flight
Be stayed by Pindus, which was his delight.
Him the fresh laurels, him the lowly heath
20  Bewailed with dewy tears; his parting breath
Made lofty Maenalus hang his piny head;
Lycaean marbles wept when he was dead.
Under a lonely tree he lay and pined,
His flock about him feeding on the wind,
As he on love; such kind and gentle sheep,
Even fair Adonis would be proud to keep.
There came the shepherds, there the weary hinds.
Thither Menalcas parcht with frosts and winds.
All ask him, whence, for whom, this fatal love?
30  Apollo came, his arts and herbs to prove.
Why Gallus, why so fond? he says; thy flame,
Thy care, Lycoris, is another's game;
For him she sighs and raves, him she pursues
Through the mid-day heats and morning dews,
Over the snowy cliffs and frozen streams,
Through noisy camps. Up, Gallus, leave thy dreams,
She has left thee. Still lay the drooping swain,
Hanging his mournful head, Phoebus in vain

---

**13–21** Based on Theocritus, *Idyll* I, 66–9, and imitated by Milton, 'Lycidas', 50–53.
**27ff.** The procession of gods and shepherds is also from Theocritus, *Idyll* I, 80–82.

Offers his herbs, employs his counsel here;
40    'Tis all refused, or answered with a tear.
What shakes the branches? what makes all the trees
Begin to bow their heads, the goats their knees?
Oh! 'tis Sylvanus, with his mossy beard
And leafy crown, attended by a herd
Of wood-born satyrs; see! he shakes his spear,
A green young oak, the tallest of the year.
Pan, the Arcadian god, forsook the plains,
Moved with the story of his Gallus' pains.
We saw him come with oaten-pipes in hand,
50    Painted with berries-juice; we saw him stand
And gaze upon his shepherd's bathing eyes;
And what! no end, no end of grief, he cries!
Love little minds all thy consuming care,
Or restless thoughts, they are his daily fare.
Nor cruel love with tears, nor grass with showers,
Nor goats with tender sprouts, nor bees with flowers
Are ever satisfied. Thus spoke the god,
And touched the shepherd with his hazel-rod:
He, sorrow-slain, seemed to revive, and said,
60    'But yet Arcadians, is my grief allayed,
To think that in these woods, and hills, and plains,
When I am silent in the grave, your swains
Shall sing my loves, Arcadian swains inspired
By Phoebus; oh! how gently shall these tired
And fainting limbs repose in endless sleep.
While your sweet notes my love immortal keep!
Would it had pleased the gods, I had been born
Just one of you, and taught to wind a horn,
Or wield a hook, or prune a branching vine,
70    And known no other love but, Phyllis, thine;
Or thine, Amyntas; what though both are brown,
So are the nuts and berries on the down;
Amongst the vines, the willows and the springs,
Phyllis makes garlands and Amyntas sings.

No cruel absence calls my love away,
Farther than bleating sheep can go astray;
Here, my Lycoris, here are shady groves,
Here fountains cool, and meadows soft, our loves
And lives may here together wear, and end:
80   O the true joys of such a fate and friend!
 I now am hurried by severe commands
Into remotest parts, among the bands
Of armed troops; there by my foes pursued,
Here by my friends; but still by Love subdued.
Thou far from home, and me, art wandering o'er
The Alpine snows, the farthest western shore,
The frozen Rhine. When are we like to meet?
Ah, gently, gently, lest thy tender feet
Be cut with ice. Cover thy lovely arms,
90   The northern cold relents not at their charms.
Away I'll go into some shady bowers
And sing the songs I made in happier hours,
And charm my woes. How can I better chuse,
Than amongst wildest woods myself to lose,
And carve our loves upon the tender trees;
There they will thrive. See how my loves agree
With my young plants. Look how they grow together,
In spite of absence and in spite of weather.
Meanwhile I'll climb that rock, and ramble o'er
100  Yon woody hill; I'll chase the grizly boar,
I'll find Diana's and her nymphs' resort,
No frosts, no storms, shall lack my eager sport.
Methinks I'm wandering all about the rocks
And hollow-sounding woods. Look how my locks
Are torn with boughs and thorns; my shafts are gone,
My legs are tired, and all my sport is done.
Alas! this is no cure for my disease;
Nor can our toils that angry god appease.
 Now neither nymphs nor songs can please me more,
110  Nor hollow woods, nor yet the chafed boar;

No sport, no labour, can divert my grief:
Without Lycoris there is no relief.
Though I should drink up Heber's icy streams,
Or Scythian snows, yet still her fiery beams
Would scorch me up. Whatever we can prove,
Love conquers all, and we must yield to love.'                    (1684)


# JOHN DRYDEN (1631–1700)

## The Entire Episode of Nisus and Euryalus, Translated from the 5th and 9th Books of Virgils Aeneids – the whole of the section from Book IX [Aen. IX. 174–449] *The story of Nisus and Euryalus*

Printed from *Sylvae: Poetical Miscellanies, the Second Part* (1685). The text differs in many details from that of the 1697 text, but is substantially, and from *Aeneid* IX, 233 to the end completely, identical with that of Richard Maitland, Earl of Lauderdale, published posthumously *c.* 1708. Dryden revised this version (and in particular the last 150 lines) for his 1697 text, sometimes for the better. (See Introduction and Appendix C.)

This is one of the noblest and most moving episodes in the *Aeneid*: though based on the exploits of Odysseus and Diomede in *Iliad* X, the treatment of the friendship between the two young heroes is wholly Virgilian.


The Trojan camp the common danger shared;
By turns they watched the walls, and kept the nightly guard.
To warlike Nisus fell the gate by lot
(Whom Hyrtacus on huntress Ida got
And sent to sea Aeneas to attend);
Well could he dart the spear, and shafts unerring send.
Beside him stood Euryalus his ever-faithful friend.
No youth in all the Trojan host was seen

More beautiful in arms, or of a nobler mien.
10 Scarce was the down upon his chin begun;
One was their friendship, their desire was one.
With minds united in the field they warr'd,
And now were both by choice upon the guard.
Then Nisus thus:
'Or do the gods this warlike warmth inspire,
Or makes each man a god of his desire?
A noble ardour boils within my breast,
Eager of action, enemy of rest,
That urges me to fight, or undertake
20 Some deed that may my fame immortal make.
Thou seest the foe secure: how faintly shine
Their scattered fires; the most in sleep supine
Dissolved in ease and drunk with victory.
The few awake the fuming flaggon ply;
All hushed around. Now hear what I revolve
Within my mind, and what my labouring thoughts resolve.
Our absent Lord both camp and council mourn;
By message both would hasten his return.
The gifts proposed if they confer on thee
30 (For fame is recompense enough to me)
Methinks beneath yon hill I have espied,
A way that safely will my passage guide.'
Euryalus stood listening while he spoke,
With love of praise and noble envy struck,
Then to his ardent friend exposed his mind:
'All this alone, and leaving me behind!
Am I unworthy, Nisus, to be joyned?
Think'st thou my share of honour I will yield,
Or send thee unassisted to the field?
40 Not so my father taught my childhood arms,

---

**27** Aeneas is absent on a mission to Evander, king of Pallanteum (see Book VIII).

Born in a siege and bred amongst alarms.
Nor is my youth unworthy of my friend
Or of the heaven-born hero I attend.
The thing called Life with ease I can disdain
And think it oversold to purchase fame.'
To whom his friend:
'I could think, alas, thy tender years
Would minister new matter to my fears,
Nor is it just thou shouldst thy wish obtain;
50   So Jove in triumph bring me back again
To those dear eyes, or if a god there be
To pious friend, propitious more than he.
But if some one, as many sure there are,
Of adverse accidents in doubtful war,
If one should reach my head, there let it fall,
And spare thy life: I would not perish all.
Thy youth is worthy of a longer date.
Do thou remain to mourn thy lover's fate,
To bear my mangled body from the foe
60   Or buy it back, and funeral rites bestow.
Or if hard fortune shall my corpse deny
Those dues, with empty marble to supply.
O let me not the widow's tears renew,
Let not a mother's curse my name pursue:
Thy pious mother, who in love to thee
Left the fair coast of fruitful Sicily,
Her age committing to the seas and wind
When every pious matron stayed behind.'
To this Euryalus: 'Thou plead'st in vain,
70   And but delay'st the cause thou canst not gain.
No more: 'tis loss of time.' With that he wakes
The nodding watch; each to his office takes.
      The guard relieved, in company they went
To find the council at the royal tent.
Now every living thing lay void of care,
And sleep, the common gift of nature share.

Meantime, the Trojan peers in council sate
And called their chief commanders to debate
The weighty business of th' endangered state.
80   What next was to be done, who to be sent
T' inform Aeneas of the foe's intent.
In midst of all the quiet camp they held
Nocturnal council; each sustains a shield
Which his o'erlaboured arm can hardly rear,
And leans upon a long projected spear.
Now Nisus and his friend approach the guard,
And beg admittance, eager to be heard:
The affair important, not to be deferred.
Ascanius bids them be conducted in.
90   Then thus, commanded, Nisus does begin:
'Ye Trojan fathers, lend attentive ears,
Nor judge our undertaking by our years.
The foes securely drenched in sleep and wine
Their watch neglect; their fires but thinly shine.
And where the smoke in thickening vapours flies,
Covering the plain and clouding all the skies,
Betwixt the spaces we have marked a way,
Close by the gate and coasting by the sea;
This passage undisturbed and unespy'd
100   Our steps will safely to Aeneas guide:
Expect each hour to see him back again,
Loaded with spoils of foes in battle slain.
Snatch we the lucky minute while we may;
Nor can we be mistaken in the way:
For hunting in the vale we oft have seen
The rising torrents with the streams between,
And know its winding course with every ford.'
He paused; and old Aletes took the word:
'Our country gods in whom our trust we place
110   Will yet from ruin save the Trojan race
While we behold such springing worth appear
In youths so brave and breasts devoid of fear.'

(With this he took the hand of either boy,
Embraced them closely both and wept for joy.)
'Ye brave young men, what equal gifts can we,
What recompense for such desert decree!
The greatest, sure, and best you can receive
The gods, your virtue and your fame will give:
The rest our grateful general will bestow
120 And young Ascanius, till his manhood, owe.'
'And I, whose welfare in my father lies
(Ascanius adds) by all the deities,
By our great country and our household gods,
By hoary Vesta's rites and dark abodes,
Adjure you both (on you my fortune stands:
That and my faith I plight into your hands);
Make me but happy in his safe return:
(For I no other loss but his can mourn).
Nisus, your gift shall two large goblets be,
130 Of silver wrought with curious imagery,
And high embossed, which, when old Priam reigned,
My conquering sire at sacked Arisba gained;
And two more tripods cast in antique mould,
With two great talents of the finest gold;
Besides, a bowl which Tyrian art did grave,
The present which Sidonian Dido gave.
But if in conquered Italy we reign,
When spoils by lot the victor shall obtain –
Thou saw'st the courser by proud Turnus pressed –
140 That, and his golden arms and sanguine crest,
And shield, from lot exempted, thou shalt share.
With these, twelve captive damsels young and fair:
Male slaves as many, well appointed all
With vests and arms, shall to thy portion fall.
And last, a fruitful field to thee shall rest,

---

**132** Nothing is known of this exploit of Aeneas, though the town (in the Troad) is mentioned once in the *Iliad* (II, 836).

The large demesnes the Latian king possest.
But thou, whose years are more to mine ally'd,
No fate my vow'd affection shall divide
From thee, O wondrous youth! Be ever mine:
150  Take full possession, all my soul is thine,
My life's companion and my bosom friend,
One faith, one fame, one fate shall both attend.
My peace shall be committed to thy care,
And to thy conduct my concerns in war.'
     Then thus the bold Euryalus reply'd,
'Whatever fortune, good or bad, betyde,
The same shall be my age, as now my youth;
No time shall find me wanting to my truth.
This only from your bounty let me gain
160  (And this not granted, all rewards are vain):
Of Priam's royal race my mother came,
And sure the best that ever bore the name:
Whom neither Troy, nor Sicily could hold
From me departing, but, o'erspent and old,
My fate she follow'd; ignorant of this
Whatever danger, neither parting kiss
Nor pious blessing taken, her I leave:
And, in this only act of all my life, deceive.
By this your hand and conscious night I swear,
170  My youth so sad a farewell could not bear.
Be you her patron; fill my vacant place;
(Permit me to presume so great a grace);
Support Her age forsaken and distreast;
That hope alone will fortify my breast
Against the worst of fortunes and of fears.'
He said; th'assistants shed presaging tears.
But above all Ascanius moved to see
That image of his filial piety,
Then thus reply'd:
180  'So great beginnings in so green an age
Exact that faith, which firmly I engage;

Thy mother all the privilege shall claim
Creusa had; and only want the name.
Whate'er event thy enterprise shall have,
'Tis merit to have borne a son so brave.
By this my head a sacred oath I swear
(My father used it): what, returning here,
Crown'd with success, I for thyself prepare,
Thy parent and thy family shall share.'

190   He said, and weeping while he spoke the word,
From his broad belt he drew a shining sword,
Magnificent with gold, Lycaon made,
And in an ivory scabbard sheath'd the blade.
This was his gift; while Mnestheus did provide
For Nisus arms, a grisly lion's hide,
And true Aletes changed with him his helm of temper tried.
     Thus arm'd they went: the noble Trojans wait
Their going forth, and follow to the gate.
With prayers and vows above the rest appears

200   Ascanius, manly far above his years,
And messages committed to their care
Which all in winds were lost and empty air.
The trenches first they passed, then took their way
Where their proud foes in pitch'd pavilions lay,
To many fatal, ere themselves were slain.
The careless host dispersed upon the plain
They found, who drunk with wine supinely snore;
Unharnessed chariots stand upon the shore.
Midst wheels and reins and arms, the goblet by,

210   A medley of debauch and war, they lie.
Observing, Nisus show'd his friend the sight,
Then thus: 'Behold a conquest without fight.
Occasion calls the sword to be prepared:
Our way lies there. Stand thou upon the guard,
And look behind, while I securely go
To cut an ample passage through the foe.'
Softly he spoke, then stalking took his way,

With his drawn sword, where haughty Rhamnus lay,
His head rais'd high, on tapestry beneath,
220   And heaving from his breast he puffed his breath.
A king and prophet by king Turnus loved;
But fate by prescience cannot be remov'd.
Three sleeping slaves he soon subdues; then spies
Where Remus with his proud retinue lies.
His armour-bearer first, and next he kills
His charioteer, entrench'd betwixt the wheels,
And his lov'd horses; last invades their Lord;
Full on his neck he aims the fatal sword:
The gasping head flies off; a purple flood
230   Flows from the trunk, that wallows in the blood,
Which by the spurning heels dispers'd around
The bed besprinkles and bedews the ground.
    Then Lamyrus with Lamus and the young
Sarranus who with gaming did prolong
The night-oppressed with wine and slumber lay
The beauteous youth, and dream'd of lucky play;
More lucky, had it been protracted to the day.
The famished lion thus with hunger bold
O'erleaps the fences of the nightly fold,
240   The peaceful flocks devours, and tears and draws.
Wrapped up in silent fear they lie, and pant beneath his paws.
Nor with less rage Euryalus employs
The vengeful sword, nor fewer foes destroys;
But on th'ignoble crowd his fury flew,
Which Fadus, Hobesus and Rhoetus slew.
With Abaris in sleep the rest did fall;
But Rhoetus waking and observing all,
Behind a mighty jar he slunk for fear;
The sharp-edg'd iron found and reached him there:

---

**247** *Rhoetus*: perhaps an error in the transmission of Virgil's text. We have just been told that Rhoetus was slain in his sleep.

250   Full as he rose he plung'd it in his side;
      The cruel sword returned in crimson dy'd.
      The wound, a blended stream of wine and blood,
      Pours out; the purple soul comes floating in the flood.
          Now where Messapus quartered they arrive;
      The fires were fainting there, and just alive.
      The warlike horses ty'd in order fed;
      Nisus the discipline observed, and said:
      'Our eagerness of blood may both betray.
      Behold the doubtful glimmering of the day,
260   Foe to these nightly thefts. No more, my friend
      Here let our glutted execution end.
      A lane through slaughter'd bodies we have made?'
      The bold Euryalus, though loath, obey'd.
      Rich arms and arras which they scattered find,
      And plate, a precious load, they leave behind.
      Yet, fond of gaudy spoils, the boy would stay
      To make the proud caparisons his prey;
      Which decked a neighbouring steed.
      Nor did his eyes less longingly behold
270   The girdle studded o'er with nails of gold
      Which Rhamnes wore: this present long ago
      On Remulus did Caedicus bestow
      And absent joyn'd in hospitable tyes.
      He dying to his heir bequeath'd the prize.
      Till by the conquering Rutuli oppressed,
      He fell, and they the glorious gift possest.
      These gaudy spoils Euryalus now bears
      And vainly on his brawny shoulders wears.
      Messapus' helm he found amongst the dead,
280   Garnish'd with plumes and fitted to his head.
      They leave the camp, and take the safest road.
          Meantime a squadron of their foes abroad,
      Three hundred horse with bucklers arm'd, they spy'd,
      Whom Volscens by the king's command did guide.
      To Turnus these were from the city sent,

And to perform their message sought his tent.
Approaching near their utmost lines they draw,
When bending towards the left, their captain saw
The faithful pair; for through the doubtful shade
290    His glittering helm Euryalus betray'd,
On which the moon with full reflection play'd.
''Tis not for nought (cry'd Volscens from the crowd)
These men go there;' then rais'd his voice aloud.
'Stand, stand! why thus in arms? and whither bent?
From whence? to whom? and on what errand sent?'
Silent they make away, and haste their flight
To neighbouring woods, and trust themselves to night.
The speedy horsemen spur their steeds to get
'Twixt them and home, and every path beset,
300    And all the windings of the well-known wood.
Black was the brake, and thick with oak it stood,
With fern all horrid and perplexing thorn,
Where tracks of bears had scarce a passage worn.
The darkness of the shades, his heavy prey,
And fear, misled the younger from his way.
But Nisus hit the turns with happier haste
Who now, unknowing, had the danger past
And Alban lakes (from Alba's name so called)
Where king Latinus then his oxen stall'd.
310    Till turning at the length he stood his ground,
And vainly cast his longing eyes around
For his lost friend.
'Ah wretch', he cried, 'where have I left behind,
Where shall I hope th' unhappy youth to find
Or what way take?' Again he ventures back
And treads the mazes of his former track
Through the wild wood: at last he hears the noise
Of trampling horses and the rider's voice.
The sound approached, and suddenly he view'd
320    His foes enclosing and his friend pursued,
Forelaid and taken, while he strove in vain

The covert of the neighbouring wood to gain.
What should he next attempt, what arms employ
With fruitless force to free the captive boy?
Or tempt unequal numbers with the sword
And die by him whom living he adored?
Resolved on death his dreadful spear he shook,
And casting to the moon a mournful look
'Fair Queen', said he, 'who dost in woods delight,
330   Grace of the stars and goddess of the night,
Be present, and direct my dart aright.
If e'er my pious father for my sake
Did on thy altars grateful offerings make,
Or I increased them with successful toils,
And hung thy sacred roof with savage spoils,
Through the brown shadows guide my flying spear
To reach this troop.' Then poising from his ear
The quivering weapon with full force he threw:
Through the divided shades the deadly javelin flew.
340   On Sulmo's back it splits; the double dart
Drove deeper onward, and transfixed his heart.
He staggers round, his eyeballs roll in death,
And with short sobs he gasps away his breath.
All stand amazed; a second javelin flies
From his stretch'd arm, and hisses through the skies.
The lance through Tagus' temples forc'd its way
And in his brain-pan warmly buried lay.
   Fierce Volscens foams with rage and, gazing round,
Descry'd no author of the fatal wound,
350   Nowhere to fix revenge. 'But thou', he cries,
'Shalt pay for both'; and at the prisoner flies
With his drawn sword. Then, struck with deep despair,
That fatal fight the lover could not bear,
But from his covert rush'd in open view,
And sent his voice before him as he flew;
'Me, me, employ your sword, on me alone:
The crime confess'd, the fact was all my own.

He neither could nor durst, the guiltless youth;
Ye moon and stars bear witness to the truth;
360    His only fault, if that be to offend,
Was too much loving his unhappy friend.'
Too late, alas, he speaks;
The sword, which unrelenting fury guides,
Driven with full force had pierced his tender sides.
Down fell the beauteous youth, the gaping wound
Gush'd out a crimson stream and stain'd the ground.
His nodding neck reclines on his white breast
Like a fair flower, in furrow'd fields oppressed
By the keen share; a poppy on the plain
370    Whose heavy head is overcharg'd with rain.
Disdain, despair and deadly vengeance vow'd
Drove Nisus headlong on the hostile crowd;
Volscens he seeks, at him alone he bends;
Borne back and push'd by his surrounding friends
He still pressed on; and kept him still in sight,
Then whirled aloft his sword with all his might.
Th'unerring weapon flew, and wing'd with death
Enter'd his gaping mouth, and stopped his breath.
Dying he slew, and staggering on the plain
380    Sought for the body of his lover slain.
Then quietly on his dear breast he fell,
Content in death to be revenged so well.
        O happy pair! for if my verse can give
Eternity, your fame shall ever live,
Fix'd as the Capitol's foundation lies,
And spread where'er the Roman eagle flies.                    (1685)

---

**367–9** Dryden's revision of this famous simile for his 1697 text is markedly superior: 'His snowy neck reclines upon his breast/Like a fair flower by the keen share opprest,/Like a white poppy sinking on the plain.'
**383–6** Virgil apostrophizes the dead heroes: a tribute unique in the poem.

# LUKE MILBOURNE (1649–1720)

[Aen. I. 159–209] *Aeneas and his shipwrecked comrades land at Carthage*

From *The First Book of Virgil's Aeneis Made English*, published anonymously in 1688. Printed from the rare first (and only) edition: see Appendix D.

    In a deep Bay, a pretty Islet forms
    A Port, secure from sight, secure from storms;
    Against whose sides the mounting Billows broke,
    Recoil in Eddyes from the noisie stroke:
    Huge rocks on both hands seem to touch the Skies,
    The Sea beneath all calm and silent lies;
    On this side Woods a gloomy Scene enclose,
    Whose thick set Leaves a reverend Shade compose;
    On that cool Grotts, by artless Hangings done,
10  Within sweet Springs, and seats of native Stone.
    Hither fair Nymphs from Summers heat retire;
    Here Ships no Chains, nor Anchors hold require.
    Here rides Aeneas with his broken Fleet,
    Reduc'd to seven; with joyful shouts they greet
    The Land, and leap to shore, their Limbs at ease,
    And clothes well dry'd, the fainting Saylors please.
      Sparks from sharp Flint Achates strikes, the same
    Fed with dry'd Chips and Leaves, commenc'd a Flame;
    Their tainted Wheat ashore they nimbly take,
20  And dry'd and ground, for craving Hunger bake.
    Aeneas climb'd the Rocks, and view'd around
    The Seas wide Prospect, could he thence have found

---

**7** *a gloomy Scene*: Dryden has 'a sylvan scene', echoing Milton, *Paradise Lost* IV, 140, itself an adaptation of Virgil's '*silvis scaena coruscis*'.

His shatter'd Galleys loose dispers'd about,
Or Capys or Caycus Ancient out.
No ship at last, no Flag, no Sail descry'd,
Three straggling Deer from his high stand he spy'd,
Behind vast Herds in fruitful Valleys feed:
Achates call'd. He snatch'd his Shafts with speed,
And knotty Bow, which with strong Arms he drew,
30    And first the lofty Branched Leaders slew:
Those kill'd, the nimble Darts at random rove,
With certain Death, among the trembling Drove:
Nor stopt his hand, till seven huge Staggs destroy'd,
With welcome shares, his hungry Mates employ'd;
Rich Wines, the kind Acestes' gift, before
He left Sicilia's hospitable shore,
With equal Care the gentle Prince bestows,
And thus with soft kind words allays their woes:
    'O Friends, by Heavens from mighty ills set free,
40    Courage at last the end of these may see:
You stormy Streights and dismal Whirlpools past,
On murderous Shores and barren Desarts cast:
Cheer up, my Mates, force off ignoble fear,
Dangers well past with cheerful hearts you'll hear;
Through toyls, and pains and various dangers hurl'd,
We'll grasp at Latium, where a smiling World;
Where Troy reviv'd, and Crowns and Scepters wait
Our hopes, the Largess of relenting Fate.'
    Thus he discours'd, though rack'd with mighty care,
50    And with forc'd smiles conceal'd his deep despair.          (1688)

# ANONYMOUS

## Amor Omnibus Idem:* or, The Force of Love in All Creatures [Georg. III. 209–85]

Printed from *Examen Poeticum: Miscellany Poems Part Three* (1693). Dryden, in the 'Postscript to the Reader' appended to his 1697 translation, said of this passage: 'Whoever has given the World the Translation of part of the third Georgic, which he calls The Power of Love, has put me to sufficient pains to make my own not inferior to his.' Dryden's version offers several similarities with this passage, e.g. in lines 31, 50–52, 68 (identical), 92–4, 95 (identical).
   Cf. the modern version of the same passage by C. W. Brodribb.

> Whether the nobler Horse's breed you raise,
> Or duller Herds your fertile Pastures graze,
> Nothing will more a vigorous strength produce
> Than to forbid them the licentious use
> Of Love's enfeebling Rites: be therefore sure
> Your Bulls are pastured by themselves secure;
> Let some broad River, or a rising Hill
> Be interpos'd; or let them take their fill
> In closer Stalls; for wanton Love's desire
> Is kindled at the Eyes; whose wasteful fire
> Consumes them by degrees, and makes them slight
> Their food, while they behold the pleasing sight.
> Besides, the fierce Encounters that ensue
> When rival Bulls th' alluring Object view
> Who, both inspir'd with Jealousie and Rage,
> For the fair Female bloody Battles wage:
> Till with black Blood their sides are cover'd o're,
> And their curl'd foreheads meet with hideous roar,

10

*The Latin words of the title are from *Georgics* III, 244 ('Love is the same for all creatures').

Which neighbouring Groves and distant Caves rebound,
20   And great Olympus ecchos back the sound;
Whilst the glad Victor does the spot maintain,
And of his warlike hazards reaps the gain:
The conquer'd Foe forsakes the hostile place,
With deep resentments of his past Disgrace:
The ignominious wounds the Conqueror gave
In his griev'd mind no slight impression leave:
Departing he his absent Love does moan,
Looks back with longing Eyes and many a groan
On those his ancient Realms where once he rul'd alone.
30   Then with redoubled Care his strength supplies,
Rough on the flinty Ground all night he lies,
And shrubs and prickling thistles for his food suffice.
Then runs his Horns into some solid Oak,
Whose reeling trunk does scarce sustain the stroke;
With vain assault provokes the yielding Air
And makes his flourishes before the War.
Then with his force and strength prepar'd does go
With headlong Rage against th' unwary Foe:
Like a white Wave that is descry'd from far
40   Rolling its vastness towards the frighted Shore,
Till with loud noise against the pointed Beaks
Of solid Rocks, the moving Mountain breaks;
Whilst the chaste Billows from the bottom throw
The rising Sands that on the Surface flow.
     All creatures thus the Force of Love do find;
For whether they be those of Human kind
Or savage Beasts, or Neptune's spawning Fry,
Or wanton Herds, or painted Birds that fly,
They all the like transporting Fury try.
50   'Tis with this Rage the Lyoness is stung,
When o'er the Forest (mindless of her young)
She sternly stalks; 'tis then the shapeless Bear
With fierce Desire does to the Woods repair
And wide destruction makes: 'tis then we see
The savage Boar's and Tyger's cruelty.

Let then the sun–burnt Traveller forbear
In Lybia's sandy Desarts to appear.
    See how the Winds the trembling Stallions fray,
When first to their sagacious Nostrils they
60 The distant Female's well-known scent convey!
Then no restraining curbs, nor cruel blows,
Nor hollow caves nor obvious Rocks oppose
Their passage, nor the Sea's objected Force,
That bears the Mountains down its violent Course.
The Sabine Boar does then prepare to wound,
And whets his foamy Tusks, and paws the ground:
His sides against the rugged Trees does tear
And hardens both his Shoulders for the War.
    What does the Youth in whose enraged Veins
70 The heat of Love's distemper'd Fever reigns?
Through stormy Seas he his bold Fortune tries,
Though in his Face the obvious Billows rise
And dash him back to Shore; whilst from the Throne
Of Heav'n its loud Artillery rattles down
On his devoted Head. Nor can the sound
Of waters which against the Rocks rebound
Recall his desperate Course, nor all the Tears
Occasion'd by his careful Parents' fears,
Nor his lov'd Nymph who soon the self-same Fortune shares.
80    'Twere long to tell the spotted Linx's wars,
By Love excited; or the furious Jars
Of prowling Wolves, or Mastives' head-strong Rage;
Ev'n timorous Stags will for their Hinds engage.
But most of all in Mares the amorous Fire
Appears; whom Venus did herself inspire.
What time that Potnian Glaucus (to improve
Their speed) withheld them from the Rites of Love.
With Rage incens'd they struck their Master dead,
And on his mangled Limbs by piecemeal fed.
90 O're craggy Mountains Love their way does guide
And spurs them through the depths of Rivers wide.

When Spring's soft Fire their melting Marrow burns
(For 'tis in Spring the lusty warmth returns)
They to the tops of steepest Hills repair,
And with wide Nostrils snuff the Western air,
Wherewith conceiving (wonderful to tell!)
Without the Stallion's help their bellies swell;
Whose frantick Fury makes them scour amain
O're solid Rocks, and through the liquid Plain,
100   Nor Hills nor straightning Vales their giddy course restrain.
Nor do they tow'rds the Sun's uprising steer
Their headstrong way, nor tow'rds the frozen Bear,
Nor tow'rds the place where tepid Auster pours
Upon the pregnant Earth her plenteous Show'rs,
Till from their lustful Groins at last does fall
Their Off-spring, which the Shepherds rightly call
Hippomanes: a slimy, poisonous Juice
Which muttering Step-Dames in Inchantments use,
And in the mystic cup their powerful Herbs infuse.
110   But time is lost, which never will renew,
Whilst ravish'd, we the pleasing Theam pursue.          (1693)

---

**101-4** A mistranslation of a difficult passage, which Dryden also gets wrong.
Virgil (following Aristotle) refers to the belief that mares run either north or
south, but never east or west.
**107** *Hippomanes*: literally 'horse-madness'

# JOHN DRYDEN (1631–1700)

## The Fourth Pastoral or, Pollio [Ecl. IV]

Printed from the 1697 text of *The Works of Virgil in English*, edited as vol. V of the California Dryden by W. Frost and V.A. Dearing (1987). Dryden published an earlier version of this poem in *Miscellany Poems: The First Part* (1684). This is the so-called 'Messianic' Eclogue, on which see Introduction. Dryden gives added grandeur to this translation by employing not only alexandrines (e.g. line 12), as he does frequently in his Virgil, but also (uniquely in this poem) fourteeners (lines 15, 42, 73, 75).

> *The Poet celebrates the Birth-day of Saloninus, the Son of Pollio, born in the Consulship of his Father, after the taking of Salonæ, a City in Dalmatia. Many of the Verses are translated from one of the Sybils, who prophesie of our Saviour's Birth.*

Sicilian Muse begin a loftier strain!
Though lowly Shrubs and Trees that shade the Plain,
Delight not all; Sicilian Muse, prepare
To make the vocal Woods deserve a Consul's care.
The last great Age, foretold by sacred Rhymes,
Renews its finish'd Course, Saturnian times
Rowl round again, and mighty years, begun
From their first Orb, in radiant Circles run.
The base degenerate Iron-off-spring ends;
10   A golden Progeny from Heav'n descends;
O chast Lucina speed the Mother's pains,
And haste the glorious Birth; thy own Apollo reigns!

---

**4** The consul is C. Asinius Pollio, who took office in 40BC. The child was sometimes said to be his, but there is no evidence for this. Pollio is named below, line 14. Dryden believed him to be the child's father: see lines 16–19.
**11** *Lucina*: goddess of childbirth

The lovely Boy, with his auspicious Face,
Shall Pollio's Consulship and Triumph grace;
Majestick Months set out with him to their appointed Race.
The Father banish'd Virtue shall restore,
And Crimes shall threat the guilty world no more.
The Son shall lead the life of Gods, and be
By Gods and Heroes seen, and Gods and Heroes see.

20 The jarring Nations he in peace shall bind,
And with paternal Virtues rule Mankind.
Unbidden Earth shall wreathing Ivy bring,
And fragrant Herbs (the promises of Spring)
As her first Off'rings to her Infant King.
The Goats with strutting Dugs shall homeward speed,
And lowing Herds, secure from Lyons feed.
His Cradle shall with rising Flow'rs be crown'd;
The Serpents Brood shall die: the sacred ground
Shall Weeds and pois'nous Plants refuse to bear,

30 Each common Bush shall Syrian Roses wear.
But when Heroick Verse his Youth shall raise,
And form it to Hereditary Praise;
Unlabour'd Harvests shall the Fields adorn,
And cluster'd Grapes shall blush on every Thorn.
The knotted Oaks shall show'rs of Honey weep,
And through the Matted Grass the liquid Gold shall creep.
Yet, of old Fraud some footsteps shall remain,
The Merchant still shall plough the deep for gain:
Great Cities shall with Walls be compass'd round;

40 And sharpen'd Shares shall vex the fruitful ground.
Another Tiphys shall new Seas explore,
Another Argos land the Chiefs, upon th' Iberian Shore:

---

**26** For lions, cf. Isaiah 11, 6.
**35** Honey on tap was a feature of the Golden Age: cf. *Georgics* I, 131.
**37** *footsteps*: traces
**41–2** Tiphys was helmsman on the *Argo*, the first ship on which Jason sailed.

Another Helen other Wars create,
And great Achilles urge the Trojan Fate:
But when to ripen'd Man-hood he shall grow,
The greedy Sailer shall the Seas forego;
No Keel shall cut the Waves for foreign Ware;
For every Soil shall every Product bear.
The labouring Hind his Oxen shall disjoyn,
50  No Plow shall hurt the Glebe, no Pruning-hook the Vine:
Nor Wooll shall in dissembled Colours shine.
But the luxurious Father of the Fold,
With native Purple, or unborrow'd Gold,
Beneath his pompous Fleece shall proudly sweat:
And under Tyrian Robes the Lamb shall bleat.
The Fates, when they this happy Web have spun,
Shall bless the sacred Clue, and bid it smoothly run.
Mature in years, to ready Honours move,
O of Cœlestial Seed! O foster Son of Jove!
60  See, lab'ring Nature calls thee to sustain
The nodding Frame of Heav'n, and Earth, and Main;
See to their Base restor'd, Earth, Seas, and Air,
And joyful Ages from behind, in crowding Ranks appear.
To sing thy Praise, wou'd Heav'n my breath prolong,
Infusing Spirits worthy such a Song;
Not Thracian Orpheus should transcend my Layes,
Nor Linus crown'd with never-fading Bayes:
Though each his Heav'nly Parent shou'd inspire;
The Muse instruct the Voice, and Phœbus tune the Lyre.
70  Shou'd Pan contend in Verse, and thou my Theme,
Arcadian Judges shou'd their God condemn.
Begin, auspicious Boy, to cast about
Thy Infant Eyes, and with a smile, thy Mother single out;

Thy Mother well deserves that short delight,
The nauseous Qualms of ten long Months and Travel to
                                                                    requite.
Then smile; the frowning Infant's Doom is read,
No God shall crown the Board, nor Goddess bless the Bed.

                                                                    (1697)


# JOHN DRYDEN

### The First Book of the Aeneis, 1–75, 277–407 [Aen. I. 1–49, 198–296]

Juno's first soliloquy expresses her hatred of the Trojans. After the storm engineered by her has driven Aeneas ashore at Carthage, he tries to encourage his men. Venus complains to Jupiter about her son's plight; Jupiter reassures his daughter in a speech outlining the destiny of Rome.

No translator surpasses Dryden in the grandeur with which these opening passages are rendered.


*The Trojans, after a seven Years Voyage, set sail for Italy, but are*
*overtaken by a dreadful Storm, which Æolus raises at Juno's*
*Request. The Tempest sinks one, and scatters the rest: Neptune*
*drives off the Winds and calms the Sea. Æneas with his own Ship,*
*and six more, arrives safe at an Affrican Port. Venus complains to*
*Jupiter of her Son's Misfortunes.* Jupiter *comforts her, and sends*
*Mercury to procure him a kind Reception among the Carthaginians.*
*Æneas going out to discover the Country, meets his Mother in the*
*Shape of an Huntress, who conveys him in a Cloud to Carthage;*

---

**67** *Linus*: son of Apollo, teacher of Orpheus
**77** The communion of gods and heroes in the first Golden Age is referred to by Catullus, and cf. lines 18–19.

*where he sees his Friends whom he thought lost, and receives a kind*
*Entertainment from the Queen. Dido by a device of Venus begins to*
*have a Passion for him, and after some Discourse with him, desires*
*the History of his Adventures since the Siege of Troy, which is*
*the Subject of the two following Books.*

Arms, and the Man I sing; who, forc'd by Fate,
And haughty Juno's unrelenting Hate,
Expell'd and exil'd, left the Trojan Shoar:
Long Labours, both by Sea and Land he bore,
And in the doubtful War, before he won
The Latian Realm, and built the destin'd Town:
His banish'd Gods restor'd to Rites Divine,
And setl'd sure Succession in his Line:
From whence the Race of Alban Fathers come,
10   And the long Glories of Majestick Rome.
    O Muse! the Causes and the Crimes relate,
What Goddess was provok'd, and whence her hate:
For what Offence the Queen of Heav'n began
To persecute so brave, so just a Man!
Involv'd his anxious Life in endless Cares,
Expos'd to Wants, and hurry'd into Wars!
Can Heav'nly Minds such high resentment show;
Or exercise their Spight in Human Woe?
    Against the Tiber's Mouth, but far away,
20   An ancient Town was seated on the Sea:
A Tyrian Colony; the People made
Stout for the War, and studious of their Trade:
Carthage the Name, belov'd by Juno more
Than her own Argos, or the Samian Shoar.
Here stood her Chariot, here, if Heav'n were kind,
The Seat of awful Empire she design'd.
Yet she had heard an ancient Rumour fly,
(Long cited by the People of the Sky;)

---

**6–10** Aeneas' first foundation in Italy was at Lavinium, subsequently moved
to Alba Longa and thence to Rome (cf. 169–76).

That times to come shou'd see the Trojan Race
30   Her Carthage ruin, and her Tow'rs deface:
Nor thus confin'd, the Yoke of Sov'raign Sway,
Should on the Necks of all the Nations lay.
She ponder'd this, and fear'd it was in Fate;
Nor cou'd forget the War she wag'd of late,
For conq'ring Greece against the Trojan State.
Besides long Causes working in her Mind,
And secret Seeds of Envy lay behind.
Deep graven in her Heart, the Doom remain'd
Of partial Paris, and her Form disdain'd:
40   The Grace bestow'd on ravish'd Ganimed,
Electra's Glories, and her injur'd Bed.
Each was a Cause alone, and all combin'd
To kindle Vengeance in her haughty Mind.
For this, far distant from the Latian Coast,
She drove the Remnants of the Trojan Hoast:
And sev'n long Years th' unhappy wand'ring Train,
Were toss'd by Storms, and scatter'd through the Main.
Such Time, such Toil requir'd the Roman Name,
Such length of Labour for so vast a Frame.
50   Now scarce the Trojan fleet with Sails and Oars
Had left behind the Fair Sicilian Shoars:
Ent'ring with chearful Shouts the wat'ry Reign,
And ploughing frothy Furrows in the Main:
When lab'ring still, with endless discontent,
The Queen of Heav'n did thus her Fury vent.
    Then am I vanquish'd, must I yield, said she,
And must the Trojans reign in Italy?
So Fate will have it, and Jove adds his Force;
Nor can my Pow'r divert their happy Course.

---

**38–41** Juno's grievances: the Judgement of Paris, the Trojan prince who preferred Venus to herself in the beauty contest; Ganymede, a grandson of King Dardanus of Troy, was abducted by Jupiter; Electra was Dardanus' mother by Jupiter.

60    Cou'd angry Pallas, with revengeful Spleen,
       The Grecian Navy burn, and drown the Men?
       She for the Fault of one offending Foe,
       The Bolts of Jove himself presum'd to throw:
       With Whirlwinds from beneath she toss'd the Ship,
       And bare expos'd the Bosom of the deep:
       Then, as an Eagle gripes the trembling Game,
       The Wretch yet hissing with her Father's Flame,
       She strongly seiz'd, and with a burning Wound,
       Transfix'd and naked, on a Rock she bound.
70    But I, who walk in awful State above,
       The Majesty of Heav'n, the Sister-wife of Jove;
       For length of Years, my fruitless Force employ
       Against the thin remains of ruin'd Troy.
       What Nations now to Juno's Pow'r will pray,
       Or Off'rings on my slighted Altars lay?

                    *

       Endure, and conquer; Jove will soon dispose
       To future Good, our past and present Woes.
       With me, the Rocks of Scylla you have try'd;
       Th' inhuman Cyclops, and his Den defy'd.
80    What greater Ills hereafter can you bear?
       Resume your Courage, and dismiss your Care.
       An Hour will come, with Pleasure to relate
       Your Sorrows past, as Benefits of Fate.
       Through various Hazards, and Events we move
       To Latium, and the Realms foredoom'd by Jove:
       Call'd to the Seat, (the Promise of the Skies,)
       Where Trojan Kingdoms once again may rise.
       Endure the Hardships of your present State,
       Live, and reserve your selves for better Fate.
90      These Words he spoke; but spoke not from his Heart;
       His outward Smiles conceal'd his inward Smart.

---

76–89 Aeneas encourages his fellow survivors.

The jolly Crew, unmindful of the past,
The Quarry share, their plenteous Dinner haste:
Some strip the Skin, some portion out the Spoil;
The Limbs yet trembling, in the Cauldrons boyl:
Some on the Fire the reeking Entrails broil.
Stretch'd on the grassy Turf, at ease they dine;
Restore their Strength with Meat, and chear their Souls with
                                                        Wine.

Their Hunger thus appeas'd, their Care attends,
100   The doubtful Fortune of their absent Friends:
Alternate Hopes and Fears, their Minds possess,
Whether to deem 'em dead, or in Distress.
Above the rest, Æneas mourns the Fate
Of brave Orontes, and th' uncertain State
Of Gyas, Lycus, and of Amycus:
The Day, but not their Sorrows, ended thus.
When, from aloft, Almighty Jove surveys
Earth, Air, and Shoars, and navigable Seas,
At length on Lybian Realms he fix'd his Eyes:
110   Whom, pond'ring thus on Human Miseries,
When Venus saw, she with a lowly Look,
Not free from Tears, her Heav'nly Sire bespoke.

   O King of Gods and Men, whose awful Hand,
Disperses Thunder on the Seas and Land;
Disposing all with absolute Command:
How cou'd my Pious Son thy Pow'r incense,
Or what, alas! is vanish'd Troy's Offence?
Our hope of Italy not only lost,
On various Seas, by various Tempests tost,
120   But shut from ev'ry Shoar, and barr'd from ev'ry
                                                        Coast.

    You promis'd once, a Progeny Divine,
Of Romans, rising from the Trojan Line,
In after-times shou'd hold the World in awe,
And to the Land and Ocean give the Law.
How is your Doom revers'd, which eas'd my Care;
When Troy was ruin'd in that cruel War?

Then Fates to Fates I cou'd oppose; but now,
When Fortune still pursues her former Blow,
What can I hope? what worse can still succeed?
130 What end of Labours has your Will decreed?
Antenor, from the midst of Grecian Hosts,
Could pass secure, and pierce th' Illyrian Coasts:
Where rowling down the Steep, Timavus raves,
And through nine Channels disembogues his Waves.
At length he founded Padua's happy Seat,
And gave his Trojans a secure Retreat:
There fix'd their Arms, and there renew'd their Name,
And there in Quiet rules, and crown'd with Fame.
But we, descended from your sacred Line,
140 Entitled to your Heav'n, and Rites Divine,
Are banish'd Earth, and, for the Wrath of one,
Remov'd from Latium, and the promis'd Throne.
Are these our Scepters? These our due Rewards?
And is it thus that Jove his plighted Faith regards?
    To whom, the Father of th' immortal Race,
Smiling with that serene indulgent Face,
With which he drives the Clouds, and clears the Skies:
First gave a holy Kiss, then thus replies.
    Daughter, dismiss thy Fears: To thy desire
150 The Fates of thine are fix'd, and stand entire.
Thou shalt behold thy wish'd Lavinian Walls,
And, ripe for Heav'n, when Fate Æneas calls,
Then shalt thou bear him up, sublime, to me;
No Councils have revers'd my firm Decree.
And lest new Fears disturb thy happy State,
Know, I have search'd the Mystick Rolls of Fate:
Thy Son (nor is th' appointed Season far)
In Italy shall wage successful War:
Shall tame fierce Nations in the bloody Field,
160 And Sov'raign Laws impose, and Cities build.

---

149–206 Jupiter foretells the future.
152 Aeneas died and was deified three years after subduing the Italians.

'Till, after ev'ry Foe subdu'd, the Sun
Thrice through the Signs his Annual Race shall run:
This is his time prefix'd. Ascanius then,
Now called Iulus, shall begin his Reign.
He thirty rowling Years the Crown shall wear:
Then from Lavinium shall the Seat transfer:
And, with hard Labour, Alba-longa build;
The Throne with his Succession shall be fill'd,
Three hundred Circuits more: then shall be seen,
170  Ilia the fair, a Priestess and a Queen:
Who full of Mars, in time, with kindly Throws,
Shall at a Birth two goodly Boys disclose.
The Royal Babes a tawny Wolf shall drain,
Then Romulus his Grandsire's Throne shall gain,
Of Martial Tow'rs the Founder shall become,
The People Romans call, the City Rome.
To them, no Bounds of Empire I assign;
Nor term of Years to their immortal Line.
Ev'n haughty Juno, who, with endless Broils,
180  Earth, Seas, and Heav'n, and Jove himself turmoils;
At length atton'd, her friendly Pow'r shall joyn,
To cherish and advance the Trojan Line.
The subject World shall Rome's Dominion own,
And, prostrate, shall adore the Nation of the Gown.
An Age is ripening in revolving Fate,
When Troy shall overturn the Grecian State:
And sweet Revenge her conqu'ring Sons shall call,
To crush the People that conspir'd her Fall.
Then Cæsar from the Julian Stock shall rise,
190  Whose Empire Ocean, and whose Fame the Skies

---

169 *Circuits*: years. Three hundred years (roughly) separated the legend of
Aeneas from Romulus, traditional founder of Rome (753 BC, though other
dates have been proposed).
177–8 The Eternal City.
185–95 The coming of Augustus.

Alone shall bound: Whom, fraught with Eastern Spoils,
Our Heav'n, the just Reward of Human Toyls,
Securely shall repay with Rites Divine;
And Incense shall ascend before his sacred Shrine.
Then dire Debate, and impious War shall cease,
And the stern Age be softned into Peace:
Then banish'd Faith shall once again return,
And Vestal Fires in hallow'd Temples burn;
And Remus with Quirinus shall sustain
200  The righteous Laws, and Fraud and Force restrain.
Janus himself before his Fane shall wait,
And keep the dreadful issues of his Gate,
With Bolts and Iron Bars: within remains
Imprison'd Fury, bound in brazen Chains:
High on a Trophie rais'd, of useless Arms,
He sits, and threats the World with vain Alarms.          (1697)


# JOHN DRYDEN

## The Sixth Book of the Aeneis, 374–520 [Aen. VI.
264–383] *The descent into the underworld; the ghost of Palinurus*

For the first part of this passage cf. the versions of Harington and
Ogilby; for the death of Palinurus in Book V see Phaer's translation.


Ye Realms, yet unreveal'd to human sight,
Ye Gods, who rule the Regions of the Night,
Ye gliding Ghosts, permit me to relate
The mystick Wonders of your silent State.
   Obscure they went thro dreery Shades, that led
Along the waste Dominions of the dead:

---

**199** *Quirinus*: the deified Romulus.
**201–6** The 'Pax Augusta'.

Thus wander Travellers in Woods by Night,
By the Moon's doubtful, and malignant Light:
When Jove in dusky Clouds involves the Skies;
10    And the faint Crescent shoots by fits before their Eyes.
    Just in the Gate, and in the Jaws of Hell,
Revengeful Cares, and sullen Sorrows dwell;
And pale Diseases, and repining Age;
Want, Fear, and Famine's unresisted rage.
Here Toils, and Death, and Death's half-brother, Sleep,
Forms terrible to view, their Centry keep;
With anxious Pleasures of a guilty Mind,
Deep Frauds before, and open Force behind:
The Furies Iron Beds, and Strife that shakes
20    Her hissing Tresses, and unfolds her Snakes.
Full in the midst of this infernal Road,
An Elm displays her dusky Arms abroad;
The God of Sleep there hides his heavy Head:
And empty Dreams on ev'ry Leaf are spread.
Of various Forms unnumber'd Specters more;
Centaurs, and double Shapes, besiege the Door:
Before the Passage horrid Hydra stands,
And Briareus with all his hundred Hands:
Gorgons, Geryon with his triple Frame;
30    And vain Chimæra vomits empty Flame.
The Chief unsheath'd his shining Steel, prepar'd,
Tho seiz'd with sudden Fear, to force the Guard;
Off'ring his brandish'd Weapon at their Face;
Had not the Sibyl stop'd his eager Pace,
And told him what those empty Fantomes were;
Forms without Bodies, and impassive Air.
Hence to deep Acheron they take their way;
Whose troubled Eddies, thick with Ooze and Clay,
Are whirl'd aloft, and in Cocytus lost:
40    There Charon stands, who rules the dreary Coast:
A sordid God; down from his hoary Chin
A length of Beard descends; uncomb'd, unclean:

His Eyes, like hollow Furnaces on Fire:
A Girdle, foul with grease, binds his obscene Attire.
He spreads his Canvas, with his Pole he steers;
The Freights of flitting Ghosts in his thin Bottom bears.
He look'd in Years; yet in his Years were seen
A youthful Vigour, and Autumnal green.
An Airy Crowd came rushing where he stood;
50   Which fill'd the Margin of the fatal Flood.
Husbands and Wives, Boys and unmarry'd Maids;
And mighty Heroes more Majestick Shades;
And Youths, intomb'd before their Fathers Eyes,
With hollow Groans, and Shrieks, and feeble Cries:
Thick as the Leaves in Autumn strow the Woods:
Or Fowls, by Winter forc'd, forsake the Floods,
And wing their hasty flight to happier Lands:
Such, and so thick, the shiv'ring Army stands:
And press for passage with extended hands.
60       Now these, now those, the surly Boatman bore:
The rest he drove to distance from the Shore.
The Heroe, who beheld with wond'ring Eyes,
The Tumult mix'd with Shrieks, Laments, and Cries;
Ask'd of his Guide, what the rude Concourse meant?
Why to the Shore the thronging People bent?
What Forms of Law, among the Ghosts were us'd?
Why some were ferr'd o're, and some refus'd?
        Son of Anchises, Offspring of the Gods,
The Sibyl said; you see the Stygian Floods,
70   The Sacred Stream, which Heav'n's Imperial State
Attests in Oaths, and fears to violate.
The Ghosts rejected, are th' unhappy Crew
Depriv'd of Sepulchers, and Fun'ral due;
The Boatman Charon; those, the bury'd host,
He Ferries over to the Farther Coast.

---

55 Dryden has echoed Milton's version of Virgil's famous simile, *Paradise Lost*
I, 301, 'thick as autumnal leaves that strow the brooks . . .'

Nor dares his Transport Vessel cross the Waves,
With such whose Bones are not compos'd in Graves.
A hundred years they wander on the Shore,
At length, their Pennance done, are wafted o're.

80   The Trojan Chief his forward pace repress'd;
Revolving anxious Thoughts within his Breast.
He saw his Friends, who whelm'd beneath the Waves,
Their Fun'ral Honours claim'd, and ask'd their quiet Graves.
The lost Leucaspis in the Crowd he knew;
And the brave Leader of the Lycian Crew:
Whom, on the Tyrrhene Seas, the Tempests met;
The Sailors master'd, and the Ship o'reset.
Amidst the Spirits Palinurus press'd;
Yet fresh from life; a new admitted Guest:

90   Who, while the steering view'd the Stars, and bore
His Course from Affrick, to the Latian Shore,
Fell headlong down. The Trojan fix'd his view;
And scarcely through the gloom the sullen Shadow knew.
Then thus the Prince. What envious Pow'r, O Friend,
Brought your lov'd life to this disastrous end?
For Phœbus, ever true in all he said,
Has, in your fate alone, my Faith betray'd.
The God foretold you shou'd not die, before
You reach'd, secure from Seas, th' Italian Shore.

100   Is this th' unerring Pow'r? The Ghost reply'd,
Nor Phœbus flatter'd, nor his Answers ly'd;
Nor envious Gods have sent me to the Deep:
But while the Stars, and course of Heav'n I keep,
My weary'd Eyes were seiz'd with fatal sleep.
I fell; and with my weight, the Helm constrain'd,
Was drawn along, which yet my gripe retain'd.
Now by the Winds, and raging Waves, I swear,
Your Safety, more than mine, was then my Care:
Lest, of the Guide bereft, the Rudder lost,

110   Your Ship shou'd run against the rocky Coast.
Three blust'ring Nights, born by the Southern blast,
I floated; and discover'd Land at last:

High on a Mounting Wave, my head I bore:
Forcing my Strength, and gath'ring to the Shore:
Panting, but past the danger, now I seiz'd
The Craggy Cliffs, and my tyr'd Members eas'd:
While, cumber'd with my dropping Cloaths, I lay,
The cruel Nation, covetous of Prey,
Stain'd with my Blood th' unhospitable Coast:
120 And now, by Winds and Waves, my lifeless Limbs are tost:
Which O avert, by you Etherial Light
Which I have lost, for this eternal Night:
Or if by dearer tyes you may be won,
By your dead Sire, and by your living Son,
Redeem from this Reproach, my wand'ring Ghost;
Or with your Navy seek the *Velin* Coast:
And in a peaceful Grave my Corps compose:
Or, if a nearer way your Mother shows,
Without whose Aid, you durst not undertake
130 This frightful Passage o're the *Stygian* Lake;
Lend to this Wretch your Hand, and waft him o're
To the sweet Banks of yon forbidden Shore.
Scarce had he said, the Prophetess began;
What Hopes delude thee, miserable Man?
Think'st thou thus unintomb'd to cross the Floods, ⎫
To view the Furies, and Infernal Gods;        ⎬
And visit, without leave, the dark abodes?     ⎭
Attend the term of long revolving Years:
Fate, and the dooming Gods, are deaf to Tears.
140 This Comfort of thy dire Misfortune take;
The Wrath of Heav'n, inflicted for thy sake,
With Vengeance shall pursue th' inhumane Coast:
Till they propitiate thy offended Ghost,
And raise a Tomb, with Vows, and solemn Pray'r;
And *Palinurus* name the Place shall bear.
This calm'd his Cares: sooth'd with his future Fame;
And pleas'd to hear his propagated Name.                    (1697)

---

**145** Capo di Palinuro lies off the coast road leading south from Salerno.

# JOHN DRYDEN

## The Sixth Book of the Aeneis, 1055–1102, 1168–77
## [Aen. VI. 777–807, 847–53]

As the pageant of souls awaiting birth passes before Aeneas in the
Elysian Fields, Anchises points to Romulus and Augustus, and
defines the nature of Rome's world-historical destiny.

> See Romulus the great, born to restore
> The Crown that once his injur'd Grandsire wore.
> This Prince, a Priestess of your Blood shall bear;
> And like his Sire in Arms he shall appear.
> Two rising Crests his Royal Head adorn;
> Born from a God, himself to Godhead born.
> His Sire already signs him for the Skies,
> And marks his Seat amidst the Deities.
> Auspicious Chief! thy Race in times to come
> Shall spread the Conquests of Imperial Rome:
> Rome whose ascending Tow'rs shall Heav'n invade;
> Involving Earth and Ocean in her Shade:
> High as the Mother of the Gods in place;
> And proud, like her, of an Immortal Race.
> Then when in Pomp she makes the Phrygian round;
> With Golden Turrets on her Temples crown'd:
> A hundred Gods her sweeping Train supply;
> Her Offspring all, and all command the Sky.

10

---

2 *his injur'd Grandsire*: Numitor, king of Alba Longa, was deposed by his
brother, who made Numitor's daughter Rhea Silvia a Vestal Virgin in the
hope of preventing the birth of a possible avenger; but she was impregnated
by Mars, and gave birth to Romulus.

13–15 The cult of Cybele, the 'Great Mother', came to Rome in 204 BC. She
was depicted with a battlemented crown, symbolic here of Rome itself.

15 *Phrygian:* Mt Berecyntus in Phrygia was a cult centre for the worship of
Cybele.

Now fix your Sight, and stand intent, to see
20   Your Roman Race, and Julian Progeny.
The mighty Cæsar waits his vital Hour;
Impatient for the World, and grasps his promis'd Pow'r.
But next behold the Youth of Form Divine,
Cæsar himself, exalted in his Line;
Augustus, promis'd oft, and long foretold,  }
Sent to the Realm that Saturn rul'd of old;  }
Born to restore a better Age of Gold.  }
Affrick, and India, shall his Pow'r obey,  }
He shall extend his propagated Sway,  }
30   Beyond the Solar Year; without the starry Way:  }
Where Atlas turns the rowling Heav'ns around;
And his broad Shoulders with their Lights are crown'd.
At his fore-seen Approach, already quake
The Caspian Kingdoms, and Mæotian Lake.
Their Seers behold the Tempest from afar;
And threatening Oracles denounce the War.
Nile hears him knocking at his sev'nfold Gates;
And seeks his hidden Spring, and fears his Nephews Fates.
Nor Hercules more Lands or Labours knew,
40   Not tho' the brazen-footed Hind he slew;
Freed Erymanthus from the foaming Boar,
And dip'd his Arrows in Lernæan Gore:
Nor Bacchus, turning from his Indian War,
By Tygers drawn triumphant in his Car,
From Nisa's top descending on the Plains;
With curling Vines around his purple Reins.

---

23 By inserting 'But next' (not in the Latin) Dryden shows that he took the
first mention of Caesar to refer to Julius. Several other translators make the
same assumption, but only one Caesar is singled out: in Virgil's eyes Augustus
was Rome's second founder, as Romulus was the first.
39–46 Virgil draws a parallel between Augustus' labours and journeys on
behalf of civilization and those of two traditional 'culture heroes', Hercules,
who civilized the west, and Bacchus, who civilized the east.

And doubt we yet thro' Dangers to pursue
The Paths of Honour, and a Crown in view?

\*

Let others better mold the running Mass ⎫
50   Of Mettals, and inform the breathing Brass;  ⎬
And soften into Flesh a Marble Face:  ⎭
Plead better at the Bar; describe the Skies,
And when the Stars descend, and when they rise.
But, Rome, 'tis thine alone, with awful sway,  ⎫
To rule Mankind; and make the World obey;  ⎬
Disposing Peace, and War, thy own Majestick Way.  ⎭
To tame the Proud, the fetter'd Slave to free;
These are Imperial Arts, and worthy thee.          (1697)


# LUKE MILBOURNE (1649–1720)

[Georg. I. 438–511] *Signs and portents of the sun; civil war
and its effect on agriculture*

From Milbourne's *Notes on Dryden's Virgil* (1698): see Appendix D.
One of the most powerful passages in the poem.

Observe the Sun too, watch his rising Signs,
And how he toward his watry Couch declines.
The Sun's Prognostics all are plain and clear,
Both when he mounts, and when the Stars appear.
If with a spotted Limb he climbs the Skies,

---

47–8 Anchises addresses Aeneas direct, encouraging him to stand firm in
Latium.
49–58 The Latin text of these celebrated lines will be found alongside Mandel-
baum's translation.

Or masques in Clouds, or half his Beams denies,
Then look for showers or for a Southern wind,
To plants and Herds a moist unwholsom Kind.
If when he rises first his languid Beams
10  Break thro the gather'd Clouds with watry Gleams,
Or if the Morning leaves her Saffron Bed,
Her faded Cheeks with deadly paleness spread,
What ratling storms of Hail their looks attend?
What Leaves can then their tender Grapes defend?
    Your Observations yet are surer far
When down Heav'ns steep he drives his burning Carr;
His Brows oft change then with a various hue,
And Winds his Red and Rains his Black pursue.
If gloomy spots mix with his ruddy Flame,
20  All mighty winds and mighty Rains proclaim
With such a Sky I'd never quit the shore,
Be drill'd to Sea, or once my Boat unmoore.
    But if his Rise unclouded Beams display,
And with unclouded Beams he close the Day,
Fear neither Rains nor Winds; the North then moves,
Drives off the Clouds and rustles thro the Groves.
In short, the Farmer by the Sun may know
Whence Clouds will rise, or gentle Gales will blow,
What storms the watry South designs to bring,
30  What weather from the falling Night may spring:
For who'd with false Prognostics charge the Sun?
He warns us oft of Mischiefs scarce begun;
Foreshows blind Insurrections, unfledg'd Jarrs,
Fermenting treacheries and brooding Wars.
He pity'd Rome when murder'd Caesar dy'd,
And to the World his chearful Beams denyd,

---

**35** The death of Julius Caesar. Milbourne rightly censured Dryden's version
of this line: 'And pity'd Rome when Rome in Caesar fell'. Rome did not
fall, and Virgil does not say so.

Behind a gloomy Scurf obscur'd his Light,
And godless men fear'd an Eternal Night.
'Twas then the Time when Seas and Air and Earth
40 Contriv'd to give prodigious Monsters birth.
Dark Heav'n on that inhuman Action scowl'd,
And Dogs obscene in every Quarter howl'd;
Ill-boding Schriech-Owls with their ominous Notes
Scream'd thro the Day and stretch'd their fateful throats;
Hot Aetna burst his fiery bounds below,
And made Sicilia's Fields with sulphur glow,
Made melted Rocks in livid torrents roll,
And shot vast fiery Globes against the Pole.
Th' affrighted Germans heard the dismal sound
50 Of clanking Arms which march'd the Welkin round.
The snowy Alps with uncouth trembling reel'd,
And silent Groves prodigious Voices fill'd,
Pale meager Ghosts broke from the rending Tomb
And glaring stalk thro Night's obscurer gloom.
Brutes (horrid strange!) with human language spoke,
And staggering Earth her shatter'd Surface broke.
Swift Brooks a passage to their Streams deny'd,
And quite forgot the Seas attending Tide;
Big with their tears the sacred Marbles stood,
60 And sweating Statues dropt a sanguine Flood.
Po, prince of Streams, with uncouth madness swell'd,
Bore down the Groves, and Forests headlong fell'd,
At once drown'd all the Fields and Herds and Stalls,
Hurry'd with violent Fury to his dreadful Falls.
Beasts, livers all with boding Lines were vein'd,
And bloody Springs their Streams with gore distain'd.
Th'unpeopled Streets were fill'd with hideous sounds,
And howling Wolves there took their Midnight rounds.
Lightnings ne'er shot so thick from cloudless Skies,
70 Nor such portentous Comets plagu'd our Eyes.

Philippi then a griev'd Spectator stood,
And saw her Fields o'erflow'd with streams of Blood,
While Roman troops in war with Romans clos'd,
And Friends their Friends with equal Arms oppos'd.
Heav'n, angry, thought it worth its while once more
T'enrich the barren soils with Roman Gore,
To glut the wide Pharsalian Fields around,
And the large Plains by lofty Haemus crown'd.
    The time shall come when, as the toiling Swains
80  With crooked Plows shall furrow up the Plains,
They'll find our Spears with eating Rust consum'd,
And hollow Helmets long in Earth inhum'd,
And pigmy Heirs shall with amazement see
The mighty Bones of their gigantic Ancestry.
    Ye kindred Gods who o'er great Rome preside,
Quirinus too, to all the Gods ally'd!
And Mother Vesta, whose protecting Hand
Makes Tiber flow, and Rome triumphant stand:
O let this one, this gallant Youth remain,
90  And the vast Ruins of the World sustain!
Enough of Blood for Perjuries we've paid,
To woes by false Laomedon betray'd.
To us the Gods, great Caesar, envy thee,
And all thy Triumphs here with Envy see.
They grudge to see a wretched Age, opprest
With lawless Guilt, by such a Guardian blest.

---

**71–80** The battle of Philippi was fought in 42 BC between the republicans
Brutus and Cassius and the Caesarians Antony and Octavian. Pharsalia was
fought earlier, in 48 BC, between Julius Caesar and Pompey. Both battlefields
were in northern Greece, near Mt Haemus.
**92** Laomedon, an early king of Troy, had cheated the gods of the payment he
had promised them for building the walls of Troy. The legend is often
referred to.
**93ff.** Miseries of civil war: the decline of agriculture. Rome does not deserve
Octavian.

For all our lower World's involved in Blood,
And horrid Sin's with impious Art pursu'd.
The Plough lies rusting by, the Soldier's scorn,
100  The Fields uncultivated, wild, forlorn;
Now Swords of Scythes the Martial Farmers make,
And, arm'd, their desolated Lands forsake,
Euphrates sounds with marching Troops from far,
And nearer Germany renews the War.                    (1698)


# JOSEPH ADDISON (1672–1719)

## Milton's Stile Imitated, in a Translation of a Story out of the Third Aeneid [Aen. III. 570–681]

Printed from *Poetical Miscellanies: The Fifth Part* (1704). The story is the adventure of the Cyclops, part of Aeneas' narrative to Dido of his voyage from Troy.

Lost in the gloomy Horror of the Night
We struck upon the Coast where Aetna lyes,
Horrid and waste; its Entrails fraught with Fire:
That now casts out dark Fumes and pitchy Clouds,
Vast Show'rs of Ashes hov'ring in the Smoak;
Now belches molten Stones and ruddy Flame
Incenst, or tears up Mountains by the roots,
Or slings a broken Rock aloft in Air.
The bottom works with smother'd Fire, involv'd
10  In pestilential Vapours, Stench and Smoak.
      'Tis said that Thunder-struck Enceladus,
Grov'ling beneath th' incumbent Mountain's weight
Lyes stretch'd supine, Eternal prey of Flames;

---

11 *Enceladus*: one of the giants who rebelled against Jupiter.

And when he heaves against the burning Load,
Reluctant to invert his broiling Limbs,
A sudden Earth-Quake shoots through all the Isle,
And Aetna thunders dreadful under Ground
Then pours out Smoak in wreathing Curls convolv'd,
And shades the Sun's bright Orb and blots out Day.
20    Here in the shelter of the Woods we lodg'd,
And frighted heard strange Sounds and dismal Yells,
Nor saw from whence they came; for all the Night
A Murky Storm deep low'ring o're our Heads
Hung imminent, that with impervious Gloom
Oppos'd itself to Cynthia's silver Ray,
And shaded all beneath: but now the Sun
With orient Beams had chas'd the dewy Night
From Earth and Heav'n; all Nature stood disclos'd.
When looking on the Neighb'ring Woods we saw
30  The Ghastly visage of a Man unknown,
An uncouth Feature, Meager, Pale and Wild,
Affliction's soul and terrible Dismay
Sate in his looks, his Face impair'd and worn.
With marks of Famine, speaking sore Distress.
His Locks were tangled, and his shaggy Beard
Matted with Filth, in all things else a Greek.
He first advanc'd in haste, but when he saw
Trojans and Trojan Arms, in mid Career
Stopt short, he back recoil'd as one surpriz'd:
40  But soon recov'ring speed, he ran, he flew
Precipitant, and thus with piteous Cries
Our Ears assail'd: 'By Heav'n's Eternal Fires,
By ev'ry God that sits Enthron'd on High,
By this good Light relieve a Wretch forlorn,
And bear me hence to any distant shore,
So I may shun this savage Race accurst.
'Tis true I fought among the Greeks that late
With Sword and Fire o're-turn'd Neptunian Troy,
And laid the labour of the Gods in Dust;

50 For which, if so the sad offence deserves,
Plung'd in the Deep for ever let me lye
Whelm'd under Seas; if Death must be my doom,
Let Man inflict it, and I die well-pleas'd.'
    He ended here, and now profuse of Tears
In suppliant mood fell prostrate at our Feet;
We bade him speak from whence, and what he was,
And how by stress of Fortune sunk thus low;
Anchises too with friendly aspect mild
Gave him his Hand, sure pledge of Amity;
60 When, thus encourag'd, he began his Tale.
    'I'm one, says he, of poor descent, my Name
Is Achaemenides, my country Greece,
Ulysses' sad compeer, who whilst he fled
The raging Cyclops, left me here behind
Disconsolate, forlorn, within the Cave
He left me, Giant Polypheme's dark cave;
A Dungeon wide and horrible, the Walls
On all sides furr'd with mouldy Damps, and hung
With clots of ropy Gore, and human Limbs,
70 His dire Repast: Himself's of mighty Size,
Hoarse in his Voice, and in his Visage Grim,
Intractable, that riots on the Flesh
Of mortal Men, and swills the vital Blood.
Him did I see snatch up with horrid Grasp
Two sprawling Greeks, in either Hand a Man;
I saw him when with huge tempestuous sway
He dasht and broke 'em on the Groundsil Edge;
The Pavement swam in Blood, the Walls around
Were spatter'd o're with Brains. He lapt the Blood,
80 And chew'd the tender Flesh still warm with Life,

---

**58** *Anchises*: shortly after this encounter, as the Trojans were sailing round the coast of Sicily, Aeneas' father died.
**62** Achaemenides seems to have been invented by Virgil in order to make use of Homer's story of the blinding of the Cyclops in *Odyssey* IX.

That swell'd and heav'd itself amidst his Teeth
As sensible of Pain. Not less meanwhile
Our Chief incens'd, and studious of Revenge,
Plots his Destruction, which he thus effects.
The Giant, gorg'd with Flesh, and Wine, and Blood,
Lay stretcht at length, and snoring in his Den,
Belching raw Gobbets from his Maw, o're-charg'd
With purple Wine and cruddl'd Gore, confus'd.
We gather'd round, and to his single Eye,
90    The single Eye that in his Forehead glar'd
Like a full Moon, or a broad burnisht Shield,
A forky Staff we dext'rously apply'd,
Which in the spacious Socket turning round,
Scoopt out the big round Gelly from its Orb.
    But let me not thus interpose Delays:
Fly, Mortals, fly this curst detested Race.
A hundred of the same stupendous size,
A hundred Cyclops live among the Hills,
Gigantick Brotherhood, that stalk along
100    With horrid Strides o're the high Mountains tops
Enormous in their Gait: I oft have heard
Their Voice and Tread, oft seen 'em as they past,
Sculking and scowring down, half dead with fear.
Thrice has the Moon washt all her Orb in Light,
Thrice travell'd o're, in her obscure sojourn,
The realms of Night inglorious, since I've liv'd
Amidst these Woods, gleaning from Thorns and Shrubs
A wretched sustenance.' As thus he spoke,
We saw descending from a Neighb'ring Hill
110    Blind Polypheme; by weary Steps and slow
The groping Giant with a Trunk of Pine
Explor'd his way; around, his woolly Flocks
Attending grazing; to the well-known Shore
He bent his Course, and on the Margin stood,
A hideous Monster, terrible, deform'd;
Full in the midst of his high Front, there gap'd

The spacious hollow where his Eye-ball roll'd,
A ghastly Orifice; He rins'd the Wound,
And washt away the Strings and clotted Blood
120  That cak'd within; then stalking through the Deep
He Fords the Ocean; while the topmost Wave
Scarce reaches up his middle side; we stood
Amaz'd, be sure, a sudden horror chill
Ran through each Nerve, and thrill'd in ev'ry Vein,
Till using all the force of Winds and Oars
We sped away; he heard us in our Course,
And with his out-stretch'd Arms around him grop'd,
But finding nought within his reach, he rais'd
Such hideous shouts that all the Ocean shook.
130  Ev'n Italy, tho' many a League remote,
In distant Ecchos answer'd; Aetna roar'd,
Through all its inmost winding Caverns roar'd.
    Rous'd with the sound, the mighty Family
Of one-ey'd Brothers hasten to the shore,
And gather round the bellowing Polypheme,
A dire assembly; we with eager haste
Work ev'ry one, and from afar behold
A Host of Giants cov'ring all the Shore.
    So stands a Forrest tall of Mountain Oaks
140  Advanc'd to mighty growth: the Traveller
Hears from the humble Valley where he rides
The hollow Murmurs of the Winds that blow
Amidst the Boughs, and at a distance sees
The shady tops of Trees unnumber'd rise,
A stately prospect, waving in the Clouds.          (1704)

# LAUDERDALE, RICHARD MAITLAND, EARL OF (1633–95)

## Virgil's Aeneids Book X, 818–1012 [Aen. X. 755–908] *The story of Lausus and Mezentius*

'This noble episode', as Dryden calls it, was one of two passages from the *Aeneid* which he translated in *Sylvae* (1685), the other being the story of Nisus and Euryalus. Lauderdale's version (printed here from the posthumous edition of his translation of Virgil, *c.* 1708) differs generally from both Dryden's 1685 and his 1697 texts, but there is one interesting correspondence. In line 54, the phrase 'noble emulation' also occurs in Dryden's 1685 text, but in 1697 this has been changed to 'generous indignation'.

The bloody fight both equally maintain
And equal numbers on both sides are slain.
They yield by turns, by turns advance again.
From heaven the gods behold the fruitless toil,
And pity restless mortals all the while.
On the side Venus, th' other Juno stands
While death is raging midst the numerous bands.
Again Mezentius shakes his massy spear
And threatening makes the field his presence fear.
10  Like huge Orion stalking through the tide,
Divides the waves, which scarce his shoulders hide:
Or like an ash, whose roots on hills are spread
Deep in the earth, so clouds obscure his head:
And so appears Mezentius thus array'd.

---

8 *Mezentius*: renegade king of the Etruscans, now exiled and fighting against his countrymen, who are allies of Aeneas. Cf. 190–91.
10 Orion, mighty hunter, a giant who in this simile resembles the Cyclops Polyphemus.

The Trojan chief at distance saw him stand
And then rejoyc'd to meet him hand in hand.
Mezentius firmly stood Aeneas' shock,
His vast foundations being like a rock;
Then with his eyes he measures out how far
20    His brawny arm can dart his ponderous spear,
And cries aloud with these profaning words:
'My sword and this right hand, these are Mezentius' gods.
That Trojan pirate's arms, my Lausus, here
I vow this day thou shalt in triumph wear.'
This said, he threw his spear with mighty force,
Which glancing from Aeneas' shield diverts its course,
And fixed its point in famed Antores' side –
He that in war t' Alcides was ally'd:
The great Antores, who from Argos chose
30    The towns of Italy for his repose,
By chance unhappily receives his death
And thinks on Argos with his latest breath.
    The pious Trojan then his javelin threw,
Which through the brazen shield and target flew;
A treble quilt and three bulls' hides it past
With powerful force, transpierc'd his groin at last.
But strength not failing yet, Aeneas draws
His shining sword, and follows on his blows;
Glad now to see Mezentius' blood, pursues,
40    And double force upon his foes renews.
Lausus sees this, and with deep grief oppress'd,
Flies to relieve his father thus distress'd.
(Here thy hard fate I must lament, dear youth,

---

23 The Trojan pirate is Aeneas; Lausus is Mezentius' son.
28 *Alcides*: Hercules
31–2 Dryden's version of these lines captures the pathos of Virgil's Latin
better than Lauderdale's: 'Now falling by another's wound, his eyes/He casts
to Heav'n, on Argos thinks, and dies' (*sternitur infelix alieno vulnere,*
*caelumque/aspicit et dulcis moriens reminiscitur Argos*).

And, to thy memory just, relate the truth.
Though time to come will doubt my lasting song
I can't forget a man so brave and young.)
Disabled now, the father quits the field,
And strives to draw the javelin from his shield;
Lausus springs forth to join the threatening foe,
50  To save his father and receive the blow;
At which loud shouts run round th' applauding field,
While Lausus does his vanquish'd father shield.
All fired with rage, all animated now,
Their darts with noble emulation throw.
The Dardan prince himself, poised like a rock,
Maintained the battle and sustained the shock.
    To some close covert so the ploughmen fly
When rattling hail or storms of wind are nigh;
But when the threatening clouds are overblown
60  And the sun shines, they to their work return.
Aeneas thus, while mastered in the field,
Rested beneath the safeguard of his shield
And Lausus warns (thus loudly does he cry):
'Why dost thou press thus close, why wilt thou die?
Urged on too rashly 'bove thy strength to move,
From filial duty and thy pious love?'
This naught abates his passion or his rage,
But moves Aeneas' patience to engage,
Whose anger, being kindled fresh, does wait
70  Only to finish Lausus' wretched fate.
Then with his powerful sword he forc'd his way
Through the fair breast where life and virtue lay.
The streaming blood through the light armour play'd
And stained the gilded coat his tender mother made.
The fleeting soul, as willing here to stay,
With heavy groans was loath to go away.
This when Aeneas saw so slowly pass
And death stand hovering o'er the beauteous face,
His bitter grief sad thoughts do in him move

80    Of Troy again and his paternal love.
     With this he tendered him his hand, and cry'd,
     'Unhappy youth, thou should'st be deify'd!
     Whate'er Aeneas can bestow, receive;
     Thy arms and sword, if valued, here I give;
     Thy body back to thy sad parents yield
     T'appease the Manes of the bloody field.
     This consolation in thy death receive,
     That great Aeneas' hands thy death did give.'
     He stops; his friends then rais'd him from the ground
90    While his hair dangled in the bloody wound.
        And now the father stood by Tyber's streams
     To cleanse his wounds, and ease his wearied limbs;
     Against a tree his fainting body leans
     And a small bough his helm of brass sustains;
     His ponderous arms lie scatter'd on the grass,
     While all his warriors round about him pass.
     He, faint and sick, hands down his head to rest,
     His neck reclines, his beard rests on his pensive breast.
     Much he of Lausus asks and much enquires,
100   Why he's not yet returned, why his desires
     Are not obeyed, to bring him to the field?
     Which they observed but dead, alas, borne on his shield.
     His weeping friends contrive to bring him home.
     He at a distance far presaged his doom;
     His hoary head with dust he covers o'er
     And lifts his hands to heav'n from Tyber's shore.
     Then the dear corpse embraces, and then cries:
     'What pleasure have I had of life, what joys,
     That I should live so wretched as to see
110   Him I begot, a sacrifice for me?
     Alas, my Lausus, I am dead in thee.
     'Tis now a woeful exile that I feel,
     Since I behold a wound I cannot heal.
     My guilt has tarnish'd much thy deathless name,
     Chas'd me from empire, exil'd as I am.

This is but what I to my country owe
And willingly again could undergo;
Tho' I ha'nt yet bid farewell to the light,
Howe'er I'll soon remove th'ingrateful sight.
120  With that his feeble limbs he rais'd from ground,
Ready to stagger with the bleeding wound;
Boldly resolv'd to mount his courser straight,
With constant care, well manag'd for the bit,
Whom he had often mounted with success,
His trust in battle, and his pride in peace.
Then thus he spake his sorrowing tale of woe:
'O Rhaebus, we too much of life do know,
If mortals would but be contented so.
Either this day bring back Aeneas' head,
130  And Trojan spoils away in triumph lead;
Or let me some revenge for murther take,
This day, some vengeance for my Lausus' sake.
But if the Fates a conquest still deny,
Then with thy conquer'd master thou wilt die;
For after me, I trust, thou wilt disdain
A Trojan for thy lord, or foreign rein.'
This said, he mounts his trusty steed again;
Does both his hands with pointed javelins load;
His brazen helm with crested horse-hair flowed;
140  He spurs the courser on, all in a flame
With grief and madness, and the loss of fame,
With conscious thought, and sense of secret shame;
Then call'd aloud three times Aeneas' name,
The Trojan knew the voice, and to the challenge came;
Then with a joyful heart, 'Great Jove,' he said:
'And thou, bright Phoebus, now to arms persuade
This boasting challenger.' He said no more,
But with his dreadful spear, mounted before,
He hastens to Mezentius, who thus cries:
150  'Thou threat'st in vain, the murthered Lausus lies
Extended on the strand; this was, I own,

The only way that I could be undone.
I fear not death, but partial fate defy;
Cease to insult, for I come here to die.
Howe'er, I'll give thee this before I go' –
And cast a whizzing dart upon his foe.
Then plies his hand, and doubles on his blow.
This way and that he wheels his horse around
And swiftly traverses the dusty ground.
160 Aeneas' golden shield the strokes sustain,
Whilst he casts darts on every side in vain.
Three times the Trojan all his force withstood,
And bore upon his shield an iron wood:
Vex'd with delay, and now impatient grown,
Thus to defend without proceeding on;
At last o'er power'd with an unequal force
He plucks a spear and darts it at his horse;
Just in the temples did the lance remain,
Gauling the steed with more than mortal pain;
170 Who bounds, and rising beats the air in vain,
Then backward tumbles from his frantic height,
And casts his rider with oppressive weight.
   From both the armies mingled shouts arise,
Trojans and Latins echo to the skies.
Aeneas quickly brandishes his sword,
And to him utters this disdainful word:
'Now where are proud Mezentius' threats? and where
His haughty words? are they all lost in air?'
He, struggling hard for breath, at last replies:
180 'My bitter foe, why dost thou tyrannize?
Why threaten death to him who scorns his fate?
Death's no discredit, though unfortunate.
I came not here a victory to find,
But to my Lausus' death my life resign'd;
When he expired, my passport too was sign'd.
Nor risk I life; I'm sure my son ne'er made
Such terms for me; but if I could persuade

My conquering foe to grant me my request,
I beg a grave to give me peaceful rest,
190   To screen me from the furious rage of those
That from my subjects are become my foes.
Grant me but this, and I contented die;
Oh! let me by my much–lov'd Lausus lie.'
Then to his throat apply'd the fatal steel
And drench'd his arms by his own bloody will.          (*c.* 1708)


# ALEXANDER POPE (1685–1744)

## Summer: the Second Pastoral, or Alexis

Pope's four pastorals (one for each of the four seasons) first appeared in *Tonson's Miscellany* (1708), from which the present text, which differs in a few places from later editions, is printed. Written in 1704, the pastorals are among Pope's earliest compositions, drawing freely on Virgil's *Eclogues* and Spenser's *Shepheardes Calender.* The poem is dedicated (see line 9) to the physician Samuel Garth.

A faithful Swain, whom Love had taught to sing,
Bewail'd his Fate beside a silver Spring;
Where gentle Thames his winding Waters leads
Thro' verdant Forests, and thro' flow'ry Meads.
There while he mourn'd, the Streams forgot to flow,
The Flocks around a dumb Compassion show,
The Naiads wept in ev'ry watry Bower,
And Jove consented in a silent Show'r.
    Accept, O Garth, the Muse's early Lays,
10   That adds this wreath of Ivy to thy Bays;
Hear what from Love unpractis'd Hearts endure,
From Love, the sole disease thou canst not cure!
    Ye shady Beeches, and ye cooling Streams,
Defence from Phoebus', not from Cupid's Beams;

To you I mourn; nor to the deaf I sing,
The woods shall answer, and their Echo ring.
Ev'n Hills and Rocks attend my doleful Lay,
Why art thou prouder and more hard than they?
The bleating Sheep with my Complaints agree,
20    They parch'd with Heat, and I inflam'd by thee.
The sultry Sirius burns the thirsty Plains,
While in thy Heart Eternal Winter reigns.
    Where are ye Muses, in what Lawn or Grove,
While your Alexis pines in hopeless Love?
In those fair Fields where sacred Isis glides,
Or else where Cam his winding Vales divides?
As in the crystal Spring I view my Face,
Fresh rising Blushes paint the watry Glass;
But since those Graces please thy Sight no more,
30    I'll shun the Fountains which I sought before.
Once I was skill'd in ev'ry Herb that grew,
And ev'ry Plant that drinks the morning Dew;
Ah wretched Shepherd, what avails thy Art,
To cure thy Lambs, but not to heal thy Heart!
    Let other Swains attend the rural Care,
Feed fairer Flocks, or richer Fleeces sheer:
But nigh that Mountain let me tune my Lays,
Embrace my Love, and bind my Brows with Bays.
That Flute is mine, which Colin's tuneful Breath
40    Inspir'd when living, and bequeath'd in Death.
He said: Alexis, take this Pipe, the same
That taught the Groves my Rosalinda's Name –
Yet soon the Reeds shall hang on yonder Tree,
For ever silent, since despis'd by thee.

---

15–16 Cf. Virgil, Eclogue X, 8, and Ogilby's translation: 'Nor to the deaf
shall we our numbers sing,/Since woods in answering us with echoes ring.'
Both Ogilby and Pope quote from Spenser's 'Epithalamium'.
23–4 Cf. Virgil, Eclogue X, 9–10; Milton, 'Lycidas', 50.
39–40 Cf. Virgil, Eclogue II, 36–8. Colin is from Spenser, *Shepheardes
Calender.*

O were I made by some transforming Pow'r,
The captive Bird that sings within thy Bow'r.
Then might my Voice thy list'ning Ears employ,
And I those kisses he receives, enjoy.
  And yet my Numbers please the rural Throng,
50  Rough Satyrs dance, and Pan applauds the Song:
The Nymphs forsaking ev'ry Cave and Spring,
Their early Fruit, and milk-white Turtles bring.
Each amorous Nymph prefers her Gifts in vain,
On you their Gifts are all bestow'd again!
For you the Swains the fairest Flow'rs design,
And in one Garland all their Beauties join;
Accept the Wreath which you deserve alone,
In whom all Beauties are compriz'd in One.
  See what Delights in Sylvan Scenes appear!
60  Descending Gods have found Elysium here.
In woods bright Venus with Adonis stray'd,
And chast Diana haunts the Forest Shade.
Come, lovely Nymph, and bless the silent Hours,
When Swains from Sheering seek their nightly Bow'rs;
When weary Reapers quit the sultry Field,
And crown'd with Corn, their Thanks to Ceres yield.
This harmless Grove no lurking Viper hides,
But in my Breast the Serpent Love abides.
Here Bees from Blossoms sip the rosie Dew,
70  But your Alexis knows no Sweet but you.
Some God conduct you to these blissful Seats,
The mossie Fountains and the Green Retreats!
Where-e'er you walk, cool Gales shall fan the Glade,
Trees, where you sit, shall crowd into a Shade,
Where-e'er you tread, the blushing Flow'rs shall rise,
And all things flourish where you turn your Eyes.

---

**67** Cf. Virgil, Eclogue III, 93.
**72** *mossie Fountains*: cf. Virgil, Eclogue VII, 45.
**73–6** These lines were set to music by Handel in his *Semele*.

Oh! how I long with you to pass my Days,
Invoke the Muses, and resound your Praise;
Your praise the tuneful birds to Heav'n shall bear,
80  And list'ning Wolves grow milder as they hear.
But would you sing, and rival Orpheus' strain,
The wondring Forests soon should dance again,
The moving Mountains hear the pow'rful Call,
And headlong Streams hang list'ning in their Fall!
But see, the Shepherds shun the Noon-day Heat,
The lowing herds to murm'ring Brooks retreat,
To closer Shades the panting Flocks remove,
Ye Gods! and is there no Relief for Love?
But soon the Sun with milder Rays descends
90  To the cool Ocean, where his Journey ends;
On me Love's fiercer Flames for ever prey,
By Night he scorches, as he burns by day.                    (1708)


# AMBROSE PHILIPS (1675–1749)

## The Sixth Pastoral: An Imitation of Virgil's Singing Contests [Ecl. III, VII]

The conventional introduction and conclusion to the actual contest are here omitted.

First printed in *Tonson's Miscellany: Part VI* (1708), in which Pope's pastorals also appeared: the style and content of Philips's alternating quatrains closely resemble Pope's first pastoral (Spring). The present text is printed from the enlarged and revised edition of Philips's *Pastorals, Epistles, Odes and Other Original Poems* (1748).

---

**79–80** This couplet was changed in subsequent editions, the poet having realized 'the absurdity of introducing wolves into England'. Spenser also mentions wolves in the *Shepheardes Calender* (July and September).

HOBBINOL
The snows are melted, and the kindly rain
Descends on every herb, and every grain.
Soft balmy breezes breathe along the sky:
The bloomy season of the year is nigh.

LANQUET
The cuckoo calls aloud his wandering love;
The turtle's moan is heard in every grove;
The pastures change; the warbling linnets sing:
Prepare to welcome in the gawdy spring.

HOBBINOL
When locusts in the ferny bushes cry,
10  When ravens pant, and snakes in caverns ly,
Graze then in woods, and quit the shadeless plain,
Else shall ye press the spungy teat in vain.

LANQUET
When greens to yellow vary, and ye see
The ground bestrew'd with fruits off every tree,
And stormy winds are heard, think winter near,
Nor trust too far to the declining year.

HOBBINOL
Woe then, alack! befall the spendthrift swain,
When frost, and snow, and hail, and sleet, and rain,
By turns chastise him, while, through little care,
20  His sheep, unshelter'd, pine in nipping air.

---

**1–8** Cf. the opening of Horace's *Odes* IV, vii, '*Diffugere nives*'.

LANQUET

The lad of forecast then untroubled sees
The white-bleak plains, and silvery frosted trees,
He fends his flock, and, clad in homely frize,
In his warm cot the wintry blast defies.

HOBBINOL

Full fain, O bless'd Eliza! I would praise
Thy maiden rule, and Albion's golden days:
Then gentle Sidney liv'd, the shepherd's friend:
Eternal blessings on his shade attend!

LANQUET

Thrice happy shepherds now! for Dorset loves
30   The country-muse and our resounding groves,
While Anna reigns: O, ever may she reign!
And bring on earth the golden age again.

HOBBINOL

I love in secret all a beauteous maid,
And have my love in secret all repaid;
This coming night she plights her troth to me:
Divine her name, and thou the victor be.

LANQUET

Mild as the lamb, unharmful as the dove,
True as the turtle, is the maid I love:
How we in secret love, I shall not say:
40   Divine her name, and I give up the day.

---

**23** *frize*: a coarse woollen cloth
**29** *Dorset*: Charles Sackville, Earl of Dorset, a Restoration poet, admired by
Pope
**36** *Divine*: guess

HOBBINOL

Soft on a cowslip-bank my love and I
Together lay: a brook ran murmuring by:
A thousand tender things to me she said;
And I a thousand tender things repaid.

LANQUET

In summer-shade, behind the cocking hay,
What kind endearing words did she not say!
Her lap, with apron deck'd, she fondly spread,
And strok'd my cheek, and lull'd my leaning head.

HOBBINOL

Breathe soft ye winds, ye waters gently flow:
50   Shield her ye trees: ye flowers around her grow:
Ye swains, I beg ye, pass in silence by:
My love in yonder vale asleep does ly.

LANQUET

Once Delia slept on easy moss reclin'd,
Her lovely limbs half bare, and rude the wind:
I smooth'd her coats and stole a silent kiss:
Condemn me, shepherds, if I did amiss.

HOBBINOL

As Marian bath'd, by chance I passed by:
She blush'd, and at me glanc'd a sidelong eye:
Then, cowering in the treacherous stream, she try'd
60   Her tempting form, yet still in vain, to hide.

---

**45–8** A reminiscence of *A Midsummer Night's Dream*, IV, i.

LANQUET

As I to cool me, bathed one sultry day,
Fond Lydia, lurking, in the sedges lay:
The wanton laugh'd, and seem'd in haste to fly,
Yet oft she stopp'd, and oft she turn'd her eye.

HOBBINOL

When first I saw, would I had never seen,
Young Lycet lead the dance on yonder green,
Intent upon her beauties, as she mov'd,
Poor heedless wretch! at unawares I lov'd.

LANQUET

When Lucy decks with flowers her swelling breast,
70  And on her elbow leans, dissembling rest,
Unable to refrain my madding mind,
Nor herds, nor pastures, worth my care I find.

HOBBINOL

Come, Rosalind, O come! for, wanting thee,
Our peopled vale a desert is to me.
Come, Rosalind, O come! My brindled kine,
My snowy sheep, my farm and all, are thine.

LANQUET

Come, Rosalind, O come! Here shady bowers,
Here are cool fountains, and here springing flowers:
Come, Rosalind! Here ever let us stay,
80  And sweetly while the livelong time away.

HOBBINOL

In vain the seasons of the moon I know,
The force of healing herbs, and where they grow:
No herb there is, no season to remove
From my fond heart the racking pains of love.

LANQUET

What profits me, that I in charms have skill,
And ghosts and goblins order as I will,
Yet have, with all my charms, no power to lay
The sprite that breaks my quiet night and day.

HOBBINOL

O that, like Colin, I had skill in rhimes,
90    To purchase credit with succeeding times!
Sweet Colin Clout, who never yet had peer,
Who sung through all the seasons of the year.

LANQUET

Let me like Merlin sing: his voice had power
To free the 'clipsing moon at midnight hour:
And as he sung the fairies with their queen,
In mantles blue, came tripping o'er the green.

HOBBINOL

Last eve of May did I not hear them sing,
And see their dance? And I can shew the ring,
Where, hand in hand, they shift their feet so light:
100    The grass springs greener from their tread by night.

LANQUET

But hast thou seen their king, in rich array,
Fam'd Oberon, with damask'd robe so gay,
And gemmy crown, by moonshine sparkling far,
And azure scepter, pointed with a star?                    (1708)

---

**89, 91** *Colin, Colin Clout*: Spenser's pastoral pseudonym
**96** *mantles blue*: cf. 'Lycidas', 192.

# JAMES THOMSON (1700–1748)

## The Seasons, 'Winter', extract from the preface

The poem contains much material taken indirectly from the *Georgics*. The following passage is from the Preface to the second (1726) edition of 'Winter', the first of the four Seasons to be published. Printed from James Sambrook's edition (1981).

. . . 'The best, both antient and modern, poets, have been passionately fond of Retirement and Solitude. The wild romantic Country was their delight. And they seem never to have been more happy, than when lost in unfrequented Fields, far from the little, busy world, they were at Leisure, to meditate and sing the Works of Nature . . .

It was this Devotion to the Works of Nature that, in his *Georgicks*, inspired the rural Virgil to write so inimitably; and who can forbear joining with him in this Declaration of his, which has been the Rapture of Ages.

> Me vero primum dulces ante omnia Musae,
> quarum sacra fero ingenti percussus amore,
> accipiant caelique vias et sidera monstrent,
> defectus solis varios lunaeque labores;
> unde tremor terris, qua vi maria alta tumescant
> obicibus ruptis rursusque in se ipsa residant,
> quid tantum Oceano properent se tingere soles
> hiberni, vel quae tardis mora noctibus obstet.
> sin has ne possim naturae accedere partis
> frigidus obstiterit circum praecordia sanguis,
> rura mihi et rigui placeant in vallibus omnes,
> flumina amem silvasque inglorius.

> (*Georgics* II, 475–86)

Which may be Englished thus.

> Me may the Muses, my supreme delight!
> Whose priest I am, smit with immense Desire,
> Snatch to their Care; the Starry Tracts disclose,
> The Sun's Distress, the Labours of the Moon:
> Whence the Earth quakes: and by what Force the Deeps
> Heave at the Rocks, then on themselves reflow:
> Why Winter-Suns to plunge in Ocean speed:
> And what retards the lazy Summer-Night.
> But, least I should those mystic-Truths attain,
> If the cold Current freezes round my Heart,
> The Country Me, the brooky vales may please
> Mid woods and streams, unknown.                    (1726)

# JAMES THOMSON

## The Seasons, 'Autumn', 1235-end

An imitation of *Georgics* II, 458–540. The final paragraph is an expanded adaptation of the version of *Georgics* II, 475–86, included in the preface to 'Winter' printed above.

> Oh knew he but his Happiness, of Men
> The happiest he! who far from public Rage,
> Deep in the Vale, with a *choice Few* retir'd,
> Drinks the pure Pleasures of the RURAL LIFE.
> What tho' the Dome be wanting, whose proud Gate,
> Each Morning, vomits out the sneaking Croud
> Of Flatterers false, and in their Turn abus'd?
> Vile Intercourse! What tho' the glittering Robe,
> Of every Hue reflected Light can give,
> Or floating loose, or stiff with mazy Gold,
> The Pride and Gaze of Fools! oppress him not?

10

What tho', from utmost Land and Sea purvey'd,
To Disappointment, and fallacious Hope:
For him each rarer tributary Life
Bleeds not, and his insatiate Table heaps
With Luxury, and Death? What tho' his Bowl
Flames not with costly Juice; nor sunk in Beds,
Oft of gay Care, he tosses out the Night,
Or melts the thoughtless Hours in idle State?
What tho' he knows not those fantastic Joys,
20   That still amuse the Wanton, still deceive;
A Face of Pleasure, but a Heart of Pain;
Their hollow Moments undelighted all?
Sure Peace is his; a solid Life, estrang'd
To Disappointment, and fallacious Hope;
Rich in Content, in Nature's Bounty rich,
In Herbs and Fruits; whatever greens the Spring,
When Heaven descends in Showers; or bends the Bough,
When Summer reddens, and when Autumn beams;
Or in the Wintry Glebe whatever lies
30   Conceal'd, and fattens with the richest Sap:
These are not wanting; nor the milky Drove,
Luxuriant, spread o'er all the lowing Vale;
Nor bleating Mountains; nor the Chide of Streams,
And Hum of Bees, inviting Sleep sincere
Into the guiltless Breast, beneath the Shade,
Or thrown at large amid the fragrant Hay;
Nor Aught besides of Prospect, Grove, or Song,
Dim Grottoes, gleaming Lakes, and Fountain clear.
Here too dwells simple Truth; plain Innocence;
40   Unsully'd Beauty; sound unbroken Youth,
Patient of Labour, with a Little pleas'd;
Health ever-blooming; unambitious Toil;
Calm Contemplation, and poetic Ease.

Let others brave the Flood in Quest of Gain,
And beat, for joyless Months, the gloomy Wave.
Let such as deem it Glory to destroy

Rush into Blood, the Sack of Cities seek;
Unpierc'd, exulting in the Widow's Wail,
The Virgin's Shriek, and Infant's trembling Cry.
50   Let some, far-distant from their native Soil,
Urg'd or by Want or harden'd Avarice,
Find other Lands beneath another Sun.
Let This thro' Cities work his eager Way,
By legal Outrage, and establish'd Guile,
The social Sense extinct; and That ferment
Mad into Tumult the seditious Herd,
Or melt them down to Slavery. Let These
Insnare the Wretched in the Toils of Law,
Fomenting Discord, and perplexing Right,
60   An iron Race! and Those of fairer Front,
But equal Inhumanity, in Courts,
Delusive Pomp, and dark Cabals, delight;
Wreathe the deep Bow, diffuse the lying Smile,
And tread the weary Labyrinth of State.
While He, from all the stormy Passions free
That restless Men involve, hears, and but hears,
At Distance safe, the Human Tempest roar,
Wrapt close in conscious Peace. The Fall of Kings,
The Rage of Nations, and the Crush of States,
70   Move not the Man, who, from the World escap'd,
In still Retreats, and flowery Solitudes,
To Nature's Voice attends, from Month to Month,
And Day to Day, thro' the revolving Year;
Admiring, sees Her in her every Shape;
Feels all her sweet Emotions at his Heart;
Takes what she liberal gives, nor thinks of more.
He, when young Spring protrudes the bursting Gems,
Marks the first Bud, and sucks the healthful Gale
Into his freshen'd Soul; her genial Hours
80   He full enjoys; and not a Beauty blows,
And not an opening Blossom breathes in vain.
In Summer he, beneath the living Shade,

Such as o'er frigid Tempè wont to wave,
Or Hemus cool, reads what the Muse, of These
Perhaps, has in immortal Numbers sung;
Or what she dictates writes; and, oft an Eye
Shot round, rejoices in the vigorous Year.
When Autumn's yellow Luster gilds the World,
And tempts the sickled Swain into the Field,
90    Seiz'd by the general Joy, his Heart distends
With gentle Throws; and, thro' the tepid Gleams
Deep-musing, then he *best* exerts his Song.
Even Winter wild to him is full of Bliss.
The mighty Tempest, and the hoary Waste,
Abrupt, and deep, stretch'd o'er the bury'd Earth,
Awake to solemn Thought. At Night the Skies,
Disclos'd, and kindled, by refining Frost,
Pour every Luster on th' exalted Eye.
A Friend a Book the stealing Hours secure,
100   And mark them down for Wisdom. With swift Wing,
O'er Land and Sea Imagination roams;
Or Truth, divinely breaking on his Mind,
Elates his Being, and unfolds his Powers;
Or in his Breast Heroic Virtue burns.
The Touch of Kindred too and Love he feels;
The modest Eye, whose Beams on His alone
Extatic shine; the little strong Embrace
Of prattling Children, twin'd around his Neck,
And emulous to please him, calling forth
110   The fond parental Soul. Nor Purpose gay,
Amusement, Dance, or Song, he sternly scorns;
For Happiness and true Philosophy
Are of the social still, and smiling Kind.
This is the Life which those who fret in Guilt,
And guilty Cities, never knew; the Life,
Led by primeval Ages, uncorrupt,
When Angels dwelt, and GOD himself, with Man!

Oh Nature! all-sufficient! over all!
Inrich me with the Knowledge of thy Works!
120 Snatch me to Heaven; thy rolling Wonders there,
World beyond World, in infinite Extent,
Profusely scatter'd o'er the blue Immense,
Shew me; their Motions, Periods, and their Laws,
Give me to scan; thro' the disclosing Deep
Light my blind Way: the mineral *Strata* there;
Thrust, blooming, thence the vegetable World;
O'er that the rising System, more complex,
Of Animals; and higher still, the Mind,
The vary'd Scene of quick-compounded Thought,
130 And where the mixing Passions endless shift;
These ever open to my ravish'd Eye:
A Search, the Flight of Time can ne'er exhaust!
But if to that unequal; if the Blood,
In sluggish Streams about my Heart, forbid
That *best* Ambition; under closing Shades,
Inglorious, lay me by the lowly Brook,
And whisper to my Dreams. From THEE begin,
Dwell all on THEE, with THEE conclude my Song;
And let me never never stray from THEE!                    (1746)

# JOSEPH WARTON (1722–1800)

## Eclogue II [Ecl. II]

Printed from the third edition (1777) of *The Works of Virgil*, with facing Latin text and English translations of the *Aeneid* by Christopher Pitt and of the *Eclogues* and *Georgics* by Warton, who also contributed an essay on pastoral and didactic poetry.

A comparison between this version and Creech's shows how little the idiom and diction of couplet discourse had changed in a hundred years, so decisively had its technique been defined by Dryden and his circle.

> Young Corydon with hopeless love adored
> The fair Alexis, fav'rite of his lord.
> Midst shades of thickest beech he pin'd alone,
> To the wild woods and mountains made his moan,
> Still day by day, in incoherent strains,
> ('Twas all he could) despairing told his pains.
> 'Wilt thou ne'er pity me, thou cruel youth,
> Unmindful of my verse, my vows, and truth?
> Still, dear Alexis, from my passions fly?
> 10  Unheard and unregarded must I die?
> Now flocks in cooling shades avoid the heats,
> And the green lizard to his brake retreats,
> Now Thestylis the thyme and garlic pounds,
> And weary reapers leave the sultry grounds;
> Thee still I follow o'er the burning plains
> And join the shrill cicada's plaintive strains.
>       Were it not better calmly to have borne
> Proud Amaryllis' or Menalcas' scorn?
> Tho' he was black, and thou art heavenly fair?
> 20  How much you trust that beauteous hue beware!
> The privet's silver flow'rs we still neglect,
> But dusky hyacinths with care collect.

Thou know'st not whom thou scorn'st – what snowy kine,
What luscious milk, what rural stores are mine!
Mine are a thousand lambs in yonder vales,
My milk in summer's drought nor winter fails;
Nor sweeter to his herds Amphion sung,
While with his voice Boeotia's mountains rung.
Nor am I so deformed! myself I viewed
30  On the smoothe surface of the glassy flood,
By winds unmov'd, and be that image true,
I dread not Daphnis' charms, tho' judged by you.
    Oh that you loved the fields and shady grots,
To dwell with me in bowers and lowly Cots,
To drive the kids to fold, the stags to pierce;
Then should'st thou emulate Pan's skilful verse,
Warbling with me in woods; 'twas mighty Pan
To join with wax the various reeds began;
Pan, the great god of all our subject plains,
40  Protects and loves the cattle and the swains;
Nor thou disdain, thy tender rosy lip
Deep to indent with such a master's pipe.
To gain that art, how much Amyntas tried!
This pipe Damoetas gave me as he died;
Seven joints it boasts, – be thine this gift, he said:
Amyntas envious sighed, and hung the head.
Besides, two dappled kids, which late I found
Deep in a dale with dangerous rocks around,
For thee I nurse; with these, O come and play!
50  They drain two swelling udders every day.
These Thestylis hath begg'd, but begg'd in vain;
Now be they hers, since you my gifts disdain.
Come, beauteous boy! the nymphs in baskets bring
For thee the loveliest lilies of the spring;
Behold for thee the neighbouring Naiad crops

---

**45** Warton has retained a Virgilian detail omitted by Creech: the pipe
consisted of seven reeds joined together with wax.
**51–2** The close similarity between Warton's version and Creech's (lines 52–3)
is probably coincidence.

The violet pale and poppy's fragrant tops;
Narcissus' buds she joins with sweet jonquils,
And mingles cinnamon with daffodils.
With tender hyacinths of darker dyes,
60    The yellow marigold diversifies.
Thee, with the downy quince, and chestnuts sweet,
Which once my Amaryllis loved, I'll greet;
To gather plums of glossy hue will toil,
These shall be honoured if they gain thy smile.
Ye myrtles too I'll crop and verdant bays,
For each so placed a richer scent conveys.
O Corydon, a rustic hind thou art!
Thy presents ne'er will touch Alexis' heart!
Give all thou canst, exhaust thy rural store,
70    Iolas, thy rich rival, offers more.
    What have I spoke? betrayed by heedless thought,
The boar into my crystal springs have brought!
Wretch that I am! to the tempestuous blast
O I have given my blooming flowers to waste!
Whom dost thou fly? the gods of heaven above,
And Trojan Paris deigned in woods to rove;
Let Pallas build, and dwell in lofty towers,
Be our delight the fields and shady bowers:
Lions the wolves, and wolves the kids pursue,
80    The kids sweet thyme, and I still follow you.
Lo! labouring oxen spent with toil and heat,
In loosened traces from the plough retreat,
The sun is scarce above the mountains seen,
Lengthening the shadows o'er the dusky green;
But still my bosom feels not evening cool,
Love reigns unchecked by time, or bounds, or rule.
What frenzy, Corydon, invades thy breast?
Thy elms grow wild, thy vineyard lies undrest;
No more thy necessary labours leave,
90    Renew thy works, and osier-baskets weave:
If this Alexis treat thee with disdain,
Thou'lt find another and a kinder swain.'

(1777)

# PERCY BYSSHE SHELLEY
(1792–1822)

## The final chorus from 'Hellas'

Shelley's poem contains many allusions to Virgil's Fourth Eclogue, in which the poet foretells the return of the Golden Age.

> The world's great age begins anew,
>     The golden years return,
> The earth doth like a snake renew
>     Her winter weeds outworn:
> Heaven smiles, and faiths and empires gleam,
> Like wrecks of a dissolving dream.
>
> A brighter Hellas rears its mountains
>     From waves serener far;
> A new Peneus rolls his fountains
> 10  Against the morning star.
> Where fairer Tempes bloom, there sleep
> Young Cyclads on a sunnier deep.
>
> A loftier Argo cleaves the main,
>     Fraught with a later prize;
> Another Orpheus sings again,
>     And loves, and weeps, and dies.
> A new Ulysses leaves once more
> Calypso for his native shore.

---

**9–12** These evocative Greek place-names occur in *Georgics* IV and *Aeneid* III.
**13–18** Cf. Eclogue IV, 34–6.

Oh, write no more the tale of Troy,
20      If earth Death's scroll must be!
Nor mix with Laian rage the joy
      Which dawns upon the free:
Although a subtler Sphinx renew
Riddles of death Thebes never knew.

Another Athens shall arise,
      And to remoter time
Bequeath, like sunset to the skies,
      The splendour of its prime;
And leave, if nought so bright may live,
30   All earth can take or Heaven can give.

Saturn and Love their long repose
      Shall burst, more bright and good
Than all who fell, than One who rose,
      Than many unsubdued:
Not gold, not blood, their altar dowers,
But votive tears and symbol flowers.

Oh, cease! must hate and death return?
      Cease! must men kill and die?
Cease! drain not to its dregs the urn
40      Of bitter prophecy.
The world is weary of the past,
Oh, might it die or rest at last!                (1822)

---

**21–4** refers to the story of Oedipus, son of Laius, king of Thebes, who solved
the riddle of the Sphinx.

# WILLIAM WORDSWORTH
(1770–1850)

Translation of Part of the First Book of the Aeneid,
1–94 [Aen. I. 657–722] *Venus plots to work on Dido's
incipient love for Aeneas*

Part of a translation of the end of Book I written *c.* 1816 and
published in the *Philological Museum*, 1832. It was not reprinted by
the poet, who also translated several other passages of Virgil.

> But Cytherea, studious to invent
> Arts yet untried, upon new counsels bent,
> Resolves that Cupid, chang'd in form and face
> To young Ascanius, should assume his place;
> Present the maddening gifts, and kindle heat
> Of passion at the bosom's inmost seat.
> She dreads the treacherous house, the double tongue;
> She burns, she frets – by Juno's rancour stung;
> The calm of night is powerless to remove
> These cares, and thus she speaks to winged Love:
> 'O son, my strength, my power! who dost despise
> What, save thyself, none dares through earth and skies
> The giant-quelling bolts of Jove, I flee,
> O son, a suppliant to thy deity!
> What perils meet Æneas in his course,
> How Juno's hate with unrelenting force
> Pursues thy brother – this to thee is known;
> And oft-times hast thou made my griefs thine own.
> Him now the generous Dido by soft chains
> Of bland entreaty at her court detains;

10

20

---

1 *Cytherea*: Venus
17 *thy brother*: Cupid and Aeneas were both Venus' sons.

Junonian hospitalities prepare
Such apt occasion that I dread a snare.
Hence, ere some hostile God can intervene,
Would I, by previous wiles, inflame the queen
With passion for Æneas, such strong love
That at my beck, mine only, she shall move.
Hear, and assist; – the father's mandate calls
His young Ascanius to the Tyrian walls;
He comes, my dear delight, – and costliest things
30    Preserv'd from fire and flood for presents brings.
Him will I take, and in close covert keep,
'Mid groves Idalian, lull'd to gentle sleep,
Or on Cythera's far-sequestered steep,
That he may neither know what hope is mine,
Nor by his presence traverse the design.
Do thou, but for a single night's brief space,
Dissemble; be that boy in form and face.
And when enraptured Dido shall receive
Thee to her arms, and kisses interweave
40    With many a fond embrace, while joy runs high,
And goblets crown the proud festivity,
Instil thy subtle poison, and inspire,
At every touch, an unsuspected fire.'


    Love, at the word, before his mother's sight
Puts off his wings, and walks, with proud delight,
Like young Iulus; but the gentlest dews
Of slumber Venus sheds, to circumfuse
The true Ascanius steep'd in placid rest;
Then wafts him, cherish'd on her careful breast,
50    Through upper air to an Idalian glade,
Where he on soft *amaracus* is laid,
With breathing flowers embraced, and fragrant shade.

---

**32** Idalia is a grove in Cyprus.
**51** *amaracus* (so in the Latin): marjoram

But Cupid, following cheerily his guide
Achates, with the gifts to Carthage hied;
And, as the hall he entered, there, between
The sharers of her golden couch, was seen
Reclin'd in festal pomp the Tyrian queen.
The Trojans too (Æneas at their head),
On couches lie, with purple overspread:
60 Meantime in canisters is heap'd the bread,
Pellucid water for the hands is borne,
And napkins of smooth texture, finely shorn.
Within are fifty handmaids, who prepare,
As they in order stand, the dainty fare;
And fume the household deities with store
Of odorous incense; while a hundred more
Match'd with an equal number of like age,
But each of manly sex, a docile page,
Marshal the banquet, giving with due grace
70 To cup or viand its appointed place.
The Tyrians rushing in, an eager band,
Their painted couches seek, obedient to command.
They look with wonder on the gifts – they gaze
Upon Iulus, dazzled with the rays
That from his ardent countenance are flung,
And charm'd to hear his simulating tongue;
Nor pass unprais'd the robe and veil divine,
Round which the yellow flowers and wandering foliage
                                                        twine.

   But chiefly Dido, to the coming ill
80 Devoted, strives in vain her vast desires to fill;
She views the gifts; upon the child then turns
Insatiable looks, and gazing burns.

---

77–8 Wordsworth has evidently borrowed from Dryden here: 'Nor pass
unprais'd the vest and veil divine/Which wand'ring foliage and rich flow'rs
entwine.'

To ease a father's cheated love he hung
Upon Æneas, and around him clung;
Then seeks the queen; with her his arts he tries;
She fastens on the boy enamour'd eyes,
Clasps in her arms, nor weens (O lot unblest!)
How great a God, incumbent o'er her breast,
Would fill it with his spirit. He, to please
90   His Acidalian mother, by degrees
Blots out Sichaeus, studious to remove
The dead, by influx of a living love,
By stealthy entrance of a perilous guest,
Troubling a heart that had been long at rest.                    (1832)


# JAMES HENRY (1798–1876)

[Aen. VI. 237–330] *The descent into the underworld*

During the years 1845–53 Henry made versions of passages from
*Aeneid* I–VI under the title 'Six Photographs of Heroic Times',
published in a miscellany entitled *My Book* (1853). See further,
Introduction, p. xxvii.

By a bláck lake protécted
And glóomy woods róund,
There gáped with a vást
Awful yáwn a deep cávern
All rúgged with shíngle,
Over which without hárm
Could no flýing thing páss,

---

**90** *Acidalian*: a rarely used epithet for Venus, only here in Virgil and
unexplained.
**91** *Sichaeus*: Dido's dead husband, to whom she had vowed lifelong fidelity.

Such a stéam from its dárk jaws
Exháled to heaven's cónvex;
10    For which réason the Gráii
The pláce called Avérnus.

Hére first the príestess
Sets fóur black steers stánding,
Ánd on their fóreheads
Póurs the wine sídeways;
And plúcking the úppermost
Háirs 'twixt the hórns,
Pláces the fístlings
On the fíre of the áltar,
20    And alóud calls on Hécate
In Érebus poténtial
As wéll as in héaven.
And óthers the júgulars
Incíse from belów,
And in wíde, shallow sáucers
Recéive the warm blóod.
To the móther of the Fúries,
And tó her great síster,
Enéas himsélf slays
30    A fléecy, black lámb,
Ánd to thee, Próserpine,
A bárren-wombed héifer;
Then tó the king Stýgian
The níght altar ráises,
And an óx's whole cárcase
Upón its fire pláces,
And óver the hót roast
Póurs the fat óil.

But, behóld! at sunríse
40    The ground únder their féet
Is begínning to béllow,

And the móuntain tops wóody
To quáke to and fró,
Ánd through the dárkness
Dog-bítches are hówling;
For the Góddess is cóming: –

'Off! óff! ye profáne ones,'
The próphetess críes:
'Let not óne of you ánywhere
50  Ín the grove línger –
But thóu, draw thy swórd,
And set óut on thy róad;
For cóurage, Enéas,
Now, nów is the tíme;
For fírmness the tíme 's now.'
These wórds having úttered,
She plúnged all infúriate
Ínto the cáve's mouth;
Hé, with no timid step,
60  Kept páce with his guíde.

Ye Góds who rule óver
The émpire of spírits,
And yé, silent Shádes,
Ye, Cháos and Phlégethon,
Régions of wíde-brooding
Stíllness and níght,
Be the prívilege allówed me
To téll what I've héard,
Your sánction accórded
70  The thíngs to revéal
That in dárkness are súnk
And the dépths of the éarth.

In the lónely night, dárkling,
They wént through the sháde,

Through the réalms unsubstántial
And mánsions of Dis,
As one trávels in the wóods
By the créscent moon's twílight,
When Júpiter plúnges
80    The ský into shádow,
And múrky night stríps
The wórld of its cólor.

In the véstibule's frónt,
And the véry begínning
And jáw's edge of Órcus,
Remórse has her cóuch placed
With Sórrow besíde her,
And thére pale Diséases
And sád Old Age dwéll,
90    And Pénury vile,
And ill-cóunselling Húnger,
And Féar, Ðeath and Tóil,
Frightful fórms to behóld,
And, Déath's cousin, Sléep,
And the críminal Pássions;
And in frónt, as thou énterest,
Déath-dealing Wárfare,
Ánd the Euménides'
Íron bedchámbers,
100    And Díscord insénsate,
With blóody band týing
The snákes of her háir.

In the midst an aged élm
Its wide-branching árms
Huge and shády spreads óut,
Under whóse every léaf,
Vain, incónsequent Dréams,
They sáy, have their dwélling

And néstle in clústers.
110 Many mónsters besídes
Of béastly forms várious
Abóut the doors kénnel;
Centaurs, Górgons, and Hárpies,
Half-mán half-fish Scýllas,
Hundred-hánded Briáreus,
Lerna's béast hissing hórrid,
Flame-bélching Chiméra,
And the thrée-bodied Sháde.

Here Enéas his swórd grasps,
120 In súdden alárm,
And presénts the drawn édge
To thém coming ónward,
And séems to be bént
(Were it nót for the wárning
His skílled comrade gíves him
That they're nóthing but thin
Unsubstántial souls flítting
Under sémblance of bódies)
To rúsh in upón them,
130 And, áll to no púrpose,
Cleave the shádows in súnder.

From hénce the road léads
Tó where Tartárean
Ácheron's wáters
In vást muddy whírlpool
Rísing belch óver
The whóle of their sánd and lees
Ínto Cocýtus.
A férryman hórrid
140 Has chárge of these wáters,
Charon, térribly squálid,
With eýes of flame stáring,

And gréat grisly béard
Uncáred on chin lýing,
And sórdid garb hánging
Tied óver his shóulder:
Althóugh somewhat áged,
The Gód is still hárdy,
And wéars his years wéll;
150   And himsélf with a lóng pole
The bóat forward scúlling,
Himsélf the sails ténding,
Acróss in his rústy craft
Férries his fréight.

With a rúsh the whole crówd
Toward the férry was póuring;
Men and mátrons were thére,
And magnánimous héroes,
The tásk of life óver,
160   And yóung lads and máidens,
And yóuths whom their párents
Saw ón the pile pláced;
As númerous as léaves fall
Detáched in the fórest,
In the first chill of áutumn;
Or as bírds from the hígh-deep
Tówards the land shóaling
When the cóld season róuts
And to súnny climes sénds them
170   Awáy beyond séa.

Acróss to be férried
The fóremost were bégging,
And in lóve with the fúrther bank
Strétched their hands óut;
But the bóatman sevére
Now sóme takes, now óthers,

And sóme from the stránd
Removes fár and keeps óff.

Then Enéas in wónder
180   And móved by the túmult: –
'What méans,' says, 'O máiden,
To the ríver such cóncourse?
What ís it these sóuls seek?
Or fróm the banks whý
Are sóme of them túrned back,
While sóme of them óver
The lívid straits rów?'
To whóm briefly thús
The áge-stricken príestess: –

190   'O són of Anchíses.
Gods' óffspring undóubted,
Of Stýx and Cocýtus
Thou sée'st the deep wáters,
Which nó God may swéar by
And nót keep his óath.
Unbúried, forlórn,
All the crówd thou see'st hére;
Yon férryman's Cháron;
Acróss sail the búried.
200   These hórrible bánks
And this hóarse stream to cróss
No sóul is permítted,
Ere his bónes in the tómb rest.
A húndred years flítting
They wánder these shóres round;
Then at lást are admítted
To vísit agáin
The so múch longed-for wáters.'

(1853)

# JOHN CONINGTON (1825–69)

[Aen. VIII. 369–453; 608–731] *Venus asks her husband*
*Vulcan to make new armour for Aeneas; Aeneas marvels at the*
*scenes of Rome's future history depicted on the shield*

Night falls, and earth and living things
Are folded in her sable wings.
But Venus, with a mother's dread
   At Latium's wild alarm,
To Vulcan on the golden bed
Spoke, breathing on each word she said
   Sweet love's enticing charm:
'When Greece was labouring to destroy
The fated battlements of Troy,
10 No aid from thee I cared to ask
   For Troy's unhappy race,
Nor chose in vain for arms to task
   Thy labour or thy grace,
Though much to Priam's sons I owed,
And oft my tears of pity flowed
   For my Æneas' case.
And now his foot, by Jove's command,
Is planted on Rutulian land.
Thus then behold me suppliant here,
20 Low at those knees I most revere:
Behold a tender mother plead:
Arms are the boon, her son's the need.
Not vainly Nereus' daughter pled:
Not vain the tears Aurora shed.
What nations, see, what towns combine,
To draw the sword 'gainst me and mine!'
She ceased: her snowy arms enwound
Her faltering husband round and round.
The wonted fire at once he feels:

30     Through all his veins the passion steals,
       Swift as the lightning's fiery glare
       Runs glimmering through the thunderous air.
       His spouse in conscious beauty smiled
       To see his heart by love beguiled.
       Smit to the core with heavenly fire
       In fondling tone returns the sire:
       'Why stray so far thy pleas to seek?
       Has trust in Vulcan grown so weak?
       Had such, my queen, been then thy bent,
40     E'en then to Troy had arms been lent,
       Nor Jove nor Fate refused to give
       To Priam ten more years to live.
       And now, if war be in the air
       And battle's need thy present care,
       What molten gold or iron can
       With fire to fuse and winds to fan,
       All shall be thine: thy power confess,
       Nor seek by prayers to feign it less.'
       He said, and to his bosom pressed
50     His beauteous queen, and sank to rest.

       The night had crowned the cope of heaven,
       And sleep's first fading bloom had driven
          The slumber from men's eyes;
       E'en at the hour when prudent wife,
       Who day by day, to eke out life,
          Minerva's distaff plies,
       Relumes her fire, o'erreaching night,
       And tasks her maidens by its light,
       To keep her husband's bed from stain
60     And for their babes a pittance gain;
       So, nor less swift, at labour's claim
       Springs from his couch the Lord of flame.
       Fast by Æolian Lipare

And fair Sicania's coast
An island rises from the sea
   With smoking rocks embossed;
Beneath, a cavern drear and vast,
Hollowed by Cyclopëan blast,
   Rings with unearthly sound;
70   Bruised anvils clang their thunder-peal,
Hot hissing glows the Chalyb steel,
And fiery vapour fierce and fast
   Pants up from underground;
The centre this of Vulcan's toil,
And Vulcan's name adorns the soil.
Here finds he, as he makes descent,
The Cyclops o'er their labour bent:
Brontes and Steropes are there,
And gaunt Pyracmon, stripped and bare.
80   The thunderbolt was in their hand,
Which Jove sends down to scourge the land;
A part was barbed and formed to kill,
A part remained imperfect still.
Three rays they took of forky hail,
   Of watery cloud three rays,
Three of the winged southern gale,
   Three of the ruddy blaze:
Now wrath they mingle, swift to harm,
And glare, and noise, and loud alarm.
90   Elsewhere for Mars they plan the car
Wherewith he maddens into war
   Strong towns and spearmen bold,
And burnish Pallas' shirt of mail,

---

64–6 The island is the modern Volcano, one of the Lipari islands off the NE coast of Sicily.
71 The Chalybes were noted metalworkers.
77 *The Cyclops*: a race of one-eyed giants. Their role as smiths is post-Homeric.

The Ægis, bright with dragon's scale
 And netted rings of gold:
The twisted serpent-locks they shape
And Gorgon's head, lopped at the nape:
 Her dying eyes yet rolled.
'Away with these,' he cried, 'away,
100  My sons, and list what now I say:
A mighty chief of arms has need:
Now prove your skill, your strength, your speed.
Begone, delay!' No further speech:
Each takes the part assigned to each,
 And plies the work with zeal:
In streams the gold, the copper flows,
And in the mighty furnace glows
 The death-inflicting steel.
A shield they plan, whose single guard
110  May all the blows of Latium ward,
And fold on fold together bind,
Seven circles round one centre twined.
Some make the windy bellows heave,
Now give forth air, and now receive:
The copper hisses in the wave:
The anvils press the groaning cave.
With measured cadence each and all
The giant hammers rise and fall:
The griping pincers, deftly plied,
120  Turn the rough ore from side to side.

*

 But careful Venus, heavenly fair,
Had journeyed through the clouds of air,
 Her present in her hands:
Deep in the vale her son she spied
Reposing by the river-side,
 And thus before him stands:
'Lo, thus the Gods their word fulfil:

Behold the arms my husband's skill
  Has fashioned in a day:
130 Fear not conclusions soon to try
  With Latium's braggarts, but defy
    E'en Turnus to the fray.'
Then to her son's embrace she flew:
The armour 'neath an oak in view
  She placed, all dazzling bright.
He, glorying in the beauteous prize,
From point to point quick darts his eyes
  With ever-new delight.
Now wondering 'twixt his hands he turns
140 The helm that like a meteor burns,
  The sword that rules the war,
The breastplate shooting bloody rays,
As dusky clouds in sunlight blaze,
  Refulgent from afar,
The polished greaves of molten gold,
The spear, the shield with fold on fold,
  A prodigy of art untold.
There, prescient of the years to come,
Italia's times, the wars of Rome,
150   The fire's dark lord had wrought:
E'en from Ascanius' dawning days
The generations he portrays,
  The fights in order fought.
There too the mother wolf he made
In Mars's cave supinely laid:
Around her udders undismayed
  The gamesome infants hung,
While she, her loose neck backward thrown,
Caressed them fondly, one by one,
160   And shaped them with her tongue.
Hard by, the towers of Rome he drew

---

**161–200** Tales of early Rome.

And Sabine maids in public view
　　Snatched 'mid the Circus games:
So 'twixt the fierce Romulean brood
And Tatius with his Cures rude
　　A sudden war upflames.
And now the kings, their conflict o'er,
Stand up in arms Jove's shrine before,
From goblets pour the sacred wine,
170　And make their peace o'er bleeding swine.
There too was Mettus' body torn
By four-horse cars asunder borne;
Ah, well for thee, had promise sworn,
　　False Alban, held thee true!
And Tullus dragged the traitor's flesh
Through wild and wood: the briars looked fresh
　　With sprinkled gory dew.
Porsenna there with pride elate
Bids Rome to Tarquin ope her gate:
180　With arms he hems the city in:
Æneas' sons stand firm to win
　　Their freedom with their blood:
Enraged and menacing his air,
That Cocles dares the bridge to tear,
And Cloelia breaks her bonds, bold fair,
　　And swims across the flood.

---

**162** Rape of the Sabine women.

**165** War with the Sabines under their king Tatius concludes with a treaty.

**171** Mettus, dictator of Alba Longa, broke his treaty with Rome, which led
to the fall of Alba Longa.

**178–9** Tarquin, the exiled last king of Rome, is helped by the Etruscan Lars
Porsenna to besiege the city.

**184** The story of how Horatius Cocles 'kept the bridge' is familiar from
Macaulay's 'Lay'.

**185** Cloelia was a hostage taken by the Etruscans: she escaped and swam the
Tiber to safety.

There Manlius on Tarpeia's steep
Stood firm, the Capitol to keep:
The ancient palace-roof you saw
190   New bristling with Romulean straw.
A silver goose in gilded walls
With flapping wings announced the Gauls;
And through the wood the invaders crept,
And climbed the height, while others slept.
Golden their hair on head and chin:
Gold collars deck their milk-white skin:
   Short cloaks with colours checked
Shine on their backs: two spears each wields
Of Alpine make; and oblong shields
200   Their brawny limbs protect.
Luperci here of raiment stripped
   And dancing Salii move,
And flamens with their caps wool-tipped,
   And shields that fell from Jove;
And high-born dames parade the streets
In pensile cars with cushioned seats.
Far off he sets the gates of Dis,
And Tartarus' terrible abyss,
   And dooms to guilt assigned:
210   There Catiline on frowning steep
Hangs poised above the infernal deep
   With Fury-forms behind:
And righteous souls apart he draws,
With Cato there to give them laws.
'Twixt these in wavy outline rolled

---

187 The Roman general Manlius defended the Capitol against the Gauls.
201–4 The Luperci and the Salii were Roman religious cults.
210–14 The conspirator Lucius Sergius Catilina was put to death in 63 BC.
Cato the Younger committed suicide rather than fall into the hands of Julius
Caesar: he became the personification of republican ideals to which Augustus
(with Julius Caesar's fate in mind) proclaimed allegiance.

The swelling ocean, all of gold,
  Though hoary showed the spray:
Gay dolphins, sheathed in silver scales,
Lash up the water with their tails,
220    And 'mid the surges play.
There in the midmost meet the sight
The embattled fleets, the Actian fight:
Leucate flames with warlike show,
And golden-red the billows glow.
Here Cæsar, leading from their home
The fathers, people, gods of Rome,
  Stands on the lofty stern:
The constellation of his sire
Beams o'er his head, and tongues of fire
230    About his temples burn.
With favouring Gods and winds to speed
  Agrippa forms his line:
The golden beaks, war's proudest meed,
  High on his forehead shine.
There, with barbaric troops increased,
Antonius, from the vanquished East
  And distant Red-sea side,
To battle drags the Bactrian bands
And Egypt; and behind him stands
240    (Foul shame!) the Egyptian bride.
Each from his moorings, on they pour,
And three-toothed beak and back-drawn oar
Plough up in foam the marble floor.
Who saw had deemed that Cyclads, torn
From their firm roots, were onward borne
  Colliding on the surge,

---

**221–80** The battle of Actium (31 BC). Augustus and his commander-in-chief Agrippa defeat Antony and Cleopatra; Augustus takes over the province of Egypt.

That hills with hills in conflict meet:
The mighty chiefs their tower-armed fleet
    With such propulsion urge.
250  With hand or enginery they throw
Live darts ablaze with fiery tow:
The sea-god's verdant fields look red,
Incarnadined with heaps of dead.
Her native timbrel in her hand,
The queen to battle calls her band,
Infatuate! – nor perceives as yet
Two snakes behind with fangs a-whet.
Anubis and each monster strange
    That Egypt's land reveres
260  'Gainst Neptune, Venus, Pallas range,
    And shake their uncouth spears.
There where they battle, host and host,
Raves grisly Mars, in steel embossed:
    The Furies frown on high:
With mantle rent glad Discord walks,
Bellona fierce behind her stalks,
    Her scourge of crimson dye.
Then Actian Phœbus bends his bow:
Scared by that terror, flies the foe,
270    Arabia, Egypt, Ind:
The haughty dame in wild defeat
Is shaking out her loosened sheet,
    And standing to the wind.
She, wanning o'er with death foreseen,
Through corpses flies, devoted queen,
    By wave and Zephyr sped:
While mighty Nile, through all his frame
Deep shuddering for his people's shame,
His ample vesture opened wide,
280  Invites the vanquished host to hide
    Within his azure bed.

Cæsar, of triple triumph proud,
Pays to Rome's gods the gift he vowed,
   Three hundred fanes of stone:
The live streets ring with shouts and games:
Each shrine is thronged by grateful dames,
   Each floor with victims strown.
Himself, bright Phœbus' gate before,
At leisure tells the offerings o'er,
290 And fastens on the gorgeous door
   The first-fruits of the prey:
There march the captives, all and each,
In garb as diverse as in speech,
   A multiform array.
The houseless Nomad there is shown,
And Afric tribes that wear no zone,
And Morini, extreme of men,
And Dahæ, masterless till then:
Gelonians too, with bended bows,
300 And Leleges, and Carian foes:
Euphrates droops his head, and flows
   With less of billowy pride:
Old Rhine extends his branching horns,
And passion-chafed Araxes scorns
   The bridge that spans his tide.
Such legends traced on Vulcan's shield
   The wondering chief surveys:
On truth in symbol half revealed
   He feasts his hungry gaze,
310 And high upon his shoulders rears
The fame and fates of unborn years.                    (1867)

---

**282** Augustus' triple triumph, in celebration of victories in Illyricum, at
Actium, and in Egypt, was held in Rome on 13–15 August, 29 BC.

# R. D. BLACKMORE (1825–1900)

## The Georgics: Book the First, 1–145 [Georg. I.
1–124] *Prologue. Invocation to the gods and to Octavian
(Augustus Caesar). On agriculture*

What makes blithe corn, beneath what starry sign
To turn the sod, and wed the elm and vine,
What care of beeves, and how the flock may thrive,
And due experience of the frugal hive –
Mæcenas, hence my song. Ye lights on high,
Who lead the rolling seasons through the sky,
Good Liber, come, and fostering Ceres too,
If earth exchanged, by power derived from you,
Chaonian mast for dainty wheat; and quaff'd
10   With new-found grapes her Achelöan draught.
Ho too, ye Fauns, that love the farming folk,
Come, tripping Fauns, and maidens of the oak,
Your boons I sing. And thou, whose trident rang
Upon young earth, and forth the war-horse sprang:
And thou, woodranger, whose three hundred steers,
All snowy white, the Cæan coppice rears:
Nay, Pan thyself, stout warder of the sheep,
Forsake ancestral grove and Arcad steep,
If still thou lovest Mænala thine own,
20   Come, Tegeän god, and make thy presence known!
Ho, Pallas, author of the olive bough,

---

5 Each of the poem's four books is dedicated to Maecenas, Virgil's patron and
Augustus' 'minister of culture'.
9 *Chaonian mast*: i.e. mashed acorns, the food of primitive man. The oaks
grown at Dodona in Chaonia were sacred to Zeus (Jupiter).
10 *Achelöan draught*: i.e. water. The Achelous was said to be the world's oldest
river.
14 Neptune created the first horse.
15 Refers to Aristaeus, who first taught men how to create new swarms of
bees: for his story, see the end of *Georgics* IV (translated by S. P. Bovie).

And boy inventor of the talon'd plough!
With cypress fresh unfibred from the sods,
Sylvanus, come! come, goddesses and gods!
All ye, whose province is the furrow'd plain,  ⎫
Who nurse unsown the infancy of grain,        ⎬
And pour upon the seedlands gracious rain.     ⎭

    And foremost thou, of whom 'tis yet unknown
What senate of the gods shall hold thy throne;
30  Or if, great Cæsar, thou shalt haply deign
To view the towns, and make the world thy reign;
Thy mother's myrtle if the globe shall bring,
To crown thee sire of corn and tempest-king:
Or com'st thou god of the unmeasur'd sea,
And sailors own no providence but thee;
Shall Thulé be thy serf, and Tethys crave
Thy hand for some sweet heiress of the wave?
Or wilt thou lend the laggard months thy star,
Where flies the Virgin from the Claws afar?
40  The Scorpion folds his fiery arms awry,
And leaves thee larger moiety of sky.
Whate'er thy choice (since Orcus hopes in vain,
Nor hast thyself so dark a lust of reign;
Though Greece admire the meads of asphodel,
And Proserpine be satisfied with hell),
Whate'er thy choice, vouchsafe my voyage good speed,
And bid my gallant enterprise succeed;
For waylost rustics deign with me to feel,
Advance, and learn to honour our appeal,
50    When Spring is new, and mountains grey with thaw,
And loam grows mealy to the zephyr's flaw,

---

**32** Myrtle was sacred to Venus, ancestral mother of the Julian family, to which Augustus belonged.
**36** *Thulé*: an island north of Britain: the edge of the world; *Tethys*: mother of the nymphs.
**38ff.** The idea is that Caesar after deification will become a new constellation.

The plough at once my groaning bull must bear,
And, chafed along the furrow, gleam the share.
That corn-land best shall pay the farmer's cost,
Which twice hath felt the sun, and twice the frost,
His wildest vows with double answer meet,
And burst his garners with a world of wheat.

But ere we plough a stranger farm, 'tis good
To learn the winds, and heaven's uncertain mood,
60    The ancient tilth, and how the country lies,
And what each quarter yields, and what denies.
Here corn exults, and there the grape is glad,
Here tress and grass, unbidden verdure add.
So mark how Tmolus yields his saffron store,
While ivory is the gift of Indian shore;
With incense soft the softer Shebans deal,
The stark Chalybian's element is steel;
With acrid castor reek the Pontic wares,
Epirus wins the palm of Elian mares.

70    So Nature framed these laws, for good or ill,
And stamp'd on each the fiat of her will,
When first Deucalion, through a world forlorn,
Cast stones, and man, a flinty race, was born.

Then come, forthwith, before the year grow old,
Let sturdy bulls turn up the buxom mould,
And dusty summer dress the clods supine,
When mellow sunbeams more maturely shine.
But if the land is poor; 'twill be enow
Beneath Arcture to skim with shallow plough,
80    Here, lest the weeds annoy the blithesome grain,
And there, lest water fail the sandy plain.

Shorn fallows each alternate year should rest,
And leisure brace the languid meadow's breast;

---

67 *Chalybian:* the Chalybes, who lived near the Black Sea, were famous workers in iron (not steel).
72 *Deucalion:* the Noah-figure in the Greek myth of the Flood.

Or change your star, and sow the yellow corn
Where bouncing peas with rattling pods were borne,
Or where, from slim vetch and from lupin rude,
You glean'd the brittle haulm and rustling wood.
For hemp and oats consume their nurture deep,
And poppies drizzled with Lethæan sleep.
90    But yet alternate years relieve the toil;
   Let no false shame however check thy hand
To glut with rich manure a droughty soil,
   And cast foul ashes o'er exhausted land.
So fields by change of crops have welcome rest,
Nor thankless proves the earth's unfurrow'd breast.
   Nay, oft 'tis good to burn the sterile leys,
And fire the stubble with a crackling blaze:
Or if thereby the soil's constituents breed
Mysterious vigour and nutritious feed;
100   Or if, by purging of the fire, they lose
Injurious properties and worthless ooze;
Or if the heat opes passages and pores
Unseen, whose moisture meets the tender spores;
Or if it hardens and contracts the veins,
That gape too widely; lest the prying rains,
Or beating sunglare fiercely shed around,
Or winter's searching frost consume the ground.
   So then, by crushing idle clods, the swain
With harrow and bush-harrow glads the plain,
110   Nor doth the golden Ceres from on high,
Without a blessing watch his industry.
Nor vain his work who cuts the straight rig's chine,
With plough set crossways to his former line,
Slashes the hummocks left by Autumn's toil,
Exerts the land, and disciplines the soil.
   For winters dry, and showery summers, pray;
The dust of winter makes the cornland gay:
'Tis this so proudly decks the Mysian wold,
And Gargara marvels at his crown of gold.

120      And what of him who, having sown the grain,
        Falls to pell-mell, and routs the flying plain,
        Crushes the clods of over-fat argill,
        And floods the seedland with the ductile rill?
        When parch'd fields gasp with dying herbage – lo,
        He tempts the runnel from the hill-side trough;
        The purling runnel brawls and falls away
        Through the smooth stones, and slakes the thirsty clay.
            Or him who, lest the stalk be overweigh'd,
        Feeds off the rankness of the tender blade,
130     When first they top the furrow's edge; and drains
        The stagnant plashes from the spongy plains?
        So much the more if, by the season's whim,
        A flooded river overswell its brim,
        A slimy mantle o'er the field diffuse,
        And fill the ditches with fermenting ooze.
            And yet, when carls and beeves have done their best,
        The reprobate goose will prove no trifling pest;
        Strymonian cranes, and bitter endive's root
        Annoy, and shade is noxious to the fruit.
140         Our heavenly Father hath not judged it right
        To leave the road of agriculture light:
        'Twas he who first made husbandry a plan,
        And care a whetstone for the wit of man;
        Nor suffer'd he his own domains to lie
        Asleep in cumbrous old-world lethargy.                    (1871)

# R. D. BLACKMORE

The Georgics: Book the Second, 1–134
[Georg. II. 1–113] *On arboriculture*

Thus far of tillage, and the starry signs –
Now thee I sing, great Bacchus, god of vines,
The birth, moreover, of the greenwood-tree,
And slow-grown olive, I will sing with thee.
Lenæan father, visit us awhile;
Here all the world is smiling in thy smile;
The vine presents her Autumn to thy sip,
And foams the vintage o'er the wine-tub's lip;
Lenæan father, come, and, buskin-free,
10 Imbrue thy feet in purple must with me.
    First, different trees have divers birth assign'd;
For some lack no compulsion of mankind,
But spring spontaneously in every nook,
Peopling the meadows and the mazy brook;
Thus osiers lithe, and brooms that gently play,
The poplar, and the willow silver-grey.
    And some arise from seed themselves have shed;
For so the chesnut rears its lofty head,
The bay-oak, towering monarch of the wood,
20 And oaks with Grecian oracles endued.
    But others densely stool up from the root,
A forest new, as elms and cherries shoot;
Nay, even thus the young Parnassian bay,
Beneath the mother's shadow, feels her way.
    These methods nature gave; hence all the sheen
Of woods, and shrubs, and bowery chapels green.
    But other modes there are which practice hath
Discover'd for herself on labour's path.

---

**9** *Lenæan father* : Bacchus, god of the wine-press.

Shoots from the mother's tender form, with skill,
30    One gardener trims, and plants along the drill;
Another roughly buries stocks uncut,
And stakes four-cleft, and poles with sharpen'd butt.
Some trees demand the arching layer's coil,
And thriving nurseries in the mother soil.
Some lack no root, no pruner need mistrust
To lay the leader in its native dust.
Nay more, the olive-stump is cleft in twain,
And, strange to tell, the dry wood roots again!
    And oft the branches of one tree we find
40    Saucily alter'd to another kind,
On wild pear-stocks engrafted pippins come,
And stony cornels blush upon the plum.
    Then list, ye swains, the culture I describe
For each, according to his class and tribe:
By culture tame the wildings, and convert,
Nor let an inch of surface lie inert:
Ismarian crags enamel with the vine,
And drape with olive mount Taburno's chine.
    Ho thou, Mæcenas! great and glorious name,
50    By right and fact, my better half of fame,
Be nigh, be pilot of the voyage with me;
A flowing sheet upon so broad a sea.
Not all things would I grasp that I can feel,
Though hundred tongues were mine and voice of steel.
Come thou, and hug the very brink of land;
    Safe in the arms of mother earth we stay,
    I will not mock thee yet with fabled lay,
Through many a winding and premisals grand.
    The trees that spring, with no man to invite,
60    And climb spontaneous to the shores of light,

---

48 *Taburno*: in the Campagna, famous in Virgil's time for its olives.
49 *Mæcenas*: see note on I, 5 (previous extract).

Unfruitful are, but lusty from their birth,
Because strong nature underlies the earth.
Yet even these, if grafted well or moved,
And set in trenches with the soil improved,
Cast by their wildwood mind, and nursed in ease,
Come blithely into any style you please.
Nay, barren suckers from the root will bear
When planted out with liberal space and air:
Their mother's foliage shrouds them now in gloom,
70  And robs the growing buds, and starves the bloom.

But slowly comes the tree which thou hast sown,
A canopy for grandsons of thine own:
Degenerate fruits forget their taste and shape,
And birds make boot upon the worthless grape.
So all cost trouble, all must be compell'd
To keep their drill, by constant labour quell'd.

But olives answer better from the stock,
And Paphian myrtles from the solid block;
The vine from layers; and from offsets spring
80  Hard hazels, and the ash the forest-king,
The tree whose chaplets shade Alcides' brow,
And Chaon Father's mast-producing bough:
And thus the lofty palm bedecks the plain,
And fir design'd for hardships on the main.

But nuts are grafted on the rough arbute,
And barren planes bear apple-trees in fruit:
With chestnut bloom the beech is silver-laid,
The mountain-ash in white pear-flowers array'd,
And swine crunch acorns in the elm-tree shade.
90  Nor is the mode to bud and graft the same –
For where the buds, (like emeralds in their frame,)
Push'd forth the bark, their filmy jerkins split,
A narrow eyelet through the crown is slit;

81 *Alcides*: Hercules, who wore a crown of poplar.
82 *Chaon Father* : i.e. Jupiter: see note on I, 9.

Herein the germ, a stranger, they compress,
And teach with juicy rind to coalesce.
To graft – the knotless trunks are lopp'd amain,
And cleft with wedges deep into the grain,
Then fruitful scions are enclosed; nor long
Till a great tree with laughing boughs leaps out,
100  And looks up with astonishment and doubt,
At stranger leaves, and fruit that must be wrong.
    Nay, passing that, more kinds than one there be
Of elm and willow, lote and cypress tree:
Plump olives, too, distinctive features own,
Orchads, and Rays, and Bruisers tart of tone.
So apples and Phæacian orchards gleam ⎞
With divers hues; and pears diversely teem, ⎬
Crustumian, Syrian, and the big voleme. ⎠
    A different grape bedecks these elms of ours
110  Than Lesbos gathers in Methymna's bowers;
And Thasian vines there are, and Mareots white,
One fit for heavy land, and one for light:
And Psythian best for raisins, and Lagene
(Shrewd sort to test the feet and tongue, I ween);
Purple, and Rathripe; Rhætic, too, shall earn
My proudest verse, yet challenge not Falern!
Vines Aminæan, firmest wine; and more,
Where Tmolus and the king Phanæüs soar:
And small Argitis, which no rival fears,
120  To gush so full, or keep so many years.
And shall I slight, ye gods of the repast,
Your Rhodian pet, and turgid-bunch'd Bumast?

---

105 Types of olive.
106 The orchards of King Alcinous were famous from Homer, *Odyssey* VII,
112 ff.
108 The voleme was a large type of pear.
109–22 Varieties of grape and wine.

    But hold – ye kinds that urge unnumber'd claims –
What use to give a catalogue of names?
Who seeks to learn it, let him score the sand
The west wind hurls upon the Libyan strand,
Or, when east winds upon the roadstead roar,
Ionian surges rolling to the shore.
    Not every soil will every tree adorn;

130    The willows by the river marge are born,
The alders still the fat morass prefer,
The barren wild-ash loves the mountain spur:
The shores with myrtle laugh; the grape-vines woo
The upland sun, north winds and frost the yew.      (1871)


# WILLIAM MORRIS (1834–96)

The Aeneids of Virgil, VII, 601–54, 783–817 [Aen.
VII. 601–54, 783–817] *Juno opens the Gates of War. Parade
of the Italian chieftains*

Morris translated the poem lineally: i.e., his line numbers correspond
to those of the original.

In Latium of the Westland world a fashion was whilome,
Thence hallowed of the Alban folk, held holy thence by
                         Rome,
Earth's mightiest thing: and this they used what time soe'er
                       they woke
Mars unto battle; whether they against the Getic folk,
Ind, Araby, Hyrcanian men, fashioned the woeful wrack,
Or mid the dawn from Parthian men the banners bade aback.
For twofold are the Gates of War – still bear they such a
                       name –
Hallowed by awe of Mars the dread, and worship of his fame,

Shut by an hundred brazen bolts, and iron whose avail
10    Shall never die: nor ever thence doth door-ward Janus fail.
Now when amid the Fathers' hearts fast is the war-rede

grown,

The Consul, girt in Gabine wise, and with Quirinus gown
Made glorious, doth himself unbar the creaking door-leaves

great,

And he himself cries on the war; whom all men follow

straight,

The while their brazen yea-saying the griding trumpets blare.

In e'en such wise Latinus now was bidden to declare
The battle 'gainst Æneas' folk, and ope the gates of woe.
But from their touch the Father shrank, and fleeing lest he do
The evil deed, in eyeless dark he hideth him away.
20    Then slipped the Queen of Gods from heaven, and ended

their delay;

For back upon their hinges turned the Seed of Saturn bore
The tarrying leaves, and burst apart the iron Gates of War,
And all Ausonia yet unstirred brake suddenly ablaze:
And some will go afoot to field, and some will wend their

ways

Aloft on horses dusty-fierce: all seek their battle-gear.
Some polish bright the buckler's face and rub the pike-point

clear

With fat of sheep; and many an axe upon the wheel is worn.
They joy to rear the banners up and hearken to the horn.
And now five mighty cities forge the point and edge anew
30    On new-raised anvils; Tibur proud, Atina staunch to do,

---

7 The Gates of War, in the temple of Janus in Rome, were closed in
peacetime. The custom was supposed to have begun around 700 BC, but
Virgil has synchronized it with the time of Aeneas. Augustus closed the gates
twice, in 29 and 25 BC.

Ardea and Crustumerium's folk, Antemnæ castle-crowned.
They hollow helming for the head; they bend the withe
                                                    around
For buckler-boss: or other some beat breast-plates of the
                                                    brass,
Or from the toughened silver bring the shining greaves to
                                                    pass.

Now fails all prize of share and hook, all yearning for the
                                                    plough;
The swords their fathers bore afield anew they smithy now.
Now is the gathering-trumpet blown; the battle-token speeds;
And this man catches helm from wall; this thrusteth foaming
                                                    steeds
To collar; this his shield does on, and mail-coat threesome
                                                    laid
40  Of golden link, and girdeth him with ancient trusty blade.

O Muses, open Helicon, and let your song awake
To tell what kings awoke to war, what armies for whose sake
Filled up the meads; what men of war sweet mother Italy
Bore unto flower and fruit as then; what flame of fight ran
                                                    high:
For ye remember, Holy Ones, and ye may tell the tale;
But we – a slender breath of fame scarce by our ears may sail.

Mezentius first, the foe of Gods, fierce from the Tuscan shore
Unto the battle wends his way, and armeth host of war:
Lausus, his son, anigh him wends; – no lovelier man than he,
50  Save Turnus, the Laurentine-born, the crown of all to see. –

---

**30–31** Towns in Latium (Lazio): Tibur is the modern Tivoli, Ardea was
Turnus' capital.
**41** Invocation to the Muses, introducing the catalogue of local chieftains,
beginning with Mezentius and his son Lausus (destined to be killed by
Aeneas) and ending with Turnus and the warrior-maid Camilla.

Lausus, the tamer of the horse, the wood-deer's following bane,
Who led from Agyllina's wall a thousand men in vain.
Worthy was he to have more mirth than 'neath Mezentius'

sway;

Worthy that other sire than he had given him unto day.

*

Now mid the forefront Turnus self of body excellent,
Strode sword in hand: there by the head all others he

outwent:

His threefold crested helm upbore Chimæra in her wrath;
Where very flame of Ætna's womb her jaws were pouring

forth;

And fiercer of her flames was she, and madder of her mood
60 As bloomed the battle young again with more abundant

blood.

But on the smoothness of his shield was golden Io shown
With upraised horns, with hairy skin, a very heifer grown, –
A noble tale; – and Argus there was wrough, the maiden's

ward;

And father Inachus from bowl well wrought the river

poured.

A cloud of foot-folk follow him; his shielded people throng
The meadows all about; forth goes the Argive manhood

strong;

Aruncan men and Rutuli, Sicanians of old years,
Sacranian folk, Labicus' band the blazoned shield-bearers:
Thy thicket-biders, Tiber; those that holy acres till
70 Beside Numicus, those that plough Rutulian holt and hill,
And ridges of Circæi: they whose meadows Anxur Jove
Looks down on, where Feronia joys amid her fair green

grove;

---

57 *Chimæra*: one of the monsters of hell-mouth, a symbol of primitive
violence appropriate for Turnus.
70 The river Numicus was holy because Aeneas died there.

Where Satura's black marish lies, where chilly Ufens glides,
Seeking a way through lowest dales, till in the sea he hides.

And after these from Volscian folk doth fair Camilla pass,
Leading a mighty host of horse all blossoming with brass;
A warrior maid, whose woman's hands unused to ply the
rock,
Unused to bear Minerva's crate, were wise in battle's shock.
The very winds might she outgo with hurrying maiden feet,
80   Or speed across the topmost blades of tall unsmitten wheat,
Nor ever hurt the tender ears below her as she ran;
Or she might walk the middle sea, and cross the welter wan,
Nor dip the nimble soles of her amid the wavy ways.
From house and field the youth pours forth to wonder and to
gaze;
The crowd of mothers stands at stare all marvelling, and
beholds
Her going forth; how kingly cloak of purple dye enfolds
Her shining shoulders, how the clasp of gold knots up her
hair,
And how a quiver Lycian-wrought the Queen herself doth
bear,
And shepherd's staff of myrtle-wood steel-headed to a spear.

(1876)

---

**75** Camilla is Virgil's own invention, unlike the other heroes of the Italian
resistance. She is half-real (she fights and dies bravely in Book XI), half a
figure of fantasy.
**79–82** Cf. Pope, *An Essay on Criticism*, 372–3: '. . . when swift Camilla scours
the plain,/Flies o'er th' unbending corn, and skims along the main.'

# ALFRED, LORD TENNYSON
(1809–92)

## To Virgil

*Written at the request of the Mantuans for the nineteenth centenary
of Virgil's death*

I

Roman Virgil, thou that singest
  Ilion's lofty temples robed in fire,
Ilion falling, Rome arising,
  wars, and filial faith, and Dido's pyre;

II

Landscape-lover, lord of language
  more than he that sang the Works and Days,
All the chosen coin of fancy
  flashing out from many a golden phrase;

III

Thou that singest wheat and woodland,
10    tilth and vineyard, hive and horse and herd;
All the charm of all the Muses
  often flowering in a lonely word;

IV

Poet of the happy Tityrus
  piping underneath his beeches bowers;
Poet of the poet-satyr
  whom the laughing shepherd bound with flowers;

---

**6** Hesiod, the Greek poet whose *Works and Days* was the first didactic epic,
the forerunner of the *Georgics*.    **9** Refers to the *Georgics*.
**13** See Eclogue I, 1.    **16** Silenus was 'bound with flowers' in Eclogue VI, 19.

V

Chanter of the Pollio, glorying
   in the blissful years again to be,
Summers of the snakeless meadow,
20    unlaborious earth and oarless sea;

VI

Thou that seëst Universal
   Nature moved by Universal Mind;
Thou majestic in thy sadness
   at the doubtful doom of human kind;

VII

Light among the vanish'd ages;
   star that gildest yet this phantom shore;
Golden branch amid the shadows,
   kings and realms that pass to rise no more;

VIII

Now thy Forum roars no longer,
30    fallen every purple Cæsar's dome –
Tho' thine ocean-roll of rhythm
   sound for ever of Imperial Rome –

IX

Now the Rome of slaves hath perish'd,
   and the Rome of freemen holds her place,
I, from out the Northern Island
   sunder'd once from all the human race,

---

**17–20** Refers to Eclogue IV, which foretells the return of the Golden Age.
**21–2** See Anchises' speech on the nature of the universe, *Aeneid* VI, 724ff.

X
I salute thee, Mantovano,
　　I that loved thee since my day began,
　　Wielder of the stateliest measure
40　　　ever moulded by the lips of man.　　　　　　　(1882)


# F. W. H. MYERS (1843–1901)

## Classical Essays: Virgil [Georg. II. 483–502] *In praise of rural retirement*

A paraphrase of Georgics II, 483–502, one of the most famous passages in the *Georgics*: cf. the imitation by James Thomson and the translation of the whole passage by L. P. Wilkinson.

If thou thy secrets grudge me, nor assign
So high a lore to such a heart as mine, –
Still, Nature, let me still thy beauty know,
Love the clear streams that thro' thy valleys flow,
To many a forest lawn that love proclaim,
Breathe the full soul, and make an end of fame!
Ah me, Spercheos! oh to watch alway
On Taygeta the Spartan girls at play!
Or cool in Hæmus' gloom to feel me laid,
10　　Deep in his branching solitudes of shade!
　　Happy the man whose steadfast eye surveys
The whole world's truth, its hidden works and ways, –
Happy, who thus beneath his feet has thrown
All fears and fates, and Hell's insatiate moan! –

---

**37** *Mantovano*: Virgil was born in Mantua.
**7–10** Virgil makes his idyllic picture of a '*locus amoenus*' specific by reference to places familiar in Greek literature.

Blest, too, were he the sister nymphs who knew,
Pan, and Sylvanus, and the sylvan crew; –
On kings and crowds his careless glance he flings,
And scorns the treacheries of crowds and kings;
Far north the leaguered hordes are hovering dim;
20 Danube and Dacian have no dread for him;
No shock of laws can fright his steadfast home,
Nor realms in ruin nor all the fates of Rome.
Round him no glare of envied wealth is shed,
From him no piteous beggar prays for bread;
Earth, Earth herself the unstinted gift will give,
Her trustful children need but reap and live;
She hath man's peace 'mid all the worldly stir,
One with himself he is, if one with her.                    (1883)

* * *

Then since from God those lesser lives began
40 And the eager spirits entered into man,
To God again the enfranchised soul must tend
He is her home, her Author is her End;
No death is hers; when early eyes grown dim
Starlike she soars and Godlike melts in Him.

---

27–8 These lines are merely a summary of the closing lines of *Georgics* II (502–40).

39ff. Myers has added these lines from Georgics IV.225–7.

# F. W. H. MYERS

Classical Essays: Virgil [Aen. VI. 724–51] *Anchises expounds the nature of the universe and the soul's progress after death*

This passage, Virgil's poetic synthesis of Stoic, Platonic, Orphic and Pythagorean doctrine, is the most important philosophical passage in the *Aeneid*.

> One Life through all the immense creation runs,
> One Spirit is the moon's, the sea's, the sun's;
> All forms in the air that fly, on the earth that creep,
> And the unknown nameless monsters of the deep, –
> Each breathing thing obeys one Mind's control,
> And in all substance is a single Soul.
> First to each seed a fiery force is given;
> And every creature was begot in heaven;
> Only their flight must hateful flesh delay
> And gross limbs moribund and cumbering clay.
> So from that hindering prison and night forlorn
> Thy hopes and fears, thy joys and woes are born,
> Who only seest, till death dispart thy gloom,
> The true world glow through crannies of a tomb.
>     Nor all at once thine ancient ills decay,
> Nor quite with death thy plagues are purged away;
> In wondrous wise hath the iron entered in,
> And through and through thee is a stain of sin;
> Which yet again in wondrous wise must be

10

---

**5–6** The Stoic principle of the *anima mundi* or world-soul.

**9–11** The Platonic idea that the body is the soul's prison was used by Wordsworth in his 'Immortality Ode'.

**14** Cf. Waller's lines: 'The soul's Dark Cottage, batter'd and decay'd/Lets in new Light thro chinks that Time hath made' ('Of the Last Verses in the Book').

20    Cleansed of the fire, abolished in the sea;
      Ay, thro' and thro' that soul unclothed must go
      Such spirit-winds as where they list will blow; —
      O hovering many an age! for ages bare,
      Void in the void and impotent in air!
         Then, since his sins unshriven the sinner wait,
      And to each soul that soul herself is Fate,
      Few to heaven's many mansions straight are sped
      (Past without blame that Judgment of the dead),
      The most shall mourn till tarrying Time hath wrought
30    The extreme deliverance of the airy thought, —
      Hath left unsoiled by fear or foul desire
      The spirit's self, the elemental fire.
         And last to Lethe's stream on the ordered day
      These all God summoneth in great array;
      Who from that draught reborn, no more shall know
      Memory of past or dread of destined woe,
      But all shall there the ancient pain forgive,
      Forget their life, and will again to live.                    (1883)

---

**20–22** The purgatorial winds and fire recur in Dante's *Inferno*.
**33ff.** The doctrine of rebirth after a thousand-year cycle is Platonic, but
Plato had drawn on Orphic and Pythagorean beliefs.

# SIR CHARLES BOWEN (1835–94)

## Eclogue X: Gallus [Ecl. X]

For the metre, see Introduction. The last eight lines, omitted in the version by Sir W. Temple, constitute a 'coda' not just to this poem but to the *Eclogues* as a whole: the last line echoes the conclusions of Eclogues I and VI.

One last labour in song, of thy grace, Arethusa, concede.
Strains, though few, for my Gallus – that even Lycoris may
read –
Yet must I sing, ere parting. Who gives not Gallus a song?
So, when beneath the Sicilian seas thou glidest along,
Doris from thine keep ever her salt sea-waters apart.
Come; let us tell of the passion consuming Gallus's heart,
While each flat-nosed goat on the young bush browses at
call,
No deaf ears shall we sing to; the woods make answer to all.

Nymphs of the stream, what glades, what forest detained ye
the day
10  When with a love unrequited my Gallus wasted away?
Never a height of Parnassus, of Pindus never a mount
Stayed ye, nor yet Aganippe, the fair Aonian fount.
Even the bay-trees wept him, the tamarisk gave him a tear;
Pine-clad Mænalus mourned as beneath his precipice drear
Lonely he lay; and the rocks of the frosty Lycæus repined.
All of his sheep stand round him; – they feel no shame of
mankind;

---

1 *Arethusa*: a sea-nymph who, while bathing in the Arcadian river Alpheus, was pursued by the river-god and turned into a fountain near Syracuse in Sicily.
9–15 Based on Theocritus, *Idyll* I, 66–9, and imitated by Milton, 'Lycidas' 50–53.

Nor thou, heavenliest singer, do thou feel shame of thy
sheep;
Flocks himself by the river the lovely Adonis did keep.

Thither the shepherds came, and the swineherds tardy at last;
20   Thither Menalcas, drenched from his winter storing of mast.
'Whence this passion?' they ask him. Apollo came, the divine:
'Gallus,' he cries, 'what madness! The lovely Lycoris of thine
Follows another love through a wild camp-life and the
snows.'
Thither arrived Silvanus, his brows with greenery fine,
Nodding his giant lilies and fennel flowers as he goes.

Pan of Arcadia next — ourselves we beheld him — he came —
Blood-red berries of elder, and all vermilion flame, —
'Grieving for ever!' he saith. 'Wild grief Love little esteems;
Neither is fierce Love sated with tears, nor the meadow with
streams,
30   Nor with the cytisus blossom the bee, nor the goat with the
leaf.'

Sadly he answers: 'At least some day ye will sing of my grief
Unto your hills, Arcadians; — alone, Arcadians, chief
Masters of song. How gently, methinks, my bones would
repose
Should your pipes hereafter relate my love and its woes!
Would of a truth I among you were one! your sheep were it
mine
Daily to tend, or be dresser in vintage-time of the vine!
Then at the least whether Phyllis it were, or Amyntas, my
spark,
Or some other, that kindled — and what if Amyntas be dark,

---

**19ff.** The procession of gods and shepherds is also from Theocritus, *Idyll* I,
80–82.

Dark is the violet's beauty, and dark is the hyacinth's pride –
40 Here they would lie among willows beneath long vines at
my side;
Phyllis gather me flowers, and Amyntas sing me his lay.
Here are the cold, clear fountains, the waving meadow is
gay;
Here are the forest shadows; and here life ever should glide,
Glide of itself, O Lycoris, beside thee gently away.

Now by insensate passion of savage war I am here
Stayed – my face to the foeman, encompassed around by the
spear.
Thou – yet far be the fancy – remote from the land that is
thine,
Lookest on Alpine snows – cold heart – and the winters of Rhine,
Lonely, without my love. May frosts thy feebleness spare!
50 Ah, may the splinters icy thy delicate feet forbear!
I will away; and the verses I wrought in the Chalcis mould
Set to the pipe and the music of Sicily's shepherd of old.
Rather had I in the forest, the wild beasts' caverns among,
Bear what awaits me, carving my love on the trees that are
young,
So, as the trees grow upward, my love shall grow with them
too.
There meanwhile with the nymphs I will roam great Mænalus
through
Hunting the savage boar. No frosts of the winter shall make
Me and my hounds cease ranging the high Parthenian brake.
Over the rocks, methinks, and the ringing covers I go,
60 Sweeping already in chase; with joy from the Parthian bow
Winging the Cretan arrow; – as though this medicine healed
Love like mine! or the Love-god to human sorrow would
yield!
Vain is the dream – Hamadryads no more, nor pastoral strain
Bring me delight. Farewell, farewell to the forests again!
Love is a god no toils can appease, no misery melt.

No, not in iciest frosts by the Hebrus waves if we dwelt,
Nor if Sithonian snows we endured, and winters of sleet;
Or, when the dying bark on the tall elm withered with heat,
Sheep for an Æthiop master beneath fierce Cancer we
drove. –
70 All things else Love conquers; let us too yield unto Love.'

Muses, enough ye will deem your poet already has sung,
Sitting and weaving a basket of slender mallows and young.
Ye of your grace will make it of worth in Gallus's eyes –
Gallus, for whom my love grows hour by hour, as arise
Hourly the alders green in the new-born spring to the skies.
Let us be going; the shade for a singer is deadly and chill;
Chill is the juniper's shade; for the corn all shade is an ill.
Homeward, for Hesperus comes – ye have fed, my goats, to
your fill.
(1887)

# CHARLES STUART CALVERLEY
## (1831–84)

### Eclogue II: Corydon [Ecl. II]

See also the versions of Warton and Creech.

For one fair face – his master's idol – burned
The shepherd Corydon; and hope had none.
Day after day he came ('twas all he could)
Where, piles of shadow, thick the beeches rose:
There, all alone, his unwrought phrases flung,
Bootless as passionate, to copse and crag.
'Hardhearted! Naught car'st thou for all my songs,
Naught pitiest. I shall die, one day, for thee.
The very cattle court cool shadows now,

10    Now the green lizard hides beneath the thorn:
     And for the reaper, faint with driving heat,
     The handmaids mix the garlic-salad strong.
     *My* only mates, the crickets – as I track
     'Neath the fierce sun thy steps – make shrill the woods.
     Better to endure the passion and the pride
     Of Amaryllis: better to endure
     Menalcas – dark albeit as thou art fair.
     Put not, oh fair, in difference of hue
     Faith overmuch: the white May-blossoms drop
20    And die; the hyacinth swart, men gather it.
     Thy scorn am I: thou ask'st not whence I am,
     How rich in snowy flocks, how stored with milk.
     O'er Sicily's green hills a thousand lambs
     Wander, all mine: my new milk fails me not
     In summer or in snow. Then I can sing
     All songs Amphion the Dircæan sang,
     Piping his flocks from Attic Aracynth.
     Nor am I all uncouth. For yesterday,
     When winds had laid the seas, I, from the shore,
30    Beheld my image. Little need I fear
     Daphnis, though thou wert judge, or mirrors lie.
     – Oh! be content to haunt ungentle fields,
     A cottager, with me; bring down the stag,
     And with green switch drive home thy flocks of kids:
     Like mine, thy woodland songs shall rival Pan's!
     – 'Twas Pan first taught us reed on reed to fit
     With wax: Pan watches herd and herdsman too.
     – Nor blush that reeds should chafe thy pretty lip.
     What pains Amyntas took, this skill to gain!
40    I have a pipe – seven stalks of different lengths
     Compose it – which Damœtas gave me once.
     Dying he said, 'At last 'tis all thine own.'
     The fool Amyntas heard, and grudged, the praise.
     Two fawns moreover (perilous was the gorge
     Down which I tracked them –!) – dappled still each skin –
     Drain daily two ewe-udders; all for thee.

Long Thestylis has cried to make them hers.
Hers be they – since to thee my gifts are dross.

Be mine, oh fairest! See! for thee the Nymphs
50   Bear baskets lily-laden: Naiads bright
For thee crop poppy-crests and violets pale,
With daffodil and fragrant fennel-bloom:
Then, weaving casia in and all sweet things,
Soft hyacinth paint with yellow marigold.
Apples I'll bring thee, hoar with tender bloom,
And chestnuts – which my Amaryllis loved,
And waxen plums: let plums too have their day.
And thee I'll pluck, oh bay, and, myrtle, thee
Its neighbour: neighboured thus your sweets shall mix.
60   – Pooh! Thou'rt a yokel, Corydon. Thy love
Laughs at thy gifts: if gifts must win the day,
Rich is Iolas. What thing have I,
Poor I, been asking – while the winds and boars
Ran riot in my pools and o'er my flowers?

– Yet, fool, whom fliest thou? Gods have dwelt in woods,
And Dardan Paris. Citadels let her
Who built them, Pallas, haunt: green woods for me.
Grim lions hunt the wolf, and wolves the kid,
And kids at play the clover-bloom. I hunt
70   Thee only: each one drawn to what he loves.
See! trailing from their necks the kine bring home
The plough, and, as he sinks, the sun draws out
To twice their length the shadows. Still I burn
With love. For what can end or alter love?

Thou'rt raving, simply raving, Corydon.
Clings to thy leafy elm thy half-pruned vine.
Why not begin, at least, to plait with twigs
And limber reeds some useful homely thing?
Thou'lt find another love, if scorned by this.'         (1908)

# ROBERT BRIDGES (1844–1930)

Ibant Obscuri,* 1–49, 227–374, 412–84 [Aen. VI.
268–316, 494–641, 679–751] *The descent into the
underworld; Deiphobus tells Aeneas how he was killed and how
Helen betrayed Troy to the Greeks; the Sibyl tells of the
damned in Tartarus; the arrival at the Elysian Fields; Anchises
tells of the principle of the universe and the soul's progress after
death*

They wer' amid the shadows by night in loneliness obscure
Walking forth i' the void and vasty dominyon of Ades;
As by an uncertain moonray secretly illumin'd
One goeth in the forest, when heav'n is gloomily clouded,
And black night hath robb'd the colours and beauty from all
            things.
   Here in Hell's very jaws, the threshold of darkening Orcus,
Have the avenging Cares laid their sleepless habitation,
Wailing Grief, pallid Infections, & heart-stricken Old-age,
Dismal Fear, unholy Famine, with low-groveling Want,
10  Forms of spectral horror, gaunt Toil and Death the devourer,
And Death's drowsy brother, Torpor; with whom, an inane
            rout,
All the Pleasures of Sin; there also the Furies in ambusht
Chamber of iron, afore whose bars wild War bloodyhanded
Raged, and mad Discord high brandisht her venomous locks.
   Midway of all this tract, with secular arms an immense elm
Reareth a crowd of branches, aneath whose leafy protection
Vain dreams thickly nestle, clinging unto the foliage on high:
And many strange creatures of monstrous form and features
Stable about th' entrance, Centaur and Scylla's abortion,
20  And hundred-handed Briareus, and Lerna the wildbeast
Roaring amain, and clothed in frightful flame the Chimæra,

---

*The title is from Aen. VI. 268, '*ibant obscuri sola sub nocte per umbram*'.

Gorgons and Harpies, ' and Pluto's three-bodied ogre.
   In terror Æneas upheld his sword to defend him,
With ready naked point confronting their dreaded onset:
And had not the Sibyl warn'd how these lively spirits were
All incorporeal, flitting in thin maskery of form,
He had assail'd their host, and wounded vainly the void air.
   Hence is a road that led them a-down to the Tartarean
                                                    streams,
Where Acheron's whirlpool impetuous, into the reeky
30   Deep of Cokytos disgorgeth, with muddy burden.
These floods one ferryman serveth, most awful of aspect,
Of squalor infernal, Chāron: all filthily unkempt
That woolly white cheek-fleece, and fiery the blood-shotten
                                                    eyeballs:
On one shoulder a cloak knotted-up his nudity vaunteth.
He himself plieth oar or pole, manageth tiller and sheet,
And the relics of mén in his ash-grey barge ferries over;
Already old, but green to a god and hearty will age be.
   Now hitherward to the bank much folk were crowding, a
                                                    medley
Of men and matrons; nor did death's injury conceal
40   Bravespirited heroes, young maidens beauteous unwed,
And boys borne to the grave in sight of their sorrowing sires.
   Countless as in the forest, at a first white frosting of autumn
Sere leaves fall to the ground; or like whenas over the ocean
Myrıâd birds come thickly flocking, when wintry December
Drives them afar southward for shelter upon sunnier shores,
So throng'd they; and each his watery journey demanded,
All to the further bank stretching-oút their arms impatient:
But the sullen boatman took now one now other at will,
While some from the river forbade he', an' drave to a distance.

                              *

50   Here too Deiphobus he espied, his fair body mangled,
Cruelly dismember'd, disfeatur'd cruelly his face,
Face and hands; and lo! shorn closely from either temple,

Gone wer' his ears, and maim'd each nostril in impious
                                                    outrage.
Barely he⁻knew him again cow'ring shamefastly' an' hiding
His dire plight, & thus he 'his old companyon accosted.
'Noblest Deiphobus, great Teucer's intrepid offspring,
Who was it, inhuman, coveted so cruel a vengeance?
Who can hav' adventur'd on thée? That last terrible night
Thou wert said to hav' exceeded thy bravery, an' only
60  On thy faln enemies wert faln by weariness o'ercome.
Wherefor' upon the belov'd sea-shore thine empty sepulchral
Mound I erected, aloud on thy ghost tearfully calling.
Name and shield keep for⁻thee the place; but thy body, dear
                                                    friend,
Found I not, to commit to the land ere sadly' I left it.'
    Then the son of Priam ' 'I thought not, friend, to reproach
                                                    thee:
Thou didst all to the full, ev'n my shade's service, accomplish.
'Twas that uninterdicted adultress from Lacedæmon
Drave⁻me to doom, & planted in hell, her trophy triumphant.
On that night, – how vain a security and merrymaking
70  Then sullied us thou know'st, yea must too keenly
                                                    remember, –
When the ill-omened horse o'erleapt Troy's lofty defences,
Dragg'd in amidst our town pregnant with a burden of arm'd
                                                    men.
She then, her Phrygian women in feign'd phrenzy collecting,
All with torches aflame, in wild Bacchic orgy paraded,
Flaring a signal aloft to her ambusht confederate Greeks.
I from a world of care had fled with weariful eyelids
Unto my unhappy chamber', an' lay fast lockt in oblivyon,
Sunk to the depth of rest as a child that nought will awaken.
Meanwhile that paragon helpmate had robb'd me of all arms,
80  E'en from aneath the pillow my blade of trust purloining; –

67 Helen, wife of Menelaus: after Paris's death she lived as Deiphobus' wife.

Then to the gate; wide flíngs she it op'n an' calls Menelaus.
Would not a so great service attach her faithful adorer?
Might not it extinguish the repute of her earlier illdeeds?
Brief⁻be the tale. Menelaus arrives: in company there came
His crime-counsellor Æolides . . . So, and more also
Déal⁻ye', O Gods, to the Greeks! an' if I call justly upon
                                                        you. –
But thou; what fortune hitherward, in turn prithy tell me,
Sent⁻thee alive, whether erring upon the bewildering Ocean,
Or high-prompted of heav'n, or by Fate wearily hunted,
90  That to the sunless abodes and dusky demesnes thou
                                                approachest?'
    Ev'n as awhile they thus converse it is already mid-day
Unperceiv'd, but aloft earth's star had turn'd to declining.
And haply' Æneas his time in parley had outgone,
Had not then the Sibyl with word of warning avized him.
'Night hieth, Æneas; in tears our journey delayeth.
See our road, that it here in twain disparteth asunder;
This to the right, skirting by th' high city-fortresses of Dis,
Endeth in Elysium, our path; but that to the leftward
Only receives their feet who wend to eternal affliction.'
100  Deiphobus then again, 'Speak not, great priestess, in anger;
I will away to refill my number among th' unfortun'd.
Thou, my champyon, adieu! Go where thy glory awaits thee!'
When these words he 'had spok'n, he⁻turn'd and hastily was
                                                        fled.
    Æneas then look'd where leftward, under a mountain,
Outspread a wide city lay, threefold with fortresses engirt,
Lickt by a Tartarean river of live fire, the torrential
Red Phlegethon, and huge boulders his roundy bubbles be:
Right i' the front stareth the columnar gate adamantine,
Such that no battering warfare of mén or immortals
110  E'er might shake; blank-faced to the cloud its bastion
                                                    upstands.
Tisiphone thereby in a bloodspotty robe sitteth alway
Night and day guarding sleeplessly the desperat entrance,

Wherefrom an awestirring groan-cry and fierce clamour
outburst,
Sharp lashes, insane yells, dragg'd chains and clanking of iron.
   Æneas drew back, his heart by' his hearing affrighted:
'What manner of criminals, my guide, now tell⁻me,' he
question'd,
'Or what their penalties? what this great wail that ariseth?'
Answering him the divine priestess, 'Brave hero of Iliûm,
O'er that guilty threshold no breath of purity may come:
120   But Hecate, who gave⁻me to rule i' the groves of Avernus,
Herself led me around, & taught heav'n's high retribution.
Here Cretan Rhadamanthus in unblest empery reigneth,
Secret crime to punish, – full surely he⁻wringeth avowal
Even of all that on earth, by vain impunity harden'd,
Men sinning have put away from thought till'impenitent death.
On those convicted tremblers then leapeth avenging
Tisiphone with keen flesh-whips and vipery scourges,
And of her implacable sisters inviteth attendance.'
– Now sudden on screeching hinges that portal accursèd
130   Flung wide its barriers. – 'In what dire custody, mark thou,
Is the threshold! guarded by how grim sentry the doorway!
More terrible than they the ravin'd insatiable Hydra
That sitteth angry within. Know too that Tartarus itself
Dives sheer gaping aneath in gloomy profundity downward
Twice that height that a man looketh-up t'ward airy Olympus.
Lowest there those children of Earth, Titanian elders,
In the abyss, where once they fell hurl'd, yet wallowing lie.
There the Alöïdæ saw I, th' ungainly rebel twins
Primæval, that assay'd to devastate th' Empyræan
140   With huge hands, and rob from Jove his kingdom immortal.
And there Salmoneus I saw, rend'ring heavy payment,
For that he idly' had mockt heav'n's fire and thunder electric;
With chariot many-yoked and torches brandishing on high
Driving among 'his Graian folk in Olympian Elis;
Exultant as a God he rode in blasphemy worshipt.

---

**136ff**. These old gods and giants tried to overthrow Jupiter.

Fool, who th' unreckoning tempest and deadly dreaded bolt
Thought to mimic with brass and confus'd trample of horses!
But 'him th' Omnipotent, from amidst his cloudy pavilyon,
Blasted, an' eke his rattling car and smoky pretences
150 Extinguish'd at a stroke, scattering ' his dust to the whirlwind.
There too huge Tityos, whom Earth that gendereth all things
Once foster'd, spreadeth-out o'er nine full roods his immense
limbs.
On him a wild vulture with hook-beak greedily gorgeth
His liver upsprouting quick as that Hell-chicken eateth.
Shé diggeth and dwelleth under the vast ribs, her bloody bare
neck
Lifting anon: ne'er loathes she the food, ne'er fails the
renewal.
Where wer' an end their names to relate, their crimes and
torments?
Some o'er whom a hanging black rock, slipping at very
point of
Falling, ever threateneth: Couches luxurious invite
160 Softly-cushion'd to repose: Tables for banqueting outlaid
Tempt them ever-famishing: hard by them a Fury regardeth,
And should théy but a hand uplift, trembling to the dainties,
She with live firebrand and direful yell springeth on them.
    Their crimes, – not to' hav lov'd a brother while love was
allow'd them;
Or to' hav struck their father, or inveigled a dependant;
Or who chancing alone on wealth prey'd lustfully thereon,
Nor made share with others, no greater company than they:
Some for adultery slain; some their bright swords had offended
Drawn i' the wrong: or a master's trust with perfidy had met:
170 Dungeon'd their penalties they await. Look not to be
answer'd
What that doom, nor th' end of these men think to determine.
Sóme aye roll heavy rocks, some whirl dizzy on the revolving

Spokes of a pendant wheel: sitteth and to eternity shall sit
Unfortun'd Theseus; while sad Phlegias saddeneth hell
With vain oyez to' all loud crying a tardy repentance,
"Walk, O man, i' the fear of Gód, and learn to be righteous!"
Here another, who sold for gold his country, promoting
Her tyrant; or annull'd for a base bribe th' inviolate law.
This one had unfather'd his blood with bestial incest:
180  All some fearful crime had dared & vaunted achievement.
What mind could harbour the offence of such recollection,
Or lend welcoming ear to the tale of iniquity and shame,
And to the pains wherewith such deeds are justly requited?'
     Ev'n when thus she' had spok'n, the priestess dear to

                                                        Apollo,
'But, ready, come let us ón, perform⁻we the order appointed!
Hast'n⁻we (saith⁻she), the wall forged on Cyclopian anvils
Now I see, an' th' archway in Ætna's furnace attemper'd,
Where my lore biddeth us to depose our high-privileg'd gift.'
     Then together they trace i' the drooping dimness a

                                                        footpath,
190  Whereby, faring across, they arrive at th' arches of iron.
Æneas stept into the porch, and duly besprinkling
His body with clear water affixt his bough to the lintel;
And, having all perform'd at length with ritual exact,
They came out on a lovely pleasance, that dream'd-of oasis,
Fortunate isle, the abode o' the blest, their fair Happy

                                                        Woodland.
Here is an ampler sky, those meads ar' azur'd by a gentler
Sun than th' Earth, an' a new starworld their darkness

                                                        adorneth.

                            *

Now Lord Anchises was down i' the green valley musing,
Where the spirits confin'd that await mortal resurrection

---

174 Theseus tried to carry off Persephone from Hades; Phlegias set fire to
Apollo's temple. These mythical sinners were all guilty of the same crime:
blasphemy against the gods.

200  While diligently he⁻mark'd, his thought had turn'd to his own
                                                                  kin,
     Whose numbers he⁻reckon'd, an' of all their progeny foretold
     Their fate and fortune, their ripen'd temper an' action:
     He then, when he' espied Æneas t'ward him approaching
     O'er the meadow, both hands uprais'd and ran to receive him,
     Tears in his eyes, while thus his voice in high passion outbrake.
     'Ah, thou'rt come, thou'rt come! at length thy dearly belov'd
                                                                 grace
     Conquering all hath won⁻thee the way. 'Tis allow'd to behold
                                                                 thee,
     O my son, – yea again the familyar raptur' of our speech.
     Nay, I look't for 't thus, counting patiently the moments,
210  And ever expected; nor did fond fancy betray me.
     From what lands, my son, from what life-dangering ocean
     Art⁻thou arrived? full mighty perils thy path hav' opposèd:
     And how nearly the dark Libyan thy destiny o'erthrew!'
     Then 'he, 'Thy spirit, O my sire, 'twas thy spirit often
     Sadly appearing aroused⁻me to seek thy fair habitation.
     My fleet moors i' the blue Tyrrhene: all with⁻me goeth well.
     Grant⁻me to touch thy hand as of old, and thy body embrace.'
     Speaking, awhile in tears his feeling mutinied, and when
     For the longing contact of mortal affection, he out-held
220  His strong arms, the figure sustain'd them not: 'twas as empty
     E'en as a windworn cloud, or a phantom of irrelevant sleep.
          On the level bosom of this vale more thickly the tall trees
     Grow, an' aneath quivering poplars and whispering alders
     Lethe's dreamy river throu' peaceful scenery windeth.
     Whereby now flitted in vast swarms many people of all
                                                                 lands,
     As when in early summer 'honey-bees on a flowery pasture
     Pill the blossoms, hurrying to' an' fro, – innumerous are they,
     Revisiting the ravish'd lily cups, while all the meadow hums.
          Æneas was turn'd to the sight, and marvelling inquired,
230  'Say, sir, what the river that there i' the vale-bottom I see?
     And who they that thickly along its bank have assembled?'

Then Lord Anchises, 'The spirits for whom a second life
And body are destined ar' arriving thirsty to Lethe,
And here drink th' unmindful draught from wells of
oblivyon.
My heart greatly desired of this very thing to acquaint thee,
Yea, and show¯thee the men to¯be¯born, our glory her'after,
So to gladden thine heart where now thy voyaging endeth.'
'Must it then be¯believ'd, my sire, that a soul which attaineth
Elysium will again submit to her old body-burden?
240   Is this well? what hap can awake such dire longing in them?'
'I will tell thee', O son, nor keep thy wonder awaiting,'
Answereth Anchises, and all expoundeth in order.
'Know first that the heavens, and th' Earth, and space fluid or
void,
Night's pallid orb, day's Sun, and all his starry coævals,
Are by one spirit inly quickened, and, mingling in each part,
Mind informs the matter, nature's complexity ruling.
Thence the living creatures, man, brute, and ev'ry feather'd
fowl,
And what breedeth in Ocean aneath her surface of argent:
Their seed knoweth a fiery vigour, 'tis of airy divine birth,
250   In so far as unimpeded by an alien evil,
Nor dull'd by the body's framework condemn'd to
corruption.
Hence the desires and vain tremblings that assail them, unable
Darkly prison'd to arise to celestial exaltation;
Nor when death summoneth them anon earth-life to
relinquish,
Can they in all discard their stain, nor wholly away with
Mortality's plaguespots. It must¯be that, O, many wild graffs
Deeply at 'heart engrain'd have rooted strangely upon them:
Wherefore must suffering purge them, yea, Justice atone
them
With penalties heavy as their guilt: some purify exposed
260   Hung to the viewless winds, or others long watery searchings
Low i' the deep wash clean, some bathe in fiery renewal:

Each cometh unto his own retribution, – if after in ample
Elysium we attain, but a few, to the fair Happy Woodland,
Yet slow time still worketh on us to remove the defilement,
Till it hath eaten away the acquir'd dross, leaving again free
That first fiery vigour, the celestial virtue of our life.
All whom here thou seest, hav' accomplished purification:
Unto the stream of Lethe a god their company calleth,
That forgetful of old failure, pain & disappointment,
270   They may again into' earthly bodies with glad courage enter.'

(1916)

# V. SACKVILLE-WEST (1892–1962)

## The Land

*The Land* is a 'georgic' poem in four books, one for each of the
seasons (cf. Thomson's georgic poem *The Seasons*). The first extract,
from 'Spring', includes advice on arboriculture (see Virgil, *Georgics*
II) and bees (see *Georgics* IV). In the conclusion, the poet specifically
invokes Virgil.

### Spring: Orchards – Young stock – Bee-master (part)

ORCHARDS
Look, too, to your orchards in the early spring.
The blossom-weevil bores into the sheath,
Grubs tunnel in the pith of promising shoots,
The root-louse spends his winter tucked beneath
Rough bark of trunks or chinks of tangled roots;
Canker, rot, scab, and mildew blight the tree;
There seems an enemy in everything.
Even the bulfinch with his pretty song,

10   And blue puffed tits make havoc in the pears
     Pecking with tiny beak and strong;
     Mild February airs
     Are full of rogues on mischievous wing,
     And orchard trees are wickedly tenanted
     By crawling pirates newly roused from sloth,
     The apple-sucker and wood-leopard moth;
     Who'd win his fight must wage a constant war,
     Have sense in his fingers, eyes behind his head;
     Therefore let foresight race ahead of time,
     Spray close and well
20   With soap and sulphur, quassia, lead, and lime,
     When buds begin to swell,
     All to defeat some small conspirator.

     Sometimes in apple country you may see
     A ghostly orchard standing all in white,
     Aisles of white trees, white branches, in the green,
     On some still day when the year hangs between
     Winter and spring, and heaven is full of light.
     And rising from the ground pale clouds of smoke
     Float through the trees and hang upon the air,
30   Trailing their wisps of blue like a swelled cloak
     From the round cheeks of breezes. But though fair
     To him who leans upon the gate to stare
     And muse 'How delicate in spring they be,
     That mobled blossom and that wimpled tree,'
     There is a purpose in the cloudy aisles
     That took no thought of beauty for its care.
     For here's the beauty of all country miles,
     Their rolling pattern and their space:
     That there's a reason for each changing square,
40   Here sleeping fallow, there a meadow mown,
     All to their use ranged different each year,
     The shaven grass, the gold, the brindled roan,
     Not in some search for empty grace,
     But fine through service and intent sincere.

YOUNG STOCK

Nor shall you for your fields neglect your stock;
Spring is the season when the young things thrive,
Having the kindly months before them. Lambs,
Already sturdy, straggle from the flock;
Frisk tails; tug grass-tufts; stare at children; prance;
50   Then panic-stricken scuttle for their dams.
Calves learn to drink from buckets; foals
Trot laxly in the meadow, with soft glance
Inquisitive; barn, sty and shed
Teem with young innocence newly come alive.
Round collie puppies, on the sunny step,
Buffet each other with their duffer paws
And pounce at flies, and nose the plaited skep,
And with tucked tail slink yelping from the hive.
Likewise the little secret beasts
60   That open eyes on a world of death and dread,
Thirst, hunger, and mishap,
The covert denizens of holts and shaws,
The little creatures of the ditch and hedge,
Mice nested in a tussock, shrews, and voles,
Inhabitants of the wood,
The red-legged dabchick, paddling in the sedge,
Followed by chubby brood;
The vixen, prick-eared for the first alarm
Beside her tumbling cubs at foot of tree, –
70   All in the spring begin their precarious round,
Not cherished as the striplings on the farm,
Sheltered, and cosseted, and kept from harm,
But fang and claw against them, snare and trap,
For life is perilous to the small wild things,
Danger's their lot, and fears abound;
Great cats destroy unheedful wings,
And nowhere's safety on the hunted ground;
And who's to blame them, though they be
Sly, as a man would think him shame?

80    Man in security walks straight and free,
        And shall not measure blame,
        For they, that each on other preys,
        Weasel on rabbit, owl on shrew,
        Their cowardly and murderous ways
        In poor defence of life pursue,
        Not for a wanton killing, not for lust,
        As stags will fight among the trampled brake
        With antlers running red; with gore and thrust,
        With hoofs that stamp, and royal heads that shake
90    Blood from their eyes, – in vain,
        Since still their splendid anger keeps them blind,
        And lowers their entangled brows again,
        For brief possession of a faithless hind; –
        Not thus, but furtive through the rustling leaves
        Life preys on little life; the frightened throat
        Squeals once beneath the yellow bite of stoat,
        Destroyers all, necessity of kind;
        Talon rips fur, and fang meets sharper fang,
        And even sleeping limbs must be alert.
100   But fortunate, if death with sudden pang
        Leaps, and is ended; if no lingering hurt,
        Dragging a broken wing or mangled paw,
        Brings the slow anguish that no night reprieves,
        In the dark refuge of a lonely shaw.

        So do they venture on their chance of life
        When months seem friendliest; so shall men
        Repair their herds in spring by natural law
        In byre and farrowing pen.
        Thus shall you do, with calves that you would rear,
110   – Heifer, not driven to the slaughterer's knife,
        And bull-calf, early cut from bull to steer, –
        Two to one udder run, till they may feed
        Alone; then turn the little foster-siblings out;

Or wean from birth, and teach to drink from pail,
With fair allowance of their mother's milk,
(But watch, for as the calf grows hale,
He's rough, and knocks the empty pail about.)
By either method shall you safely breed
Moist muzzles, thrifty coats of silk,
120   Well-uddered heifers, bullocks strong and stout.

BEE-MASTER

The wise man, too, will keep his stock of bees
In a sheltered corner of his garden patch,
Where they may winter warmly, breed and hatch
New swarms to fill his combs and fertilize his trees.

I have known honey from the Syrian hills
Stored in cool jars; the wild accacia there
On the rough terrace where the locust shrills,
Tosses her spindrift to the ringing air;
Narcissus bares his nectarous perianth
130   In white and golden tabard to the sun,
And while the workers rob the amaranth
Or scarlet windflower low among the stone
Intent upon their crops,
The Syrian queens mate in the high hot day,
Rapt visionaries of creative fray,
Soaring from fecund ecstasy alone,
While through the blazing ether, drops
Like a small thunderbolt the vindicated drone.

I have known bees within the ruined arch
140   Of Akbar's crimson city hang their comb;
Swarm in forsaken courts in a sultry March,
Where the mild ring-doves croon, and small apes play,
And the thin mangy jackal makes his home;
And where, the red walls kindling in the flares,

Once the great Moghul lolling on his throne,
Between his languid fingers crumbling spice,
Ordered his women to the chequered squares,
And moved them at the hazard of the dice.

But this is the bee-master's reckoning
150  In England. Walk among the hives and hear.

Forget not bees in winter, though they sleep,
For winter's big with summer in her womb,
And when you plant your rose-trees, plant them deep,
Having regard to bushes all aflame,
And see the dusky promise of their bloom
In small red shoots, and let each redolent name –
Tuscany, Crested Cabbage, Cottage Maid –
Load with full June November's dank repose;
See the kind cattle drowsing in the shade,
160  And hear the bee about his amorous trade,
Brown in the gipsy crimson of the rose.

                    *


# Autumn

VINTAGE
The wooden shovels take the purple stain,
The dusk is heavy with the wine's warm load;
Here the long sense of classic measure cures
The spirit weary of its difficult pain;
Here the old Bacchic piety endures,
Here the sweet legends of the world remain.
Homeric waggons lumbering the road;
Virgilian litanies among the bine;
170  Pastoral sloth of flocks beneath the pine;
The swineherd watching, propped upon his goad,

Under the chestnut trees the rootling swine.
Who could so stand, and see this evening fall,
This calm of husbandry, this redolent tilth,
This terracing of hills, this vintage wealth,
Without the pagan sanity of blood
Mounting his veins in young and tempered health?
Who could so stand, and watch processional
The vintners, herds, and flocks in dusty train
180   Wend through the molten evening to regain
The terraced farm and trodden threshing-floor
Where late the flail
Tossed high the maize in scud of gritty ore,
And lies half-buried in the heap of grain, –
Who could so watch, and not forget the rack
Of wills worn thin and thought become too frail,
Nor roll the centuries back
And feel the sinews of his soul grow hale,
And know himself for Rome's inheritor?


190   O Mantuan! that sang the bees and vines,
The tillage and the flocks,
I saw the round moon rise above the pines
One quiet planet prick the greening west,
As goats came leaping up the stony crest
And the crook'd goatherd moved between the rocks.
That moon, that star, above my English weald,
Hung at that hour, and I not there to see;
Shining through mist above the dew-drenched field,
Making a cavern of the plumy tree.
200   Then all my deep acquaintance with that land,
Crying for words, welled up; as man who knows
That Nature, tender enemy, harsh friend,
Takes from him soon the little that she gave,
Yet for his span will labour to defend
His courage, that his soul be not a slave,

Whether on waxen tablet or on loam,
Whether with stylus or with share and heft
The record of his passage he engrave,
And still, in toil, takes heart to love the rose.

210    Then thought I, Virgil! how from Mantua reft,
Shy as a peasant in the courts of Rome,
You took the waxen tablets in your hand,
And out of anger cut calm tales of home.         (1926)

# C. W. BRODRIBB (1878–1945)

## [Georg. III. 209–85] *The power of love*

From *Virgil: the Georgics in English Hexameters* (1928). In a prefatory note the author writes that 'an attempt has been made to reproduce the original metre as nearly as the structural differences between the two languages will permit'. The result may be compared with the earlier experiment of Robert Bridges: both writers use archaisms, including the third-person-singular verb in —eth.

And never is discipline more forcefully invigorating
Than when unexcited love's blind provocation is absent:
Steers be it or stallions, as custom mostly commendeth.
Wherefore men set apart their bulls and give them a pasture
In solitude, a river's prisoners or penn'd on a hillside;
Or shut up in their stalls they find them plenty withindoors:
Else the presence will waste them away: seen nearly the
                                       female
Rouseth a flame; her charms will allure; nor stays the
                                       remembrance
Of fodder or woodland any more; and often atwixt them
10    She, the heifer, wakes strife, forcing them proudly to
                                       warfare.

Beautiful on Sila's broad pastures grazeth a damsel:
Her duelling suitors alternate dash to the combat,
And many are the buffets exchang'd; blood darkly bedews
                                              them;
And their loud bellowings, while horn conflicteth against horn,
Fill the forests and groves and set long Olympus in uproar.
No common encampment yields courtesy; but the defeated
Beats a retreat and moveth away a wandering exile:
Grievous is his disgrace, his victor's haughtiness irks him,
His wounds all unaveng'd, his love lost: wistfully casting
20   Glance upon ancestral kingdoms he leaves them, an outlaw.
Whereupon, all diligence, he trains his forces, on unstrewn
Ground finds flinty bedding, there nightlong lying uneasy,
Champs the roughest herbage, the rushes' sharp prickliness
                                              eating,
And trieth ev'ry device, wrath's new scholar e'en to the
                                              horntips,
Now battering tree-trunks, and now to the wind's
                                              provocation
Spurning as in prelude to the fray his sandy parade ground.
Then rallying powers freshly resumed he moves to the onset,
Advancing the colours on an unsuspecting opponent:
As when afar the billow that whiteneth in the midocean
30   Marches on, and thence draws to an arch, and soon with
                                              immense bulk
Rolleth ashore, crashing over the reefs, not less than a
                                              mountain
Crestfal'n, while the nether waters with yeasty resurgence
Tumble about and cast their sombre sand-eddy upwards.

   All the living creatures upon earth, or wilding or human,
All fishes, all beast-kind, and birds of motley adornment,
Rush to the flame and phrenzy: the same passion equally
                                              rules them.
And never else prowleth lioness, forgetful of her cubs,
More ravenously abroad; never else more murderous are
                                              bears,

Rude ruffians, working many deaths and mischief on all sides
40    In the forest; then fierce is a hog, most spiteful a tigress.
Ah! 'tis an ill conduct Libyan wastes lend to the lonely!
Dart-like through the bodies (hast thou not markt it?) of horses
Runs a tremor when a scent as of old comes wafted upon
                                                        them:
No rein of rider, no lash plied angrily serveth;
Nor precipice nor stony crevasse shall stay them a moment,
Nor the river that swirls its mountain scenery down-stream.
Out rusheth he, the Sabine wild-boar, and sharpeneth his tusk,
Plants foot aground and rooteth in earth, rubs sides on a
                                                    treetrunk,
And shoving here and there hardens his shoulder against scars.
50    What will a youth whose frame feels love's imperious ardour
Burn as a fire? Storms break, and straits loom darkly before
                                                        him;
Late at night he stems the current, while thundering o'erhead
Heav'n's high portal echoes, and rocks cry against him as on
                                                        them
Spray dasheth; and agoniz'd parents shall vainly recall him,
And bride doom'd to perish where ruthless destiny lays him.
See the dappled ounces that Bacchus brings as an escort,
Wolves, dogs and mild deer to the lists all bravely repairing.
Sooth, above all the passion rages most fiercely among mares:
She, the goddess, moved them when those four Potnian horses
60    Turned to devour Glaucus, rending their master asunder.
Them the passion conducts o'er Gargara, o'er the resounding
Ascanius; they cross mountains and watery reaches;
And ever as the desire kindles to a fury within them,
Most in spring, since spring once more bringeth heat to
                                                    them, as one
Toward the zephyr they turn, taking their station on high
                                                        crags,

---

59–60 Glaucus kept a herd of mares at Potniae: they went mad and devoured him.

And drink in the pleasant breezes, thence (truly a marvel!)
Made pregnant, though males be away, conceiving an air-
                                                     draught;
Then scatter o'er steep bluffs, down cliffs, and sloping races
Hastily, not to the east's quarters nor yet to the sunrise,
70   But north and north-west, and darkest cradle of Auster
Where blackening whirlwinds are born and rain-heavy
                                                     tempests.
Thence cometh *hippomanes*, so titled rightly of herdsmen:
Slowly running from a mare's haunches 'tis a poisonous issue:
*Hippomanes* many times in witchcraft's noisome alembic
Brew'd with mixed simples and incantation accursèd.   (1928)


# ALLEN TATE (1899–1979)

## The Mediterranean

The poet juxtaposes the timeless world of Aeneas' voyage to Italy
(Hesperia, land of the west) and the historical world of his ancestors'
voyage to the New World.

*Quem das finem, rex magne, dolorum?**

Where we went in the boat was a long bay
A slingshot wide, walled in by towering stone –
Peaked margin of antiquity's delay,
And we went there out of time's monotone:

---

**69–70** Virgil refers to the belief (found in Aristotle) that mares run either
north or south (Auster), but never east or west.
*The Latin quotation is from *Aeneid* I, 241: the correct reading is *laborum*, not
*dolorum*; Venus asks Jupiter when Aeneas' trials will end.

Where we went in the black hull no light moved
But a gull white-winged along the feckless wave,
The breeze, unseen but fierce as a body loved,
That boat drove onward like a willing slave:

Where we went in the small ship the seaweed
10   Parted and gave to us the murmuring shore,
And we made feast and in our secret need
Devoured the very plates Aeneas bore:

Where derelict you see through the low twilight
The green coast that you, thunder-tossed, would win,
Drop sail, and hastening to drink all night
Eat dish and bowl to take that sweet land in!

Where we feasted and caroused on the sandless
Pebbles, affecting our day of piracy,
What prophecy of eaten plates could landless
20   Wanderers fulfil by the ancient sea?

We for that time might taste the famous age
Eternal here yet hidden from our eyes
When lust of power undid its stuffless rage;
They, in a wineskin, bore earth's paradise.

Let us lie down once more by the breathing side
Of Ocean, where our live forefathers sleep
As if the Known Sea still were a month wide –
Atlantis howls but is no longer steep!

---

12–20 The allusion is to the prophecy in *Aeneid* III that the Trojans will
know they have reached their homeland when they find themselves consum-
ing the plates (i.e. flat cakes) on which they picnicked. The prophecy comes
true at the beginning of Book VII when the Trojans land at the mouth of the
Tiber.

What country shall we conquer, what fair land
30   Unman our conquest and locate our blood?
    We've cracked the hemispheres with careless hand!
    Now, from the Gates of Hercules we flood

    Westward, westward till the barbarous brine
    Whelms us to the tired land where tasseling corn,
    Fat beans, grapes sweeter than muscadine
    Rot on the vine: in that land were we born.                    (1936)


# C. DAY LEWIS (1904–72)

## [Georg. IV. 125–46; I. 493–511]

Like Ogilby and Dryden, Day Lewis translated the complete works
of Virgil, beginning with the *Georgics*, composed during the Second
World War: the parallel with Virgil's time is referred to in the
dedicatory stanzas to Stephen Spender, and is particularly striking in
the closing lines of Book I. The first extract, the description of
the old gardener, picks up the theme of happiness through self-
sufficiency which permeates Book II.

### FROM DEDICATORY STANZAS TO STEPHEN SPENDER
. . . Meanwhile, what touches the heart at all, engrosses.
Through the flushed springtime and the fading year
I lived on country matters. Now June was here
Again, and brought the smell of flowering grasses
To me and death to many overseas:
They lie in the flowering sunshine, flesh once dear
To some, now parchment for the heart's release.
Soon enough each is called into the quarrel.
Till then, taking a leaf from Virgil's laurel,
10   I sang in time of war the arts of peace.

Virgil – a tall man, dark and countrified
In looks, they say: retiring: no rhetorician:
Of humble birth: a Celt, whose first ambition
Was to be a philosopher: Dante's guide.
But chiefly dear for his gift to understand
Earth's intricate, ordered heart, and for a vision
That saw beyond an imperial day the hand
Of man no longer armed against his fellow
But all for vine and cattle, fruit and fallow,
20   Subduing with love's positive force the land.

Different from his our age and myths, our toil
The same. Our exile and extravagances,
Revolt, retreat, fine faiths, disordered fancies
Are but the poet's search for a right soil
Where words may settle, marry, and conceive an
Imagined truth, for a regimen that enhances
Their natural grace. Now, as to one whom even
Our age's drought and spate have not deterred
From cherishing, like a bud of flame, the word,
30   I dedicate this book to you, dear Stephen.

Now, when war's long midwinter seems to freeze us
And numb our living sources once for all,
That veteran of Virgil's I recall
Who made a kitchen-garden by the Galaesus
On derelict land, and got the first of spring
From airs and buds, the first fruits in the fall,
And lived at peace there, happy as a king.
Naming him for good luck, I see man's native
Stock is perennial, and our creative
40   Winged seed can strike a root in anything.

*

I remember once beneath the battlements of Oebalia,
Where dark Galaesus waters the golden fields of corn,

I saw an old man, a Corycian, who owned a few poor acres
Of land once derelict, useless for arable,
No good for grazing, unfit for the cultivation of vines.
But he laid out a kitchen garden in rows amid the
                                                    brushwood,
Bordering it with white lilies, verbena, small-seeded poppy.
He was happy there as a king. He could go indoors at night
To a table heaped with dainties he never had to buy.
His the first rose of spring, the earliest apples in autumn:
And when grim winter still was splitting the rocks with cold
And holding the watercourses with curb of ice, already
That man would be cutting his soft-haired hyacinths,
                                                    complaining
Of summer's backwardness and the west winds slow to come.
His bees were the first to breed,
Enriching him with huge swarms: he squeezed the frothy
                                                    honey
Before anyone else from the combs: he had limes and a
                                                    wealth of pine trees:
And all the early blossom, that clothed his trees with promise
Of an apple crop, by autumn had come to maturity.
He had a gift, too, for transplanting in rows the far-grown
                                                    elm,
The hardwood pear, the blackthorn bearing its weight of
                                                    sloes,
And the plane that already offered a pleasant shade for
                                                    drinking.
But these are matters the strict scope of my theme forbids me:
I must pass them by, and leave them for later men to enlarge
                                                    on.

*

Surely the time will come when a farmer on those frontiers
Forcing through earth his curved plough

Shall find old spears eaten away with flaky rust,
Or hit upon helmets as he wields the weight of his mattock
And marvel at the heroic bones he has disinterred.
70   O Gods of our fathers, native Gods, Romulus, Vesta
Who mothers our Tuscan Tiber and the Roman Palatine,
At least allow our young prince to rescue this shipwrecked era!
Long enough now have we
Paid in our blood for the promise Laomedon broke at Troy.
Long now has the court of heaven grudged you to us; Caesar,
Complaining because you care only for mortal triumphs.
For Right and Wrong are confused here, there's so much
war in the world,
Evil has so many faces, the plough so little
Honour, the labourers are taken, the fields untended,
80   And the curving sickle is beaten into the sword that yields not.
There the East is in arms, here Germany marches:
Neighbour cities, breaking their treaties, attack each other:
The wicked War-god runs amok through all the world.

(1940)


# ROBERT LOWELL (1917–77)

## Falling Asleep over the Aeneid

From *Poems 1938–49*. See Patric Dickinson's translation of *Aeneid* XI,
1–212 (the funeral of Pallas).

(*An old man in Concord forgets to go to morning service. He falls
asleep, while reading Vergil, and dreams that he is Aeneas at the
funeral of Pallas, an Italian prince.*)

The sun is blue and scarlet on my page,
And *yuck-a, yuck-a, yuck-a, yuck-a*, rage
The yellowhammers mating. Yellow fire
Blankets the captives dancing on their pyre,

And the scorched lictor screams and drops his rod.
Trojans are singing to their drunken God,
Ares. Their helmets catch on fire. Their files
Clank by the body of my comrade – miles
Of filings! Now the scythe-wheeled chariot rolls
10   Before their lances long as vaulting poles,
And I stand up and heil the thousand men,
Who carry Pallas to the bird-priest. Then
The bird-priest groans, and as his birds foretold,
I greet the body, lip to lip. I hold
The sword that Dido used. It tries to speak,
A bird with Dido's sworded breast. Its beak
Clangs and ejaculates the Punic word
I hear the bird-priest chirping like a bird.
I groan a little. 'Who am I, and why?'
20   It asks, a boy's face, though its arrow-eye
Is working from its socket. 'Brother, try,
O Child of Aphrodite, try to die:
To die is life.' His harlots hang his bed
With feathers of his long-tailed birds. His head
Is yawning like a person. The plumes blow;
The beard and eyebrows ruffle. Face of snow,
You are the flower that country girls have caught,
A wild bee-pillaged honey-suckle brought
To the returning bridegroom – the design
30   Has not yet left it, and the petals shine;
The earth, its mother, has, at last, no help:
It is itself. The broken-winded yelp
Of my Phoenician hounds, that fills the brush
With snapping twigs and flying, cannot flush
The ghost of Pallas. But I take his pall,
Stiff with its gold and purple, and recall

---

**29–32** Cf. *Aeneid* XI, 70–71.
**35–9** Cf. *Aeneid* XI, 72–7.

How Dido hugged it to her, while she toiled,
Laughing – her golden threads, a serpent coiled
In cypress. Now I lay it like a sheet;
40   It clinks and settles down upon his feet,
The careless yellow hair that seemed to burn
Beforehand. Left foot, right foot – as they turn,
More pyres are rising: armoured horses, bronze,
And gagged Italians, who must file by ones
Across the bitter river, when my thumb
Tightens into their wind-pipes. The beaks drum;
Their headman's cow-horned death's-head bites its tongue,
And stiffens, as it eyes the hero slung
Inside his feathered hammock on the crossed
50   Staves of the eagles that we winged. Our cost
Is nothing to the lovers, whoring Mars
And Venus, father's lover. Now his car's
Plumage is ready, and my marshals fetch
His squire, Acoetes, white with age, to hitch
Aethon, the hero's charger, and its ears
Prick, and it steps and steps, and stately tears
Lather its teeth; and then the harlots bring
The hero's charms and baton – but the King,
Vain-glorious Turnus, carried off the rest.
60   'I was myself, but Ares thought it best
The way it happened.' At the end of time,
He sets his spear, as my descendants climb
The knees of Father Time, his beard of scalps,
His scythe, the arc of steel that crowns the Alps.
The elephants of Carthage hold those snows,
Turms of Numidian horse unsling their bows,
The flaming turkey-feathered arrows swarm
Beyond the Alps 'Pallas,' I raise my arm

---

**54** *Acoetes*: a compatriot of Evander (see *Aeneid* XI, 85).

And shout, 'Brother, eternal health. Farewell
70   Forever,' Church is over, and its bell
Frightens the yellowhammers, as I wake
And watch the whitecaps wrinkle up the lake.
Mother's great-aunt, who died when I was eight,
Stands by our parlour sabre. 'Boy, it's late.
Vergil must keep the Sabbath.' Eighty years!
It all comes back. My Uncle Charles appears.
Blue-capped and bird-like. Phillips Brooks and Grant
Are frowning at his coffin, and my aunt,
Hearing his coloured volunteers parade
80   Through Concord, laughs, and tells her English maid
To clip his yellow nostril hairs, and fold
His colours on him . . . It is I, I hold
His sword to keep from falling, for the dust
On the stuffed birds is breathless, for the bust
Of young Augustus weighs on Vergil's shelf:
It scowls into my glasses at itself.                    (1950)

---

**69–70** Cf. *Aeneid* XI, 97–8.

# ROLFE HUMPHRIES

[Aen. VIII. 306–415] *Aeneas at the site of Rome*

In this pastoral interlude before the fighting begins, Aeneas visits Pallanteum, on the site of the future Rome, to seek alliance with its king, Evander, an Arcadian settler, once a friend of Aeneas' father Anchises. In the famous 'walk round the site of Rome', Evander points out landmarks of the future city, while the poet emphasizes the contrast between the primitive simplicity of the early settlement and the metropolitan splendour of Augustan Rome. Meanwhile, Venus commissions her husband Vulcan to make new armour for Aeneas.

> Then back to the city again; and old Evander
> Kept his son Pallas near him and Aeneas,
> Talking of various matters, so the journey
> Was lightened, and the landscape charmed Aeneas,
> Who wondered as he watched the scene, and questioned,
> And learned its early legend. King Evander
> Began the story: – 'Native Nymphs and Fauns
> Dwelt in these woodlands once, and a race of men
> Sprung from the trunks of trees, or rugged oak,
> 10   Men primitive and rude, with little culture:
> They had no knowledge of ploughing, none of harvest;
> The fruits of the wild trees, the spoils of hunting,
> Gave them their nourishment. Then Saturn came here,
> Fleeing Jove's arms, an exile from his kingdom.
> He organized this race, unruly, scattered
> Through the high mountains, gave them law and order.
> He gave the place a name; Latium, he called it,
> Since once he lay there safely, hiding in shelter.
> Under his rule there came those golden ages
> 20   That people tell of, all the nations dwelling
> In amity and peace. But little by little
> A worse age came, lack-luster in its color,
> And the madness of war, and the evil greed of having.

Then came the Ausonian bands, Sicanian peoples,
And the land of Saturn took on other names,
And the kings came, and the fierce giant Thybris
For whom we named our river; we forgot
Its older title, Albula. Here I came
An exile from my country, over the seas,
30   Driven by fate and fortune, which no man
Can cope with or escape. The nymph Carmentis,
My mother, led me here with solemn warnings
Under Apollo's guidance.'

                    So Evander
Finished the tale, resumed the walk. They came,
First, to an altar and a gate: Carmental
The Romans call it, in honor of that nymph
Who first foretold the greatness of the Romans,
The glory of Pallanteum. Past the portal
They came to a spreading grove, a sanctuary
40   Restored by Romulus, and under the cold cliff
The Lupercal, named, in Arcadian fashion,
For the great god Pan. And then Evander showed him
The wood of Argiletum, and told the legend
Of the death of Argus, once a guest. From there
They went to the Tarpeian house, and a place
Golden as we now know it, once a thicket,
Once brush and briar, and now our Capitol.
Even then men trembled, fearful of a presence
Haunting this wood, this rock. 'A god lives here,'
50   Evander said, 'What god, we are not certain,
But certainly a god. Sometimes my people
Think they have seen, it may be, Jove himself
Clashing the darkening shield, massing the storm-cloud.
Here you can see two towns; the walls are shattered,
But they remind us still of men of old,
Two forts, one built by Janus, one by Saturn,
Janiculum, Saturnia.'

                    So they came,
Conversing with each other, to the dwelling
Where poor Evander lived, and saw the cattle
60   And heard them lowing, through the Roman forum,
The fashionable section of our city,
And as they came to the house itself, Evander
Remembered something, – 'Hercules,' he said,
'Great victor that he was, bent head and shoulders
To enter here, and this house entertained him.
Dare, O my guest, to think of wealth as nothing,
Make yourself worthy of the god, and come here
Without contempt for poverty.' He led him,
The great Aeneas, under the low rafters,
70   Found him a couch, nothing but leaves, and the bedspread
A Libyan bear-skin. And night came rushing down
Dark-wingèd over the earth.

                                        And Venus' heart
Was anxious for her son, and with good reason,
Knowing the threats and tumult of the Latins.
She spoke to Vulcan, in that golden chamber
Where they were wife and husband, and her words
Were warm with love: – 'When the Greek kings were tearing
Troy's towers as they deserved, and the walls were fated
To fall to enemy fire, I sought no aid
80   For those poor people, I did not ask for weapons
Made by your art and power; no, dearest husband,
I would not put you to that useless labor,
Much as I owed to Priam's sons, however
I sorrowed for my suffering Aeneas.
But now, at Jove's command, he has made a landing
On the Rutulian coast; I come, a suppliant
To the great power I cherish, a mother asking
Arms for her son. If Thetis and Aurora
Could move you with their tears, behold what people
90   Unite against me, what cities sharpen weapons

Behind closed gates, intent on our destruction!'
So Venus pleaded, and as she saw him doubtful,
The goddess flung her snowy arms around him
In fondlement, in soft embrace, and fire
Ran through him; warmth, familiar to the marrow,
Softened his sternness, as at times in thunder
Light runs through cloud. She knew her charms, the goddess,
Rejoicing in them, conscious of her beauty,
Sure of the power of love, and heard his answer: —
100  'No need for far-fetched pleading, dearest goddess;
Have you no faith in me? You might have asked it
In those old days; I would have armed the Trojans,
And Jupiter and the fates might well have given
Another ten years of life to Troy and Priam.
Now, if your purpose is for war, I promise
Whatever careful craft I have, whatever
Command I have of iron or electrum,
Whatever fire and air can do. Your pleading
Is foolish; trust your power!' And he came to her
110  With the embrace they longed for, and on her bosom
Sank, later, into slumber.

                    And rose early
When night was little more than half way over,
The way a housewife must, who tends the spindle,
Rising to stir and wake the drowsing embers,
Working by night as well as day, and keeping
The housemaids at the task, all day, till lamplight,
A faithful wife, through toil, and a good mother,
Even so, like her, with no more self-indulgence,
The Lord of Fire rose early, from soft pillows
120  To the labor of the forge.                    (1951)

# OLIVER ST JOHN GOGARTY
(1878–1957)

Printed from *Collected Poems* (1952).


## Virgil

From Mantua's meadows to Imperial Rome
Came Virgil, with the wood-light in his eyes,
Browned by the suns that round his hillside home
Burned on the chestnuts and the ilices.
And these he left, and left the fallows where
The slow streams freshened many a bank of thyme,
To found a city in the Roman air,
And build the epic turrets in a rhyme.
But were the woodland deities forgot,
10  Pan, Sylvan, and the sister nymphs for whom
He poured his melody the fields along?
They gave him for his faith a happy lot:
The waving of the meadows in his song
And the spontaneous laurel at his tomb.


## Sub Ilice*

Who will come with me to Italy in April?
Italy in April! The cherries on the hill!
The sudden gush of rivers where the valleys rib the

                         mountains;
The blue green mists, the silence which the mountain valleys

                         fill!

---

*The title 'Sub Ilice' (under the ilex) is from Eclogue VII, 1.

Is that Alba Longa? Yes; and there's Soracte.
Soracte? Yes; in Horace: don't you 'vides ut,' you fool?
No! She's not a model . . . you will have her husband on us . . . !
Though her buttocks are far better than the Seven Hills of
                                                                    Rome!

Cherries ripe and mountains! Young wives with the gait of
10    Goddesses; and feelings which you try in vain to say
To the gay vivacious calculating native;
If you knew Italian you would give the show away.
What is the attraction? Why are we delighted
When we meet the natives of a race that's not our own?
Is that which we like in them our ignorance about them;
And we feel so much the better where we know we are not
                                                                    known?

Well, it does not matter. I am thinking of a stone-pine
Where an Empress had her villa on the great Flaminian Way;
And the blond Teutonic students who have come so far for
                                                                    knowledge,
20    And the fräuleins who come with them on a reading holiday.

If I met a tall fair student girl from Dresden,
Whiter than a cream cheese, credulous, and O
Earnest, and so grateful for the things that I might teach her,
And I took her touring, would she have the sense to go?

I would through a ringlet, whisper . . . 'This is Virgil's
Confiscated farmstead which his friend in Rome restored.
The Mastersinging races from the North came down here
                                                                    merging;
And your hair was heir to colour that great Titian preferred.

---

5–6 Refers to the opening of Horace's 'Ode on Mount Soracte' (I, 9).

How my pulses leap up! I can hardly curb them,
30    Visiting the places which a poet loved . . . Ah, well!
Never fear the nightfall . . . Veniemus urbem!
My friend can take our taxi and go look for an hotel.'

Here between the last wave of the hills subsiding
And the river-beeches which are growing bald with age,
Gentle as the land's rise, lofty and abiding,
Rhythm's mountain ranges rose to sunshine from his page.

'"Is this Virgil's birthplace?"' Scholars are uncertain –
You cannot be a scholar if a thing is too well known –
There's the Idylls' ilex: if we use it for a curtain,
40    You can sit on half my raincoat and my half will be a throne.
Virgil was Menalcas: let me call you Phyllis.
Now look up the Idyll where they tried what each could do:
There! "Vis ergo inter nos," and "turn about's," "vicissim";
My pipe though not wax-jointed yet can play a tune or two.'

Friends, you must forgive me for this utter nonsense.
To-day I saw an ilex where the Dodder streels along;
And that togaed exile made me so despondent
That I called the light and glory which it shadows into song.

Thwart in the world I control are many seasons,
50    Many climes and characters obedient to a spell;
I turn to human grandeur's most exalted voice for reasons,
And not the least, that Virgil led a soul estranged from Hell.

(1952)

---

**43** See Eclogue III, 28.

# SMITH PALMER BOVIE

[Georg. IV. 315–566] *The story of Orpheus and Eurydice*

On this famous episode, which forms the conclusion of the *Georgics*, see Introduction, p. xiii.

What god, O Muses, forged this art for us?
Who placed this new experience in our path?
The shepherd Aristaeus lost his swarm,
Our story goes, through hunger and disease,
And fled from Tempe toward the stream Peneus.
Beside the sacred head of the river's source
He stood disconsolate and told his tale
Of woes, addressed his mother in these words:
　'Mother, Cyrene mother, dwelling here
10　Within these swirling depths, why was I born
To suffer from the fates, if, as you say,
Apollo is my father, and I am
A member of the famous race of gods?
The love you had for me is banished – where?
Why did you once extend my hopes to heaven?
See, mother though you are, how I have lost
This crown of mortal life, experience
With bees that practice taught me, barely gained
Along with skill in tending herds and crops.
20　Uproot then with your hands my fruitful trees,
Bring on your hostile fire against my barns,
Lay my harvest low, consume my crops,
And wield a ruthless axe against my vines,
Since all my praise has bred disgust in you.'
　　His mother in her river room below
Heard the sound. Around her sat the nymphs

---

**9–51** Based on Achilles' appeal to his mother Thetis in Homer, *Iliad* I. Virgil here shifts his poem out of the didactic into the heroic mode.

All spinning Milesian wool dyed glossy-green;
Drymo, Xantho, Phyllodoce, Ligea,
Whose dazzling hair flows round their snow-white necks;
30   Cydippe, golden-haired Lycorias,
The first a maiden still, the other then
Acquainted with the labors of first birth;
Beroe, Clio, Ocean's daughters both,
Both clad in gold and varicolored skins;
Ephyre, Opis, Asian Deiopea;
Swift Arethusa, now returned from the chase.
Among them, Clymene was holding forth
On Vulcan's baffled love, the stolen sweets
And tricks of Mars, relating the countless loves
40   Of all the gods from Chaos to the present.
Entranced by her account, they spin the wool,
When Aristaeus' grief a second time
Strikes on his mother's ear, transfixing all
Upon their glossy chairs. Before the rest,
Arethusa raised her golden head
To look above the water's crest, and called:
'Cyrene, sister, such profound lament
Might well alarm you, for your protégé
Himself, your Aristaeus, stands beside
50   Father Peneus' wave, disconsolate
And tearful, citing you for cruelty.'
     The mother, filled with unnamed dread, replied:
'Lead him down to us; he has the right
To touch the gods' threshold'; she then commands
The river's depths to yield the boy a path.
The curling wave arched round him like a mountain,
Enfolded him, and set him down below.
And now he viewed with awe his mother's home,
And paced the watery empire, walking round
60   The lakes locked inside caves, the resonant groves;
The powerful rush of water made him reel
To see the mighty rivers underground

All gliding in their separate directions:
The Phasis and the Lycus of Caucasia,
The Enipeus River's source in northern Greece,
And father Tiber's head, swift Anio's,
The Mandragora watering the Levant,
The Slavic Boug that roars across its rocks,
The bull-faced River Po with gilded horns,
70    Whose flow is most impetuous of all
That wind through fertile lands to the dark blue sea.
When Aristaeus reached his mother's room,
Its ceilings arched with vaults of porous stone,
Cyrene heard out his tale of idle tears;
The sisters poured fresh water on his hands,
And offered smooth wool towels, as is meet.
They spread a feast, replenished all the cups.
The mother spoke: 'Now, take the goblets full
Of Lydian wine; we'll pour a drop to Ocean!'
80    Cyrene made her vows at once to Ocean,
Father of all, and to the sister nymphs
Who guard a hundred woods, a hundred streams.
Three times she spilled out on the blazing hearth
A draft of purest nectar, three times back
The flame shot glancing upward off the ceiling:
Encouraged by the omen, she began:
    'A sea-blue prophet dwells in the Aegean,
Proteus, who rides the mighty deep behind
A string of fish and brace of water-horses.
90    At present, he is looking in on ports
In Thessaly and his native land, Pallene.
We nymphs and ancient Nereus praise this seer
For, as a prophet, he knows everything,
What is, what has been, what is soon to come.
It pleased Neptune to grant the gift to him,
For Proteus tends the monsters of the deep

---

**87ff.** The story of Proteus is from Homer, *Odyssey* IV.

And feeds the ugly seals beneath the waves.
Now, son, first capture Proteus and chain him,
That he divulge the reason for your plague
100 And show its cure. But he will not give counsel
Until forced: for words he'll not relent.
So bind him fast with force and chains, and then
His tricks will clash against their bonds in vain.
I'll lead you to the place the old man hides
When the sun enkindles flaming heat at noon,
When grass is parched and cattle seek the shade.
You'll steal upon him as he lies asleep,
Tired from his morning's journey with the waves.
But when you have him anchored down with chains,
110 He'll alter into various forms of beast:
First to savage boar, then to jet-black tiger,
To scaly dragon, tawny lioness;
Or, hissing like greedy flame, he slips the bounds
Or dissolves into vaporous flood and so makes off.
But all the more the shapes that he assumes
Hold on, my son, and draw the chains more tight,
Until once more he turns back to the form
He had at first when sleep obscured his sight.'
    She poured ambrosial fragrance on her son
120 That seeped through every corner of his frame;
His shapely locks exhaled the gentle savor
And supple strength found ways to seize his limbs.
There lies a deep cave, hollowed in a mountain
Where wind-driven waves break into harmless parts,
In former times a safe and sure retreat
For storm-tossed mariners: inside this cave
Proteus hid behind a jutting rock.
Cyrene brought the shepherd to the spot,
Concealed him in the shadows out of view
130 And drew off at a distance, wrapped in cloud.
    The pitiless Dog Star blazed away in heaven
Roasting India's parched inhabitants,

The fiery sun had used up half his course,
The grass lay scorched, the heat rays baked and cooked
On the hollow streams' dried channels and mud-bed.
And now old Proteus coming in from sea
Made for his usual haunt within the cave.
Round him frisked the damp tribes of the deep,
Sprinkling far and wide the bitter brine.
140    Sleepy seals stretched out along the shore,
While he, like some old shepherd of the hills
Who leads his flock at evening to the barns
(Wolves lick their chops at the sound of the bleating lambs),
Sits on a rock in their midst and counts them over.
Now that occasion favored Aristaeus.
He barely let the old man fall asleep
And rest his weary limbs, before he swooped
On the lying hulk with a shout, and chained it fast.
Proteus now, remembering all his tricks,
150    Transformed himself into most miraculous shapes
To fire, to fearful beast, to liquid flood.
But since no trick could save him, Proteus
Resumed his form and spoke with human voice:
'Oh rash young man, who sent you to our home?
What are you after here?' The boy replied:
'You know well, Proteus; don't pretend you don't.
Cease trying, then, to fool me. We have come,
Instructed by the gods, to seek from you
An oracle to restore our flagging fortunes.'
160    He said this much. Then the prophet, bowing to force
Rolled his eyes ablaze with grey-green light
And gnashed his teeth as he released the fates:
'A god's wrath makes you pay this heavy price
(Though even this is less than you deserve)
And would make you still, did Fate not intervene:
Unhappy Orpheus roused this punishment,
Who rages still with grief for his stolen bride.
Headlong past a stream, the fated girl

In fleeing your advances, failed to see
170  The monstrous serpent lurking on the shore.
Her Dryads filled the mountain heights with moans;
Summits wept in Thrace and Macedon,
And in Rhesus' martial land; the Hebrus wept,
The Danube, and the fair princess of Athens.
Orpheus soothed his love with the hollow lyre,
Singing to thee, sweet bride, along the strand
Alone, with rising day and falling night.
He breached the jaws of Hell, the home of Dis,
The pitch-black groves of fear; approached the dead,
180  To win the frightful king, and all the hearts
That know not how to answer human prayer.
At his song, from Hell's deep places rustled forth
The slender shades of those whose light has failed,
Like birds that flock by thousands to the leaves
When Winter rain or nightfall sends them down
From mountainsides: the mothers and their husbands,
Noble heroes' bodies void of life,
Boys, unwedded girls, and youthful sons
Consigned to fire before their parents' eyes.
190  Around them wind Cocytus' twisted reeds
And grisly mud; the sluggish, hateful swamp
Confines them, as the ninefold swirling Styx
Encompasses them about. The very halls
Of Hell and inmost Tartarus stand open
In surprise; the Furies are astounded,
Their bluish tresses intertwined with snakes.
Cerberus, in amazement, holds his three
Mouths open, and even the wind subsides;
Ixion's wheel stands still. Now Orpheus had
200  Retraced his steps, avoiding all mischance,
Eurydice approached the upper air
Behind him (as Proserpina had ruled),

---

**184–93** Some of this material was used again in *Aeneid* VI.

When all at once a mad desire possessed
The unwise lover – pardonable, indeed,
If Hell knew how to pardon. Overcome
By love, he stopped and – oh, forgetful man! –
Looked back at his, his own, Eurydice,
As they were drawing near the upper light.
That instant, all his labor went to waste,

210 His pact with the cruel tyrant fell apart,
And three times thunder rocked Avernus' swamps.
She cried out, "What wild fury ruins us,
My pitiable self, and you, my Orpheus?
See, once again the cruel fates call me back
And once more sleep seals closed my swimming eyes.
Farewell: prodigious darkness bears me off,
Still reaching out to you these helpless hands
That you may never claim." And with her words
She vanished from his sight like smoke in air,

220 Not seeing him clutch wildly after shadows
And yearning still to speak. Hell's ferryman
Refused him further passage through the swamp
That intervened. What could he do? Where turn,
A second time bereft of her? What tears
Might sway the dead, what human voice might alter
Heaven's will? Her body, stiff and cold,
Reposed long since adrift in the Stygian bark.
Seven continuous months, they say, he wept
By Strymon's lonely wave under soaring cliffs,

230 Unfolding his tragic song to the frozen stars,
Enchanting tigers, moving oaks with his theme:
Like a nightingale concealed in the poplar's shade,
Who sings a sad lament for her stolen brood
Some stony-hearted ploughman saw and dragged
Still naked from the nest: she weeps all night
And, perching on the bough, renews her song

---

**221** *Hell's ferryman*: Charon.

Of elegiac woe; her grave complaint
Fills places far and wide. No thought of love
Or wedding rites could bend his inflexible will.
240    He wandered lonely through the icy North,
Past the snow-encrusted Don, through mountain fields
Of unadulterated frost, conveyed the grief
At Hell's ironic offerings, and rapt
Eurydice. By such unwavering faith
The Thracian women felt themselves outraged,
And at their sacred exercise, nocturnal
Bacchanals, they tore the youth apart,
And scattered his limbs around the spacious fields.
But even then his voice, within the head
250    Torn from its marble neck, and spinning down
The tide of his paternal River Hebrus,
The cold-tongued voice itself, as life fled away,
Called out "Oh, my forlorn Eurydice!
Eurydice!" and the shoreline answered back
Along the river's breadth, "Eurydice!" '

  With these words, Proteus plunged back in the deep
And where he dove, the water swirled with foam.
Cyrene stayed, and addressed her startled son:
'My son, dismiss your worries from your mind.
260    This was the plague's whole cause, for this the Nymphs
With whom she danced far into woodland groves
Devised your bees' bleak end. Entreat their peace
By humbly offering gifts, and venerate
The gracious Dryads; they will pardon you,
Repress their wrath in favor of your vows.
I'll tell you first precisely how to pray:
Select the four best bullocks from the herd
Now grazing on Arcadia's verdant crest.
And choose four matching heifers, still unbroken.
270    By the goddesses' lofty shrines erect four altars,

---

**249–51** Cf. Milton, 'Lycidas', 61–2.

Where the sacred blood may trickle from their throats,
And leave the creatures' hulks in a shady grove.
When the ninth succeeding Dawn displays her course
You'll send to Orpheus, as his funeral dues,
Oblivion's poppies: slay a jet-black ewe,
And find the grove again; and sacrifice
A calf to reconcile Eurydice.'

    Without delay he does his mother's bidding,
Comes to the shrine, creates the altars there
280    That she prescribed; selects his four best steers,
Leads in four matching heifers, still unbroken.
When the ninth succeeding Dawn led on her course,
He sent off Orpheus' due and found the grove.
Here a wonder strange to tell appears,
When from the bellies, over the rotten flesh
Of the corpses, bees buzz out from caved-in flanks,
Swarm in heavy clouds to treetops, group,
And hang in clusters down from the pliant boughs.

    All this I've sung of cultivating fields,
290    Of tending flocks and caring for the trees,
While by the deep Euphrates noble Caesar
Thunders triumph, grants the reign of law
To grateful subjects, clears his path to heaven.
All this time sweet Naples nourished me,
Her Virgil, in the flower of humble peace,
In study: I who played at shepherds' songs
In callow youth, and sang, O Tityrus,
Of you at ease beneath your spreading beech.      (1956)

---

**289–98** Epilogue. Virgil rounds off his poem with a reference to Augustus' campaigns in the east, enabling us to date the poem to 30 BC. The final words are a self-reference to the opening of the First Eclogue.

# W. H. AUDEN (1907–73)

## Secondary Epic

An ironic comment on the 'prophetic' passages in *Aeneid* VIII (the shield of Aeneas) and VI (Anchises' vision in the underworld).

No, Virgil, no:
Not even the first of the Romans can learn
His Roman history in the future tense,
Not even to serve your political turn;
Hindsight as foresight makes no sense.

How was your shield-making god to explain
Why his masterpiece, his grand panorama
Of scenes from the coming historical drama
Of an unborn nation, war after war,
10  All the birthdays needed to pre-ordain
The Octavius the world was waiting for,
Should so abruptly, mysteriously stop,
What cause could he show why he didn't foresee
The future beyond 31 BC,
Why a curtain of darkness should finally drop
On Carians, Morini, Gelonians with quivers,
Converging Romeward in abject file,
Euphrates, Araxes and similar rivers
Learning to flow in a latinate style,
20  And Caesar be left where prophecy ends,
Inspecting troops and gifts for ever?
Wouldn't Aeneas have asked: – 'What next?
After this triumph, what portends?'

---

11 *Octavius*: the birth name of Octavian, afterwards Augustus.
16–19 See *Aeneid* VIII, 725–8.
20–21 See *Aeneid* VIII, 720–22.

As rhetoric your device was too clever:
It lets us imagine a continuation
To your Eighth Book, an interpolation,
Scrawled at the side of a tattered text
In a decadent script, the composition
Of a down-at-heels refugee rhetorician
30      With an empty belly, seeking employment,
Cooked up in haste for the drunken enjoyment
Of some blond princeling whom loot had inclined
To believe that Providence had assigned
To blonds the task of improving mankind.


. . . Now Mainz appears and starry New Year's Eve
        As two-horned Rhine throws off the Latin yoke
        To bear the Vandal on his frozen back;
        Lo! Danube, now congenial to the Goth,
        News not unwelcome to Teutonic shades
40      And all lamenting beyond Acheron
        Demolished Carthage or a plundered Greece:
        And now Juturna leaves the river-bed
        Of her embittered grievance – loud her song,
        Immoderate her joy – for word has come
        Of treachery at the Salarian Gate.
        Alaric has avenged Turnus . . .


No, Virgil, no:
Behind your verse so masterfully made
We hear the weeping of a Muse betrayed.

---

**36** *two-horned Rhine*: *Aeneid* VIII, 727; so called because of its division into
two mouths.
**42** *Juturna*: Turnus' nymph-sister, who tried in vain to help him against
Aeneas in *Aeneid* XII.
**45** *Salarian Gate*: exit from Rome by the Via Salaria, the ancient Sabine salt-
road leading out to Reate, the modern Riete.
**46** *Alaric*: Visigothic leader who captured Rome in AD 410.

50    Your Anchises isn't convincing at all:
      It's asking too much of us to be told
      A shade so long-sighted, a father who knows
      That Romulus will build a wall,
      Augustus found an Age of Gold,
      And is trying to teach a dutiful son
      The love of what will be in the long run,
      Would mention them both but not disclose
      (Surely, no prophet could afford to miss,
      No man of destiny fail to enjoy
60    So clear a proof of Providence as this.)
      The names predestined for the Catholic boy
      Whom Arian Odovacer will depose.                    (1960)


# PATRIC DICKINSON (1914–94)

## The Aeneid, Book XI, 1–296 [Aen. XI. 1–212]
*The funeral of Pallas*

One of the most moving set-pieces in the *Aeneid*: an immense
symphonic adagio.

      Meanwhile the Goddess of dawn had left the ocean and risen,
      And the thoughts of death preyed on Aeneas' mind
      And he wished for leisure to bury his companions.
      The first rays of the dawn lit on him paying
      Vows to the gods, as befits a conqueror.
      He lopped its branches from an enormous oak
      And set it up on a mound and hung upon it

---

**61–2** Odo(v)acer, the first barbarian king of Italy, deposed Romulus Augustu-
lus, last emperor of the West, in AD 476.

The spoils of Mezentius the chief, the bulk of his shining

armor —

A trophy, God of War, to your majesty.

10    He fixed the crests still dripping blood and the broken
Weapons, the dinted cuirass twelve times pierced,
He bound the brazen shield to the left-hand side of the

trophy

And hung from its neck the ivory-hilted sword.
Then he began to exhort his cheering friends,
For his whole band of captains was close around him,
'My friends we have won a resounding victory!
Put from your minds all fear of future trials,
These are the spoils of a proud king, the first fruits —
See what my hands have made of Mezentius!
20    Now we must march to the very walls of Latium
And King Latinus. Be ready in fighting trim,
Look to the coming clash with hope in your hearts,
Let there be no delays through lack of forethought,
No dilatory halfheartedness when the Gods
Give us the sign to pluck our standards up,
Strike camp, and march. But meanwhile let us consign
The unburied bodies of our friends to earth —
The only honor that avails them now
In the deep pit of Acheron. Go!' he cried,
30    'Pay your last tributes to these glorious souls
Who have bought us our new country with their blood.
And first let Pallas be borne to Evander's sorrowing city,
A warrior carried off by an evil day
And drowned before his time in the dark of death,
Though he had no lack of valor.' He spoke weeping,
And turned to his tent door again where the body
Of lifeless Pallas was laid out, watched over
By the veteran Acoetes, who in the old days

---

8 *Mezentius*: renegade Etruscan leader slain by Aeneas in Book X

Was Evander's armor-bearer in Arcadia
40    And later, under less auspicious stars,
Had been appointed guardian of his beloved
Young protégé. Around the bier was gathered
The whole of Aeneas' retinue and a crowd
Of Trojans and with their hair unbound
In mourning mode women of Ilium.
But when Aeneas entered the tall doors
They beat their breasts and raised the keen to the stars
And the royal dwelling echoed the bitter woe.
Aeneas gazed on the pillowed head of Pallas
50    And his snow-white countenance; and the gaping wound
Cleft in his marble breast by the Ausonian spear.
Tears started to his eyes and he began,
'Did Fortune envy you, poor luckless boy,
That she bereft me of you when she came
To me and smiled her favors, forbidding you
To see my kingdom or ride home in triumph
To your father's home? Not such were the promises
I gave on your behalf when I left Evander
And he embraced me, speeding me on my way
60    To a great empire, and warned me anxiously
That we should find our enemies fierce, and fight
Grim battles with an obdurate race. And now
In the grip of hopeless hopes perhaps even now he is offering
Vows to the gods, heaping the altars with gifts,
While we with the vain office of our griefs
Dead-march with the dead boy who owes
No debt to heaven's powers; now or henceforward.
O wretched father to see with your own eyes
The agonizing funeral of your son!
70    Is this the promised, this the returning triumph?

---

**58** King Evander entrusted his son Pallas to Aeneas' protection (see Book
VIII, 514–19).

This, all my pledge was worth? Ah yet, Evander,
It is no coward you shall look upon
With despicable wounds – you shall not be
A father craving death for the dishonor
A living son has brought so safely home.
Italy, cry alas for the great defender
Lost to you now, and lost to you, Iulus!'

When he had wept his fill Aeneas ordered
The poor corpse to be lifted up, and picking
80   A thousand mourners from his whole array
He sent them to attend the final rites,
And with their presence soothe a father's tears –
Scant solace for such weight of grief, but the due
Of the wretched parent. Others with quick fingers
Plaited the pliant framework for a litter
From shoots of strawberry-tree and twigs of oak
Shading the raised-up bed with sprays of leaves.
High on the rustic bier, they laid the boy
And he lay there like a flower plucked by the fingers
90   Of a young girl, a delicate violet
Or a wilting fleur-de-lis before their hue
And living form are lost to them, though the earth
No longer gives them strength and sustenance.
Aeneas next brought forth two garments stiff
With gold and purple which in a day gone by
Had been a labor of love to Sidonian Dido
As she made them for him, working the thin threads
Of gold along the hems with her own hands.
As a last act of homage sadly Aeneas
100   Wound the young warrior's body in one of these
And with the other muffled up his head

---

**89–93** One of the most beautiful similes in Virgil: cf. the reworking of the
same lines by Robert Lowell (above).

So soon to be consumed on the funeral pyre.
Also he piled the many spoils of battle
Pallas had won in Laurentum, and commanded
The long train of his loot to be led forth.
He added also the horses and the weapons
Stripped from the foe. There stood the victims too,
Hands bound behind their backs, whose doom it was
To appease in death the spirit of the dead
110   And with the blood of sacrifice imbue
The holy flames. Then next he ordered the leaders
To carry tree trunks hung with enemy arms
Each labeled with its owner's hated name.
Acoetes was led tottering along
Worn out with age and grief, beating his breast,
Clawing his cheeks till he collapsed and lay
Full length on the ground. They also pulled along
Chariots soaking in Rutulian blood,
Then came his charger Aethon, stripped of his trappings,
120   Tears pouring down his face. Then other bearers
Carried his spear and helmet – his conqueror Turnus
Had kept the rest of his arms. Then came the whole
Host of the Trojan mourners, all the Etruscans,
And the Arcadians, arms reversed, and finally
When the whole cavalcade had passed in its long procession
Aeneas paused and said with a heavy sigh,
'The Fates call me away to other tears,
The same implacable destinies of war.
I bid you hail for ever, heroic Pallas,
130   For ever farewell!' There was no more to say.
He turned back to his own high ramparts, he strode
Back into camp.

---

**118** *Rutulian*: the Rutuli were an ancient Latin tribe; their leader was Turnus.
**124** Evander came to Italy from the real Arcadia (not the imaginary one of
the *Eclogues*).

And now from the city of Latium
Ambassadors arrived, with olive branches,
Begging a favor from Aeneas: *would he return*
*The dead who lay about the plain as the sword*
*Had strewn them, and allow their burial*
*In proper graves? Nobody may sustain*
*A quarrel with the dead and lost-to-light.*
*Let him show mercy to his onetime hosts*
140  *And kinsmen of the bride betrothed to him!*
This was no prayer to merit a rebuke
And generously Aeneas granted it
Adding these words: 'What utter ill luck led you
So undeservedly to become embroiled
In a war so terrible, men of Latium – you –
And forced you to abjure your friendship with us?
Is it you that ask for peace for the dead, for the losers
In the grim hazard of war? For my part I
Had rather grant it to the living! Indeed
150  I would never have come here had not destiny
Allotted me this land to be my home.
It is not on your nation I make war.
It was the King abused our proffered friendship
Preferring to rely on Turnus' army –
Fairer if Turnus himself had faced the death
That these have suffered; if he means to end
The war by force of arms and expel the Trojans
It would become him better to meet me
In single combat – and let that man survive
160  Whose life was earned from Heaven or by his prowess!
But now depart and kindle the funeral fires
Under your wretched fellow citizens!'
He ended there and they, eying each other,
Stood in dumfounded silence. Finally Drances,

---

**164** Drances' speech against Turnus at the Latin war-council is at
XI, 343–75.

An older man who never forewent a chance
To smirch young Turnus with taunts and objurgations,
Opened his mouth and answered, 'Man of Troy!
By repute so mighty, mightier in the deeds
We have known you do, what words of praise shall I use
170 To exalt you to heaven? Shall I admire first
Your love of justice or your exertions in war?
On our side we are delighted to be the bearers
Of such an answer to our native city
And, if we light on an auspicious moment,
To ally you to our King Latinus – Indeed,
Let Turnus try to make peace for himself!
We would be proud to help raise up those fated walls
To their full height and hump on our own shoulders
The stones of your new Troy!' These sentiments
180 Drew from the rest a murmur of assent.
Twelve days were set for truce, and under the warrant
Of peace the Trojans and the Latins wandered,
Mutually harmless, mingling in the woods
Or on the mountain slopes. The tall ash trees
Rang to the stroke of the two-edged ax, and pines
With tops among the stars came crashing down.
Incessantly they drove their wedges in
To oak and resinous cedar tree and hauled
The trunks of rowans on their groaning wagons.

190 Now flying Rumor, but a moment ago
Proclaiming Pallas Latium's conqueror,
Was harbinger of grief unbearable
And now the news came to Evander's ears,
Then to his household, then to all the city.
The Arcadians rushed to the gates and as they went
They snatched up funeral torches in accordance with ancient
                                                      custom,
The highway glowed with the long lines of flame
That clove the countryside in two. To meet them

Came the cortege of Trojans and they mingled
200   Into a single mourning throng. And as soon
As the elder women saw them approach the houses
They kindled the whole city with their keening.
There was no power could hold Evander back.
He rushed into their midst and directly the bier
Was set upon the earth he hurled himself
On Pallas and clung to him, weeping, groaning,
Till, at long last, he forced out through his grief:
'O Pallas, Pallas, this was not the promise
You gave me once. You swore you would take care,
210   Nor blindly fling yourself into the arms
Of the savage God of War! But well I know
That yearning for the first day of glory in action,
The ineffable taste of honor won in a first engagement!
Alas the ill-starred first fruits of your youth!
The bitter lesson of a war so near!
And not one god of all the gods gave heed
To my vows and prayers! O my most blessed wife,
Lucky the death that spared you of these sorrows!
An opposite fate is mine; by living on
220   I have defeated my destiny, only to be
A father left in solitariness.
Had I but followed the friendly flag of Troy
And fallen to a hail of Rutulian weapons!
If only it had been my life in forfeit,
My body borne in this procession home,
Not Pallas. But I lay no blame on you
My Trojan friends, nor on our mutual treaty,
Nor in the hands we joined to seal it with.
This was the lot inevitably destined
230   To fall on my old age. But if my son
Was doomed to an early death what better death
Could I wish for him than falling as he led
His Trojans against Latium, having killed
The Volscians in their thousands?

I could not ask for a nobler funeral
Than good Aeneas and the Phrygian nobles
And the whole Etruscan army and their leaders
Have accorded to you. They have brought mighty trophies,
Those whom your strong right arm despatched to Death.
240 And you too, Turnus, would have found your place there,
Yes, as a mighty tree-trunk hung with your armor –
Had Pallas been your equal in age and strength.
And let no grief of mine delay you Trojans
From waging the war. Go now, and bear this message
Back to your King: If I prolong a life
That is hateful to me now that Pallas is dead,
It is because of your sword-arm which, you admit
Owes us, father and son, the death of Turnus.
This is the one, the only, deed undone –
250 The key to your success and my deserts.
I seek no joy in life (nor rightly should I);
But to my son, down there among the shades,
I would be glad to bear some joyful news.'

Meanwhile the dawn had raised her tonic light
For suffering mortals, bringing back the round
Of task and toil. And now Aeneas the leader
And Tarchon built their funeral pyres along
The winding shores: and here the living brought
Each man the bodies of his dead according
260 To the custom of his ancestors. Thickly smoking
The torches were applied and the whole sky
Became one pall of smoke, black and opaque.
Three times they circled round the blazing pyres
Their armor glittering; three times they rode
Their horses round the grievous funeral fires
Uttering lamentations. The earth was wet
With tears, their weapons dripping with their tears.
Their cries and trumpet-peals rose to the sky.
Some tossed on the fires spoils stripped from the Latin dead,

270    Helmets and elegant swords, bridles and chariot wheels:
       Others brought offerings of personal gear,
       Things dear to the dead, their helmets and the weapons
       That had not saved them. Many the carcasses
       Of oxen immolated there to Death:
       They slit the throats of bristly boars and cattle
       Seized out of every field, and gouts of blood
       Were poured onto the flames. And now along
       The whole length of the shore they stood and watched
       The burning of their comrades and kept guard
280    Over half-burnt pyres and nothing could tear them away
       Till dewy night fell and the sky was studded
       With the cold fires of the stars.
                                        The unhappy Latins
       In a different quarter were no less engaged
       In building countless pyres. Of the many bodies
       Of their warriors some they buried in earth, some
       They carried away to fields nearby to send them
       Home to their cities; the rest, an enormous heap
       Of entangled corpses, they then and there cremated
       Uncounted and unhonored. Everywhere
290    For miles the countryside gleamed with the flare
       Of more and yet more fires.
                                        And now the third
       Daybreak had lifted from the sky its chilling shadows.
       And the mourners came to level the piles of ashes
       And muddle of bones from the beds of the funeral fires
       And heap upon them mounds of earth which their heat
       Still had the power to warm.                    (1961)

# C. DAY LEWIS (1904–72)

## Eclogue III: The Singing Match [Ecl. III. 60–111]

One of Virgil's earliest pastorals: its structure – a conversation (here omitted) leading to a singing match – is modelled on Theocritus.

### The Singing Match (tune: 'O Waly Waly')

DAMOETAS
From Jupiter my song begins
                    for Jupiter is everywhere,
Making the earth all fruitful to be
                    and to my ditties lending his ear.

MENALCAS
And I'm the man that Phoebus loves,
                    my garden is Apollo's seat:
I give him gifts – the bay-tree and
                    the hyacinth do blush so sweet.

DAMOETAS
Now Galatea throws at me
10                  an apple – she's a wanton maid:
Off to the sally trees she do run
                    wishing I spy whereto she's fled.

MENALCAS
But dear Amyntas is my flame:
                    he is my flame, and never coy.
My little dog, he knows the Moon,
                    and just as well he knows that boy.

DAMOETAS

I have a present for my Venus,
                        I've a present for my dear,
Since I did mark a treetop high
20                      and doves a-building nesties there.

MENALCAS

Ten golden apples did I pluck,
                        ten golden apples a wild tree bore:
All that I could, I sent to my boy,
                        tomorrow he shall have ten more.

DAMOETAS

Oh many times, oh charming words
                        she's spoke to me, my Galatea!
Whisper a few, a few of them,
                        you breezes, into heaven's ear!

MENALCAS

Ah what avails it, Amyntas dear,
30                      that after me your heart's inclined,
If while you hunt the ravening boar,
                        you leave me the nets to mind?

DAMOETAS

Send Phyllis here, Iollas, do –
                        send Phyllis here, for it's my birthday:
And when I sacrifice for the crops
                        a heifer, come yourself this way.

MENALCAS

Phyllis I love before the rest,
                        and Phyllis wept to see me go:
Long did she say farewell to me,
40                      farewell, farewell, my handsome beau.

**DAMOETAS**

The wolf is cruel to the sheep,
                              cruel a storm to orchard tree,
Cruel is rain to ripened crops,
                              Amaryllis' rage is cruel to me.

**MENALCAS**

A shower is sweet to growing crops,
                              to weanling goats an arbutus tree;
Willow is sweet to breeding herds,
                              none but Amyntas sweet to me.

**DAMOETAS**

My Muse is but a country girl,
50                            yet Pollio has sung her praise.
Fatten a calf, ye Muses all,
                              for Pollio who loves your lays.

**MENALCAS**

But Pollio sings his own songs too:
                              so feed a bullock for him, say I –
Fatten a bull with venturesome horns
                              and hooves that make the soft sand fly.

**DAMOETAS**

May he who loves you, Pollio,
                              delighting, share your paradise:
Let honey flow for him in streams
60                            and brambles bear a delicate spice.

---

**50–53** Pollio was consul in 40 BC (see Eclogue IV) and himself a poet.

MENALCAS

May he who loathes not Bavius be
           delighted, Maevius, by your ditties:
Let him yoke foxes to his plough,
           and milk he-goats that have no titties.

DAMOETAS

Oh children dear, who gather flowers,
           who gather flowers and wild strawberries
                    near,
Run away quick – away from that grass,
           a cold cold snake is lurking there.

MENALCAS

Oh sheep, beware – graze not too far,
70           and never trust that river bank:
Look at the ram, your leader, oh sheep,
           drying his fleece that still is dank.

DAMOETAS

Now Tityrus, keep back your goats
           from grazing near the river's brim:
I mean to dip them all in a pool –
           dip them myself, when comes the time.

MENALCAS

Now fold the flocks, my shepherd lads,
           for if the heat dries the milk again
As it has done these latter days,
80           then we shall squeeze their teats all in
                    vain.

---

**61–2** Nothing is known of these poets except that the latter incurred the displeasure of Horace.

DAMOETAS
Ah my poor bull, he peaks and pines
                                though rich for him the vetches grow:
Love is the same for man or beast —
                                'tis death to herd and herdsman also.

MENALCAS
My flock are naught but skin and bone;
                                it is not love has injured my ewes:
Some evil eye has overlooked
                                my pretty lambs, I know not whose.

DAMOETAS
I have a riddle. Where on earth
90                                is heaven only twelve feet broad?
Answer my riddle, and I'll say
                                Apollo's not a greater bard.

MENALCAS
I have a riddle. Where on earth
                                are flowers signed with kings' names
                                                                grown?
Answer my riddle, and I'll say
                                that Phyllis shall be yours alone.

PALAEMON
I cannot decide between you, after so keen a contest.
Both of you deserve a heifer — and so does each man
Who trembles before love's sweetness or tastes her bitter rue.
100  Lads, let down the hatches, the fields have drunk their fill.

                                                                (1963)

---

89–96 Various solutions have been proposed for the first riddle (e.g. an
astronomical sphere), none of them conclusive. The answer to the second
riddle is the hyacinth, whose markings were said to derive from the blood
either of Hyacinthus, a prince accidentally killed by his lover Apollo, or of
Ajax, who committed suicide.

# ALLEN MANDELBAUM (1926– )

The Aeneid, Book VI, 1191–1203, and Book VII, 1–171 [Aen. VI. 893–901; VII. 1–134] *The Promised Land*

Printed from the 1971 edition. Perhaps the most magical transition in the poem: at the end of Book VI Aeneas and the Sibyl ascend from the underworld. Aeneas and his party re-embark, sailing along the Italian coast from Cumae to the mouth of the Tiber, where they land in Latium, Latinus' kingdom. Two prophecies are now revealed: this is the Promised Land.

> There are two gates of Sleep: the one is said
> to be of horn, through it an easy exit
> is given to true Shades; the other is made
> of polished ivory, perfect, glittering,
> but through that way the Spirits send false dreams
> into the world above. And here Anchises,
> when he is done with words, accompanies
> the Sibyl and his son together; and
> he sends them through the gate of ivory.
> 10  Aeneas hurries to his ships, rejoins
> his comrades, then he coasts along the shore
> straight to Caieta's harbor. From the prow
> the anchor is cast. The sterns stand on the beach.

*

> In death, you too, Aeneas' nurse, Caieta,
> have given to our coasts unending fame;
> and now your honor still preserves your place

---

1–9 Aeneas and the Sibyl leave the underworld as mysteriously as they entered it: by the ivory gate, perhaps because they are not 'true shades' (*verae umbrae*).

of burial; your name points out your bones
in broad Hesperia — if that be glory.

But having paid her final rites as due,
20   the mound above her tomb in order, pious
Aeneas, when the heavy seas have stilled,
sets out his sails to voyage, quits the harbor.
Night falls; the winds breathe fair; the brilliant moon
does not deny his way; the waters gleam
beneath the quivering light. The Trojans sail
close by the shore of Circe's island, where
the wealthy daughter of the Sun, with song
unending, fills her inaccessible groves;
she kindles fragrant cedarwood within
30   her handsome halls to light the night and runs
across her finespun web with a shrill shuttle.
The raging groans of lions fill her palace —
they roar at midnight, restless in their chains —
and growls of bristling boars and pent-up bears,
and howling from the shapes of giant wolves:
all whom the savage goddess Circe changed,
by overwhelming herbs, out of the likeness
of men into the face and form of beasts.
But lest the pious Trojans have to suffer
40   such horrors and be carried to this harbor
or land along these cruel coasts, Neptune
had swelled their sails with saving winds and helped
their flight. He carried them past the seething shoals.

And now the sea was red with sunrays, saffron
Aurora shone in her rose chariot;
the winds fell off, and from the high air every
harsh blast was ended suddenly, the oars

---

**26–38** *Circe's island*: for the enchantress see Homer, *Odyssey* X. The island is
now a promontory (Monte Circeo).

beat down against the waters' sluggish marble.
Then from his ship Aeneas spies a spacious
50  forest; and through the trees the Trojan sees
the Tiber, gracious river, hurrying
to sea, with yellow sands and rapid eddies.
And varied birds that knew the river's channel
and banks flew through the grove; and overhead
they soothed the air with song. Aeneas orders
his men to change their course; the prows are turned
to land; he enters, glad, the shadowed river.

Now, Erato, be with me, let me sing
of kings and times and of the state of things
60  in ancient Latium when the invaders
first beached their boats upon Ausonia's coasts,
and how it was that they began to battle.
O goddess, help your poet. I shall tell
of dreadful wars, of men who struggle, tell
of chieftains goaded to the grave by passion,
of Tuscan troops and all Hesperia
in arms. A greater theme is born for me;
I try a greater labor.

King Latinus,
an old man now, ruled over fields and tranquil
70  towns in long-lasting peace. He was the son
of Faunus and Marica, a Laurentian
nymph – so we have been told. And Faunus' father
was Picus – he who calls you, Saturn, parent:
you are the earliest author of that line.
The edicts of the gods had left Latinus
no male descent; for as his son grew up,
he was cut off in early youth. One daughter

---

58–68 A second invocation ushers in the second half of the poem, the 'greater work' of war. *Erato*: the muse of love, perhaps invoked because of the quarrel over Lavinia between Aeneas and Turnus.

was all he had as heir for house and holdings;
and she was ripe now, ready for a husband;
80   her years were full for marriage. Many wooed her
from all Ausonia, wide Latium.
And Turnus, handsomest above all others,
had wooed her, too: he had mighty grandfathers
and great-grandfathers, and Latinus' royal
wife wished to see him as her son-in-law.
But in that wedding's way there stand the omens
of gods with many sinister alarms.
For in the inner courtyard of the palace
there stood a laurel tree with sacred leaves,
90   preserved with reverence for many years.
They say that it was found by King Latinus
himself, when he built his first fortresses,
and he had made it holy to Apollo;
from it, he gave the colonists their name:
Laurentians. At that laurel's crown – how strange
to tell – a thick and sudden swarm of bees,
borne, shrill, across the liquid air, had settled;
they twined their feet and hung from leafy branches.
At once the prophet cried: 'In that direction
100   from which the swarm has come I see a stranger
approaching and an army nearing us;
I see them reach the palace, see them ruling
in our high citadel.' More, while the virgin
Lavinia with pure and fragrant torches
kindled the altars, standing by her father,
she seemed – too terrible – to catch that fire
in her long tresses; all her ornaments
were burning in that crackling blaze, and burning,
her queenly hair, her crown set off with jewels;
110   then wrapped in smoke and yellow light, she scattered
her flames throughout the palace. This indeed
was taken as a sign of fear and wonder:
they sang she would be glorious in fame
and fate but bring great war to her own people.

Much troubled by these signs, Latinus visits
the oracle of Faunus, of his fate-
foretelling father; he consults the groves
of high Albunea. Deepest of forests,
it echoes with a holy fountain, breathing
120  a savage stench in darkness. Here the tribes
of Italy and all Oenotria
seek answers in uncertainty. And here
the priest would bring his gifts, then lie along
the outspread hides of slaughtered sheep, beneath
the silent night, asking for sleep, and see
so many phantoms hovering strangely
and hear various voices and enjoy
the conversation of the gods and speak
to Acheron in deep Avernus. Father
130  Latinus also came here, seeking answers.
He sacrificed a hundred woolly sheep,
as due, then rested on their hides and fleece.
A sudden voice was sent from that thick forest:
'O do not seek, my son, to join your daughter
in marriage to a Latin; do not trust
the readied wedding bed. For strangers come
as sons-in-law; their blood will raise our name
above the stars; and their sons' sons will see
all things obedient at their feet, wherever
140  the circling Sun looks on both sides of Ocean.'
Latinus does not keep within himself
these answers told him by his father Faunus,
these warnings given under silent night.
But racing wide across Ausonia's cities,
swift Rumor had already carried them,

---

**122ff**. This form of oracular consultation was known as '*incubatio*': the seeker receives the oracle's response while asleep. Lavinia is destined to marry a stranger whose descendants will rule the world.

just at the time the Trojan crewmen fastened
their fleet along the grassy riverbank.

Aeneas, his chief captains, and the handsome
Iülus rest beneath a tall tree's branches
150     as they make ready for a feast with cakes
of wheat set out along the grass (for so
had Jove himself inspired them); and these
they use as platters, heaped with country fruits.
And here it happened, when their scanty food
was done, that – hungry still – they turned upon
the thin cakes with their teeth; they dared profane
and crack and gnaw the fated circles of
their crusts with hand and jaw; they did not spare
the quartered surfaces of their flat loaves.
160     'We have consumed our tables, after all,'
Iülus laughed, and said no more. His words,
began to bring an end to Trojan trials;
as they first fell from Iülus' lips, Aeneas
caught them and stopped his son's continuing;
he was astounded by the will of heaven.
He quickly cries: 'Welcome, my promised land!
I hail the faithful household gods of Troy!
This is our home and country. For my father,
Anchises – now I can remember – left
170     such secrets of the fates to me, saying:
"My son, when you are carried overseas
to stranger shores, and when, your food consumed,
your hunger forces you to eat your tables,
remember in your weariness to hope
for homes, to set your hands to building dwellings
and raising walls around them." And this was
the hunger that he had foretold; this was

---

173 The 'tables' are probably plates made of edible matter, a kind of chapatti.

the final trial to end our sorrows. Come,
and with the sun's first light let us explore
180   in different directions from this harbor –
and gladly – what these lands are, who lives here,
and where their city lies. Now let us pour
our cups to Jupiter, entreat my father
Anchises, set our wine back on the tables.'     (1971)


# ALLEN MANDELBAUM

Aeneid VI, 1129–37 [Aen. VI. 847–53] *The destined mission of Rome*

These famous lines constitute the epilogue to Anchises' prophecy in the Elysian fields. Cf. Dryden's version, and also Virgil's original (below).

For other peoples will, I do not doubt,
still cast their bronze to breathe with softer features,
or draw out of the marble living lines,
plead causes better, trace the ways of heaven
with wands and tell the rising constellations;
but yours will be the rulership of nations,
remember, Roman, these will be your arts:
to teach the ways of peace to those you conquer,
to spare defeated peoples, tame the proud.     (1971)


excudent alii spirantia mollius aera
(credo equidem), uiuos ducent de marmore uultus,
orabunt causas melius, caelique meatus
describent radio et surgentia sidera dicent:
tu regere imperio populos, Romane, memento
(hae tibi erunt artes), pacique imponere morem,
parcere subiectis et debellare superbos.

# ANTHONY JAMES BOYLE

## Eclogue VI [Ecl. VI] *The Song of Silenus*

This strange poem is unique among Virgil's Eclogues. It begins by rejecting, on the advice of Apollo, any temptation to desert the pastoral genre, yet the song of Silenus, which occupies most of the piece, is an extraordinary mixture of cosmology and mythological tales, many describing erotic fantasies and metamorphoses, themes fashionable at the time. For the introduction of Gallus into the poem, cf. Eclogue X.

> My first Muse saw fit to play in Syracusan verse,
> And Thalea was not ashamed to inhabit the woods.
> When I sang kings and battles, Cynthius plucked
> My ear and warned: 'A shepherd's duty, Tityrus,
> Is to feed his sheep fat, to keep his song lean-spun.'
> Now I (for there'll be more than enough who desire,
> Varus, to tell your praises and set doleful wars to verse)
> Shall study the rustic Muse on a thin reed.
> I do not sing unordered. Yet if someone, someone
> 10  Seized by love reads these lines too, our tamarisks, Varus,
> Every grove will sing of you. Phoebus finds no page
> More welcome than that inscribed with Varus' name.
>
> Proceed, Pierians. The boys Chromis and Mnasyllos
> Saw Silenus lying asleep in a cave,

---

1 *Syracusan*: Theocritus, the Greek pastoral poet, came from Sicily.
2 *Thalea*: the muse of comic (i.e. light) verse
3 *Cynthius*: Apollo
4 *Tityrus*: see Eclogue I.
5 Virgil follows the Alexandrian poet Callimachus (not a pastoral poet) in rejecting heroic epic in favour of short poems.
9–12 The poet offers his poem to the soldier-statesman Alfenus Varus and says it is inspired by Apollo.

Veins swollen, as always, by yesterday's Iacchus.
Garlands lay nearby, just fallen from his head,
And dangling by a worn handle his heavy wine-jug.
They set on him – for often the old man had teaséd them
                                                        both
With the hope of song – and bind him in his own garlands.
20 An ally joins and aids the timid pair, Aegle,
Aegle, fairest of Naiads, and, though he's now awake,
With blood-red mulberries daubs his temples and brow.
Smiling at the trick, he asks: 'Why tie the bonds?
Release me, lads; to seem to have the power is enough.
Here are the songs you want: get to know them. The songs
                                                        are yours,
For her there'll be another prize.' With that he begins.


Then truly you could have seen in rhythmic dance the Fauns
And wild beasts play, then even rigid oaks wave their
                                                        crowns.
Far less Parnassus' crag rejoices in Phoebus,
30 Far less Rhodope and Ismarus thrill to Orpheus.


For he sang how through great void were driven together
The seeds of earth and of breath and of ocean
And seeds of streaming fire; how from these elements
All beginnings and the world's tender orb itself took shape.
Then how the land began to harden and to shut Nereus
In the sea and gradually to assume the forms of things;
Now how the earth is dazed by the new sun's growing light,
And as the clouds lift to greater heights the rains fall,
And forests first begin to rise, and here and there
40 Living creatures wander across nescient hills.

---

**15** *Iacchus*: wine
**19** The binding of supernatural beings to make them tell stories is an old folk motif. It also occurs in the story of Proteus in Homer, *Odyssey* IV, and in *Georgics* IV.

Next he relates the stones cast by Pyrrha, Saturn's reign,
The Caucasian birds and theft of Prometheus.
To these he links the spring where sailors called for Hylas
Left behind, till the whole shore rang 'Hylas! Hylas!'
And Pasiphaë – fortunate, if cattle hadn't existed –
He consoles in her love for the snowy bull.
Ah, hapless girl, what derangement has seized you?
Proetus' daughters filled the fields with imitation-lowings;
Yet not one pursued such foul copulation
50   With the herd, however much each feared the plough
On her neck and often felt for horns on smooth brow.
Ah, hapless girl, now you wander among the hills,
While he, his snowy flank pillowed by soft hyacinth,
Under a black ilex chews the pale-hued grass,
Or pursues some heifer in the great herd. 'Close off,
                                                    Nymphs,
Dictaean Nymphs, close off now the woodland pastures,
In the hope somewhere our eyes may light upon
The bull's wandering tracks. Perhaps, captivated
By the green grass or trailing after the herds,
60   He'll be led by heifers right to Gortyn's stalls.'

Then he sings the girl whom Hesperidean apples thrilled,
Then encases Phaëthon's sisters in moss of bitter
Bark and raises them from the soil as tall alders.

---

**41** Pyrrha and her husband Deucalion re-created the human race after the
Flood (cf. the story of Noah and his wife).

**42** Prometheus stole fire from the gods and was punished by being hung on a
mountain in the Caucasus where birds ate his liver.

**43** Hercules carried off Hylas on the voyage of the Argonauts but lost him to
the river-nymphs of Propontis.

**45–6** Minos king of Crete refused to sacrifice a white bull to Neptune, who
in revenge made his wife Pasiphaë fall in love with the animal.

**48–50** Proetus' daughters went mad and thought they were cows, but unlike
Pasiphaë did not feel sexual passion.

**61** Atalanta, famous for her swiftness of foot, was defeated in a race by the
trick of the golden apple, thrown at her feet by a rival.

**62** Phaethon was killed driving the sun's chariot; his sisters were turned into
trees.

Then he sings of Gallus wandering by Permessus' stream,
How one of the Sisters led him to Aonian hills,
And how for this man the whole choir of Phoebus rose;
And how Linus, the shepherd of divine song,
Hair garlanded with flowers and bitter celery,
Said to him: 'These reeds – take them – the Muses give you,
70   Which once they gave the old Ascraean, who used them
To lead downhill in lean-spun song the rigid ash.
Use them to tell the Grynean Wood's origin,
So there'll be no grove in which Apollo glories more.'

Why should I speak of Scylla, Nisus' child, of whom the tale
Persists that, gleaming thighs girt with barking fiends,
She vexed Dulichium's ships, and in the whirlpool's depths –
Ah! – ripped the flesh of trembling men with sea-dogs' fangs?
Or how he narrated Tereus' transformed limbs,
The feast, the gifts Philomela prepared for him,
80   The swift flight to the desert and the wings on which first
The hapless creature hovered above her roof?

All the themes that Phoebus once studied and joyous
Eurotas heard and told its laurels to learn by heart
He sings (the valleys catch the sound and toss it to the stars),
Until Vesper gave the order to pen the sheep
And count them and climbed into Olympus' unwilling sky.

(1976)

---

64 The intrusion of a real poet, Gallus (see Eclogue X), into this mythological
sequence is extraordinary.
67 *Linus*: legendary singer, teacher of Orpheus.
70 Refers to the Greek poet Hesiod.
74 Virgil has conflated Scylla, daughter of Nisus, who was turned into a bird,
with the monster Scylla (of Scylla and Charybdis).
78–9 Tereus raped Philomela, who was turned into a nightingale after killing
Tereus' son Itys and serving him up to his father at a feast.

# PAUL ALPERS

## Eclogue VII [Ecl. VII] *The Singing Match*

From *The Singer of the Eclogues: A Study of Virgilian Pastoral with a New Translation of the Eclogues* (1979).

MELIBEE  CORIN  THYRSIS

*M.*Under a whispering holm-oak, Daphnis sat,
  Corin and Thyrsis drove their flocks together,
  Thyrsis his sheep, Corin goats swollen with milk,
  Both in the flower of youth, Arcadians both,
  Equal in song and eager to respond.
  Here, while I screened young myrtles from the frost,
  My flock's he-goat had strayed, and I catch sight
  Of Daphnis; he sees me and 'Quick,' he says,
  'Come here, Melibee; your goat and kids are safe.
10  If you can stop a while, rest in the shade.
  To drink here, willing bullocks cross the fields;
  Here slender reeds border the verdant banks
  Of Mincius, and the cult-oak hums with bees.'
  What to do? with no Alcippe, no Phyllis
  At home to pen my spring lambs, newly weaned?
  Yet 'Corin versus Thyrsis' was a match!
  My serious business gave way to their playing.
  So they began the contest, in alternate

---

**2** *Corin*: Corydon in the original. When Shakespeare adapted Lodge's *Rosalynde* for his *As You Like It*, he changed Lodge's classical Corydon into Corin, a name which also recalls Spenser's Colin.

**4** *Arcadians*: the earliest reference to Arcadia as the idyllic location of the pastoral world. The 'shepherds' through their skill in song become citizens of this ideal world, though they live in Italy.

**12–13** A local touch: the Mincio flowed near Mantua, Virgil's birthplace. Arcadia is thus identifiable by any reader with his own '*locus amoenus*' (ideal place).

Verses, which the Muses wished recalled.

20     Corin's turn first, and Thyrsis then replied.

    C.    Beloved nymphs of Helicon, grant me
       A song such as my Codrus made – his verses
       Rank next to Phoebus'; if we're not up to him,
       On this votive pine, my whistling pipe will hang.

    T.    Arcadians, deck with bays the budding poet,
       Shepherds, let Codrus burst his guts with envy;
       If his praise is lavish, bind my brows, lest his
       Ill-meaning tongue should harm the rising bard.

    C.    This bristling boar's head, Delia, little Micon

30     Presents, and the hardy stag's wide-branching horns;
       If this is rightly yours, all of smooth marble,
       Calves bound and scarlet-booted, you shall stand.

    T.    This yearly bowl of milk, these cakes, Priapus –
       That's what you get, protecting our poor garden;
       We've made you marble for the moment, but if
       New offspring fill the flock, you shall be gold.

    C.    Nymph Galatea, sweet as Hyblaean thyme,
       Shining as swans, lovely as ivy pale,
       When bulls, well fed, shall to their stalls return,

40     If you still care at all for Corin, come.

    T.    Nay, think me bitter as Sardonic herbs,
       Shaggy as gorse, worthless as beached seaweed,
       If this day seems not longer than the year.
       Go home well fed, if you've any shame, you bullocks.

    C.    You mossy founts, and grass as slumber soft,
       You green arbutus, spreading checkered shade,
       Screen my flock from the heat; the scorching season
       Comes: now curling vine shoots swell and bud.

    T.    Here is a hearth, a fire of pitchy pine,

50     Steadily burning, smoking the doorposts black.
       Here Boreas' chills concern us just as much
       As numbers wolves or banks the raging floods.

    C.    Junipers and shaggy chestnuts stand erect;
       Strewn everywhere, fruits lie beneath their trees;

Now all rejoices; but should fair Alexis
Forsake these hills, you'd see the streams run dry.
T.   Fields parch; in tainted air, grass thirsts and dies;
Bacchus begrudges hills vines' leafy shade;
At Phyllis' coming, every grove turns green,
60    Jove will descend in showers of kindly rain.
C.   Poplars delight Alcides, vines please Bacchus,
Myrtles fair Venus and his laurel Phoebus;
Phyllis loves hazels and while Phyllis loves them,
Myrtle nor Phoebus' laurels shall match hazels.
T.   Loveliest in woods the ash, in gardens pine,
Poplars by streams and firs on lofty mountains;
Fair Lycidas, if you return to me,
Wood ash will yield to you and garden pines.
M.   All this I recall, and Thyrsis strove in vain.
70    From then on, it's been Corin, Corin with us.            (1979)

# L. P. WILKINSON (1907–85)

## The Georgics, Book II, 458–540 [Georg. II. 458–540] *In praise of rural retirement*

This famous passage was imitated by James Thomson in *The Seasons*.

How lucky, if they know their happiness,
Are farmers, more than lucky, they for whom,
Far from the clash of arms, the earth herself,
Most fair in dealing, freely lavishes
An easy livelihood. What if no palace
With arrogant portal out of every cranny
Belches a mighty tide of morning callers
And no one gapes at doors inlaid so proudly
With varied tortoiseshell, cloth tricked with gold
10  And rare Corinthian bronzes? What if wool
Is white, not tainted with Assyrian poison,
And honest olive oil not spoilt with cassia?
Yet peace they have and a life of innocence
Rich in variety; they have for leisure
Their ample acres, caverns, living lakes,
Cool Tempês; cattle low, and sleep is soft
Under a tree. Coverts of game are there
And glades, a breed of youth inured to labour
And undemanding, worship of the gods
20  And reverence for the old. Departing Justice
Left among these her latest earthly footprints.

---

**11** Dyes and plants from Assyria were a byword for luxury among the Romans: cf. Eclogue IV, 25.
**16** Tempe: ancient beauty-spot in Thessaly.
**20–21** In the myth of the declining ages of man from gold to iron, the departure of Justice from the earth signalled the start of the iron age.

For my own part my chiefest prayer would be:
May the sweet Muses, whose acolyte I am,
Smitten with boundless love, accept my service,
Teach me to know the paths of the stars in heaven,
The eclipses of the sun and the moon's travails,
The cause of earthquakes, what it is that forces
Deep seas to swell and burst their barriers
And then sink back again, why winter suns
30  Hasten so fast to plunge themselves in the ocean
Or what it is that slows the lingering nights.
But if some chill in the blood about the heart
Bars me from mastering these sides of nature,
Then will I pray that I may find fulfilment
In the country and the streams that water valleys,
Love rivers and woods, unglamorous. O to be
Wafted away to the Thessalian plains
Of the Spercheūs, or Mount Taÿgetus
Traversed by bacchant feet of Spartan girls!
40  O who will set me down in some cool glen
Of Haemus under a canopy of branches?
Blessèd is he whose mind had power to probe
The causes of things and trample underfoot
All terrors and inexorable fate
And the clamour of devouring Acheron;
But happy too is he who knows the gods
Of the countryside, knows Pan and old Silvanus
And the sister Nymphs. Neither the people's gift,
The fasces, nor the purple robes of kings,
50  Nor treacherous feuds of brother against brother
Disturb him, not the Danube plotting raids
Of Dacian tribesmen, nor the affairs of Rome
And crumbling kingdoms, nor the grievous sight
Of poor to pity and of rich to envy.

---

**49** *fasces*: bundles of rods, symbols of authority (whence fascism).

The fruit his boughs, the crops his fields, produce
Willingly of their own accord, he gathers;
But iron laws on tablets, the frantic Forum
And public archives, these he has never seen.
Some vex with oars uncharted waters, some
60   Rush on cold steel, some seek to worm their way
Into the courts of kings. One is prepared
To plunge a city's homes in misery
All for a jewelled cup and a crimson bedspread;
Another broods on a buried hoard of gold.
This one is awestruck by the platform's thunder;
That one, enraptured, gapes at the waves of applause
From high and low rolling across the theatre.
Men revel steeped in brothers' blood, exchange
The hearth they love for banishment, and seek
70   A home in lands beneath an alien sun.
The farmer cleaves the earth with his curved plough.
This is his yearlong work, thus he sustains
His homeland, thus his little grandchildren,
His herds and trusty bullocks. Never a pause!
The seasons teem with fruits, the young of flocks,
Or sheaves of Ceres' corn; they load the furrows
And burst the barns with produce. Then, come winter,
The olive-press is busy; sleek with acorns
The pigs come home; the arbutes in the woods
80   Give berries; autumn sheds its varied windfalls;
And high on sunny terraces of rock
The mellow vintage ripens.
Meanwhile his darling children hang upon
His kisses; purity dwells in his home;
His cows have drooping udders full of milk,
And in the fresh green meadow fatling kids
Spar with their butting horns. The master himself
Keeps holiday, and sprawling on the grass,
With friends around the fire to wreathe the bowl,
90   Invokes you, Lord of the Winepress, offering

Libation, and nails a target to an elm
For herdsmen to compete in throwing darts,
While hardy rustic bodies are stripped for wrestling.
Such was the life the ancient Sabines lived
And Remus with his brother; thus it was
That Rome became the fairest thing in the world,
Embracing seven hills with a single wall.
And earlier still, before the Cretan king,
Dictaean Jove, held sway and an impious age
100   Of men began to feast on slaughtered oxen,
This life was led on earth by golden Saturn,
When none had ever heard the trumpet blown
Or heard the sword-blade clanking on the anvil.     (1982)


# ROBERT FITZGERALD (1910– )

## The Fortunes of War, 1069–1298 [Aen. XII. 791– 952] *The death of Turnus*

The conflict, and the poem, are resolved: first on the divine plane, when Juno ends her hostility to the Trojans, and then on the battlefield, when Aeneas kills Turnus.

Omnipotent Olympus' king meanwhile
Had words for Juno, as she watched the combat
Out of a golden cloud. He said:
                        'My consort,
What will the end be? What is left for you?

---

**95** *Remus*: Romulus' brother.

**99** Jupiter was born in a cave on Mount Dicte in Crete (still shown to tourists).

**101** Saturn presided over the Golden Age, until his rule was usurped by his son Jupiter (after which, according to Virgil's account in *Aeneid* VIII, he fled to Italy). In Eclogue IV Virgil foretells the return of this age.

You yourself know, and say you know, Aeneas
Born for heaven, tutelary of this land,
By fate to be translated to the stars.
What do you plan? What are you hoping for,
Keeping your seat apart in the cold clouds?
10  Fitting, was it, that a mortal archer
Wound an immortal? That a blade let slip
Should be restored to Turnus, and new force
Accrue to a beaten man? Without your help
What could Juturna do? Come now, at last
Have done, and heed our pleading, and give way.
Let yourself no longer be consumed
Without relief by all that inward burning;
Let care and trouble not forever come to me
From your sweet lips. The finish is at hand.
20  You had the power to harry men of Troy
By land and sea, to light the fires of war
Beyond belief, to scar a family
With mourning before marriage. I forbid
Your going further.'
                          So spoke Jupiter,
And with a downcast look Juno replied:

'Because I know that is your will indeed,
Great Jupiter, I left the earth below,
Though sore at heart, and left the side of Turnus.
Were it not so, you would not see me here
30  Suffering all that passes, here alone,

---

10–11 Aeneas had been wounded earlier in Book XII, but Venus had healed
the wound.

11–13 Juturna, Turnus' sister, had been granted immortality by the gods. She
had given Turnus back his sword after he had accidentally taken and lost his
charioteer's sword. These two divine interventions cancelled each other out:
the two leaders now face each other alone, as Drances had proposed at the
Latin war-council in Book XI.

Resting on air. I should be armed in flames
At the very battle-line, dragging the Trojans
Into a deadly action. I persuaded
Juturna — I confess — to help her brother
In his hard lot, and I approved her daring
Greater difficulties to save his life,
But not that she should fight with bow and arrow.
This I swear by Styx' great fountainhead
Inexorable, which high gods hold in awe.
40   I yield now and for all my hatred leave
This battlefield. But one thing not retained
By fate I beg for Latium, for the future
Greatness of your kin: when presently
They crown peace with a happy wedding day —
So let it be — and merge their laws and treaties,
Never command the land's own Latin folk
To change their old name, to become new Trojans,
Known as Teucrians; never make them alter
Dialect or dress. Let Latium be.
50   Let there be Alban kings for generations,
And let Italian valor be the strength
Of Rome in after times. Once and for all
Troy fell, and with her name let her lie fallen.'

The author of men and of the world replied
With a half-smile:
                'Sister of Jupiter
Indeed you are, and Saturn's other child,
To feel such anger, stormy in your breast.
But come, no need; put down this fit of rage.
I grant your wish. I yield, I am won over

---

**50** According to Jupiter's prophecy in Book I (of which this scene is a kind of mirror image) Ascanius will found Alba Longa, where the Trojans will reign for three hundred years, until the founding of Rome by Romulus.

60    Willingly. Ausonian folk will keep
      Their fathers' language and their way of life,
      And, that being so, their name. The Teucrians
      Will mingle and be submerged, incorporated.
      Rituals and observances of theirs
      I'll add, but make them Latin, one in speech.
      The race to come, mixed with Ausonian blood,
      Will outdo men and gods in its devotion,
      You shall see – and no nation on earth
      Will honor and worship you so faithfully.'

70    To all this Juno nodded in assent
      And, gladdened by his promise, changed her mind.
      Then she withdrew from sky and cloud.
                                        That done,
      The Father set about a second plan –
      To take Juturna from her warring brother.
      Stories are told of twin fiends, called the Dirae,
      Whom, with Hell's Megaera, deep Night bore
      In one birth. She entwined their heads with coils
      Of snakes and gave them wings to race the wind.
      Before Jove's throne, a step from the cruel king,
80    These twins attend him and give piercing fear
      To ill mankind, when he who rules the gods
      Deals out appalling death and pestilence,
      Or war to terrify our wicked cities.
      Jove now dispatched one of these, swift from heaven,
      Bidding her be an omen to Juturna.
      Down she flew, in a whirlwind borne to earth,
      Just like an arrow driven through a cloud

---

**60** *Ausonian*: Italian

**62–5** The Teucrians (Trojans) will lose their name and their language; all will
become Latin.

**70–71** The final metamorphosis of Juno from inveterate enemy of Troy into
one of the deities of the Capitoline triad (with Jupiter and Minerva) to whom
the Romans paid special honour.

From a taut string, an arrow armed with gall
Of deadly poison, shot by a Parthian –
90   A Parthian or a Cretan – for a wound
Immedicable; whizzing unforeseen
It goes through racing shadows: so the spawn
Of Night went diving downward to the earth.

On seeing Trojan troops drawn up in face
Of Turnus' army, she took on at once
The shape of that small bird that perches late
At night on tombs or desolate roof-tops
And troubles darkness with a gruesome song.
Shrunk to that form, the fiend in Turnus' face
100  Went screeching, flitting, flitting to and fro
And beating with her wings against his shield.
Unstrung by numbness, faint and strange, he felt
His hackles rise, his voice choke in his throat.
As for Juturna, when she knew the wings,
The shriek to be the fiend's, she tore her hair,
Despairing, then she fell upon her cheeks
With nails, upon her breast with clenched hands.

'Turnus, how can your sister help you now?
What action is still open to me, soldierly
110  Though I have been? Can I by any skill
Hold daylight for you? Can I meet and turn
This deathliness away? Now I withdraw,
Now leave this war. Indecent birds, I fear you;
Spare me your terror. Whip-lash of your wings
I recognize, that ghastly sound, and guess
Great-hearted Jupiter's high cruel commands.
Returns for my virginity, are they?
He gave me life eternal – to what end?
Why has mortality been taken from me?
120  Now beyond question I could put a term
To all my pain, and go with my poor brother

Into the darkness, his companion there.
Never to die? Will any brook of mine
Without you, brother, still be sweet to me?
If only earth's abyss were wide enough
To take me downward, goddess though I am,
To join the shades below!'
                              So she lamented,
Then with a long sigh, covering up her head
In her grey mantle, sank to the river's depth.

130    Aeneas moved against his enemy
And shook his heavy pine-tree spear. He called
From his hot heart:
                        'Rearmed now, why so slow?
Why, even now, fall back? The contest here
Is not a race, but fighting to the death
With spear and sword. Take on all shapes there are,
Summon up all your nerve and skill, choose any
Footing, fly among the stars, or hide
In caverned earth —'
                        The other shook his head,
Saying:
            'I do not fear your taunting fury,
140    Arrogant prince. It is the gods I fear
And Jove my enemy.'
                        He said no more,
But looked around him. Then he saw a stone,
Enormous, ancient, set up there to prevent
Landowners' quarrels. Even a dozen picked men
Such as the earth produces in our day
Could barely lift and shoulder it. He swooped
And wrenched it free, in one hand, then rose up
To his heroic height, ran a few steps,
And tried to hurl the stone against his foe —
150    But as he bent and as he ran
And as he hefted and propelled the weight

He did not know himself. His knees gave way,
His blood ran cold and froze. The stone itself,
Tumbling through space, fell short and had no impact.

Just as in dreams when the night-swoon of sleep
Weighs on our eyes, it seems we try in vain
To keep on running, try with all our might,
But in the midst of effort faint and fail;
Our tongue is powerless, familiar strength
160 Will not hold up our body, not a sound
Or word will come: just so with Turnus now:
However bravely he made shift to fight
The immortal fiend blocked and frustrated him.
Flurrying images passed through his mind.
He gazed at the Rutulians, and beyond them,
Gazed at the city, hesitant, in dread.
He trembled now before the poised spear-shaft
And saw no way to escape; he had no force
With which to close, or reach his foe, no chariot
170 And no sign of the charioteer, his sister.
At a dead loss he stood. Aeneas made
His deadly spear flash in the sun and aimed it,
Narrowing his eyes for a lucky hit.
Then, distant still, he put his body's might
Into the cast. Never a stone that soared
From a wall-battering catapult went humming
Loud as this, nor with so great a crack
Burst ever a bolt of lightning. It flew on
Like a black whirlwind bringing devastation,
180 Pierced with a crash the rim of sevenfold shield,
Cleared the cuirass' edge, and passed clean through
The middle of Turnus' thigh. Force of the blow
Brought the huge man to earth, his knees buckling,
And a groan swept the Rutulians as they rose,
A groan heard echoing on all sides from all
The mountain range, and echoed by the forests.

The man brought down, brought low, lifted his eyes
And held his right hand out to make his plea:

'Clearly I earned this, and I ask no quarter.
190   Make the most of your good fortune here.
If you can feel a father's grief – and you, too,
Had such a father in Anchises – then
Let me bespeak your mercy for old age
In Daunus, and return me, or my body,
Stripped, if you will, of life, to my own kin.
You have defeated me. The Ausonians
Have seen me in defeat, spreading my hands.
Lavinia is your bride. But go no further
Out of hatred.'
                    Fierce under arms, Aeneas
200   Looked to and fro, and towered, and stayed his hand
Upon the sword-hilt. Moment by moment now
What Turnus said began to bring him round
From indecision. Then to his glance appeared
The accurst swordbelt surmounting Turnus' shoulder,
Shining with its familiar studs – the strap
Young Pallas wore when Turnus wounded him
And left him dead upon the field; now Turnus
Bore that enemy token on his shoulder –
Enemy still. For when the sight came home to him,
210   Aeneas raged at the relic of his anguish
Worn by this man as trophy. Blazing up
And terrible in his anger, he called out:

'You in your plunder, torn from one of mine,
Shall I be robbed of you? This wound will come

---

**199ff.** The final confrontation: might Aeneas have spared Turnus if Turnus
had not been wearing the sword-belt he had taken from Pallas after he killed
him (in Book X)? The moral dilemma remains unresolved.

From Pallas: Pallas makes this offering
And from your criminal blood exacts his due.'

He sank his blade in fury in Turnus' chest.
Then all the body slackened in death's chill,
And with a groan for that indignity
220  His spirit fled into the gloom below.                    (1983)


# GUY LEE (1918– )

## Eclogue VI [Ecl.VI] *The Song of Silenus*

Cf. the version by A. J. Boyle, above, p. 305 (with headnote).


With Syracusan verses our Thaléa first
Thought fit to play, nor blushed to live among the woods.
When I was singing kings and battles, Cynthius pulled
My ear in admonition: 'A shepherd, Tityrus,
Should feed his flock fat, but recite a thin-spun song.'
I now (for you'll have many eager to recite
Your praises, Varus, and compose unhappy wars)
Will meditate the rustic Muse on slender reed.
I sing to order. Yet if any read this too,
10  If any love-beguiled, Varus, our tamarisks
Will sing of you, each grove of you, nor any page
Please Phoebus more than that headed by Varus' name.
    Proceed, Piéridës. Young Chromis and Mnasyllos
Once saw Silenus lying in a cave asleep,
His veins, as ever, swollen with yesterday's Iacchus;
Only, the garlands lay apart, fallen from his head,
And from its well-worn handle a heavy tankard hung.
Attacking (for the old man had often cheated both
With hope of song) they bind him with his own garlands.
20  Aeglë joins in, arriving as they grew alarmed,

Aeglë of Naiads loveliest, and, now he's looking,
With blood-red mulberries paints his temples and his brow.
The trick amuses him, but 'Why the bonds?' he asks;
'Release me, lads; it is enough to have shown your power.
Now hear the song you want; your payment shall be song,
Hers of another kind.' And with that he begins.
Then truly you could see Fauns and wild animals
Playing in rhythm, then stubborn oaks rocking their crowns.
Not so much joy does Phoebus bring Parnassus' crag,
30    Nor Orpheus astonish Rhódopë and Ísmarus.
    For he was singing how through a great emptiness
The seeds of earth and breath and sea and liquid fire
Were forced together; how from these first things all else,
All, and the cosmos' tender globe grew of itself;
Then land began to harden and in the deep shut off
Nereus and gradually assume the shapes of things;
And now the dawn of the new sun amazes earth,
And showers fall from clouds moved higher overhead,
When first the forest trees begin to rise, and when
40    Rare creatures wander over unfamiliar hills.
Here he recounts the stones by Pyrrha thrown, Saturnian
Kingship, Caucasian eagles and Prometheus' theft;
Adds at what fountain mariners for Hylas lost
Shouted till all the shore re-echoed *Hylas, Hylas*;
And (fortunate if herds of kine had never been)
Consoles Pasíphaë for love of a white steer.
Unlucky maiden, ah, what madness mastered you!
The Proetides with mimic lowing filled the fields,
But yet not one pursued so base an intercourse
50    With beast, although she feared the plough's yoke for her
                                        neck
And many a time would feel on her smooth brow for horns.
Unlucky maiden, ah, you wander now on mountains,
But he, with snow-white flank pressing soft hyacinth,
Beneath black ilex ruminates the sallow grass,
Or tracks some female in a great herd. 'Close, you Nymphs,

Dictéan Nymphs, now close the clearings in the woods.
Somewhere, perhaps, the wandering hoof-prints of a bull
Will find their own way to our eyes; possibly he,
Attracted by green grass, or following the herd,
60    Is led on by some cow to Gortyn's cattle-sheds.'
Then sings he the maid who admired Hesperidéan apples;
Then with the moss of bitter bark surrounds and lifts
The Phaëthóntiads from earth as alders tall;
Then sings of Gallus wandering by Permessus' stream,
How one of the Sisters led him to Aonia's mountains,
And how all Phoebus' choir stood up to greet a man;
How Linus there, the shepherd of inspired song,
His locks adorned with flowers and bitter celery,
Told him: 'The Muses give you this reed pipe (there, take it)
70    Which once they gave the old Ascréan, whose melody
Could draw the stubborn rowans down the mountainside.
Tell you with this the origin of Grynia's grove,
Lest any sacred wood be more Apollo's pride.'
    Why should I speak of Nisus' Scylla, who (so runs
The rumour), white groin girdled round with barking
                                                    monsters,
Tossed the Dulichian ships and in her deep whirlpool
With sea-hounds, ah, would savage frightened mariners?
Or how he told the tale of Terêus' limbs transformed,
What feast, what present Philomel prepared for him,
80    By what route sought the wilderness, and on what wings
Before that swooped unhappy over her own roof?
All, that from Phoebus' meditation, in old days, blest
Eurotas heard and bade his laurels memorize,
He sings (the smitten valleys tell it to the stars),
Till Vesper came to view in a reluctant sky
And bade the flock be folded and their number told.    (1984)

# SEAMUS HEANEY (1939– )

## The Golden Bough [Aen. VI. 98–148]

From *Seeing Things* (1991). Whether it is an invention of the poet's, or based on some lost folklore, the talisman by which Aeneas gains entry into the underworld remains a mystery. It provided the starting-point for Sir James Frazer's anthropological researches in *The Golden Bough*, but these have little relevance to Virgil.

So from the back of her shrine the Sibyl of Cumae
Chanted fearful equivocal words and made the cave echo
With sayings where clear truths and mysteries
Were inextricably twined. Apollo turned and twisted
His spurs at her breast, gave her her head, then reined in her
                                                      spasms.

As soon as her fit passed away and the mad mouthings
                                                      stopped
Heroic Aeneas began: 'No ordeal, O Priestess,
That you can imagine would ever surprise me
For already I have foreseen and foresuffered all.
But one thing I pray for especially: since they say it is here
That the King of the Underworld's gateway is to be found,
Among these shadowy marshes where Acheron comes
                                                      flooding through,
I pray for one look, one face-to-face meeting with my dear
                                                      father.
Teach me the way and open the holy doors wide.
I carried him on these shoulders through flames
And thousands of enemy spears. In the thick of battle I saved
                                                      him

---

**9** Heaney here echoes T.S. Eliot, *The Waste Land*, 243. The Latin is '*omnia praecepi atque animo mecum ante peregi*'.

And he was at my side then through all my sea-journeys,
A man in old age, worn out yet holding out always.
And he too it was who half-prayed and half-ordered me
20  To make this approach, to find and petition you.
So therefore, Vestal, I beseech you take pity
On a son and a father, for nothing is out of your power
Whom Hecate appointed the keeper of wooded Avernus.
If Orpheus could call back the shade of a wife through his
                                                            faith
In the loudly plucked strings of his Thracian lyre,
If Pollux could redeem a brother by going in turns
Backwards and forwards so often to the land of the dead,
And if Theseus too, and great Hercules . . . But why speak of
                                                            them?
I myself am of highest birth, a descendant of Jove.'

30  He was praying like that and holding on to the altar
When the prophetess started to speak: 'Blood relation of
                                                            gods,
Trojan, son of Anchises, the way down to Avernus is easy.
Day and night black Pluto's door stands open.
But to retrace your steps and get back to upper air,
This is the real task and the real undertaking.
A few have been able to do it, sons of gods
Favoured by Jupiter the Just, or exalted to heaven
In a blaze of heroic glory. Forests spread midway down,
And Cocytus winds through the dark, licking its banks.

---

24–8 Aeneas refers to other heroes who have descended alive into the underworld. Orpheus went down to recover his wife Eurydice (see Virgil's account at the end of *Georgics* IV); Pollux took the place of his brother Castor in the underworld on alternate days; Theseus went to carry off Persephone; Hercules, on his last labour, went to bring back the dog Cerberus.
32–5 Famous lines: the Latin is '. . . *facilis descensus Averno:/ noctes atque dies patet atri ianua Ditis;/ sed revocare gradum superasque evadere ad auras/ hoc opus, hic labor est.*'

40   Still, if love torments you so much and you so much need
     To sail the Stygian lake twice and twice to inspect
     The murk of Tartarus, if you will go beyond the limit,
     Understand what you must do beforehand.
     Hidden in the thick of a tree is a bough made of gold
     And its leaves and pliable twigs are made of it too.
     It is sacred to underworld Juno, who is its patron,
     And it is roofed in by a grove, where deep shadows mass
     Along far wooded valleys. No one is ever permitted
     To go down to earth's hidden places unless he has first
50   Plucked this golden-fledged growth out of its tree
     And handed it over to fair Proserpina, to whom it belongs
     By decree, her own special gift. And when it is plucked,
     A second one always grows in its place, golden again,
     And the foliage growing on it has the same metal sheen.
     Therefore look up and search deep and when you have found
                                                                 it
     Take hold of it boldly and duly. If fate has called you,
     The bough will come away easily, of its own accord.
     Otherwise, no matter how much strength you muster, you
                                                         never will
     Manage to quell it or cut it down with the toughest of
                                                         blades.'
                                                         (1991)

---

**46** *underworld Juno*: epic periphrasis for Proserpine.

# APPENDIX A: VIRGIL AND SPENSER

In presenting *The Shepheardes Calender* as his first publication, Spenser acknowledged both a vernacular debt to Chaucer and a cultural debt to Virgil, who had also begun his career with pastoral. William Webbe thought that Spenser came as close to Virgil 'as the coarseness of our speech permitted'. Stanyhurst praised Virgil's skill 'in telling as it were a Canterbury tale': so easily did Renaissance writers find parallels between Virgil and Chaucer as the supreme poetic models for their own age. Spenser's archaic style and his deliberately homely language accord with the contemporary view that pastoral dealt in a 'rude' style with 'humble' matter: but Sidney in *The Defence of Poesie* criticized Spenser for 'framing of his style to an old rustic language . . . since neither Theocritus in Greek, Virgil in Latin nor Sannazaro in Italian did affect it'.

In the 'October' Eclogue of the *Calender*, Spenser alludes to Virgil's progress from pastoral to epic, a sequence he consciously imitated in his own career. His epic *The Faerie Queene* is full of echoes and imitations of the *Aeneid*, often mediated through the romance epics of the Italian Renaissance. Its opening lines are modelled on the uncanonical opening of the *Aeneid*, lines often included in early texts of the poem and in some early translations. They disappeared by the time of Dryden. They are sometimes regarded as spurious, sometimes as genuine verses cancelled by Virgil himself or by his first editors.

> Lo I the man, whose Muse whilome did maske,
> As time her taught, in lowly shepheards weeds,
> Am now enforst a far unfitter taske,
> For trumpets sterne to chaunge mine Oaten reeds . . .

[Ille ego, qui quondam gracili modulatus avena
carmen, et egressus silvis vicina coegi
ut quamvis avido parerent arva colono,
gratum opus agricolis, at nunc horrentia Martis]
arma virumque cano . . .

# APPENDIX B: DENHAM ON TRANSLATION

In 1648 Sir John Denham published a verse letter to Sir Richard Fanshawe on the latter's translation of Guarini's *Il pastor fido*. Fanshawe later translated *Aeneid* IV, part of which Denham also translated. His praise of Fanshawe clearly incorporates his own views on translation: the words italicized would seem to set a well-nigh impossible standard for translators of Virgil (perhaps only Dryden attained it).

> Such is our Pride, our Folly, or our Fate,
> That few but such as cannot write, translate.
> But what in them is want of Art or voice,
> In thee is either modesty or choice . . .
> Secure of Fame, thou justly dost esteem
> Less honour to create than to redeem.
> *Nor ought a Genius less than his that writ*
> *Attempt translation*; for transplanted wit
> All the defects of air and soil doth share,
> And colder brains like colder climates are:
> In vain they toil, since nothing can beget
> A vital spirit, but a vital heat.
> That servile path thou nobly dost decline
> Of tracing word by word and line by line . . .
> A new and nobler way thou dost pursue
> To make translations and translators too.
> They but preserve the ashes, thou the Flame,
> True to his sense, but truer to his Fame.

In the preface to his 'Destruction of Troy' (1656) Denham makes the same point: 'I conceive it a vulgar error in translating poets, to affect being Fidus Interpres: whosoever aims at it in poetry, as he attempts what is not required, so he shall never perform what he attempts; for it is not his business to translate language into language but poesie into poesie.'

# APPENDIX C: DRYDEN AND LAUDERDALE

'The late Earl of Lauderdale,' says he [i.e. Dryden], 'sent me over his new translation of the *Aeneids*, which he had ended before I engaged in the same design. Neither did I then intend it; but some proposals being afterwards made me by my Bookseller I desired his Lordship's leave that I might accept them, which he freely granted, and I have his letter to shew for that permission. He resolved to have printed his work, which he might have done two years before I published mine: and had performed it, if death had not prevented him. But having his manuscript in my hands, I consulted it as often as I doubted of my author's sense: for no man understood Virgil better than that learned Nobleman. His friends have yet another and more correct copy of that translation by them, which had they been pleased to have given the public, the judges must have been convinced that I had not flattered him.'

(From Dryden's *Dedication to the Aeneis*)

Thus you find that there was a correcter copy, Mr Dryden owns, than that he had by him. And it is this copy that the noble author's friends thought would prove acceptable to the learned world, and therefore have no reason to doubt a favourable reception. It was not undertaken with any design to oppose or thwart Mr Dryden, this being done before his was thought of, and there is no reason the world should be robbed of the performance of so considerable a man, because another translation was published before this, whose author has acknowledged his obligation to our Copy for the assistance it has given him in the understanding of Virgil.

(From the Preface to the Works of Virgil translated by Lauderdale, undated,

*c.* 1709)

Lauderdale's editors further emphasized Dryden's debt to him by printing on the title-page the words '*sequiturque sequentem*' (*Aeneid* XI, 695, 'he follows the follower').

# APPENDIX D: DRYDEN AND MILBOURNE

According to the *Dictionary of National Biography*, no copy of Milbourne's translation of *Aeneid* I is known. There is, however, a copy in the British Library. Milbourne's name does not appear on the title-page, but the attribution to him is confirmed by an extract from Motteux's *Gentleman's Journal* for August 1692, which includes a quotation from the Preface to the translation and identifies the author as Milbourne. In this Preface Milbourne writes that he was spurred on to attempt his work by 'love of the best of poets who has for so long unhappily continued a stranger to tolerable English; and ambition to make trial upon that which Mr Dryden represents as a wholly impossible task . . . He observed how Phayer [Phaer] and Stainhurst [Stanyhurst] of old, and Ogilby of late, had murder'd the most absolute of poets; how Sandys, Denham and Waller had undertaken some scatter'd Parcels, without any design of prosecuting the work . . .'

Milbourne's attempt seems to have met with no encouragement, and he evidently abandoned it. When nine years later Dryden's complete version appeared, jealousy and frustration prompted Milbourne to publish his highly critical *Notes on Dryden's Virgil* (1698) in which he included specimens by himself of the Fourth Eclogue and the First Georgic. The opening paragraph of the latter was reprinted by Dr Johnson in his 'Life of Dryden' in order that 'according to his own proposal his verses may be compared with those which he censures'. Pope mentions Milbourne in his *Essay on Criticism* (line 463) as an example of a 'tedious and carping critic'.

# BIOGRAPHICAL INDEX

**Addison,** Joseph (1672–1719). Poet, essayist, statesman; also translated *Georgics* IV.

**Alpers,** Paul. Author of *The Singer of the Eclogues* (1979).

**Anonymous.** The translator of 'The Power of Love' from *Georgics* III (1693) was not known to Dryden and has not since been identified.

**Auden,** W. H. (1907–73). The leading Anglo-American poet of his generation.

**Blackmore,** R. D. (1825–1900). Novelist, barrister and classical scholar, best known as the author of *Lorna Doone*.

**Bovie,** S. P. American scholar and translator.

**Bowen,** Sir Charles (1835–94). Judge and Lord of Appeal.

**Boyle,** A. J. Has also edited a collection of essays on ancient pastoral (1975).

**Bridges,** Robert (1844–1930). Poet Laureate. His interest in prosody was reflected in his edition (the first) of Hopkins's poems (1918).

**Brodribb,** Charles William (1878–1945). His poems were published posthumously (1946), with an introduction by Edmund Blunden.

**Calverley,** Charles Stuart (1831–84). Best known as the author of much light verse. His versions of Theocritus and Virgil were published posthumously in 1908.

**Caryll,** John (1625–1711). Diplomat and minor Restoration poet, uncle of the John Caryll who was Pope's friend.

**Chaucer,** Geoffrey (*c.* 1343–1400). Like other medieval writers, he was more concerned with the stories and moral sentiments of classical poets than with their style.

**Conington,** John (1825–69). Classical scholar; edited the *Aeneid* (1858–69). He also translated the *Odes* of Horace. A memoir of his life appears as a preface to his *Miscellaneous Writings* (ed. J. A. Symonds, 1872) in which his essay on translating Virgil is included.

**Cotton,** Charles (1630–87). Restoration poet and wit.

**Cowley,** Abraham (1618–67). His many poems include a biblical epic, *Davideis*.

**Creech,** Thomas (1659–1700). Best known for his translations of Lucretius and Horace: see the opening lines of Pope's 'Imitation of Horace', the sixth epistle of the first book.

**Day Lewis,** C. (1904–72). The only modern poet to have translated the complete works of Virgil. His version of the *Aeneid*, with its mixture of archaisms and dated modernisms, is less successful than his *Eclogues* and *Georgics*.

**Denham,** Sir John (1615–69). Poet and royalist: his best-known poem *Cooper's Hill* (1642, revised 1655) was praised by Herrick, Dryden and Pope (who imitated it in his *Windsor Forest*).

**Dickinson,** Patric (1914–94). Poet, author of many radio plays; also translated several plays of Plautus.

**Douglas,** Gavin (*c.* 1474–1522). Poet and Bishop of Dunkeld, best known for his pioneering version of the *Aeneid*.

**Dryden,** John (1631–1700). Poet and critic: the most important literary figure of his time, he made many translations from Latin poetry.

**Duke,** Richard (*c.* 1659–1711). Poet and divine; he published various translations and a posthumous volume of original verse (1711).

**Fanshawe,** Sir Richard (1608–66). Poet and diplomat; best known for his translations of Guarini's *Il pastor fido* ('The Faithful Shepherd') (1647) and of Camoens' *Lusiad* (1655).

**Fitzgerald,** Robert (1910– ). Poet and translator; has also made versions of Homer and of several Greek plays.

**Fleming,** Abraham (*c.* 1522–1607). Poet and antiquary: translated the *Eclogues* ('Bucolics') twice, the second time with the *Georgics*.

**Morris,** William (1834–96). Poet, artist, craftsman and socialist.

**Myers,** Frederick William Henry (1843–1901). Poet, essayist and classical scholar.

**Ogilby,** John (1600–1676). Translator, printer and publisher: the first English translator of Virgil's complete works.

**Phaer,** Thomas (c. 1510–60). Lawyer, doctor, and author of the first English translation of the *Aeneid*, which he did not live to finish. Thomas Twyne (q.v.) completed and revised the work.

**Philips,** Ambrose (1675–1749). His poems were at one time included in all standard collections of English poetry.

**Pope,** Alexander (1685–1744). Poet and satirist. His early pastorals were influenced by Virgil.

**Sackville-West,** Victoria (1892–1962). Poet, novelist and biographer. Her *Collected Poems* appeared in 1933.

**Sandys,** George (1578–1644). While a member of the colonial council of Virginia, he completed the translation of Ovid's *Metamorphoses* for which he is best known.

**Shelley,** P.B. (1792–1822). A leading poet of the Romantic movement; in his *Defence of Poetry* he ranked Lucretius above Virgil and was generally more influenced by Greek literature than by Latin.

**Spenser,** Edmund (1552–99). The Virgil of the English Renaissance: see Appendix.

**Surrey,** Henry Howard, Earl of (1516–47). Along with Wyatt, the best-known poet of the Tudor Renaissance. His version of *Aeneid* II exists in one version only, that of *Aeneid* IV in three.

**Tate,** Allen (1899–1979). American poet and man of letters.

**Temple,** Sir William (1628–99). Writer and statesman. Most of his writing was in prose, done after he retired from politics. He was a friend and patron of Swift, and a noted gardener.

**Tennyson,** Alfred, Lord (1809–92). Poet Laureate. His few translations include some passages from Homer.

**Thomson,** James (1700–1748). His best-known poem is *The Seasons*; it forms the basis of the libretto of Haydn's oratorio. Virgil's *Georgics* thus indirectly entered the world of music.

**Twyne,** Thomas (1543–1613). Physician; translated a number of scientific and medical texts; completed and revised Thomas Phaer's version of the *Aeneid*.

**Warton,** Joseph (1722–1800). Poet and critic; brother of the historian of English poetry Thomas Warton.

**Webbe,** William (fl. 1568–91). His *Discourse of English Poetrie* (1586) throws light on the theories of poetry current at Cambridge in Spenser's time.

**Wilkinson,** Laurence P. (1907–85). Classical scholar; author of many books on Latin poetry.

**Wordsworth,** William (1770–1850). Poet Laureate. He made translations of several passages of Virgil, none of which he reprinted.

# TABLE OF TRANSLATED PASSAGES

## *Works written in imitation of, or response to, Virgil*

# INDEX OF TRANSLATORS
# AND POETS

# ACKNOWLEDGEMENTS

Grateful thanks are due to University of California Press for permission to reprint 'Eclogue VII' ('The Singing Match') by Paul Alpers from *The Singer of the Eclogues: A Study of Virgilian Pastoral with a New Translation of the Eclogues* (1979), copyright © 1979 The Regents of the University of California; to Faber & Faber Limited and Random House, Inc., for 'Secondary Epic' by W. H. Auden from *Homage to Clio* (1960), copyright © 1960 by W. H. Auden; to Smith Palmer Bovie and University of Chicago Press for 'The Story of Orpheus and Eurydice' from *The Georgics of Virgil* (1956); to Dutton Signet, a division of Penguin Books USA, Inc., for 'The Funeral of Pallas' by Patric Dickinson from *The Aeneid* (1961), translation copyright © 1961, renewed © 1989 by Patric Dickinson; to Random House, Inc., for 'The death of Turnus' by Robert Fitzgerald from *The Aeneid* (1983), translation copyright © 1980, 1982, 1983 by Robert Fitzgerald; to Faber & Faber Limited for *Aeneid VI* ('The Golden Bough') by Seamus Heaney from *Seeing Things* (1991); to Francis Cairns (Publications) Limited for 'Eclogue VI' ('The Song of Silenus') by Guy Lee from the revised edition of *Virgil: The Eclogues. The Latin Text with a Verse Translation*, originally published in *Virgil's Eclogues. The Latin Text with a Verse Translation and Brief Notes* by Guy Lee (Francis Cairns, Liverpool, 1980), reprinted in *Virgil. The Eclogues* (Penguin Books, Harmondsworth, 1984); to Random House UK Limited for translations by C. Day Lewis of 'Georgics I' and 'Georgics IV' from *Georgics of Virgil* (Jonathan Cape, 1940) and 'Eclogue III' ('The Singing Match') from *Eclogues of Virgil* (Jonathan Cape, 1963); to Faber & Faber Limited for 'Falling Asleep over the Aeneid' by Robert Lowell from *Selected Poems* (1976); to Curtis Brown, London for *The Land* by Vita

Sackville-West (1926), copyright 1926 Vita Sackville-West; to Penguin Books Limited for 'Georgics II' ('In Praise of Rural Retirement') from *The Georgics*, translated by L. P. Wilkinson (Penguin Books, 1982), copyright © L. P. Wilkinson, 1982; to Anthony J. Boyle for his translation of 'Eclogue VI' from *The Eclogues of Virgil* (Hawthorn Press, 1976); to Simon and Schuster, Inc. for *The Aeneid of Virgil*, translated by Rolfe Humphries. Copyright 1951 by Prentice-Hall, Upper Saddle River, New Jersey.

Every effort has been made to trace or contact all copyright holders. The publishers will be glad to make good any omissions brought to our attention in future editions.

# READ MORE IN PENGUIN

In every corner of the world, on every subject under the sun, Penguin represents quality and variety – the very best in publishing today.

For complete information about books available from Penguin – including Puffins, Penguin Classics and Arkana – and how to order them, write to us at the appropriate address below. Please note that for copyright reasons the selection of books varies from country to country.

**In the United Kingdom**: Please write to *Dept. EP, Penguin Books Ltd, Bath Road, Harmondsworth, West Drayton, Middlesex UB7 ODA*

**In the United States**: Please write to *Consumer Sales, Penguin Putnam Inc., P.O. Box 999, Dept. 17109, Bergenfield, New Jersey 07621-0120.* VISA and MasterCard holders call 1-800-253-6476 to order Penguin titles

**In Canada**: Please write to *Penguin Books Canada Ltd, 10 Alcorn Avenue, Suite 300, Toronto, Ontario M4V 3B2*

**In Australia**: Please write to *Penguin Books Australia Ltd, P.O. Box 257, Ringwood, Victoria 3134*

**In New Zealand**: Please write to *Penguin Books (NZ) Ltd, Private Bag 102902, North Shore Mail Centre, Auckland 10*

**In India**: Please write to *Penguin Books India Pvt Ltd, 210 Chiranjiv Tower, 43 Nehru Place, New Delhi 110 019*

**In the Netherlands**: Please write to *Penguin Books Netherlands bv, Postbus 3507, NL-1001 AH Amsterdam*

**In Germany**: Please write to *Penguin Books Deutschland GmbH, Metzlerstrasse 26, 60594 Frankfurt am Main*

**In Spain**: Please write to *Penguin Books S. A., Bravo Murillo 19, 1° B, 28015 Madrid*

**In Italy**: Please write to *Penguin Italia s.r.l., Via Benedetto Croce 2, 20094 Corsico, Milano*

**In France**: Please write to *Penguin France, Le Carré Wilson, 62 rue Benjamin Baillaud, 31500 Toulouse*

**In Japan**: Please write to *Penguin Books Japan Ltd, Kaneko Building, 2-3-25 Koraku, Bunkyo-Ku, Tokyo 112*

**In South Africa**: Please write to *Penguin Books South Africa (Pty) Ltd, Private Bag X14, Parkview, 2122 Johannesburg*

# READ MORE IN PENGUIN

*Poets in Translation – a selection*

Penguin Classics now publishes a series that presents the best verse translations in English, through the centuries, of the major Classical and European poets. With full introductions and explanatory notes, the Poets in Translation series is a unique addition to the wealth of poetry within Penguin Classics.

**Homer in English**
Edited and introduced by George Steiner
with the assistance of Aminadav Dykman

'The *Iliad* and *Odyssey*,' writes Professor George Steiner, 'are perennially active in the pulse of the English languages'; these translations and variations on Homeric themes offer nothing less than a 'concise chronicle of English'. From Chaucer's *Troylus and Criseyde* and Shakespeare's *Troilus and Cressida* to Joyce's *Ulysses* and Walcott's *Omeros*, Homer has been the most translated author in our literature, eliciting a fantastic wealth and quality of response. This superb selection assembles highlights and representative moments from six and a half centuries.

**The Psalms in English**
Edited with an introduction by Donald Davie

The Psalms are Ancient Hebrew songs of devotion, lament, confession and thanksgiving whose composers probably included King David, 'the sweetest psalmist of Israel'. In their English versions they continue to assert profound influence in the Christian as well as the Jewish traditions. This volume contains contributions from Sir Thomas Wyatt, Shakespeare, Donne, Milton, Christopher Smart, Hardy, Isaac Rosenberg and Clive Wilmer among many others.

**Martial in English**
Edited with an introduction by J. P. Sullivan and A. J. Boyle

From Elizabethan times, writers such as Jonson, Herrick, Cowley and Byron translated Martial's portraits of poseurs, prostitutes and philosophers, legacy hunters and social climbers. Martial always retained a reputation as an underground classic; his influence on English literature, both direct and indirect, has been immense.